A Hard Fall From Grace

A novel by Michael O. Murray

Cricket Cottage Publishing, LLC

ISBN: 978-0-9991224-2-6

Dedication

To God the glory! He has blessed me with many remarkable people in my life, who have guided, loved, assisted, and inspired me. To be sure, there are far too many to list, but leading the way are my parents, Melma and Edward, who reared and loved me without limit; my wife, Toan who has enjoyed and sometimes suffered the journey with me for nearly three decades; Michael and Chloe, my wonderful *chillern*–as Grandma Alford used to say; My sibs, Roni, Jackie, and Edward—my childhood *partners-in-crime* who share my songs, inside jokes, and fond memories; My fantastically amazing brothers-in-law, Bob and Leo, whose depth of character and commitment as men and fathers truly inspire; Judith Kitz, my endlessly amazing Aunt, who edited for me and lavished me with her unbounded love, and; my dear friend Rob, the brother I chose, who has supported me through thick and thin since our 14th year of life.

I give a special nod to my grandparents, Henrietta, George, Josephine, and Edward: many years gone, but never forgotten, always loved, and eternally great. I honor their hard work, perseverance, and character.

The zeal which begins with hypocrisy must conclude in treachery; at first it deceives, at last it betrays.

--Sir Francis Bacon

Chapter 1: What's Past is Prologue

Clad head to toe in an obscuring dark rubber suit, Alex turned and moved through the darkened hallway toward the bedroom door, the bloody, dying body in the bungalow's front room of no further concern. The sounds of intense passion in progress emanated from inside the bedroom, and a gingerly touch on its door handle let the door open without a peep. Alex stepped inside to what was essentially a live porn show. Candlelight flickered on the bedside table, casting orange hues off of a pair of empty crystal wine flutes and three bottles of Chateau Something-or-Other, two of which rolled on their sides to and fro across the nightstand. The other remained upright but wobbled precariously with each thrust of the man's hips. An energetic woman made exuberant noises beneath him as he made what seemed like angry love to her. The pair simultaneously reached a moment of bliss and expressed themselves rather loudly. *What perfect timing*, Alex thought.

With feline agility, Alex closed the final ten paces to the couple and stopped at the foot of the bed, its duvet and white satin sheets haphazardly twisted into a messy braid. Alex leveled the silenced weapon at ninety degrees, and then fired two muffled shots, sending a single round into the back of the man's head and another through the woman's closed left eye. Their motion and passionate expressions fell silent, as garnet liquid poured liberally onto the bed and spilled over its edge, fast creating a soggy mess of the sheets, mattress, and carpet. Alex checked the time. The chopper patrol would return in ninety seconds. It was time to go.

"Mommy?" a tiny voice called.

Alex wheeled around to find a small boy standing in the doorway, rubbing sleepy eyes as he embarked on a mission to find comfort from the only one who could chase away the beast haunting his nightmare. He lowered his hand, stared at Alex, and grinned from ear to ear.

"Mommy, why you wearin' that mask? It's not Halloween yet," the little boy said, giggling.

He stepped toward *Mommy* with outstretched hands that reached lovingly for Alex's neck. A wisp of air sent a single bullet across the room at hypersonic speed, striking the child squarely between the eyes. His little body jerked backward from the impact and collapsed on the floor, his neck breaking as it struck that point where wall and floor conjoined. His young life was over almost before it began. Alex removed the goggles to get an unobstructed though dim look at the bloody carcass.

"Nothing personal, kid," Alex said. "Life's a piece of shit anyway—you won't miss much!"

After staring a few more seconds, the killer put the goggles back on, and lifted a small radio, talking quickly into its microphone. "It *in the pipe five-by-five, so I good to go.*"

Alex deactivated the radio, shoved it into a small pant leg pocket, then stepped over the miniature corpse and headed quickly out of the bedroom. As the killer approached the front door, someone stepped inside carrying a Styrofoam cup of dark liquid that smelled like a triple mocha espresso probably with enough caffeine to cause insomnia in all of New York City. It was intended to keep only Deputy Marshal Declan O'Keefe awake for his all-night shift, but he was already asleep, eternally. Another wisp of air launched the fifth silenced round of the night, killing the coffee-bearer before he ever knew cause for alarm. His lifeless body collapsed on the door's threshold with a thud heavy enough to send vibrations through the ground.

***

"You okay there, Sam?" a voice from outside jokingly asked. Deputy Marshal Rick Henri figured his colleague had merely missed a step and stumbled as he entered the cabin. He planned to give the man all kinds of hell about his clumsiness, but he received no reply. "Sam?" he repeated.

Again, there was no answer.

Protocol required the Marshal to investigate even slight irregularities that happened on watch rather than merely assume they were just random events. Henri had been on his way to relieve another teammate further up the path leading to the bungalow, but instead, he set his coffee cup on the ground, withdrew his Glock, and reversed his course. As he fast-walked up the path, it only took a few steps under the bright moon before he saw a dark heap on the ground, which he correctly assumed was his colleague, and a dark figure moving rapidly off to the left. Henri panicked momentarily and rushed to his downed colleague.

"Sam!" he yelled, kneeling beside the body.

The Marshal lay quiet, bloody, and motionless except for the nerve twitches that seized his dead body like the amputated tail of a gecko. Henri felt for his friend's pulse but found none. Rage surged through him and propelled him to action. He leveled his weapon and tried to draw a bead on the shadow, but its rapid pace and its blend into the darkness made a clean shot unlikely. Henri burst into chase, and at the same time, pressed the transmitter on the headset behind his ear.

"This is Henri! Fakmann's down at the bungalow. I've got an unidentified target fleeing west of the bungalow toward the beach. I'm in pursuit, but he's coming your way, Liang!"

"Come again, Henri?" a voice cracked from the small speaker in his ear.

"Fakmann's dead. I'm pursuing a suspect headed west on foot!"

"What's the status of Pigmeat and company?" the voice asked.

"Probably dead! Get someone in there to confirm," Henri replied as he dodged branches that seemed to pop up from the dark to whip his face and arms.

"Negative, Henri. You take the bungalow. We'll intercept the target."

"By the time you reach the beach, the target'll be gone. I have a better chance!" he pleaded.

"No, Henri!" a voice yelled. "Get your ass back to Pigmeat."

"That's bullshit, Terri. I can get this guy. He's not that far ahead of me." Henri puffed as he ran.

"Negative, Deputy Marshal Henri. I said *I'll* get him. That's an order."

As an all-state 100-meter champ in high school, and a guy who finished the Boston and New York Marathons and the Ironman competition in enviable times, Rick Henri had no doubt he could catch the suspect, but the Supervisory Marshal apparently had another idea in mind. Henri thought it, like most of her ideas, was a dumb plan that allocated resources recklessly, just like her *brilliant* plan for deploying the protection detail tonight. But, Stupleton was the senior Marshal and his boss, and he couldn't afford to get written up again.

The air escaped his spirits even more than his lungs as Henri sighed heavily, resigned to doing as ordered. He slowed to a jog and then to a walk as he saw the shadow pull away from him on the trail ahead and then disappear into the bushes. Seconds later, he saw the guy scale the twelve-foot wall separating the private bungalow from the adjacent public beach with the apparent ease of someone overstepping an ant. The suspect was gone, but hopefully, Stupleton and Oseefah would intercept him. Henri turned and dashed back to the bungalow, already certain of what he'd find.

Chapter 2: Rising Expectations

Grace Tran closed the file in her lap and leaned back into the cushions of her seat as she waited for the rest of her team to close theirs and look up. That would indicate they were ready to discuss in more detail the new mission handed to her team by the President of the United States himself. Mentally, she shook her head as she marveled at the path that brought her to be sitting on a private plane in the wee hours of the morning, jetting across the Atlantic on an unplanned trip.

Although Tran had done well in high school, she wasn't sure whether to go to college like all her friends. A stint flipping patties at The Burger Joint helped clarify her path. Even though near-perfect SAT scores won her several scholarship offers from the Ivy Leagues, her dad's and pop-pop's proud service in the U.S. Air Force and its predecessor, the Army Air Corps, made the Air Force Academy her only real choice. Four years later, she left its hallowed halls with the gold bars of a Second Lieutenant glistening on her shoulders, and orders in hand assigning her to OSI—the Office of Special Investigations.

That held her interest through the rank of Major, when she was accepted to Harvard Law. A *Summa Cum Laude* finish won her a lucrative offer from a big D.C. firm that fattened her bank account, but it didn't give her the sense of purpose for which she longed. That's when General Sharp swooped in. He'd followed her career even after she left his command, and when the President gave him the top seat at the National Security Agency, he wanted her on his team. Period. She was smart, ethical, trustworthy, and effective at everything she did—just the person Sharp needed to guard his flanks in the snake pit called Washington.

That was years ago. Now, as a member of the Senior Executive

Service, Tran led the NSA's Field Team Six, which only worked the most sensitive NSA assignments—those from the Director or his boss, the President. It's the reason she'd gotten the call from the Director at 2:00 a.m. after he'd been summoned to the White House by the President.

"Listen, Grace," Sharp had growled in a less than polished sleepy voice, "seems like I say this almost every damn time I give you a new mission, but this is a *Priority* case. The President personally asked for you on this—he's noticed the great work you've done on difficult cases over the years, and as you know, the reward for doing great work is more work."

He went on to explain her new assignment in short, staccato sentences. He ended by apprising her of the courier who'd arrive at her door within minutes.

The courier did so in efficient military fashion and then disappeared as quickly as he'd come, leaving Tran to peruse the thick mission file from the General. When she finished, Tran first called Vivian Lawrence to get her started on assembling the team's Mission Brief.

"I guess the shit always rolls downhill, don't it, Boss Lady?" Lawrence said, a smile present in her tone.

Acknowledging her Administrative Assistant's cheery early morning dedication, Tran ended the call and typed a message into her phone. It sent a short, encrypted message through cyberspace like a bolt of white-hot lightning: *Wheels up in ninety*. Then, she initiated the recall roster by voice-calling Ian Lockwood, her Number Two. He'd call the next person on the team's roster, who'd call the next, and so on until the entire team had spoken voice-to-voice about their newest urgent mission.

By 0400, an NSA G6 jet rocketed into the pre-dawn skies over Joint Base Andrews, the tarmac falling quickly into the darkness below. At ten-thousand feet, the aircraft arced 180 degrees and vectored southeast for a two hour and one minute flight to New Providence Island. Amid the dull drone of the plane's muted jet engines, Tran let her agents have a few minutes of quiet aboard the well-appointed plane so they could adjust to being snatched from their beds in the middle of the night, again. Besides, she wanted them ready to work the moment they landed.

After twenty minutes, Tran passed the Mission Brief folders to each member of the team, without offering instructions. Except for the rookie, they'd all been through this drill many times over the years and each knew what to do. The hyper-observant newbie could learn on the fly.

Stefan Kenison was first to look up. With the obvious brawn of an Atlas, most people thought the twenty-seven-year-old former Army Ranger was recruited to the team for his combat skills, which he had, but the real reason Tran wanted him on the team was the fact that his thick head housed the mind of an Einstein, especially for anything mathematical or technical. A fast reader, he finished reading the brief, looked up, and made eye contact with Tran. He nodded and then waited patiently for the others to finish. A short time later, the eldest, most experienced member of the team looked up.

"Ready Boss," Ian Lockwood announced, his voice a gravely tone typical for him in the morning.

Moments later, Dr. Deanna Starr raised her head and removed her horn-rimmed reading glasses. Crossing her legs over one another, she eased into the back of her seat, and noticed Tran watching everyone. A verbal acknowledgement was unnecessary.

"Good to go, Boss," Enrique Ito eventually said.

Tran nodded and leaned toward Ito, fashioning her thumb and index finger as though she would twist an unseen knob back and forth in the air. She pointed at the tablet computer hanging from Ito's neck, displaying an image of a woman sitting at her kitchen table, engaged in something outside the view of the camera's lens. "Is she on?" Tran whispered.

The woman on the screen looked up abruptly. "Yeah, I can hear ya', Grace," she answered, loudly cracking the quiet in the cabin.

"Okay, Viv," Tran answered softly. "Stand by."

Lawrence looked like a former athlete who kept herself in prime condition as she marched into her golden years, but the occasionally intractable woman refused to recognize that her years had taken any hue beyond youth. No living person except Vivian herself seemed to know her age, and she protected that information as vigorously as the NSA did the nation's secrets. But whenever Lockwood pontificated about the wisdom he'd gained with age, she was quick to roll her eyes and tell him—and anyone else within earshot—she had underwear older than he. She also hinted at her age when she justified her often impatient disposition by explaining she was running out of years to waste time waiting for people to do things.

Lawrence made a habit of saying whatever came to mind whenever it came to mind, regardless of common notions of politeness and political correctness. Nobody ever accused her of being tactful, but as rough and unpolished as she could be, she was nearly always right, and her heart was as golden as her years. Lawrence routinely went out of her way to help people—even those she didn't know—and she seemed to have her own brand of magic that helped her complete even difficult tasks ahead of time and under budget. This made her a vital asset to the team, and it was one of the reasons Tran brought her to the NSA along with her when she left the Air Force. If Lawrence had any significant drawback, her deathly fear of flying might be it. *If God meant humans to fly, we'da been born with wings*, she often said. *Besides, I ain't a'scaart' a flyin'; I'm a'scaart' a hittin' the ground.*

It took Enrique "Rique" Ito only three days to conceive, design, and construct a solution to the problem. He engineered a flat-screen mobile computer that could hang from a fashionable lanyard or sit on a tabletop. The *Ito-pad*, as he dubbed it, let Lawrence see and hear everything that happened in the field from the comfort of her home or office. Its design similar to the tablet computers selling like hotcakes in the mobile device market, Ito often claimed that the big electronics manufacturers had stolen his idea. He planned to one-up them eventually by developing technology to let users also smell and feel what their teammates in the field did, after which he'd patent and sell it to the big guys at ridiculously high prices. But even in its current form, the Ito-pad worked effectively as Lawrence's avatar.

"You 'bout done there, Evelyn Wood?" Lockwood joked, gently pressing his elbow into Stan Lauxner's side as he chided him for reading so slowly. He chuckled aloud. "You're probably not even old enough to remember those late-night TV commercials for Evelyn Wood speed reading courses, are you?"

Lauxner, the newest member of Field Team Six, had served three tours of duty in Army Explosive Ordinance Disposal, EOD. He could tell his teammates anything about improvised explosive devices, blast radiuses, firearms, and kill ratios, but paperwork and case files weren't among his strengths. He joined Field Team Six after a medical discharge from the Army, a serious bout with PTSD, and a lengthy period of unemployment. As a witness in a prior investigation, he'd caught the eye of Agent Kenison, who took him to Tran. Kenison pressed hard to get help for the humbled veteran, but the hard press wasn't necessary. Tran liked him too and thought he could bring value to FT6. As a result, his accession to the team happened quickly. Now, with only two weeks' experience on the team, quickly gleaning relevant information from a Mission Brief after being whisked away to a strange location wasn't yet in Lauxner's skill set. He seemed embarrassed that he was the last person ready for the mission briefing.

"Sorry," he said. "I've never been a fast reader and never heard of that Evelyn chick."

"No worries, Tool Man," Lockwood quipped. "We have all day!"

"I'm really sorry. It's just—"

Tran pursed her lips and rolled her eyes as she glanced at her Number Two, quietly chastising him for poking fun at the rookie. "Ignore him. He's just pulling your leg! I prefer quality over speed. In a year, nobody will remember how fast you read that file, but they may remember if you screw-up and miss something important! Take time to do it right so you don't have to make time to do it again!"

14

"Yeah, Tool Man," Lockwood added. "I'm just giving you a hard time!"

"As you get to know him better, you'll see that's his favorite hobby," Ito warned. Lockwood laughed in delight.

"Why do you call him Tool Man, Agent Lockwood?" Starr asked.

"I can't bring myself to call him Stan or Stanley," Lockwood answered, "so I gave him a new name."

"You gave him a new name?" Starr repeated, furrowing her brow.

"Yeah. You know I like woodworking, right?" Lockwood asked.

Lockwood's oddball remark caught Lauxner off-guard, but it didn't faze the other teammates. Years of working with him made them familiar with Lockwood's unorthodox ways. The heavyset, sixtyish New Yorker frequently made borderline racist or sexist comments, and his sometimes boorish demeanor was anything but predictable. As a result, people occasionally thought him a simpleton whom they needn't take seriously. It was an image many would angrily refute, but Lockwood suppressed his true intelligence and deep human compassion so he could put the misperception to skillful use.

"Are you going somewhere with this?" Kenison prompted.

"Of course. I don't even fart without a plan," Lockwood said. He turned to Starr. "See, Doc, my favorite woodworking tools are made by a company called Stancraft Tools—they make the best hand tools in the world. So, whenever I see the word, *Stan*, I tend to think of my tools."

Deanna Starr nodded in the stereotypical way a therapist might when actively listening to a patient. Despite her obvious and sometimes awkward efforts not to sound like a shrink when talking to lay people, she often did. "That explains your association of tools with Agent Lauxner, but it doesn't speak to your unwillingness to use his proper name. Perhaps there's something deeper? Maybe you're telegraphing latent disrespect for some reason, or perhaps he evokes latent memories of childhood trauma?"

Lockwood chuckled. "Damn, Doc. You got all that because I said *Tool Man*?"

15

The Ph.D. raised her brow. "Bigger breakthroughs have come from less."

"Sorry to disappoint," Lockwood said. "It's nothing so complicated as all that. It's just that, when I was a boy, there was a kid named Stan Gregory in my neighborhood. He was the biggest asshole I ever saw—"

"So wait," Ito interrupted. "Just how many assholes have you inspected in your life, Gramps?"

Lockwood rolled his eyes. "You mean besides the one talking to me?" he rebutted. "Anyways, Stan Gregory is the reason I hate the name Stan. I like *Tool Man* here, so I gave him a name that doesn't remind me of an asshole!"

"If y'all don't mind," Lauxner interrupted. "I'd actually prefer to be called *Trigg*," he announced.

"Trigg?" Starr repeated.

"Yeah—short for *Trigger*. It's a nickname I picked up in the Army. I liked pulling the trigger to detonate unexploded ordnance when we found it."

"I'm surprised you didn't say something sooner," Starr said. "We've been calling you Stan for the last few weeks."

"It's okay," Trigg said. "I didn't want to be a burr up anyone's— I mean, I didn't want to be a bother."

"All right," Tran said. "Trigg it is. With this crowd, you'll need to speak up or they'll have you for lunch. Don't worry about offending us—we can take it, whatever it is."

Tran didn't mind the banter because it helped them gel as a team. Theirs were unusually demanding jobs that well-deserved being called an occupation. Spending as much time as they did on the road or in the air tended to intrude on families, relationships, and hobbies, so Tran gave them wide latitude to destress whenever and however they could. She checked her watch and then turned to the group as a whole. "Now, if we're done beating on each other, we have about thirty minutes 'til touchdown, and I want to review the Mission Brief before then."

"Let's have it, Boss," Lockwood answered for the group.

"All right then," Tran said as she reopened the file in her lap. "As you read in the Mission Brief, Federal Judge Jack Oberlin, his girlfriend Monique Brandon, her toddler son Charlie, and two deputy U.S. Marshals were murdered in a private cabin on Paradise Island. The killer inflicted a single shot to the head of each victim, yet no one reported hearing anything. Our primary mission is to determine who killed Judge Oberlin and why, and if the opportunity presents, bring the assassin to justice. We have leave to kill the target if necessary, but we need answers and dead men don't talk. So, if there's a way to do this without killing anyone, we do that, understand?" It wasn't really a question.

"Heard and understood," Lockwood said.

"We'll fly into Lynden Pindling International on New Providence Island and disembark at a US government hangar where we'll rendezvous with the supervisory United States Marshal assigned to the judge's protection detail—a woman named Stupleton."

"Might that be Terri Stupleton by chance?" Starr asked.

"Yes," Tran answered, nodding. "You know her?"

Starr hesitated as she stumbled over the best way to answer the question. "I wouldn't say I really know her, but a few years before joining NSA, I consulted on a case she worked."

"Do you have any insights to offer?"

"I might be able to add something as the case develops," the psychologist replied.

Tran nodded. "I want to start our work promptly. So, after we meet up with Marshal Stupleton, we'll load our gear and go directly to the scene on Paradise Island, just across the water from Nassau. The scene has been secured by Marshal Stupleton's team and local law enforcement. The FBI field office in Nassau has loaned us their Evidence Recovery Team to assist us while we're here."

"Boss," Kenison said. "I thought Federal judicial security and fugitive apprehension belonged to the Marshals?"

"To be blunt, the President is extremely irate about this case," Tran said, nodding in resigned agreement. "The Marshal's Service would

17

usually handle this kind of matter, but there are critical aspects of this particular case you don't yet know. It's not public information at this point, but Chief Justice Jonathan Brenneman of the U.S. Supreme Court has privately informed the President of his intention to retire at an unspecified date in the near future. Judge Oberlin was the President's choice to fill the open seat, and some speculated he'd even be appointed Chief Justice. Judge Oberlin and the President were personal friends from ninth grade all through college. The President summoned The Old Man to the Oval Office this morning, and personally assigned this case to us. He feels he got the judge killed by nominating him for the Court, and he wants answers. Need I say more?"

The direct involvement of General Sharp—the head of the NSA—was impressive, but the fact that the President of the United States had a personal interest in the case put it over the top for most folks, including Kenison. He swallowed hard and sat up a little straighter in his chair. "I think not," he said.

"You used the word *assassin*," Lockwood noted. "I guess we've concluded this was a political assassination because of the precision kill tactics and the clean get-away? Is there any other evidence of that?"

"It is a capital mistake to theorize before one has data. If you do, you're prone to twist facts to suit theories, instead of theories to fit facts," Tran corrected, paraphrasing the great Sherlock Holmes, the one human being—albeit fictional—whom she came closest to idolizing. "We'll have to confirm that supposition but based on what I've read and heard about the case so far, it's not a big stretch to conclude this was a professional job. It's unlikely some random local thug could have gotten passed the Marshals protecting the judge and his party, committed five murders, and gotten away without a trace."

"So we suspect there's a conspiracy at work here?" Starr surmised.

"Why do you ask that?" the novice agent asked.

Starr reoriented her body slightly to face Trigg. "There were six highly trained United States Marshals guarding Judge Oberlin, and the Mission Brief said they were plain-clothed and hidden in and around the bungalow. To take them all out and get away clean is an incredible feat of logistics. Even the most highly trained assassin would need at least one other person and maybe a team to help him accomplish that."

Tran nodded. "Besides that, only a select few people knew Judge Oberlin was set to become a Supreme Court nominee, and even fewer knew he was vacationing here at this time. The killer evidently had that information and executed what appears to be a flawless plan—that's a sophisticated operation."

"I agree, boss lady," Lockwood piped. "What do we know about Marshal Stupleton and her team?"

Tran tacitly passed the question to Dr. Starr, the only person amongst them with any familiarity with the detail's lead officer. The professional profiler seized her cue.

"Mind you, I haven't seen or spoken with Marshal Stupleton in nearly a decade, and without having more direct observation, tests, or documents to go on, my prognostication here might be inaccurate…"

With a law degree that hung on her wall, Tran could appreciate fine print and the art of hedging one's bets. "Your disclaimer is noted," she said. "Give us your best guess about Stupleton as you currently know, and feel free to revise your opinion as the case progresses, Dr. Starr."

"Sure, Grace," the psychologist began, sitting more erect. "Terri Stupleton is a highly intelligent, street-smart, ambitious Caucasian woman of roughly fifty-eight or fifty-nine. She's a retired Marine Master Gunnery Sergeant who spent most of her career in the 3rd Marine Division Combat Assault Group. She's seen heavy combat—"

"She sounds like my kind of girl," Lockwood said. "Is she single?"

"Dr. Starr said the woman is highly intelligent," Ito said. "What the hell would she want with you?"

"You're an idi-Ito!" Lockwood joked.

Starr continued. "She was drummed out of the Marine Corps after a court-martial for assaulting a commissioned officer. She must have had a great lawyer because her conviction was later overturned by

19

the Commandant of the Marine Corps, who let her retire with her rank and pension. She didn't want to retire, but figured it was a better alternative than spending time in the brig. She claimed she'd been railroaded, and now seems to have an enormous chip on her shoulder. She could have written and starred in *Diary of a Mad White Woman*."

"What do you mean, Doc?" Tran asked.

"She's not a warm-and-fuzzy type, and she's not generally receptive to different ways of thinking, seeing, and acting. She's an angry hard-charger who comes across as bossy and difficult, and she often takes a my-way-or-the-highway approach."

"I take it back," Ito said to Lockwood. "She sounds like a female you."

"That doesn't always produce the best results, but Stupleton does seem to get a fair share of good results—she did, after all, rise through the ranks of the U.S. Marshal Service pretty fast. When I last worked with her, she was a novice Deputy U.S. Marshal, and now she's apparently a full Marshal."

Tran absorbed Dr. Starr's rundown on Stupleton and mentally filed the information for later use, if and when needed. She'd learned early in her career to hear what people said of others, but reserve final judgment until the people showed themselves. "Thank you, Doctor. So, Judge Oberlin was a fifty-five-year-old, thrice-divorced father of two. He had a long line of girlfriends, before, during, and after his marriages—"

"Hell, that's probably why he had three marriages to begin with," Lockwood joked.

Tran nodded and continued speaking. "His girlfriends have included celebrity supermodels, a pop singer, three actresses, and two heiresses—one to a multi-million-dollar make-up fortune and the other to a multi-billion-dollar tech fortune."

"Damn," Trigg said, "daddy had game!" His enthusiastic grin suggested he felt awe at Oberlin's ability to lure beautiful, rich women to his bed.

Tran watched Dr. Starr shoot a steely gaze at their rookie colleague. The tall, lanky Iowan with nearly translucent skin gave the appearance of a wall flower, but she exemplified the adage that one can't judge a book by its cover. The quiet, smallish woman held a Ph.D. in clinical psychology and five national Judo championships. Indeed, Tran first met Starr on the Judo mat—they attended the same Dojo and earned their third-degree black belts at the same time.

Starr had spent much of her career as a criminal profiler for various law enforcement agencies before accepting Tran's invitation to join Field Team Six. Starr had a reputation for incredible accuracy, and she could read people as easily as she could a large-print book. She often received praise from people she'd just tactfully insulted, and they hadn't even perceived the sleight.

Trigg glanced quickly in Tran's direction and then back at Starr, apologizing under his breath.

"Grace," Starr interrupted. "I'm not a political wonk or anything but with such a sordid background, Judge Oberlin doesn't seem a very likely Supreme Court nominee, and certainly not for the Chief Justice seat. Why would the President make a seemingly controversial nomination like that?"

Tran laughed. She'd had those very same thoughts when she first began reading up on Judge Oberlin. "The President's Chief of Staff didn't want Oberlin for the job either," she began. "But, the Judge was extremely smart, very efficient, and well-respected in judicial circles. He handled some of the most difficult cases over the last few years and issued rulings that have proven to be well-reasoned and influential. The President apparently had faith enough in him to fight the political battles to get him on the highest court in the land. And besides, the President doesn't believe the focus on federal appointees' personal lives is appropriate. He's publicly urged that the Senate's evaluations of nominees for federal appointments should focus on their job skills and abilities, and their capacity for effective leadership. Lastly, I'm told the President thinks that since his party holds majorities in both the House and Senate, he can push this through Congress without losing any political capital."

"Yeah, yeah, yeah, I'm sure that's the official line," Lockwood said, "but just between us and the fencepost, the *real* reason is that Oberlin and the President were cronies, and Washington is still a town that trades on the power of who you know."

For the most part, Tran shared Lockwood's cynical assessment of all things political, but she kept her opinion to herself. Her job didn't require that she agree with her superiors' reasons, only that she carry out her duties. As long as they didn't ask her to do anything unethical, immoral, or illegal, she would do her duties to the best of her ability. She rolled her eyes and flexed her tone as she resumed the briefing. "*As I was saying*, you may recall from the local Society pages that Judge Oberlin's most recent failed marriage was to Kathleen Johnson, daughter of Dwight Johnson, the wealthy, high-powered entrepreneur businessman."

"Should I know these people?" Trigg asked.

"What rock have you been living under?" Ito asked. "When they were dating, the tabloids couldn't stay away from the tale of a super-rich, black beauty socialite with highly connected parents, and a hot, hunky, wicked-smart, white, bad boy lawyer with a promising career. When they announced their engagement…oh my God! You'd have thought they were American royalty or something."

"Uh, I haven't even finished moving my stuff up from Florida yet, so I wasn't around when all that, that…whatever was going on," Trigg said, waving his hand dismissively.

"Well I was," Kenison volunteered, "and I still didn't give a shit about it."

The group chuckled lightly as Tran pressed forth. "The Judge's divorce from Ms. Johnson was finalized a few months ago, and judging by the tabloids, she may have gotten the short end of the stick. He got the kids, the house, half their marital property, and because she's filthy rich and he's a mere civil servant, she has to pay him spousal support!"

"That's enough to make a woman kill a man dead for sure!" Lawrence joked from the screen on Ito's chest.

"Hell hath no fury like the wrath of a woman scorned," Lockwood said. "I learned that from my three ex-wives!"

22

"So the ex-wife is a suspect?" Trigg asked.

"Everyone's a suspect," Kenison answered, "including her."

"Her father died recently," Starr said. "All of these stressors together are more than enough to push a vulnerable person into a dissociative state where extreme reactions like murder are possible."

"And there may be some evidence of that," Tran added. "Kathleen purportedly had drug and alcohol problems that contributed to her loss of custody of her kids."

"I also read that she threatened to kill him!" Ito added, glee apparent in his tone.

"Where did you read that?" Kenison asked.

Ito sat quickly back in his seat and looked skyward as he stumbled over his words, a reaction that signaled his trained interrogator teammates that he was fabricating rather than recalling an answer. "Uh, not sure…one of the papers around, I guess."

"Right," Lockwood chided. "You mean the National Query, don't you? That's not a paper, you idiot! That's a gossip rag!"

Ito blushed. His secret was out.

"You're such a girl!" Kenison teased.

Tran shook her head and rolled her eyes in pseudo exasperation before continuing. "Kathleen's supporters say she got a raw deal because she's a black woman and he's a white man who's been on the DC bench for the last four years, and he's friends with all the local judges."

"You'd think her money would have evened the playing field," Lockwood said.

"Y'all white people just don't unnerstand," Lawrence chimed. "It don't make no difference how much money black folks get, how many letters they got behind their names, or what titles they wear. In the eyes of the ole' white establishment, pigmented people won't never be as good as even the dumbest, most ignorant white guy just because `a da color of their skin!"

"Yeah," Ito added. "We Asians don't fare much better. We're usually portrayed as the simple little laundry attendant or the jester making wonton soup, unless someone's feeling generous, when we become the Kung-Fu master or Yakuza thug. And don't even let me get started about my Mexican side!"

23

Rique Ito's mother had been a Mexican-American house maid before she married his father, the Japanese Ambassador to the United States. Young Rique grew up in the metro DC melting pot, but his forays outside such cosmopolitan areas had left him several reminders that minorities weren't as equal in America as the Constitution would suggest. Whenever the issue of racism surfaced, he often repeated a story of a college spring break excursion to the Florida theme parks many years earlier. A yokel at a rest stop south of Daytona Beach had told him, *"If you ain't pure white A-murican, then you's jus' a light-skin nigga 'ta me, boy."* As usual, he quickly told a summary version of the experience with passion as though it had happened yesterday.

As two of four white men aboard the plane, Kenison and Trigg seemed to squirm uncomfortably as their non-Caucasian colleagues told of their brushes with racism, but Scott, the pilot up in the cockpit, didn't hear it, and judging from his flat, impervious expression, Lockwood didn't care enough to be bothered.

"All that may be true, but my hunch is these murders had nothing to do with his wife and the divorce," Lockwood pondered. "What kind of cases did the Judge handle?"

"That's a great angle," Tran said. "…Something he's already decided, was in the process of deciding, or had yet to decide. Viv, contact the Judge's clerk and begin going through everything on his docket, recent or upcoming. Forward anything interesting to Dr. Starr for additional screening."

"We shouldn't discount the women with whom he's been involved or their male relations," Starr added. "Judge Oberlin was a highly visible playboy who seemed to come out on top in his relationships with these women. If they or their fathers, brothers, or other men in their lives felt the Judge had taken advantage of them or portrayed them unfairly, that too could have been a powerful motive. A sense of moral injustice has historically been a powerful motivator for people who felt they had no other recourse."

"I always say, follow the money," Kenison volunteered. "No disrespect to the President's buddy, but in my experience, people do funny things for money, including getting into bed with strange partners—sometimes figuratively and sometimes literally."

"You think there's a business deal gone bad here?" Lockwood asked.

24

Kenison sat forward in his chair. "It is a capital mistake to theorize before one has data. If you do, you're prone to twist facts to suit theories, instead of theories to suit facts," he said, parroting one of Tran's mantras.

"I couldn't have said it better myself," Tran agreed.

"Excuse me, Boss," Trigg timidly asked. "This might be a dumb question—"

"There are no dumb questions, Trigg," Starr reassured.

"They called their Protectee *Pigmeat*. I mean…well…That sounds kind of disrespectful. Why would they call him that?" the newbie asked.

Tran smirked as she looked down at the file in her lap and shook her head. "I asked the same question, Trigg," she admitted. "And to be candid, I don't know…but, we can certainly find out."

A slight hiss from the ceiling mounted speakers telegraphed that a message from the cockpit was about to air. Tran fell silent as she waited. "Ladies and gents, this is Scott," the speaker blared. "Sorry to interrupt all your secret spy planning and stuff back there, but we're cleared to land at Pindling. We'll be on the ground—hopefully in one piece—in about five or ten minutes. Since NSA Airways is a no-frills carrier that doesn't spring for flight attendants, I guess this is the part where I ask you to return to your seats, fasten your seatbelts, and bring your tray tables and seatbacks to an upright position."

The hiss cracked again to signal that Scott had completed his announcement and deactivated the radio. Now, they needed to prepare for landing, followed by the real work they came to do. Tran quickly summarized her comments.

"Okay folks, as soon as we land, we're headed to the scene to get our first look at the situation. Trigg, you come with me, and the rest of you can scour the scene. After we're done there, we'll rendezvous to determine next steps. For now, let's strap in and enjoy the scenery as we approach. Questions?"

Of course, the team members had a bevy of questions, but deferred them until a more opportune moment. They each turned their chairs forward, and just like normal people on a normal airline, they gazed out the widows as the regional jet approached the island. The sun burned brightly in a clear blue sky. It made for an excellent distraction to their mission.

***

The island's enormous, towering resort hotels were the first views that grabbed the team's attention as they descended gracefully through the bright sky. But the buildings soon gave way to stunning vistas of crystal clear aquamarine water shimmering under mild Caribbean winds that churned white frothy waves at the beach. Living in the DC metro area, they'd all seen the ocean before, but somehow, this much further south, under the tropical sun, the water seemed bluer, the skies brighter, and the sun warmer. Throngs of people frolicked in the surf and built castles in the sand, seemingly oblivious to the aircraft streaking overhead and then gliding gently onto the airstrip beyond a road that paralleled the beachfront.

A last-minute crosswind made the plane touch down more firmly than anyone expected, jostling everyone aboard as the aircraft transitioned from flight to taxiing. The intrepid small plane travelers were undaunted, perhaps with the exception of Trigg whose face turned flush with momentary excitement.

"You know what they say about landings, don't you Tool Man?" Lockwood asked. Though the immediate danger had passed, a pallid Trigg didn't speak, but instead merely shook his head. "Any landing you can walk away from is a good one!" Lockwood said, answering his own question.

Having heard the adage from Lockwood nearly every time they had a less-than-smooth landing, the members of the team all laughed, but none as heartily as Lockwood.

The G6 taxied to a private hangar directly across from the main airport terminal, and as the passengers peered out the windows, three black SUVs rolled to a stop and formed a semi-circle near the aircraft. Four suit-clad people in sunglasses emerged from within, closed the doors, and leaned against the sides of their vehicles. Almost in unison, they folded their arms and stood motionless as they watched the jet roll to a complete stop.

Tran unsnapped her seatbelt and maneuvered to the door. She peered out at the Marshals and sighed deeply as she grasped the door handle. *It's show time*, she thought.

Chapter 3: And So It Begins

Looking out the round window in the jet's door, Tran saw a middle-aged Caucasian woman leaning against the lead vehicle, arms folded over her chest as she visually tracked the aircraft. She chewed a wad of gum like a cow chewing its cud. A thin younger man stood stoically at her side, also watching the jet roll to a stop. Their colleagues in the other cars did likewise.

Tran figured the authoritative figure at the front vehicle had to be Marshal Stupleton. Her suit, which looked as though it had come off-the-rack of a men's clothier, accented a thick, somewhat masculine build, capped by bowl-cut salt-and-pepper hair. Her broad shoulders and square build masked any hint of femininity. The Marshal's dark glasses were stereotypical of federal agents on television shows, and her plain, flat shoes would likely make her the butt of jokes at a comedy club.

When the plane stopped moving, Grace Tran turned the latch, lowered the door, and immediately descended the stairs. The bright light and warm tropical breeze made it feel like she'd stepped into vacation, grossly at odds with the reason she'd come to the Bahamas. She walked directly to the woman at the front of the formation. "You must be Marshal Stupleton," she said, extending her hand. "I'm Special Agent Grace Tran, NSA Field Team Six."

Marshal Stupleton paused and maybe sneered a bit as she looked Tran up one side and down the other. With an African-American father and a Vietnamese mother, Tran had a dark, creamy complexion, long black hair, high cheekbones, green eyes, and other features that made her exotic in the eyes of many. That and her shapely, athletic, five-eleven physique made her accustomed to being ogled, mostly by men. But the Marshal's overt examination seemed especially rude and it made Tran uncomfortable. At that moment, Tran felt the birth of mutual disdain between her and Stupleton.

After an awkward pause, Stupleton finally took Tran's hand and shook it without smiling or offering the usual pleasantries exchanged by people meeting for the first time. "This way, Tran," she said, motioning to the lead vehicle. "You ride with me. Your team will be in the other two as they please."

Tran turned and waved at the jet, spurring her team to disembark and offload their gear. The young man who'd stood at Stupleton's side held open the rear door of the car and Stupleton stepped inside and slid across the seat. Tran paused a moment as the driver held the door, and then raised her pointer finger.

"One second, please," she said, smiling and turning back to her team. They were already loading their gear into the backs of the SUVs.

"We got it, Grace," Lockwood yelled, politely waving Tran off.

"Oh, okay," she replied, reticent about not helping. She watched a second more as her team packed the last items into the truck, and quickly dispersed into the two remaining SUVs in a smooth, nearly silent operation. Satisfied her team was situated, Tran turned back to the young man at the door. "May I ask your name?"

"Uh, yes ma'am. I'm Deputy Marshal Mengyao Liang," he answered.

Tran smiled. "All right, Marshal Liang. I'm Special Agent Grace Tran," she said, lightly patting the arm with which he held the door. "Thank you."

Tran turned and slid into the SUV's middle row of seats, buckling herself in as Marshal Liang closed the door. He seated himself up front, buckled in, and fired up the truck's powerful engine. Behind them, two more engines growled to life, and seconds later, the small caravan sped off the airport grounds. Stupleton remained stoic during the initial leg of the journey, but as they pulled further from the airport, she abruptly spoke.

"Where are you staying?" Stupleton asked. "We'll get you checked in and—"

"Thanks," Tran interrupted, "but I want to get to the scene immediately. We can check-in to our rooms later."

"My folks are still processing the scene. When they're done, we'll get a report together for you, and—"

"I'm sorry," Tran again interrupted. "Did you say your team is processing the scene?"

"Yes. In my experience, getting right on the scene preserves evidence better than—"

"With all due respect, Marshal, I know the proper procedures for collecting evidence," Tran said. "My issue is that *you've* got people processing the scene. I don't want anyone trampling evidence that may be critical to my investigation. Please call and have your folks immediately stop what they're doing and withdraw to the perimeter. We'll also want to speak with your folks."

Stupleton slid a manila folder across the seat to Tran's side of the car. "All their statements are here," she said, "and when they've completed processing the area, you'll get a report of their findings just as I've provided you their statements."

"Thanks, but I don't want a summary of their findings, Marshal. I want to look at the scene myself and make my own observations, just as I'd like to speak with your Deputies and prepare my own summaries of their statements," Tran explained.

Stupleton had been staring out the windshield through her dark glasses which she'd not removed at any point since Tran arrived. She turned abruptly and snatched them from her face, sighing heavily and rolling her eyes. "We gonna' have a problem here, Tran?"

"As long as you don't interfere with my investigation, I wouldn't think we'd have any problems at all."

"That's the second time you've used that phrase, *my investigation.*"

"Yes," Tran agreed. "I was under the impression you'd been briefed that NSA has point in this matter, and that means *me.*"

"Oh sweetie," the Marshal began. "I guess you need a little lesson on executive branch structure. Judicial security belongs to the Marshal Service—and *that* means *me.* You people are here to assist."

"I don't need a civics lesson from you, and don't call me sweetie. You may call me *ma'am, Agent Tran,* or even *Ms. Tran.* Now, I don't want to get in a pissing match with you about this, so you need to understand from the start that I'm calling the shots here," Tran lectured.

"How is this a national security issue?" Stupleton asked. "That dead judge isn't a spy, he wasn't an NSA agent carrying national security secrets, and this certainly isn't an intelligence operation. It's clearly a matter of judicial security and such mat—"

"I'm not debating this with you, Marshal," Tran said tersely. "My authority comes directly from the President. He personally tasked me to lead this investigation. I'll report my findings directly to him. If you'd like, I'll tell him that you expect him to call and justify his decision to you."

Tran stopped speaking and stared dead into Stupleton's eyes, letting the silence hang heavy in the air. The Marshal fell quiet as she glowered. Tran assumed Stupleton was mentally debating the situation. Through the cold stare, Tran could almost see the thoughts churning in Stupleton's mind: *Is this skinny bitch giving me a load of shit or did the President really assign her to this?* The stakes were high, and Stupleton would be foolish to wager. A Presidential edict would easily explain the NSA's hush-hush involvement in the case and its quick arrival on scene.

"Okay," Stupleton finally said aloud, "but if I find you've lied…"

"Save it," Tran said, raising her palm almost to Stupleton's face. "Consider your threat made. Now, please get your people out of my crime scene and brief me on everything you know about this case. Let's start with exactly who's at the scene now. Of your six-member protection detail, two are dead, I presume three are driving these vehicles, and you're arguing with me. So, who's at the crime scene and what are they doing?"

Stupleton glared at Tran while Tran returned the eye lock, patiently awaiting answers to her questions. Finally, Stupleton offered them. "I procured assistance from the US Navy base across the water. The installation commander detailed some sailors from the Shore Patrol," she said. "I ordered them to secure the perimeter and patrol for explosives or incendiaries that may have been left to destroy evidence or cover tracks."

"Call ahead and order them to the perimeter, and keep everyone out," Tran repeated.

"No need," Stupleton said.

"Excuse me?"

Tran nearly slipped into anger, but Stupleton nodded, tacitly directing Tran's attention through the windshield. "We're here."

The black SUVs rolled through an ornate wrought iron gate in an iron and stone fence that stretched wide to the left and right, then turned and extended toward the beach over dunes beyond which Tran couldn't see. The caravan traveled up a gradual incline in the sand driveway, crested a hill, and down to the front of a small bungalow. The driveway curved around a large, three-tiered, stone fountain. The SUVs followed the drive half-way around the fountain and stopped between it and an intricate carved-wood double door framed by sidelights and a transom. The bungalow's most impressive feature was the vast expanse of beachfront and grassy dunes inside its fence line. Given its enormity, this had to be an expensive retreat for someone.

"This is the crime scene," Stupleton said.

The driver hopped from the vehicle and rushed to the right rear door, where he quickly took position behind the door and opened it like a proper chauffer would. Stupleton stepped from the car without speaking a word and walked briskly into the bungalow's open front door, leaving the rest of her team outside along with Tran and Field Team Six. The driver closed Stupleton's door and hurried to round the vehicle to get Tran's door, but the NSA agent had already alighted before he reached her. She politely thanked him for his effort and turned to look for her team, already disembarking their SUVs, grabbing their gear, and converging on her. As she waited for the team to assemble, Tran heard Stupleton barking orders at the people inside.

"Okay, folks," Tran began when everyone had gathered near. "Let's disperse and make our initial observations—standard approach. I'm afraid the Marshals had a team in the scene already. Hopefully, they didn't trample valuable evidence, but just keep that in mind as you make your observations and reports. We've got an Evidence Recovery Team en route from the local FBI field office to help us. Trigg, you're with me."

With little chatter, the team poured into the bungalow and across the property like water flooding over the grounds, the playful banter from the aircraft replaced by a singular purpose of mind about which there was no joke. Kenison and Ito moved in opposite directions around the outside of the bungalow while everyone else followed Tran inside. Lockwood continued on to the beachside door directly opposite the front entry, and Starr made a beeline for a few Deputy Marshals hovering in the area. Tran watched her team begin its initial assessment, and then turned her attention to her rookie who casually observed whatever he could see from the door.

"Welcome to Field Team Six, Trigg," she said. "You're lucky this is the crime scene for your first investigation."

"Why's that, ma'am?" he asked.

"Given the nature of our work, we don't always have the opportunity to examine an actual crime scene. Our work often involves the discovery and analysis of emails, conversations, phone calls, secret meetings, and other unspecified criminal actions for which there's often no actual location where a crime occurred. Here, we have a chance to observe a physical area relevant to our mission."

The newbie nodded as Tran jutted her chin toward the rear door. Trigg's eyes followed her nod to a body on a blood-soaked floor in the center of the room. Beyond it, a second body lay in a puddle of blood, partly inside but mostly outside the beachside cabin door. Lockwood knelt over it, gently moving hair that had fallen into the body's face. Tran closed the distance to the body inside the bungalow, and then stared down at it for some time. Trigg did likewise. After several minutes, Tran knelt to get a closer look. She studied it in silence for an enduring period, and then glanced around the room. Her eyes locked on additional blood splatter on the wall twenty feet away in the interior hall, suggesting another body would be found there. She turned to her trainee.

"What do you see?" she asked.

"Uh…dead white guy, maybe 40, wearing a sweat suit," Trigg answered pensively.

Tran nodded. "I see a deceased Caucasian male of approximately six feet, two inches in height, two-hundred ten pounds with highly defined lean muscle mass, roughly forty-five years of age. He has a single small caliber entry wound center mass of the back of his head, and I anticipate a larger exit wound center mass of the forehead. The body is in a forty-degree anterior oblique position, the left arm pinned beneath while the right is lying in forward lateral position at forty-five degrees. Judging from the bulge in his back, he was armed, probably with a Glock-22, standard issue for the US Marshal Service." She leaned forward and stepped to the side for a more direct view of the body's face. "The bullet hole in his forehead looks to be about nine or ten millimeters."

Tran stood and examined the wall and floor. Trigg stood too and looked in the direction of her gaze, as she jutted her chin toward the hall. "Blood spray on the wall and the spread on the floor indicates he was hit while standing, and then collapsed and bled out. He probably didn't see it coming and had no indication of danger or he'd have reached for his weapon."

Tran changed positions and looked around the room again. She saw into the adjoining hallway where the body of a small child lay on the floor in the doorway of a bedroom, with additional blood splatter streaked over the walls and floor there. She jutted her chin in that direction, and in unison, the pair meandered toward the child's corpse. As they approached, Trigg turned his head, his demeanor growing observably affected. Tran didn't know her rookie as well as she knew the others on her team, but she knew Trigg was close to his two young sons. She guessed he'd seen their eyes in the face of the dead toddler at their feet. She pulled him gently by his shoulder and moved closer to examine the body in more detail.

She stooped to the ground and looked up at Trigg. "It's not pleasant, but you've got to look," she said. "If you're going to be good at this job, you'll have to confront things you'd rather not. It's how you keep other people from having to see stuff like this."

Haltingly, Trigg stooped and faced the dead child. Despite his obvious effort to repress the tear forming in the corner of his eye, Tran saw it, but pretended she didn't. Parts of this hard-boiled soldier weren't so tough after all, but only a rare man wouldn't be moved by something like this. Tran made sure to keep her firearm handy when in the presence of that type of man— a person like that surely had something genetically wrong with them.

"Small caliber weapon," Trigg observed.

"Yep." Tran stood and walked into the bedroom, stopping at the foot of the bed where the bodies of Judge Jack Oberlin and Monique Brandon lay stiffening into rigor mortis. She stared a moment, and then looked back toward the hall. "The killer probably finished off these two and turned around to find the kid standing there."

"Why would someone do this to a kid?" Trigg bemoaned. "He can't be more than two or three," he said, gently moving the blond hair from the boy's face.

"I guess he wanted to eliminate any risk the kid might have seen something that would eventually lead us to him," Tran said. "From everything I can tell so far, he covered his tracks pretty well." Deep in thought, she stood and peered down at the small dead child. "We need to find out where the judge's children are."

She rounded the bed and observed the pallid bodies of Oberlin and Brandon. She observed their wounds and blood patterns there too. She motioned for Trigg to join her and walked him through her observations. He asked a few questions, some of which Tran thought were good, and she answered them as best she could. He seemed surprised by the number of "I don't knows" Tran offered, but she explained it clearly: one of the worst things an investigator can do is presume she knows things she doesn't really know. At such times, Tran said, *I don't know* is the right answer because spouting off at the mouth leads to faulty conclusions, missed opportunities, and national security threats.

"There's a joke to be made here," Lockwood bellowed as he entered the bedroom behind them, "but for the sake of decorum, I won't say anything about him coming and going at the same time." Lockwood smiled as he pointed at Oberlin.

Tran rolled her eyes, shook her head, and sighed. "What do you have, Ian?"

The older agent motioned over his shoulder through walls and doors to the beach side of the cabin. "The guy in the doorway is Deputy Marshal Sam Fakmann, in the service three years now. Looks like he came up on the place as the killer was leaving, opened the door, and immediately took a nine or ten-millimeter round to the center of his forehead. I'm sure the guy didn't see it coming."

"Same for the one in the living room—Deputy Marshal Declan O'Keefe," Tran said. "This poor lady here got the same while the Judge took one to the back of the head—definitely a professional job. What did you notice about the wounds, Trigg?"

The newbie momentarily paused with a deer-in-the-headlight expression on his face, not unlike a grade-schooler called on by his teacher. After a second, he seemed to collect himself and forced out a reasonably intelligent if pensive reply. "Uh, they're all the same size and same spots?"

"Precisely," Tran agreed. "In eyeballing it, it looks like all the wounds are in precisely the same locations on the forehead, even on Oberlin, who took a cap from the rear. You don't find that level of precision in a run-of-the-mill thug."

"Damn straight!" Lockwood agreed. "And there were no reports of anything unusual until Marshal Henri heard Fakmann go down," he said.

"And I presume they didn't hear anything?" Tran asked.

"No gunshots, if that's what you mean," Lockwood replied. "Henri heard the thud when Fakmann caught it in the head."

Tran nodded.

"A silenced weapon?" Trigg pensively asked.

Tran nodded again. "It's the best theory we've got right now."

She turned to Lockwood. "What's the story?"

Lockwood turned and abruptly exited the bedroom. He walked through the small hallway outside of it and stopped in the middle of the living room near the body of Deputy Marshal O'Keefe. He looked toward the rear door where a second body lay half-in and half-outside the cabin. Tran and Trigg followed, wanting to understand his thoughts. "Marshal Henri told me that he and Fakmann over there had just returned from a coffee run. Fakmann was supposed to relieve O'Keefe," he said, nodding to the body at his feet, "and Henri was supposed to relieve Liang out in the yard. Shortly after they separated on the path outside, Henri heard Fakmann go down."

"You have a time?"

"A little before midnight."

"So that's our working window, then. The killer wouldn't hang around after the job was done," Tran said. "And Fakmann caught it head-on as he entered the cabin, so the killer was on his way out at that point."

"Agreed."

"So we need to find evidence or witnesses to something just before 12 a.m."

"Speaking of witnesses…"

"Don't tell me you've located someone who saw the whole thing?" Tran joked.

"Close—Miss Brandon's other kid."

"I thought there were only five bodies?"

"There are. This kid survived."

Tran opened the file in her hand and scanned the pages inside once more, not believing she would've missed that piece of information in the umpteen times she'd read the report. It made no mention of a second child. "Stupleton," she yelled.

Tran turned abruptly and stormed out of the bedroom. As she reached the juncture of the hallway and living room, she stopped to scan for her target. Seeing the supervisory Marshal huddling with one of her team's technicians just outside the beachside door, she approached them with obvious purpose.

"If you'll please excuse us, I need a private word with your boss here," she barked, not-so-tactfully dismissing the technician.

For an awkward second, the man stared at her in seeming disbelief and Tran stared back without expression as she waited for him to withdraw. After a time, he backed up and then walked away. When he'd gone, she turned to Stupleton. The latter hesitated and then looked askance at Tran, her expression signaling her annoyance at Tran's interruption of her conversation with the man.

"That was rude, Agent Tran," the Marshal barked.

"I said *please*. What more do you want?" Tran said, dismissively. "Why didn't your report state that there was another child in the bungalow?"

"Excuse me?"

"Your report failed to note the second child in the bungalow, the one who survived the night's events," Tran barked. "Why?"

"I'm not accustomed to being interrupted when I'm working a case, Agent Tran," the Marshal chastised.

"I don't care what you're accustomed to, Marshal. I care that your report omitted relevant information that could be of critical importance to my investigation."

"What're you talking about?"

"Ms. Brandon's surviving child isn't noted in your report."

"I, I thought it was," Stupleton defended. "In fact, I'm sure of it."

"It's not," Tran countered. "This is the second significant inaccuracy I've noted about your report, and—"

"My report is directly on point, Agent Tran."

"I beg to differ. Your report also indicated your team would be securing the scene, not processing it. There's a difference. Had I known you would have people traipsing in and out of my scene, I'd have taken action sooner," Tran lectured. "This kind of inattention to detail doesn't give me confidence in your work, Marshal Stupleton. It makes me wonder what else you missed or neglected."

"Now listen here, Agent Tran!" Stupleton fired back. "I'm a lot of things, but careless in my work isn't one of them. I'm not about to stand here and listen to you insult me for—"

"You can stand anywhere you want, but you'll damn well listen when I speak," Tran corrected. "Now take this, review it, and make sure *all* relevant facts are there," she said, shoving the Marshal's report into her chest. "If there's anything missing, fix it and let me know at once. Am I clear?"

Stupleton snatched the report, looked at it briefly, then turned and stormed away without answering. Tran anticipated a curse word or two, or several, but they didn't come.

"Boss, I'm ready to render my initial report," a voice called from the rear.

Tran turned to see Kenison approaching briskly from the beachside door. "Go ahead."

"I've surveyed the grounds and talked with several of the Marshals on duty at the time," he said. "I found no shells or other evidence outside, except a few partial footprints on the path. I asked one of the Navy techs to take castings of the prints so we can examine them later. Anyway, of the six Marshals in the security detail, two were on a break at the time of the murders. Four Marshals were on sentry duty: one inside the house with the Judge and his girlfriend, one orbiting the grounds immediately around the bungalow, and two were aboard a patrol boat twenty yards offshore. The two on break returned to relieve the two on the grounds just after the murder."

"A patrol boat?"

"Yeah, the Command Post for this operation. It was assigned by the US Navy base across the bay to support the protection detail."

"Why the hell were there *two* agents aboard the boat?" Tran wondered aloud. "That reduces the concentration of force around the Protectee in the bungalow."

"Agreed," Kenison said. "It was a mediocre allocation of resources under the circumstances. I'd have pulled the second Marshal off the boat and had him orbiting the bungalow too. Only thing I can say in their defense is that they also deployed a portable laser sensor grid around the cabin too, which they might have thought would make up for the lack of coverage."

Tran considered the information. The laser sensor grid was a good idea because it shot invisible lasers across its field of vision. Any disruptions to the field—like say, a person moving across the grid—would cause an alarm back at the monitoring panel, which Tran guessed was in the Command Post. The Marshals who were supposed to be walking through it wore small transponders on their legs that made them invisible as disruptions when they moved. As Tran was about to ask her next question, Kenison anticipated her.

"Yeah, I checked the grid system's log. It was functioning perfectly but recorded no disruptions before the first indication that anything was wrong, and lots of them afterward. The disruptions are first detected about three feet beyond the cabin near the beachside door, and they go down the pathway through the trees on the southwest side and directly to the fence. Nothing after that."

"That corroborates what the Marshals said about the perpetrator's escape route. Assuming that grid disruption was in fact our killer, it's curious why the system didn't detect him when he entered the scene but did as he exited."

"So maybe the killer was already in the bungalow before they deployed the sensor grid," Trigg suggested.

"Possible, but the Marshal's report says they cleared the cabin before they allowed the Judge's party to enter it for the first time," Lockwood said. "There was always a Marshal inside after they arrived, so nobody could have infiltrated after that point."

"What if the perp was already inside, like hidden in the attic or under the floorboards or something?" Trigg asked.

"Possible, but doubtful," Kenison answered. "Per standard protocol, the Marshals used biometric scans to help them clear the

40

building; they didn't just do a look-see. If there was anybody in the house, the scans would have detected their body temperature, their breathing, and their heartbeat, so I kinda' doubt the Marshals just missed a hidden assassin."

"Unless one or more of them were in on it," Lockwood said. "That's a classic tactic for political assassinations—an inside man."

Tran raised her head and looked beyond the members of her team. Across the room, three Deputy Marshals huddled in a tight circle, talking to Agent Starr. Several feet to their right, Marshal Stupleton spoke into her cell phone, and judging by her expressions and sharp movements, the conversation displeased her to no end.

"...or maybe an inside woman," Tran added.

Chapter 4: Broma in Serio

"Dr. Starr?" Tran called across the room.

The psychologist looked toward Tran as she hastened to finish her conversation with the Marshals.

"Dr. Starr, a word please?" Tran said, motioning for Starr to join her.

Starr excused herself as she politely pushed between the shoulders of Deputy Marshals Henri, Liang, and Oseefah. After a few broad strides, Starr crossed from one side of the bungalow almost to the other and stopped a comfortable distance from Tran.

"Yes Grace?" she asked.

"How's your talk with the Marshals going?"

Starr pursed her lip, half-nodded, and shrugged her shoulder, obviously not grasping Tran's underlying question. "Okay, I suppose."

"Anything jump out at you?" Tran pressed.

"Not especially, but I think you must mean something in particular," Starr answered.

"Do you get the sense any of them are being evasive or guarded?"

Starr nodded as she realized what Tran meant. "Ah, as if they may have been part of what happened here," she surmised. "I wasn't particularly screening for that, but so far, their behaviors strike me as within the norm under the circumstances." She glanced quickly over her shoulder at the trio to whom she'd been talking and then turned back to Tran. "They're all unnerved, angry, and energized, like they're ready to go hunt down the bad guy. One seems a little more of all of that than the others, but as I said, those are probably typical reactions."

42

"Who?"

"Marshal Liang strikes me as a bit more affected by last night's events than the others, but he's also the youngest, most inexperienced among them. This is his first protection detail since he graduated training. Marshal Henri seems the angriest."

Tran nodded and studied the Marshals as she processed Starr's assessments for a moment. "Okay, Dr. Starr. Carry on with what you're doing. I'm particularly interested in any signs of evasiveness. When you're done, coordinate with Viv and comb through the service records of every member of the protection detail, including the deceased. If anything strikes you as even remotely unusual, I want to know it."

"You really think one of them was in on it?" Trigg asked.

"It's a capital mistake to theorize before one has data, lest you twist the facts to suit your theories, Trigg," Tran said.

"An enemy at the gates is less formidable, for he is known and carries his banner openly," Lockwood added. "...but the traitor moves freely amongst those within the gate."

Trigg contorted his face. "Huh?"

Lockwood laughed and clapped him gently on the shoulder. "It's from Marcus Tullius Cicero, the ancient Roman philosopher, my young, unlearned friend," he joked. "Someone inside a group can harm the group more easily than someone outside. People expect attack from outside, but not from one of their own."

"It's one possible theory of many at the moment," Tran said, turning to Starr. "Doctor," she prompted.

"I'm on it, Grace," Starr replied. The doctor turned and strolled back to the Marshals she'd been talking with earlier, quickly re-engaging them in conversation.

"All right," Tran said to the rest of the team. "I think we—"

As Tran began her discussion anew, rumbles from the front of the bungalow demanded her attention. She looked through the open front door just as a white vehicle rolled into view. As soon as it stopped, Tran heard doors opening and closing and the crescendo of an authoritative voice barking instructions. She fell silent and walked briskly to the door to investigate, her hand instinctively finding the holster on her hip. Lockwood, Kenison, and Trigg fell in behind her.

As she stepped through the threshold onto the stoop, Tran saw two plain white vans now parked alongside the SUVs that brought her team to the bungalow. A small contingent of people, the sun reflecting off the polished brass badges hanging from their sides, disembarked the vans and immediately began unloading all manner of equipment. The one who'd been droning instructions to the others broke off from the group and headed directly for Tran, smiling widely as he approached.

"You must be Agent Tran," he said, extending his hand. "I'm Special Agent Bob Darden, FBI. We're your ERT, and I promise you, we're the best damn Evidence Recovery Team in the Bureau."

Tran shook his hand firmly. "Good meeting you, Agent Darden. I appreciate you guys changing your schedule around to help us out here."

"When the SAC gets a call from the Deputy Assistant Director who received a call from the Director, who received a call from the Director of National Security and the White House Chief of Staff, well, we make that a priority," he said, chuckling.

Tran had never been comfortable with VIPs throwing their weight around to get special treatment for her. She much preferred to make her own way in the world, even if it meant she had to fight to do it. But, she recognized that sometimes, that's just the way things were. Besides, Tran had a long history with the Bureau's new Deputy Assistant Director, going back to their days at the Air Force Academy. They'd dated off and on throughout college and remained close friends even after their careers moved in separate directions. They'd worked together on interagency task forces a few times, including the team's last case that took them through swamps and beach towns in Florida. Newly promoted to Deputy Assistant Director, Mark Allen had said Darden was a rigid, by-the-book guy who was also damn near the best, if not THE best in the world at evidence recovery. In forensic investigations, Tran knew attention to detail and adherence to process were vital. Knowing Allen was as scrutinizing as she, Tran trusted his judgment nearly as much as she did her own. She thus felt comfortable accepting Allen's help, especially since she didn't have her own ERT.

"The Deputy Assistant Director and I go way back, but I'm sorry he pressured your Special Agent-in-Charge to help us. Nonetheless, I appreciate your assistance with this case, Agent Darden."

He waved his hand nonchalantly. "Bob, please."

"Okay, Bob, and I'm Grace. In any event, the Marshals and Navy personnel have been all throughout the place for several hours, so keep that in mind as you process the scene," she said, pointing over her shoulder to the bungalow. "I'll need the standard processing of the entire scene, inside and out, plus the five dead bodies inside. Make sure nobody but your team and mine touches anything in here again."

"Yes ma'am. We're on it."

"And Bob?"

"Ma'am?"

"You know how visible this matter is, right?"

"Oh yes, ma'am. I can't tell you how many times my boss used the phrase, 'no screw-ups,' before sending us out here." He quickly considered how his comment might be misperceived. "...It's not that I have a problem with screwing things up...well, I don't mean that I'm good at screwing things up because I don't have a history of doing that at all. It's just that..."

Tran chuckled. "I get it, Bob. No worries. Just...do what you do best," she said, stepping to the side and extending her arm toward the cabin door.

"Yes ma'am. I'm...just...gonna' stop talking now and get to work, how's that?" he asked, trying to bring his awkward commentary to a close.

Tran smiled and nodded at Darden, who turned to greet several members of his evidence team as they approached the cabin door. He conferred with them about their assigned tasks. The technicians greeted Tran and her team as they walked into the cabin and quickly dispersed as though they'd rehearsed the maneuver a million times before.

Tran turned and observed the bevy of activity and people in the small structure, which now resembled a beehive—many workers crawling about in a flurry of seemingly uncoordinated activity that was in reality a highly-orchestrated ballet. The quiet beachside bungalow had quickly become a very busy place.

At Tran's side, Lockwood said, "Well, Boss, looks like too many cooks in the kitchen in there, so how 'bout I take Tool Man and poke around the beach to see what we can find."

Tran nodded. "Sounds like a plan, Ian."

Lockwood looked at the rookie and jerked his head toward the beachside doors. A second later, the pair walked through the bungalow's front door, into its main living room, and then disappeared out its back door on the other side. Tran scanned the area for Ito but didn't see him anywhere. She lifted her phone and punched a speed dial number. Ito answered after two rings.

"Boss?"

"Where are you, Rique? I don't see you anywhere in the cabin."

"That's 'cause we're not in the cabin, Grace. We're on the dunes out back. I'll come down."

"No need if you're in the middle of something," Tran said.

"Viv and I are running a hunch to ground. We might have something—not sure yet."

"No worries, Rique. You've got excellent instincts. Follow them. I'm going to poke around down here, and we can catch up later." Tran disconnected the call and tucked the phone in her pocket.

Kenison excused himself. "While you do that, I'm going to walk the perimeter."

Kenison turned to head for the property's main gate. Tran turned toward the cabin. Peering at the swarm of workers buzzing about, she decided to start her work in the backyard. As she walked through the house toward the back door, she recalled the Mission Brief. Stupleton's report said the killer escaped over the wall between the bungalow's yard and a public beach. He purportedly ran along the pathway, scaled the wall, and ultimately escaped into the water.

Stepping into the yard from the cabin's back door, Tran inhaled slowly as she closed her eyes, sending her consciousness deep into her mind. She imagined herself as the assassin, emerging from the scene, desperate to make her getaway, knowing that any second, a Marshal she hadn't killed might soon come upon her. She followed the killer's likely route, carefully studying the ground as she moved. A few steps from the door, she found an indentation in the sand tinged with a scarlet hue in its ridges and valleys. She knelt to study it more closely: shallow, but broad and mushy with consistent, round, squiggly ridges across the entire tread. *A work boot?* Tran wondered. She leaned closer to the ground and, squinting one eye, looked with the other down the path ahead. She saw a run of larger, heavier, footprints at consistent intervals, but only one additional print like the one at her knee.

After a certain point, Tran saw only the heavier prints as they led off toward the wall. She stood and followed them until they stopped and circled back toward the bungalow. She guessed these footprints belonged to the Marshal who gave chase but broke pursuit and returned to the cabin on orders from his superior. She knelt again and searched for more of the odd footprints but found none. Searching all the way to the wall at the edge of the property, she still found no more of them, but noted several areas of smashed grass with the same scarlet hue. Tran estimated the solid, gray, earthen wall at the rear of the property stood twelve feet high. She stood at its base and craned her neck to see the top edge. She didn't think she could scale it without help, even with a running start, thus making her wonder how the killer had gotten over it so quickly. She considered whether the killer would have been able to do it so easily if the Marshal on his tail had chased him all the way to the wall. Shaking her head, Tran wondered why Stupleton had given such an order. Tran would never have sacrificed the opportunity to nab a bad guy under circumstances like these. Even if he were only nominally competent, the Marshal in pursuit could no doubt have captured or wounded the fleeing suspect given the distance between them and the confines of the yard.

"Marcus Tullius Cicero might have been onto something," she

said aloud, oscillating her gaze from the wall to the cabin and back again.

She pondered the possibilities a few minutes more, and then retraced her steps to the top of the path. With cell phone in hand, she took multiple pictures of the prints and marks on the ground along the way. As she studied the photo images she captured to assure she'd not put her thumb into the picture or done some other equally inane thing, someone yelled her name and title from the cabin. The unexpected interruption sent a flash of irritation through her body, but she suppressed it in an instant. She knew her natural impatience wasn't among her finer qualities, and though she'd worked hard to change it over the years, it occasionally emerged. The discourteous response she felt well up in her gut dissipated the second she realized it was Kenison who'd called out to her, but his tone and manner carried an unusual formality.

"Special Agent-in-Charge Tran?" he repeated.

Tran watched as Kenison escorted a woman in the unmistakable dress-uniform of the United States Navy. Even at a distance, with hair tucked in her unflattering cap, the young, shapely woman looked the picture of a supermodel, and Tran didn't need her crack investigative skills to see that Kenison had noticed it too. If his goofy expression hadn't revealed as much, his awkward manner with the beautiful young officer surely did. Tran mentally shook her head as she marveled at the way an attractive woman's mere presence instantly transformed one of the sharpest young agents she'd ever known into a stuttering, stammering fool. She hoped the Lieutenant's focus on her steps over the sandy, difficult-to-walk-in-while-wearing-heels path had rendered her oblivious to Kenison's temporary idiocy. Tran put her phone away and started toward the pair, wondering why a Navy officer would be at the scene.

"Special Agent-in-Charge Grace Tran," Kenison repeated when they reached speaking distance. "It's my honor to introduce Lieutenant Jessie Torres from the AUTEC Protocol office. Lieutenant Torres, this is Special Agent-in-Charge Grace Tran, National Security Agency Field Team Six."

"Lieutenant," Tran greeted. The women exchanged firm handshakes.

"Pleasure meeting you, ma'am. I'm your liaison officer. My office will support your team while you're here. We have two sets of vehicles and drivers at your disposal, and we'll take care of your chow arrangements and anything else you need."

Tran still didn't understand why a Navy officer had been assigned as liaison to Field Team Six and by whom. "You requested this?" she asked of Kenison.

The officer snapped her head to the grinning Fed beside her and then back to Tran. "Uh, no ma'am," she said. "I'm sorry. I thought your assistant would have spoken with you already."

"Excuse me?"

Torres checked a note on her smartphone. "Yes, a Ms. Vivian Lawrence made your lodging arrangements at the base and—"

"Be that as it may, Lieutenant," Tran interrupted. "I appreciate the offer, but it really isn't necessary. I'm sure you have a lot more important things to do than babysit us."

"No ma'am. You're my one and only mission."

Tran thought for a moment and then chuckled. "Join the Navy, see Grace Tran?" she asked, mocking the distinguished service's old advertising slogan.

Torres smiled. "Something like that. When my C-O tells me to personally take care of you because he received a call from the Chief of Naval Operations, who received a call from the Sec-Def, who received a call from the Director of National Security and the White House Chief of Staff, I see no upside in failing to do just that to the very best of my ability, ma'am."

Tran sighed. "Any chance I can persuade you to ignore your Commanding Officer, the CNO, the Secretary of Defense, the White House, and the DNS?" she asked facetiously.

"Sure there's a chance…a snowball's chance, ma'am."

Tran shook her head and laughed lightly. "So I guess there's no getting rid of you then?"

"No ma'am."

Tran had once been an eager young military officer like Torres. She'd had to confront people—insecure old men mostly—who tried to thwart her in the achievement of her missions, and Tran didn't want to be one of those people to Torres. She much preferred to inspire and help younger professional women coming up behind her. So, she sighed and relaxed her resistance more easily than she otherwise might. "Okay, Lieutenant Jessie Torres," Tran said. "In that case, I'll agree, but if you want to get along with me, there are three rules you must observe. First, don't get in my way. Second, if I tell you to do something, do it. Third, stop calling me *ma'am*. You may call me Grace."

Torres stared a moment, a blank expression on her face. Tran guessed her deadpan delivery of impossibly uncompromising *rules* left Torres wondering whether she was serious. Tran was of course completely serious that Torres not interfere with the case, but she didn't truly expect any professional to pledge unquestioned obedience to whatever orders might come from someone else's mouth, no matter what. There existed one Power to whom Tran would offer such an unconditional pledge, and it certainly wasn't anyone on Earth. She smiled at Torres to relieve the tension. *"Broma in serio,"* she said.

Recognizing the Spanish words, Torres smiled back. "Yes ma'am. I get it," she said. "Joking but serious."

As a member of the Federal Government's Senior Executive Service, Tran held a rank equal to a Vice Admiral. A company grade officer with any sense would feel some level of discomfort calling someone of such superior rank by their first name, so Tran would give Torres some time to adjust.

"Okay then," Tran said, checking her watch. Almost 1830 hours. Tran suddenly realized they'd not taken a break since arriving on the island early that morning. When absorbed in a mission, she occasionally worked all day without eating or taking a break, but she didn't expect her team to live her idiosyncrasies. "That's cruel and unusual punishment by any standard," she said aloud.

"Ma'am…I, I mean, Grace?" Torres asked.

"Uh, just thinking aloud," Tran said. She looked to Kenison. "You guys eat today?"

Kenison snapped from his gorgeous woman-induced stupor and looked quickly to his watch. "I guess that explains this feeling in my stomach."

"You sure that's it?" Tran asked. "I thought maybe you were feeling nervous or awkward about...something." She winked and grinned as it appeared both Kenison and Torres at once grasped her meaning, their cheeks flushing red.

Tran scanned the area but didn't see the other members of Field Team Six. Whipping out her phone, she sent a group text, asking everyone to rendezvous at the bungalow's back door. Almost as soon as she hit *Send*, Ito yelled from the cabin's side yard as he walked toward them.

"Ask and ye shall receive," he said.

Tran, Kenison, and Torres turned in his direction. "That was fast."

"We were on the way here anyway. I think we might have something interesting," Ito said. He opened the well-worn laptop he packed along with him almost everywhere he went.

"You gonna' love this," Lawrence said from the screen hanging from Ito's neck.

"When we first arrived on-scene, I noticed the radio towers in the area," Ito said, nodding at several of the structures atop nearby dunes. "They provide cell coverage to the beach, cabins and businesses around here. That made me guess that there's likely a good deal of electronic traffic in the area, so my old friend and I—" He patted the laptop, "—hacked into the local communication networks. They all have logs of the activity sent through their servers, which are normally used for diagnostic purposes. But, my particular brand of genius can make them work for us. The radar tower at LPIA covers civilian air traffic and the servers at AUTEC—"

He jutted his chin toward the Atlantic Undersea Test and Evaluation Center a few miles across the bay. The presence of a woman in uniform suddenly registered in his mind and stilled his thought. "I'm sorry," he said, "but who are you?" he asked of Torres.

Kenison puffed up his chest. "Special Agent Rique Ito, this is Lieutenant Jessie Torres, our Liaison to the Navy base while we're here."

"Yeah," Ito answered. "Well, I couldn't get into AUTEC's system from here because their security is pretty sophisticated—"

"Not to mention that it would be an act of cyber-terrorism to hack a US military installation," Torres added.

The group glanced quickly at Torres, but otherwise gave her comment no heed. Ito continued undaunted. "—but the airport's system was pretty easy to penetrate. Their server logs from last night show a lot of com-traffic in this area. I need to do some additional analysis to separate out the noise, but I think I've pinpointed radio traffic that originated just off the beach."

"The Marshal's patrol boat?" Tran asked.

"Could be," Ito replied. "But something isn't adding up."

"What are you thinking?"

"I, I—"

He closed the laptop and firmly shoved it into Kenison's stomach, the latter forced to grab hold of it or fall on his backside. Ito released the computer and lifted the device on his chest, manipulating its controls with lightning speed. "Sorry, Viv," he said at the face peering back from its screen, "you'll have to excuse us a minute."

Without waiting for her reply, he swept his fingers across the device, and pushed Lawrence's visage aside. In her place glowed a detailed aerial grid map of the area two miles around the bungalow. Everyone leaned in closer to see the screen more clearly and shield it from the sunlight.

"My calculations put the locus of two transmissions about here," he said, pointing to a flashing blue dot just off the beach. "As you can see, the radar log shows the patrol boat here," he explained, moving his fingers a half-inch to the left."

Kenison noted the data in the display's legend and made some quick calculations in his head. Considering distance from the tower, the coordinates of the radar contact, and the scale of the display, he said, "that would be about two-hundred yards away in real-time."

"Yeah, and as you see, there's nothing there," Ito agreed.

"Nothing in any of the Marshals' reports said a thing about another boat out there," an unseen Lawrence chimed. "Based on what I've learnt over the years, radar wouldn't pick up a zodiac or one 'a them other rubber military boats."

"I'm not a radar expert," Tran said, "but I assume the airport radar isn't sophisticated enough to capture an actual image of whatever was at those coordinates last night. It would only get a transponder signal or pick up a reflection."

"You're right," Ito answered. "Traditional radar systems send out pulses of energy which bounce off of objects in their field and return to the source of the pulse. The radar analyzes the returning energy to detect the presence, position, and motion of objects. It's old technology that gives only basic information about the things it detects. We have more sophisticated radars now, but the facility at LPIA is pretty ancient, and not in top condition."

"It was good enough to detect the Marshals' patrol boat, so why didn't it detect whatever was at that location?" Tran asked.

"I figure either the readings from the log are wrong or whatever was there was invisible to radar."

"Stealth technology?" Kenison asked incredulously.

Ito shrugged. "Yeah."

Kenison snickered. "So there's no chance your calculations are wrong?"

"None. I've already made my mistake for this decade."

Tran knew Ito jested about the mistake of the decade, but not about the possibility of his own error. The man took great pride in his accuracy—almost neurotically— and to his credit, he was always right.

"You know Occam's Razor—the simplest explanation is most likely, right?" Kenison said.

"So what's simpler than a small radar-evading boat that went unnoticed by highly trained US Marshals two-hundred yards away?" Lawrence asked.

Silence filled the air a moment before Torres offered an answer. "A submarine!"

Ito nodded. "That would do it."

"You mean an actual submarine, like a US Navy submarine?" Kenison choked.

"Something doesn't have to be a Virginia-class attack boat to qualify as a submarine," Torres explained. "The term *submarine* includes the long, metal torpedo-launching warships you're picturing, Agent Kenison, but it also includes single-person submersibles and remotely operated drones. NOAA, commercial fishing fleets, and college marine biology departments use submarines too."

"So you think there was a sub out there?" Kenison asked.

"I don't know," Torres said. "I'm just saying it would fit your facts."

Tran shook her head. "It's too early to think anything at this point. All we know is, the facts suggest it's a possibility. We need to see where this takes us."

"Well AUTEC is home to the most advanced deep-water hydrophones in the universe. If there were a sub in these waters last night, the base will know about it," Torres said.

"And I'm sure they'll be happy to share that information with civilians," Kenison replied, sarcastically. "I know how my fellow Army officers and I used to feel about civilians of any kind meddling in our affairs."

"Maybe," the Navy officer said. "But they'll explain it to me."

"You'd do that for me?" Kenison asked.

"I'd do it to support this team," Torres corrected. "My orders are to take care of this team's needs while you're in town."

Considering the attractive young lady's response and the long, lonely nights his job so often inspired, Kenison smiled at the thought of what he could say next, but his better judgment prevailed. Knowing him as she did, Tran rolled her eyes at his unspoken remark.

"Okay, people," Tran said. "Lieutenant, if you wouldn't mind running that to ground and getting back to me, it would be helpful. In the meantime, we need to get some dinner and then settle into quarters. Viv, I understand you've made arrangements for us at the Navy base."

Ito tickled the Ito-pad's buttons to make Viv's face slide back to the screen. "Yeah Grace. I got y'all set up in the Bachelor Officer Quarters."

"The BOQ is fine, Viv, but we need to talk about this babysitter you've arranged for us." Tran jokingly thumbed at Torres.

"I tried to tell 'em you wouldn't need or want it, but the Base Commander insisted. He said he'd gotten a call direct from the White House 'bout you, so he'd be damned if he didn't roll out the red carpet. Sorry, Grace, but he wouldn't take *hell no* for an answer," Viv explained.

"Captain Ashmead—my C-O—can be rather…stubborn," Torres validated.

"Don't worry about it," Tran said. "We have to pick and choose our battles, and that's just not one we need to fight."

"You sure?" Lawrence asked. "I always love me a good fight!"

Certain her scrappy Administrative Assistant was only half-joking, Tran smiled. Pleasant cantankerousness was the woman's nature. "I'm sure, Viv. But I do need you to do something for me. Find out who owns the cabin where the crime occurred, and where the Judge's kids are. We've not seen or heard anything about them in all of this. He won custody of them in the divorce, but it doesn't appear they came down here. Either someone else is caring for them or we've got a kidnapping on top of everything else."

"I'd rather pick a fight with somebody, Boss Lady, but I guess that'll hafta' do if that's whatcha' need."

"It is," Tran said as she turned to canvass the area. She saw Dr. Starr approaching from the front of the cabin, but no trace of the others. "Now, where are Lockwood and Trigg?"

She punched Lockwood's speed dial button on her phone.

"Ian, the Navy base sent a car for us," she said when he answered. "We're about ready to head to the BOQ and dinner. Where are you?"

"We're a ways up the beach, Boss," Lockwood answered. "We're in the middle of somethin'. You guys go on. Trigg and I will catch up when we're done."

Tran looked to the Lieutenant, tacitly asking whether she could return to the cabin to retrieve the remaining members of the team. The officer nodded. "Okay, Lockwood. We'll take your stuff and get you checked into your rooms, then grab some grub. Text or call when you're ready to come back."

"You got it, Grace. I think it may be worth our effort."

"Yeah? What is it?" Tran asked.

"Huh...rather not say 'til we see if it pans out, if you don't mind," Lockwood said.

"You want to keep me in suspense, I suppose." Tran knew that as much of a flippant, playful guy as he could be, Lockwood preferred to bring firm information to the table instead of speculation. Given his experience and track-record, Tran trusted his judgment. "All right, but it better be good," she replied, hanging up her phone. She turned to the others. "I need to take care of something before we go. You folks head to the car—I'll meet you there."

Tran watched most of her team start for the vehicles out front, and then turned to look at the people moving about inside the bungalow. Zeroing-in on the ERT leader, she made her way to him, gently grabbing his arm and pulling him aside when she reached him. She apprised him of their plans for the evening and tidied up some final details before preparing to depart the scene.

"Okay Bob," she said, "it's not easy for me to release my crime scene to anyone, but D.A.D. Allen assures me you're the best evidence supervisor in the Bureau."

"Oh stop," Darden replied, feigning embarrassment. "The Deputy Assistant Director is a nice guy, but that's gonna' make me blush."

"Right," Tran dismissed, chuckling. "Please have someone take casts of the prints out back and get up on top of the fence to see if there's anything useful there. Lastly, get the bodies to the morgue and be sure the scene is absolutely secure throughout the night. I want nobody inside the perimeter but my team and yours—at least for now."

"I'm sure you meant mine too, right?" a voice asked, its owner walking up on Tran and Darden.

Tran turned as Marshal Stupleton approached. "Excuse me?"

"Access to the scene…You meant to include me and my team in the list of authorized people, right?"

"I meant exactly what I said, Marshal," Tran answered. "For the time being, it's best that your folks stay out of the scene unless accompanied by a member of my team."

"What are you suggesting?" Stupleton challenged.

Tran winced in mild exasperation. "Really?" she balked. "You're really pretending to take offense at the use of proper procedure? Need I remind you that *your* Protectee was assassinated right under your nose! You know as well as I that no one on your team can have independent access to the scene until you're completely cleared!"

"How dare you sugg—"

"Stop," Tran snapped, raising her splayed palm in the air before Stupleton's face. "If you're as sharp as you seem to think, you know I must protect the integrity of this investigation. People on the other end of this thing must be confident that it was unbiased and complete, and that its conclusions are sound. If your team's hands are all over it any more than they already are, people will doubt the outcome and I won't have that, Marshal. So, we're doing this the right way. Period. End of discussion."

"Are you trying to—"

"Have you finished scrubbing your report for errors?"

Stupleton glowered. "You're gravely mistaken if you think your authority over this investigation gives you authority over me."

The NSA agent hovered silently as she stared at the Marshal, a mix of irritation and astonishment gripping her gut. She released a half-chuckle as she spoke. "As long as you don't screw with my investigation, Marshal, I don't think about you at all. If I need something from you, I expect you'll provide it promptly. Otherwise, stay out of my way, and we'll have no problems."

Stupleton glared at Tran, clearly debating what to say or do next. "You're quite the control freak, aren't you, Agent Tran?"

"That's right, and I'm a bitch too!" Tran said. "If you get on my bad side, you'll find out just how formidable I can be!"

"I'll just bet you are," Stupleton said.

"You only *think* I'm joking," Tran said, "but I'm serious."

Stupleton held her gaze on Tran a few seconds more, and Tran met the measure moment by moment, both staring one another down like rival commanders assessing the enemy across the battlefield. When Tran felt she'd made her point but was starting waste too much time on the childish endeavor, she spoke.

"You're dismissed, Marshal."

Chapter 5: Feeding a Fire

Burdened by her briefcase, portfolio, room key, and the handle of the wheeled suitcase on the floor behind her, Tran jerked the bag in an arc to make it clear the door. She stepped inside the room, kicking the door closed behind her. She leaned against it, sighed, and paused to catch her breath. Then, she heaved the heavy briefcase onto the bed, dropped everything else to the floor, and collapsed face-first to the mattress, her upper body resting comfortably on the bed while her knees braced against the floor. Feeling tension leave her body and relaxation coming over her for the first time in several days, see exhaled and softly muttered, "*God blesses us in many different ways.*"

The BOQ's bed felt far better than she anticipated, probably because she was exhausted. As long as she'd been fully engaged in her work, she hadn't noticed how tired she felt, but the moment she slowed down, even a little, the wariness hit her like a barreling locomotive. She'd gone to bed much later than usual the night before and didn't sleep well. She'd tossed and turned for a long time before ceding to the futility of trying to sleep, after which she'd jumped out of bed and began reading a field report on which her boss had requested her opinion. Forty minutes into it, the call from the White House shattered the silence in her apartment, thus bringing her this current assignment. A courier arrived a short time later, triggering the start of her day that ended with her faceplant on the mattress. Save for unavoidable bathroom breaks, this had been the first time in nearly forty hours she'd had to relax, even a bit. Tran inhaled and exhaled deliberatively, consciously minding her autonomic body functions and summoning the teachings of her years of martial arts. Deep breathing was the first part of effective meditation.

A sudden knock at the door roused her. "Yes, just a second," she answered, shaking the grogginess from her voice.

"Grace, it's me," the familiar voice on the other side informed.

Tran quickly collected herself and hurried to open the door. Dr. Deanna Starr stood there in blue jeans, a beautiful silk blouse, and a smile foreign to her when clad for her usual workday. Deanna looked relaxed—totally transformed from Agent-Dr. Starr. Tran checked her watch. It had been an hour since they checked-in to the 'Q and evidently, Tran's meditation session had gotten too relaxing.

"We're waiting for you downstairs. You want to grab a bite?" Starr asked.

Tran did her best to hide that she'd fallen asleep but doubted whether she'd effectively done so from Deanna. Though off-duty at the moment, Starr was still a highly accomplished professional people-reader.

"Yeah, be right there," Tran said. "Let me do one thing first." She grabbed her phone and dialed a number as she gathered her purse and righted the briefcase she'd tossed to the floor when she entered the room.

"NRO Field Support. Secure line," a voice answered on the other end of the line. "Stand-by to authenticate…"

"Standing by," Tran said.

"Go."

"Grace Tran, ACN: 092-465, MD 44-E-002," she answered, recalling information from the envelope the White House courier gave her.

An awkward silence hung in the air as Tran awaited a response from the National Reconnaissance Office on the other end. It came after nearly a minute. "Confirmed. This is Owen, 061-195, manning station 1-2-8. What is your request?"

Listening carefully, Tran satisfied herself that the man to whom she spoke was in fact who he claimed to be. "I need forty-eight hour overhead tracking on the area at or near the coordinates I'm transmitting." She keyed into the phone the number-sets Ito had given her, and then pressed *Send*.

"Data received," the voice confirmed. "I will revert within the standard timeframe unless greater urgency applies."

"Standard is fine," Tran said as she deactivated the line. She turned to Starr, waiting patiently near the door.

"Ready?"

Tran nodded.

"All right then," Starr said. "Lieutenant Torres said someone from her office will bring Lockwood and Trigg back from the scene shortly. They'll meet us."

Tran stepped through the door, hesitating briefly as she looked at the items left haphazardly around her room. It's not how she liked things, but she'd deal with the mess after dinner. Closing the door and locking it behind her, she fell in step with Deanna. They passed an elevator along the BOQ's open-air corridor and walked to the stairs. Ahead, Tran saw Kenison and Ito standing with Torres in the parking lot below, awaiting the dinner group stragglers.

"Have we chosen a venue for dinner?" Tran asked.

"The Lieutenant recommended a place—Pirate Cove Café," Starr explained. "It's a hole-in-the-wall but it supposedly has the best food on the whole island."

Tran shrugged. "I'm not one for chain restaurants anyway." The pair walked in silence a few paces. Then, Tran asked, "did you learn anything in your talks with the Marshals?"

"I think I'm getting a good read on the Deputy Marshals."

"Not Stupleton?"

"I didn't speak with her in any depth. Aside from some condescending barbs she threw at me, she seemed to go out of her way to avoid me."

"Does that tell you anything useful?"

"It could mean a lot of things, Grace. She may be avoiding me out of fear of discovery, or perhaps embarrassment over the last case we worked together." Starr was quiet for a few steps. "...or it could be that she's the same old bitch she used to be."

A shocked Tran snapped her head around to look the normally reserved, non-judgmental psychologist directly in the eye. The latter raised her brow, and the women broke into laughter as they reached the top of the stairs. Descending them, Starr returned to Tran's original question.

"The Deputy Marshals all seem pretty close. Unless I'm missing something by a wide margin, Liang is pretty easy to read. He's second-generation Chinese-American, the first in his family born and raised completely in the States. He's highly intelligent, and as a first-born son in a traditional Asian family, he feels he carries his family honor on his shoulders. That makes him deathly afraid of failure, though he'd not admit it, and he's worried that the murders of the judge's party will forever scar him in the agency. He doesn't want to work in his family's restaurant and restaurant supply businesses back in Chicago."

"Nothing unusual there," Tran said.

"Deputy Marshal Oseefah is similar, but obviously from a different culture. He's the first-born son of a first-born son of a Nigerian tribal king. He's an east-coast kid who came from an accomplished family on both sides. He has an engineering background and seems like a bit of a jokester at heart. If I read him right, I'd say he feels…perhaps hen-pecked."

"Hen-pecked?"

"Yes. I'm not entirely sure yet, but I think he feels Marshal Stupleton's interest in him goes beyond work."

Tran chuckled at the thought of the stodgy Stupleton and this handsome, hip young man together. "What makes you think that?"

"He mentioned Stupleton's decision to have the two of them alone on the boat at the time of the murders. He said she asked a lot of intrusive personal questions and stood uncomfortably close to him. She found reasons to touch him—nothing overtly inappropriate, but enough to give him the heebie-jeebies."

"He just came right out and said these things?"

"No, I had to pry it out of him. He was actually quite tight-lipped, but I'm that good." Starr smiled.

"Go on," Tran prompted.

"Then there's Deputy Marshal Rick Henri. He...well, he... He's a little harder to read."

"How so?"

"I wouldn't say he's uncooperative," Starr said as she thought aloud. "He's quite personable and talkative, but he comports himself like that to keep control of the conversation. If he can keep the focus on things he wants to discuss, he doesn't have to worry about answering anyone's questions. I have a hunch he's hiding something, but I don't know what."

"What don't you know?" Ito asked as the ladies approached. "I'm the smartest one of us all, so maybe I can help." He grinned.

"Dream on, dude," Kenison challenged, lightly back-handing Ito's stomach.

"Dr. Starr was just sharing her thoughts about the Marshals," Tran explained.

She grabbed the handle of the van's front passenger door, cuing everyone to load inside. Kenison jockeyed his way to the front door and gently grabbed Tran's hand, guiding her to the rear sliding door. "Let me help you, Boss," he said, smiling and acting concerned she might otherwise trip.

Shaking her head, Tran grinned at the exuberant young man, and then complied with his suggestion. Having redirected the only other real contender for the front passenger seat, Kenison turned and climbed into the van. As Torres rounded its front end, Kenison admired the way in which her civilian attire accented her beauty queen qualities much better than her uniform had. She hopped up into the driver's seat, started the engine, and began maneuvering the clunky vehicle through the Q's small parking lot.

They rode from the relatively smooth streets of the Navy base, out the main gate, and into town. The off-base ride tested the van's shocks as it traveled deeper into civilian parts of town, including some with dark, trash-laden streets and ramshackle buildings that didn't look inviting for tourists. After twenty minutes, Torres parked the van in front of an unmarked building with large plate glass windows on the lower level and plantation-shuttered balconies above. Tran slid from the van onto the sidewalk, her ears greeted at once by echoes of energetic Soca music carried on a warm evening ocean breeze that gently caressed her cheeks. As she waited for the others to pile out, Tran's eyes locked on a white car that meandered behind them momentarily and then continued up the road until it disappeared around a corner. Its white headlight beams degraded Tran's night vision, but after a few seconds, her eyes readjusted.

The sun had retreated beyond the horizon, and darkness seeped into the recesses of the pastel row-house buildings lining the narrow brick street. Scanning the area, Tran saw a hunched woman holding the hand of a small child as they slowly negotiated the sidewalk a short distance to the north. To the south, two loud, inebriated men staggered across the street heading away from her, pausing now and then to pass something between them, each putting it to his lips and tilting his head.

Most of the establishments in the area were dark, but lights glowed from the windows of what Tran surmised were apartments above them. The absence of street vendors, bric-a-brac shops, festive lights, and flashing signs indicated the area wasn't frequented by tourists but was instead reserved to residents. To someone with tactical training, the area created a high risk of collateral fallout and unnecessary witnesses to anything that might happen here. The denseness of the buildings and presence of numerous balconies offered a tremendous advantage to a shooter from above against targets on the street, and scarce avenues of escape would make an ambush here as easy as shooting fish in a barrel. Nothing about it felt right to Tran, but she wanted to believe their liaison officer—another woman, a fellow American, and a fellow military officer—wouldn't bring them to somewhere unsafe on foreign soil. Nonetheless, her hand instinctively crept up her hip, probing for her holstered emergency response.

"I know it doesn't look like much," Torres conceded as she sidled up to Tran on the sidewalk, "but the food here is *so good, it'll make ya' slap yo' momma*, as they say. It's only been here about six months, so it remains a hidden treasure only for the well-informed—for now."

Tran smiled at the adage. Growing up, Tran knew if she'd even thought about raising her hand to her mother, she'd have found herself flat on her back, dazed and wondering why all her teeth were on the floor. She was sure that held true even to this day, despite her extensive combat training. Both her parents were lovely, kind-hearted people whom she'd never hurt under any circumstances, but they were also resilient, determined, tough old birds who wouldn't brook improper treatment from anyone.

Looking through the windows of the cafe, Tran saw a few people huddled over plates piled high with food, but for the most part, the place looked sparse—in patronage, furnishings, and décor. They were arriving a bit beyond prime dinner hours, but it still seemed odd that an eatery billed as the best food on the island would be this desolate. Nonetheless, Tran followed Torres to the front door, which Kenison hastened to open for her. A jingly chime announced their arrival.

"Hey Mon," an accented voice shouted from somewhere in back.

"Hey Mon, yourself," Torres cheerfully answered. "I've brought some friends for dinner, Marco."

"Yah now, you jus' hold on dair, Missy," an unseen Marco yelled. "I coming out dair raight now."

A moment later, a short, thin man dashed into the dining room, smiling widely as he hurried toward Torres. His dark skin contrasted highly with his off-white suit, tan tone-on-tone silk shirt and tie, and matching snakeskin shoes. Multiple gold rings on his fingers along with the heavy gold watch and bracelet on his wrists signaled that Marco had a sense of style, albeit more pimp than restaurateur. Tran pegged his age at forty or so, but his buzzed haircut made him look younger. The man gently grabbed the lieutenant's hand and brought it to his lips. "As always, iss so good see you, Missy Lieutenant. You's radiant this night like always you is. Too long since I see you last. I tink you muss met handsome sailor boy and forget ole' Marco."

"Marco, you're unforgettable," she answered, grinning.

"So you say."

Torres motioned in sequence to the members of Tran's team. "Marco, these are my distinguished visitors from Washington—Grace, Deanna, Stefan, Rique, and the young lady on the screen there—" she said, pointing at Ito's chest "—is Vivian."

"Muddasick!" Marco exclaimed, jerking back as his eyes fell to the Ito-pad. "What dis madness?"

"Well damn, Mr. Marco," Lawrence said. "I had people jus fall-out 'cause 'a my beauty an' all, but never quite like that!"

Ito stepped forward and explained the Ito-pad while his colleagues watched him and Marco *geek out* over the technology. After a few minutes, Marco glanced up and saw Tran observing them, and immediately popped-to with an excited expression.

"I's sorry," he said. "I's forgettin' muh manners. Suh nice to meetchoo, lovely lady on da' computah." Marco bowed to Lawrence quickly, and then politely pushed passed the group as he maneuvered to the dining room. "So I's got jus five for eatin' t'night, yes? I mean, da' fancy machine don' let da pretty lady in Washin'ton eat my food, no?"

"Not yet," Ito said, emphasizing the *yet*. "But I'm working on it."

"A table for seven, Marco," Torres corrected.

Marco stopped and turned back to his guests. In exaggerated motion, he counted the members of the party. "Wan, two, tree, fo', five—I don' see nobody else, Missy Lieutenant. Ya' got some fancy Ito-machines for dem too or what?"

Torres chuckled. "Two others will join us any minute."

"Ah, okay den. Iss our busy hour and we kinda' packed, but 'cuz you special impo'tant peeples from Washin'ton and friends to my lovely Missy Lieutenant, I tink we fine' yoo space up in here somewheres, yes?" Marco joked. He turned and resumed his journey to a large booth in the corner. "Dis way."

He led them to the table, and then stood to the side as they slid one by one onto its green, arched leatherette bench, each person scooting around the half-circle until everyone fit. "Okay den," Marco

66

said after everyone seemed situated. "I bring ya' friends when dey come, but now I getchoo some nice Switcha and some eats bettah dan anyting ya' eva' et ba-for."

"Switcha?" Starr asked, wrinkling her brow.

"It's a local drink made with water, sugar, and lime juice," Torres answered. "It's pretty good."

"Excuse me, Marco. Could we get some menus please?" Kenison called as Marco walked away.

The restaurateur stopped dead in his tracks, seemingly shocked by Kenison's request. "Watchoo tink dis is, Brudda Mon—da' Waldorf Astoria?" Marco asked. "I's not dat' and I's got no menus foya'. Dis' here jus da' bess place on de island ta getchoo some good eats, plain an' simple as dat!"

Kenison laughed. "No doubt, but how are we supposed to choose what we want to eat?"

"Jus' ya' neva' mind, Brudda Mon," Marco replied. "I jus' gon' make yoo some good eats, yoo eat, den yoo say how great I is. Das how tings go 'roun here."

"That'll be just fine, Marco," Tran answered for the group.

The man smiled, looked toward the kitchen, and sharply clapped his hands as he released a sound like a birdcall. Under Tran's watchful eye, he stepped off briskly toward the back of the house. She studied him carefully but relaxed somewhat when a young girl bearing a tray of drinks came in response to his call. The teenager brought seven glasses of Switcha and served them without speaking a word or looking anyone in the eye. When she finished, she shallowly curtsied and hurried off to the back.

"Hey," Kenison said, looking around the table. "I've been thinking about why the laser grid system didn't detect the killer when he first entered the scene."

Tran quickly glanced around the room. Three other people graced the establishment at the moment, the nearest of which sat twenty feet away, clearly interested in the plate on his table. The other two seemed more interested in one another than anything else, including their food. Tran nodded her tacit consent for the discussion to continue there, and in front of Torres.

"I have another theory—it's kind of a WAG, but here goes…"

Wild-Ass Guesses often formed the bases of brilliant solutions to complex problems. Many times, they weren't the answer in and of themselves, but they often led to ideas that led to evidence that led to solutions. For that reason, Tran encouraged her team to heed their gut feelings and make WAGs as appropriate.

"It occurred to me that the killer could have gotten to the bungalow by air drop. Coming from above the grid and landing on the bungalow's roof, he could have avoided the ground detection system completely and thus wouldn't have set off any alarms. He couldn't get out the same way, because the Marshals on the ground, and maybe on the boat would have seen a chopper hovering above the cabin."

"So where would he have come from?" Tran asked. "And what would he have done with the parachute? There was no indication of a parachute recovery in Stupleton's report."

"Assuming she didn't omit that from her report too," Starr added. "But none of the Deputy Marshals mentioned it during our talks today."

Kenison tapped his finger against his forehead and smiled. "Thought that through too," he said. "In Special Ops, when we needed to infiltrate enemy lines without leaving any traces, we used wing suits because we could launch from a high-altitude aircraft far outside the target zone, and glide like a flying squirrel silently into the operational theater. If the assassin did that here, it would have been easy for him to pack his parachute out with him because he would've been wearing it like the footie pajamas you wore as a kid."

"Assuming that's the case, he would have come from some kind of aircraft," Torres added. "The base has radar coverage of the whole island, so I can check whether there were any small planes in the area at the time. I'll just add that to my list of to-dos."

68

Marco shuttled back to the table with an enormous tray balanced precariously between his right shoulder, ear, and hand. "Now time for good eats, Mon," he announced.

Pink shrimp and red-orange spiny lobsters spilled over the edges of several wide platters on the periphery of the tray, and in its center sat a large terrine filled with a creamy red soup, the aroma of which telegraphed that they'd soon enjoy some conch chowder. Peas and rice, Johnnycakes, and a selection of tamarinds, pineapples, and bananas rounded out the fare, which Marco declared the first of several courses yet to come. He lowered the tray and deftly moved plate after plate from tray to table, not once dropping, tilting, or spilling anything, or losing control of his wares. Once done, he looked up through the ceiling to the sky outside and said, "Praise to God for His goot bounty, and for Marco who cook it up sa' gut. Now eat. Enjoy."

He stood by smiling from ear to ear as to watch his guests enjoy the meal he'd prepared for them, but after a few seconds, he felt concerned that they'd not begun.

"Whyoo waiting for?" he asked. He waved his hands erratically, signaling his guests to begin eating, then paused to ensure they did. Satisfaction seemed to grip him as Tran led the way, sampling some of the smaller appetizers. The others followed. "Das much betta," he said, smiling widely as he clamored off to the back room once again.

"How often do you dine here, Jessie?" Tran asked.

"About once a week now, but when they first opened, I'd say maybe three times a week."

"What's your favorite selection?"

The officer pointed. "The chowder without a doubt. My grandma used to make it when I was a kid."

Tran ladled out a bowl of conch chowder for Torres and served it up to her with a bad Julia Child impression. "Bon appetite, Mon Ami," she said. The Lieutenant accepted it with a big smile and threw etiquette to the curb, not waiting for others to get theirs before eagerly lifting spoon to mouth. Tran smiled at how much Torres seemed to enjoy her comfort food. She ladled several more bowlfuls and passed them in succession to the members of her team. "Bon appetite to you all," she bid, raising her empty spoon to toast them.

Realizing the depth of their hunger, the team dove into the meal and had nearly finished the first course by the time Lockwood and Trigg stepped through the door. Typical, Lockwood made a boisterous entrance as they headed briskly to the table.

"That's some kind of rude to start without us, y'all," he said, pulling a nearby chair to the side of the booth. At once, he reached for the last lobster tail on the table and pulled it close. Trigg sat on the bench and scooted as far in as he could.

"We had to be sure there'd be enough for everyone," Ito teased, "so we got our plates before you, Lockwood."

"Really—a fat joke?" Lockwood asked, rubbing his belly. "Like that would have any effect on me."

Lockwood quickly shoved the lobster to his mouth, simultaneously pulling the meat from the shell, biting off a sizable chunk, and allowing the remainder to fall haphazardly to the plate beneath him. Both Tran and Starr winced at the sight.

"So, Tool Man and I found a guy and his lady who were on the beach last night," he said, not having fully swallowed. "He said they saw someone come from the grassy hill behind the bungalow and run to the water."

Tran stopped eating, her expression alone giving voice to her question.

"No, they didn't get a good look at the guy," Lockwood said. "Too far and too dark, and they weren't especially interested in him anyway. All they saw was a shadow moving across their field of vision at a fast clip."

"Why were they out there at that time?" Kenison asked.

Lockwood smirked and winked. "They just got engaged, so they were about to...celebrate, shall we say."

"How far away?" Tran asked.

"He guessed about 100 feet or so."

70

"Maybe they didn't see his face, but did they notice anything else about him?" Kenison asked. "Was he carrying anything? Did they hear anything?"

"Nothing. They said he appeared there all-of-a-sudden. They were in the middle of disrobing one another energetically when they heard a heavy thud from the direction of the fence. Thinking it might have been the beach patrol, they froze in place hoping not to be noticed."

"How did they see him in the dark?" Starr asked.

"They heard him first, but as the guy moved down the beach, he was silhouetted against the moon at one point. They said the guy wasn't concerned about them and didn't appear to be searching for anything. He paused for a second at the top of the hill, fidgeted with something, and then made a beeline for the water. A few seconds after that, a boat came up onto the beach and two people with flashlights jumped out and ran up to the bungalow. That's when they decided they should get out of there."

"Marshals Stupleton and Oseefah were on the boat," Starr said, quickly withdrawing her notepad. "That would have been them coming ashore to head off a suspect about whom Marshal Henri had alerted them."

"So, how the hell did they miss the guy?" Lockwood asked.

"Marshal Henri was in hot pursuit but Stupleton ordered him to return to the bungalow to check on Pigmeat," Tran explained. "— Oberlin's code name."

"Well that makes no damn sense," Kenison said.

"Yeah, why did they call him Pigmeat anyway?" Trigg asked.

"No, Rookie," Kenison scoffed. "Why would Stupleton order Henri to break pursuit?"

"It also makes me wonder about the Marshals' competence," Tran said. "They knew their Protectee and at least a couple members of their detail had been killed and that there was a fleeing suspect in the area, yet they overlooked a couple of overheated lovebirds on the beach in the immediate vicinity right after the crime occurred?"

"So, the guy," Kenison said. "Did he swim out to a boat or something or did he just go into the water?"

"Like I said, the witnesses were a little pre-occupied," Lockwood said, winking exaggeratedly.

"Yeah, we get it, Ian," Tran answered, rolling her eyes slightly. "Did you check out the rest of the beach?"

"Of course, Boss," Lockwood said. "Didn't find anything but a few tracks where the love-birds said the shadow first appeared. I sent their names and prints to Viv to run background checks on them, and asked ERT to take casts of the prints."

Tran nodded approval. "Jessie, how far is it from the beach in that area across the water to the main island?"

"From the cabin straight across," Jessie pondered, "I'd guess it's maybe a mile or two. It's swimmable in theory, but these waters are full of bull and tiger sharks, and bright moonlit nights are prime times for them to hunt. That particular beach is protected by a netted reef, so sharks can't get close in. Authorities regularly warn people not to swim at night, dusk, or dawn in unprotected areas beyond the nets."

Tran shook her head. "It doesn't sound like we're dealing with a recreational swimmer here. Suddenly, the idea of some sort of sub doesn't seem so outlandish. But, one way or the other, the fleeing suspect, if he went into the water, would have had to get over or under the nets and then somewhere out into the bay."

Marco returned to the table bearing another tray of his culinary artwork. "Looking like yoos still hungry," he said, smiling widely. "I gotchoo roun' two eats," he said, deftly offloading his cargo. He didn't bother to explain the dishes, and by the way everyone at the table began snatching up the items as quickly as he put them down, no explanation was needed.

He smiled widely as he maneuvered around Lockwood and Trigg. "And wat dis here? More mouths to feed, eh? Well dat no problem fur ole' Marco. Welcome, welcome brothas. Welcome to Marco's where we serve da' bess' eats on da' whole island."

Marco politely chastised his guests for talking shop while eating. He lectured that God meant for people to enjoy and appreciate His bounty, not endure it while working on issues of the world that have no meaning in the Kingdom.

Hearing his words, Tran knew the case would be all-consuming until they completed it, after which they'd likely be assigned some new high-visibility mission that would also be all-consuming. Her team needed to be sharp and refreshed to handle such tasks effectively, so occasional down-time was essential. Reasoning that tomorrow would surely be another long day, she reluctantly assented to Marco's encouragement.

"He's right," Tran announced. "No more talk about the case for the rest of our dinner. Let's eat, drink and be merry, instead."

With only a random reference to the mission here and there, the team had mild success in following Tran's no-shop instruction. For the most part, the table talk revolved around their personal lives and events. Frosty beers helped Lockwood and Kenison relax even more, but Tran's equally frosty glare reminded them that, especially when deployed, they might have to spring into action without warning. Anything remotely similar to a buzz could compromise the mission or get people killed, so only two mildly alcoholic drinks could cross the lips of anyone on the Team, not in an approved-leave status. Around eleven, they stood from the table and piled back into the van in orderly fashion. Despite Tran's initial misgivings upon arrival, the evening had gone well. Dawn would arrive before they knew it.

Chapter 6: The Light of Day

The next morning, Tran awoke early and donned her running gear. The warm Caribbean breezes and soothing sounds of waves crashing against the beach promised a pleasant, mind-clearing workout to start her day. Their hurried departure from DC followed by a long day and a heavy meal the night before made her eager for the release of exercise. From the parking lot of the base hotel, she jogged the main road through the base toward the heart of the installation, past the flagpole in front of the base headquarters, to the Officer's Club on the beach. She ran along the soft sands for several miles, and then turned onto a paved road, heading inland to the North. Tran didn't know exactly where she'd run, but figured the installation wasn't large enough for her to get lost.

After a time, she came to a fenced area beyond which she could see docks where various types of vessels berthed. Thinking of the prior evening's conversation, she slowed her jogging to a walk and then made her way to the fence, on which a placard hung, warning that the area beyond was a *Restricted Area,* access to which required the base commander's permission. Tran peered at the small fleet inside the fence, wondering whether AUTEC could help explore her team's supposition about a possible submarine in the area the night of Oberlin's assassination. Being where it was and considering its function, AUTEC surely possessed the most up-to-date marine detection technology in the U.S. arsenal of weapons. And, the base commander had offered support to her team. He'd even detailed them a Protocol Officer.

She pushed away from the fence and meandered back to the road surface. A few hundred feet from her location, she spied a paved road spur that jutted off over a seagrass-covered dune. It looked like it might take her back around to the front gate, or at least to a more populated part of the base. She resumed her run and in quick time reached a comfortable cruising pace. She began to feel herself slip into that zone that gave her and so many other runners that feeling that they could run all the way around the world, but before it could take complete hold of her, something triggered her senses. As she panned her surroundings, she saw the hood of an unremarkable, boxy, white sedan come round the bend in the road some fifty feet behind her, and slowly emerge from the cover of the grassy sandhills that skirted the beach she'd run to get to this part of the base. It creeped at the pace of someone who was lost, sight-seeing, or trying not to tail their surveillance target too closely. Tran stopped running and turned to face the vehicle full-on, making it obvious she'd seen them, but it didn't stop, turn, and speed-off as if doing so would make it suddenly unseen. Instead, the car continued coming slowly toward her as she watched it, its hood ornament moving slightly to her right, toward the middle of the road and suggesting its driver wouldn't try to hit her. As her eyes escorted the vehicle in, Tran engaged her peripheral vision to search for anything she could use as a weapon, should the need arise. Since she stayed on the base, Tran didn't anticipate possible circumstances that would call for a weapon, so she'd need to improvise if this became one. She saw several pieces of driftwood and several palm-sized rocks within her immediate area, but she concluded that her best option would be a discarded beer bottle half-buried by sand and vegetation at about 315 degrees from her, roughly fifteen feet away.

Tran stood at the ready as the car eventually pulled alongside her and the two young men inside overtly eyeballed her. Under different circumstances, Tran would have anticipated a cat-call or some sexually charged remark from an idiot who fancied himself debonair. But, the obvious government-owned vehicle, the uniforms worn by its occupants, and the fact that they were on a US military installation in broad daylight all bode against that being the case. These were Navy personnel, but Tran didn't know their intent. The car stopped inches from Tran's leg, and the passenger opened his door. He unfolded himself from the vehicle and stepped briskly toward Tran. She reached into her hip pouch for her NSA credentials, at the same time her muscles tensing in case immediate action became necessary. "Stop right there, sailor," she said. "I'm Special Agent—"

"Good morning, ma'am," the young man said, not bothering to look at the badge Tran had brandished. "We know who you are, Agent Tran, but I'm afraid you're in a secured area of base."

The Petty Officer in front of her wore a black and gray camouflage Navy War Uniform bearing the insignia of the Shore Patrol, and the driver who remained in the car wore the Navy dress blue uniform. Tran couldn't see his nametag, rank, or insignia. Nonetheless, she felt reasonably satisfied of their legitimacy.

"All due respect, ma'am, but you're not permitted to be here without the installation commander's approval. We're glad to show you back to your quarters."

Tran cocked her head slightly. "You realize I'm not actually in the secured area, right, Petty Officer Jones?" she asked, noting his nametag. "Is there a problem?"

"No ma'am, Agent Tran. We just don't want there to be any accidental issues."

"You needn't worry about that," she assured. "My security clearance is second only to that of the President and the Directors of the NSA and CIA. I have legal authority to be anywhere on any US military installation I choose." She flashed her credentials again, and again, the SPs showed no interest in seeing them.

"I'm sorry, ma'am, but we're on heightened alert," the driver yelled from inside the car.

"Why?"

"Why?" the nearest SP repeated, staring at Tran for a moment. Then, he glanced to the driver and then briefly looked toward the docks behind the fence, which he continued to do as he replied. "Um…I'm uh…we're not, uh, at liberty to disclose everything, ma'am, but I can…I can just say it's a terror alert."

"Yes, ma'am," the driver yelled from inside the car. "CIA picked up some communication traffic that Al-Qaeda is going to try to steal a

US military vessel in this region in the next few weeks to support a major offensive."

"Yes," the first SP confirmed. "I guess they're gonna' try a new attack or something like 9-11 again. What better way to hurt us than with our own ships, right ma'am?"

The hard-sell of a vague answer, their reticence to look her in the eye, their verbal stalling, and the way the first SP looked to the other for help in answering Tran's question screamed that the young men had just lied to her. Besides, NSA regularly notified all its field agents of terror alerts, but she'd received no such notice. She smiled and nodded as though she'd bought the lies they peddled. "Right. Well, if you'd be kind enough to point me toward the hotel, I'll just jog on back there now."

The men did as Tran asked, and then waited as she resumed her run toward the Bachelor Officer Quarters. She fell back into her thoughts as she completed the final leg of her morning excursion, her thoughts about the case bouncing around in her head as she fleshed out possible theories. She remained painfully aware that the Navy car had fallen some distance back, but it continued to follow her nonetheless.

Tran kept pace right to her room door, shunning her normal practice of warming down before completely ending her run. As she got inside, she closed the door and peered out the sidelight, taking care not to disturb its curtain. The car drove a couple blocks beyond the hotel, made a U-turn, and parked across the street, where it had a clear line of sight to Tran's door. The problem for them was, it gave her a clear line of sight to them too.

She watched them until she felt satisfied they weren't about to storm her door. Then, she went about the rest of her morning routine—a hundred pushups, a hundred crunches, shower, coffee—although the in-room offerings paled in comparison to the trendy MoonScents brand she and a billion other caffeine addicts loved so much—and then dress for the day. She paused intermittently to check whether her new fans were still stalking her from across the road. An hour later, she stepped outside to join the always-early Dr. Starr at the foot of the stairs, where they awaited the rest of the team and their Protocol officer, about whom she realized she may now have to wonder—the line between a helper and a minder could be very thin. The two exchanged the usual morning pleasantries, but all the while, Tran subtly maneuvered her position so she could see up the road without looking like she was looking up the road. The Navy car remained parked there, too far away for her to see the occupants' faces, but she imagined they were watching her face their way.

Kenison and Ito arrived a few minutes after Tran, followed by Trigg and Lockwood. As they joked and bantered, the now-familiar white van pulled into the lot and rolled to a stop, Torres predictably effervescent even at this early hour. "Good morning, everyone," she beamed.

"Well hello there, Jessie," Kenison said, putting to good use the extra bass his voice took on in the mornings.

"I hope you all slept well last night and you're ready for an exciting new day today," Torres continued.

"Who says it's a good morning?" Lockwood growled. The others uttered their morning tidings.

"I'm gonna' get you over to the mess hall for breakfast and then get you right back to the bungalow," Torres said.

"I think I'd prefer to go off base for breakfast," Tran said. "I saw a McMurree's just outside the main gate—let's grab something quick and handy and then get to the Embassy."

"Thought you didn't like chain restaurants," Lockwood muttered.

Tran turned and cast a disapproving stare at Lockwood, tacitly barking an order she almost never verbalized: "*Shut Up!*"

Lockwood tensed his neck and distorted his face, confessing an *Oops, my bad,* in a shutting-up kind of way.

"You sure, Grace?" Torres asked. "Our Mess Hall is pretty good—it only sounds gross."

"Off-base, Lieutenant," Tran said.

Torres shrugged in acquiescence. "You want to go to the Embassy, not the bungalow?"

"Yes—we're borrowing some working space there. We'll need to get back over to the scene at some point, but I want to get to the Embassy first."

"My C-O has set aside some space on base for y'all to use if you want it," Torres said.

"Please thank him for me, but the Embassy has everything we need to work, and it's been prearranged by the White House."

"Well," Torres jokingly relented, "that settles it. The Embassy it is."

A loud, unexpected chime rang out, everyone but Torres knowing the source at once. Ito toggled a switch on the Ito-pad dangling from his neck, and Lawrence's beaming face faded into view.

"Mornin', y'all," she said as she backed away from the camera on her side of the transmission.

"Good morning back at you, Sunshine," Lockwood greeted. "How's my Sweetie this morning?"

"Don't you start with me, Lockwood," Lawrence playfully warned. "I ain't in no mood for your brand a' malarkey this early the mornin'."

"What's the matter? Rough night, baby girl?"

"While y'all been lollygagging around all night, I been working my derriere off," she replied. "I got hold a' the judge's clerk last night, and he sent me the briefs for all the cases on his docket. Seems the judge planned this fateful voyage 'bout two months ago, an' worked real hard to clear up everything 'fore he left. Most of it is stuff that probably don't matter a hill 'a beans to what we're doin', but I found a few that might be somethin'."

"Like what?" Trigg asked.

"I'm gettin' there, junior. Don't rush me."

As Lawrence drew a breath in preparation to share what she'd learned, Tran interrupted. "Uh…Viv, you know I don't like talking business before breakfast. We're just about to grab something, so why don't you do likewise, and we'll reconvene shortly."

Lawrence snapped her head in Tran's direction and stared into the camera as though she stared directly in Tran's eyes. Lockwood also turned abruptly and looked quizzically at his boss.

"Oooo-kay, Grace," Lawrence slowly answered, drawing out the length of the word. "I'll jus' send the 'lectronic files to y'all's Secure-Star boxes, so they'll be waitin' when you get a minute to look at em'," she said. "For now, somethin' na' eat sounds real good. It's time for my special beauty breakfast anyways."

"It's too early for bourbon, Viv," Lockwood said.

"You such a fool, Lockwood," she sneered. "I'm talkin' 'bout my special smoothie, with spinach, kale, raspberry, banana, flax seed, green tea, and chia seed."

Ito wrinkled his face. "I'm not gonna' lie, Viv—that sounds disgusting."

"It's really good for the figure, and this kinda' beauty don' happen on its own, you know." She ran her hands playfully down her sides, gently swaying her hips as though performing a sensuous ballet. "Besides, anyone who eats raw fish got no right criticizing somethin' anybody else eats!"

Lockwood inhaled and prepared to offer a thought, but Lawrence held her pointed finger in a threatening posture, her expression daring him to say something. He didn't.

"And jus' for the record, Lockwood," Lawrence said, "it ain't never too early for bourbon."

With that, Lawrence turned and waltzed into her kitchen, leaving her teammates smiling at her special brand of sass. With anyone else, it might have been inappropriate and insubordinate, but not Lawrence. Her uniqueness powered the outstanding results she brought. No one dared mess with that, not even the Colonels, Generals, and high-ranking civilians she'd worked with over the years.

"There it is," Tran said in feigned excitement as she pointed out the windshield. "McMurree's has the best egg and cheese muffins on Earth."

After ordering their food, the team didn't talk much for the rest of the ride, except for random remarks about things outside or playful jabs about one another's dining etiquette. Tran limited her morning fare to a large, piping-hot black coffee. Occasionally, she turned to look behind them or casually stole glances in the rearview and side mirrors. The non-descript fed-mobile following three cars behind them stuck out like a sore thumb among the locals' more colorful, personalized vehicles.

As the van pulled up to the gate at the US Embassy, the fed car behind them rolled passed and continued up the road until it drove out of Tran's sight. A young Marine stepped from the guardhouse and held his hand in the *halt* position, a nine-millimeter weapon holstered on his hip. A second, more grizzled Marine stood several feet behind him, holding an M4 carbine assault rifle at the ready. Tran could see two other Marines on the roof of the Embassy, also monitoring on-goings at the gate. She wondered how many Marine guards she didn't see. The younger Marine politely greeted the officer, who offered her military ID and explained she was bringing NSA agents to the Embassy. Tran and the others displayed their badges as the guard leaned into the van to inspect them. Another, previously unseen Marine appeared and guided a leashed German Shepherd around the car, and quickly returned to the guardhouse.

All apparently seeming in order, the Marine stepped back from the van, saluted the Lieutenant, and waved her through the gate. The driveway barrier sank into the ground, giving the van easy access to the Embassy.

The van stopped at the main entrance of the lime sherbet–colored multi-story building. As the team piled out, an Embassy staffer came out to greet them. He introduced himself as the Aid-De-Camp to the Consul, apologized for his boss's absence, and then invited the team inside where he'd show them to the offices set aside for their use. Tran motioned for the team to follow the staffer. Starr, Kenison, Trigg, and Ito fell in behind him and climbed the low-rise stairs, but Lockwood hung back and hovered near Tran. He fell in step beside her as she started toward the door.

"I presume the car that tailed us is the reason you didn't want to discuss whatever Viv uncovered last night."

Tran raised a finger to silence him as she watched Torres round the front end of the van.

Her bright smile beaming as usual, Torres said, "Grace, if you have no objections, I'll head over to the Operations Center and get you that information we talked about last night. I'll be back in a couple hours, but if you need me, just call my cell. It's on the card I gave you—presuming you still have it."

Tran's phone vibrated and emitted a peculiar series of tones, signifying the arrival of a *priority* message she needed to see. She lifted her phone, entered her passcode, and opened the message. After reading a bit, she entered an additional set of numbers to decrypt the transmission, and then began reading, all the while ignoring the Navy officer. After scanning it, she turned back to the Lieutenant.

"Sorry, Jessie—"

"No problem," the officer excused.

"—Yes, I have your number and will call if we need you. Thanks for your help."

"Great. See you in a couple hours."

With that, Torres climbed back in the van, started its engine, and drove away. Tran turned to Lockwood, motioning for him to walk with her.

"So, who are they?" he prompted.

"Probably Navy from the base, but on whose orders and why?"

"You think Torres is part of it?"

"It would be a capital mistake to—" Tran began.

Lockwood interrupted her. "—theorize before one has data."

Tran smiled and nodded. "Exactly. But it could make sense," she said. "We didn't ask for her help, yet she and her staff were assigned to support us while we're here. Why?" she mused. "And when I went for my run this morning, the SPs challenged me when I went near the docks—I wasn't even in the secure area."

"Maybe they're just being cautious," Lockwood suggested. "I'd expect them to stop any unfamiliar face showing a keen interest in US military vessels. Besides, AUTEC is a semi-secret tech research installation."

"But they knew who I was before I identified myself," Tran resisted. "They've got to know everyone on AUTEC is cleared to be there, and since they knew who I was, I'm sure they also knew my authority level."

"Well, they say the devil's greatest trick is convincing mankind he doesn't exist."

"You're equating me with the devil?"

"I'm just saying that deception is the key weapon of people up to no good."

"You're probably right. It just raises my suspicions."

"It's highly unusual that the commanding officer at AUTEC gets calls from the Secretary of Defense, the Chief of Naval Operations, the Director of the NSA, and who-the-hell-else may have called here about us," Lockwood explained. "With all the budget wars going on in DC, he might think we're scouting out his operation for some scissor-happy politician wanting to make a name for himself or score some political points. He's probably just keeping tabs on what we're looking at."

"Yeah maybe," Tran conceded. "You get any flash messages about a terror alert in the region?"

"Just the usual *always-be-alert* kind of messages," Lockwood said. "Why?"

They fell silent as they caught up to the rest of the team. The Aid-De-Camp assumed the false enthusiasm of a tour guide, explaining where they'd go inside the embassy and what they should expect when they stepped through the doorway. When he finished, he turned and showed his embassy badge to a trio of armed, stone-faced Marines and announced that Tran and her team were special-access visitors cleared by the White House. Then, he motioned his tagalongs through the employee entrance, and passed a metal detector, a sinister-looking patrol dog, and its handler. A guard seated at the other end of the security line reached into his desk drawer and withdrew embassy security badges, already showing the team members' names and photos. He passed them to each member of the team, instructing them to assure the badges were always visible while they were in the building or anywhere on the grounds.

The team followed the Aid-De-Camp down the first adjoining hallway to a suite of empty offices on the first floor. He stopped at a gunmetal gray door with an empty slot that might otherwise have been filled by a name placard, announcing the department or bureau in residence there. He opened the door, and then stood aside as he motioned Field Team Six to enter. He followed the last of them inside the room and closed the door behind him.

"We've set aside these offices for your use, Agent Tran."

They'd stepped into a small reception area with deep pile carpeting, two maroon leather nail-head sofas and four matching single-person chairs, lamps, and other normal accouterments one would find in the lobby of a well-to-do plaintiff's attorney. The walls were a rich, dark hardwood all around, with landscape paintings here and there, and the pictures of the President and Vice President of the United States, the Secretary of State, and the Consul General displayed prominently on the only wall with a door, except for the one they'd entered.

"We've got this lobby here for any guests you might receive," the Aid said, "and back here—" He opened the single wood door and waved his arm to suggest the team step into the back of the suite. "—we have individual offices, a conference room, and a kitchenette. There's a packet of information in each office telling you some things you might need while here in the Embassy, most importantly, where the bathrooms are," the man said, evidently trying to be funny. "If you need secretarial support, we have an admin pool on the second floor, and for anything else, just dial the help desk at 777."

The six offices behind the wall were unusually posh considering that they were unused offices in a federal building. Real wood desks, leather sofas and chairs, and attractive paintings appointed the space. Had she not seen the very same paintings in several other federal executive offices, Tran might have thought the art was original. She was impressed, but then reasoned that the State Department put its better foot forward in Consulates and Embassies because those facilities often hosted visitors, dignitaries, and VIP functions. No matter, Tran wouldn't complain, and wouldn't have even if they'd been ratty. They were, after all, incidental to her mission, and they were free. Tran thanked the Aid, indicated that her team was ready to get to work, and then waited for him to depart. He uttered a few awkward pleasantries, but eventually took the hint as the team planted flags in individual offices they'd call home for the next few days. Tran followed him to the door, and then closed it firmly behind him. She turned and walked through the small lobby to the office space beyond. Ito met her at the threshold.

"Boss, I scanned the area for listening devices," he said. "We're good."

It was standard practice for Ito to run electronic counter-surveillance scans in workspaces the team used outside of their headquarters at Fort Meade, but it probably wasn't necessary in a diplomatic office of the U.S. government. Still, it didn't hurt. Tran acknowledged the information as they walked deeper into the warren of small offices. Everyone had chosen an office except Tran, but the team's choices left the largest, most well-appointed office at the end of the hall available for her. She walked there with Ito at her side.

"Y'all forget about me?" a voice called into the air.

Tran stopped and let her gaze fall to the darkened screen hanging around Ito's neck. She'd not forgotten about Lawrence, but this was their first opportunity for the team to talk candidly since disembarking the van and ditching all non-team observers. Ito touched the device to wake it from sleep-mode, and Lawrence's smiling face shined immediately on the screen.

"Sorry, Viv," Tran said. "We're just now getting to a place where we can talk."

"Oh, I see how it is," Lawrence playfully jabbed. "Got no use for the old black lady, so you just turn me off and put me in a closet.

Hmm-mmph—go on an' do me like that, but just remember, payback's a bitch."

Tran chuckled. "I know, Viv, but sometimes it's unavoidable."

"You know I don't mean nothin', Grace. I'm just givin' ya' a hard time."

Ito piped, "You've been hanging around Lockwood too much."

Viv turned her eyes upward as it to look directly at Ito's face. "Boy, you such a fool," she said. Then, looking ahead to Tran: "so can I ask now, what the hell was all that *'you know I don't like to talk business before breakfast'* stuff?" Lawrence said. "Besides your daily caffeine injection, you don't even eat breakfast, usually."

Tran paused as she considered the most appropriate explanation of her previous comment. "Let's just say I thought we should be a little more judicious about sharing with the Lieutenant until we iron out a few things. I'll explain after I give it some more thought. In the meantime, I'm excited to hear what you found in the Judge's docket."

She, Ito, and Lawrence continued the remaining few steps to Tran's office, and then took comfortable positions on the chairs and sofa inside. She motioned in the air to catch the notice of the rest of the team, and then waved them over to hear Lawrence's report.

Viv reached to somewhere outside the screen's purview and grabbed a small stack of files. She studied them a second and then continued. "Judge Oberlin was a busy man 'fore his vacation, including trials an' hearings on some big cases. It's a lot a' legal mumbo-jumbo in the files, but bein' the genius I am, I managed to cull out a few that look like something."

"Just give us a précis of what you found, Viv. We'll read through the details in our Secure-Star accounts," Tran said.

"Sure, if that would be helpful to you," Lawrence replied. "The biggest case he had in the weeks before his death was a sentencing hearing in <u>US v. Cabrillo</u>. In that one, the CIA nabbed the head of the Sudamis drug cartel off the streets of Bogata and brought him to DC for trial on a bunch of serious charges for federal and international offenses."

"Yes, I recall," Tran said. "This is a case of extraordinary rendition over which the Columbian government raised a big stink because we went into their country, captured Cabrillo, and whisked him to the US for trial, without their permission or knowledge. They've taken us to the UN, alleging we violated their national sovereignty."

"Cabrillo is a big-time scuzz-bag," Lockwood added, "second only to Bin Laden. When I was still at the Bureau, I worked six cases where that cartel was involved. Even by drug lord standards, the Sudamis Cartel is brutal."

"Judge Oberlin presided over Cabrillo's trial which convicted him on 138 counts of drug and human trafficking, torture, and corruption," Lawrence advised. "When Oberlin sentenced him to thirty-three successive life terms a month ago, Cabrillo said in open court that Oberlin was a dead man walking."

"That certainly qualifies as interesting," Tran said. "What else?"

"Another case that might be sumthin' involves a lady doctor convicted of doing secret experiments on people by re-writing their DNA. Some of the patients became mutants with nasty diseases, including some pregnant ladies. They charged her with doing unauthorized abortions on some a' da' babies, but a few were born looking more like creatures from the damn lagoon than people."

"Are you pulling my leg?" Lockwood groaned.

"It would take a damn tractor to do that," Lawrence retorted. "I joke about a lot a' things, Lockwood, but you know my work ain't one of 'em."

"It does sound like something from a sci-fi flick," Kenison said.

"Well, you know what they say—truth is stranger than fiction. Some folks call this lady Goddess Frankenstein 'cause she plays with peoples' lives like she got some right to do so."

"I think I saw protestors on that case," Trigg volunteered. "My apartment isn't far from the jail where they were holding Goddess Frankenstein. Protestors blocked traffic when I was moving in."

"I've read a little about that case, but I'm not sure I see its possible connection to Oberlin's assassination just yet," Tran said.

"There's a lot of folks on the religious extreme who don't like that this lady tinkered with the natural order of what the Almighty intended, ya' know, and a lot who think people who abort babies deserve death themselves. I'm a God-fearin' woman who thinks this lady should go straight to hell without passin' go or collectin' her $200 if the charges are true, but that ain't for me to decide. I think only He can judge us, but some folks get down-right militant 'bout ther' religion," Lawrence explained.

"People can get religious about tying their shoes," Lockwood opined.

"Don't joke about the Almighty," Lawrence admonished. "'Cause if He don't strike you down, I sure might."

The senior agent chuckled. "I believe you would, Viv. I take it back."

Tran interjected. "So, you're suggesting someone killed the judge in retaliation? For what?"

"Preventively," Lawrence said. "This lady appealed her conviction 'cause a' some legal technicality, and 'da Oberlin heard the appeal. He hadn't given out his decision yet, but he was gonna' set her free."

"And that's who the President was going to nominate to the Supreme Court?" Kenison asked. "It seems like Oberlin would have a hard time getting through a confirmation hearing. I'm no political wonk, but even I know people would've come out of the woodwork to oppose a guy like that."

"The President's party controls both houses of Congress, and he's not one to shy away from a fight if he wants something badly enough," Tran said. "But that's neither here nor there as far as we're concerned."

Starr added, "I was just thinking, if Judge Oberlin's decision isn't yet public, how do you know about it? How would the assassin?"

"His written opinion was locked in a safe at his home, and the clerk said nobody but him and Oberlin knew about it, and now me...and I guess all y'all now. He swore me to secrecy 'cept from y'all. It woulda' been released the day after Oberlin got back, but the clerk doesn't want it gettin' to the media now 'cause he's wants to protect the judge's mem'ry an' all."

"For that case to be a motive in the murders, *someone* would have to have known about his decision far enough in advance to have planned what appears to be a carefully orchestrated assassination," Tran pondered aloud.

"The plot thickens," Lockwood announced.

Chapter 7: Personnel is Policy

The more she learned about the periphery of the case, the more eager Tran felt about getting into the investigation in depth. Although connecting the dots from overnight activity helped paint a clearer picture of what really happened, Tran wanted to get out into the field to find evidence and question witnesses, and secretly, the idea of apprehending a fleeing bad guy out on the streets thrilled her. But experience taught that rushing to judgment or prematurely jumping into action often made for bad results. In a year or two, when the obligatory appeals of criminal convictions were filed, nobody would remember how fast Tran uncovered the perpetrator's identity, but they'd surely remember—and remind her—if she screwed up the case, because they'd be living with the consequences of the choices she'd make now.

"I know you're rarin' to get at it an' all, Grace, but I got one more topic to cover," Lawrence said.

"What's that?"

"I pulled the personnel jackets on the Marshals like you asked. I sent em' to you and Dr. Starr, in Secure-Star."

"Yes, thank you, Viv," Starr answered. "I got them in my mailbox and have been through two of them already."

"Oh, I bet this'll be good," Lockwood sneered.

"Well, it ain't nothin' to talk about with most of them, but two of em' are interesting. Rick Henri and Terri Stupleton both got some junk in their trunk."

"What do you mean, Viv?" Tran asked.

"Henri, well, he's a piece of work, to use Lockwood's phrase," Lawrence began. "When he was sixteen, he got arrested for hackin' into the computer servers of an online gaming site. He claimed he was only trying to help them out because he could fix a flaw in their programming that they hadn't been able to do in three updates."

"Henri's a computer nerd?" Kenison asked.

Ito's head snapped up from his laptop. "Hey, I resemble that remark."

"Call it what you want, but Henri was right," Lawrence said. "He fixed the mistake in the company's programming. The juvenile judge in his case withheld judgment, warned him not to get into anymore hacking, and promised that if he kept his nose clean until he graduated college, then the charges would disappear as though they never existed. But, if he screwed up before graduating college, the judge would convict him, put him in jail for six months, and fine him $50,000."

"How'd that work out for him?" Lockwood asked.

"He got a Bachelor's degree in two years with a double major in criminology and computer science," Lawrence answered. "And he made dean's list all semesters of undergrad and grad school."

"Score one for computer nerds everywhere," Ito said.

"Maybe," Lawrence continued. "Your boy did good for a while, but after joining the Marshals, he got two letters of counseling, a formal reprimand, and a suspension in his file. He just returned to work about three months ago after a thirty-day time-out."

"What for?" Kenison asked.

"Breach of protocol and insubordination," Lawrence answered.

"Words on a paper don't tell the real skinny," Kenison said. "What's the backstory?"

"A fugitive arrest out west. An escaped militiaman held a twelve-year-old girl at knifepoint on a train platform just as the Marshals were closing in. The bastard slit the little girl's throat and then jumped in the path of an on-comin' train to avoid going back to prison."

"What did Henri have to do with it?" Trigg asked. "I mean, it's a bad outcome and all, but sometimes we lose people, right?"

"Henri went off on Stupleton right there at the scene, calling her stupid and reckless in front of all the onlookers. Said the girl died because of Stupleton's idiotic decisions. He said he had a bead on the guy and could have dropped him, but Stupleton ordered him an' the resta' the Deputy Marshals at the scene to back off. She wanted to negotiate the guy's surrender. The whole thing got even uglier when the Office of

Professional Responsibility got into it. They said Stupleton probably didn't use the best judgment in deciding how to handle the situation, but Henri was insubordinate and publicly embarrassed the agency. I think they were most pissed 'cause the girl's parents have filed a lawsuit suit and identified Henri as one of *their* witnesses."

"So, Henri's a loose cannon," Tran surmised.

"Hmmm," the psychologist groaned. "I didn't get that impression from him. I perceive him to be dedicated to his work and his country, and eager to make a difference—he really thinks he can save the country in many ways. He has strong opinions, especially on things he considers moral absolutes. He respects authority but isn't afraid to confront it if he thinks it's wrong."

"So, you're saying he can go rogue if he doesn't get his way?"

"Well, yes, Grace, but I have to qualify that. The issue he disagrees with, in your scenario, would have to rise to the level of right or wrong, ethical or unethical. If it does, then yes, he's a guy who'd openly defy authority," Starr clarified.

"Openly defy," Lockwood repeated, laughing aloud. "You mean he'd tell his bosses to F-off."

Starr nodded. "Well…yes, literally."

"His boss ain't no Mother Teresa either," Lawrence added. "The Marine Corps court-martialed Miss Thang for deckin' a superior commissioned officer—damn near lost her pension too but she pulled a rabbit out the hat at the last minute. Besides her skirmish with Henri, her jacket shows some stuff from her early days with the Marshal Service, but she seems to have recovered okay."

Tran turned to Starr. "You indicated a history between you and Stupleton, too."

Starr inhaled and exhaled purposely, as though psyching herself up to speak about something she'd rather not. "Unfortunately," she answered. "We were on the same case several years ago when I worked as a law enforcement consultant. As I prepared to enter a holding room to assess a suspect's mental state, then-Deputy Marshal Stupleton pulled me aside and told me to play *good doc* to her *bad cop*. She wanted me to pretend I was there to help the suspect, to establish a trusting relationship with him so he'd tell me the truth about what really happened, after which I was to tell her and nobody but her what he said. She wanted to make the collar badly."

"Why's that a problem?" Trigg asked.

"It's unethical, Trigg. I wasn't there to treat him. I was there to assess him, which might ultimately have led to his imprisonment."

"That's some kind of *Shrink* rule or something?" Trigg asked.

"Confidentiality is a foundational ethical principle for mental health professionals. Creating the impression in the mind of a suspect that I was there to help him when in fact I wasn't would violate the confidentiality of the doctor-patient relationship. I'd have created that relationship if I did anything to objectively create the impression that I was his therapist. Not only could I lose my credentials for that kind of behavior, it's just wrong."

"How did Stupleton take that?" Tran asked.

"Not well. She pointed her finger at me, raised her voice, and told me in no uncertain terms exactly what I would and wouldn't do. When I insisted that I wouldn't do as she asked, she got in my face, told me she wasn't asking, as she not-so-subtly moved her hand to her holster."

"She threatened you?" Lockwood asked.

"Perhaps not in her mind, but I certainly interpreted her actions that way, yes," Starr answered.

"And what did you do?" Tran pressed.

"I let her think I'd been intimidated into doing what she asked, but rather than going into the holding room, I brought her supervisor back to her. With him present, I articulated what had happened in the moments before and told both her and her supervisor I wouldn't do what Stupleton demanded. I also documented the incident in my subsequent report. The Office of Professional Responsibility formally censured her, and her boss had her reassigned off of his team. I know the suspect's defense lawyer made an issue of it too in the trial. The suspect was ultimately convicted of several of the charges the government laid against him, but Stupleton's name was dragged through the mud during the case largely due to what I wrote in my report about her actions. That's probably one of the items Viv found in Stupleton's personnel file. I haven't seen or spoken to her since then."

Tran nodded. "I'm no profiler, but it seems like the Marshal has a pattern of wanting to be the hero who pulls the situation out in a clinch."

"Possibly. At the time, I informed her superiors that her behavior demonstrated strong traits of Narcissistic Personality Disorder," Starr said.

Lawrence injected, "yeah, well whatever her pattern is, she suddenly got some nice bank in the Cayman Islands—"

"I knew it," Kenison gloated. "Follow the money."

"A blind guy could follow this trail," Lawrence said. "Looks like $250,000 went into the account three weeks ago and another $250,000 yesterday morning."

Tran sat up straight. "Now that's interesting. Is there any legitimate reason she'd have come into that much money? Did she recently receive an inheritance or stock dividend or something?"

Vivian shook her head. "Nope. I have a contact at the Office of Terrorist Financing and Financial Crimes helping me track the money, but from what I see so far, there ain't no reason a GS-14, hundred thousand dollar a year employee would suddenly get a half-million bucks out of nowhere."

"Good work, Viv. Perhaps you can put your contact at OTFFC in touch with Mr. Mathematics here," Tran said, nodding at Kenison, "and let the two of them run that down."

"Happy to," Lawrence replied. "No offense, Kenison, but that math-geek stuff ain't my cup a' tea."

Tran turned to Kenison. "It's about time I had a little sit-down with Marshal Stupleton, and I want to have that information in hand when I do. Check her calls, federal filings—everything."

"It's my top priority, Boss," he replied, enthusiasm in his manner.

Kenison had a mind for numbers and all things convoluted and complicated. Tracing money across the globe into and out of bank accounts with long numbers would be right up his alley, Tran knew.

"I already had the Legal department serve a subpoena on her wireless carrier this morning," Lawrence said. "I should be getting the electronic records within the next few hours."

"Thank you, Viv," Kenison said. "You make my life so much easier."

"I'm jus' that good," Lawrence answered.

"Well since we're all sharing, I've made further headway on the radar contact," Ito said.

"Hold on a minute there, Nerd-boy," Lawrence said. "I was still talkin'."

"Sorry, Viv," Ito said. "It's hard to get in a word edge-wise when you're on a roll, so I have to jump in where I can."

"You're lucky I ain't right there, Ito," Lawrence joked.

"You were saying, Viv?" Tran prompted.

"The judge's kids are staying with his aunt while he was on this trip," Lawrence said. "His clerk said he didn't want them with their mother and thought it too early in the relationship to introduce them to Ms. Brandon."

"That answers one outstanding question," Tran said.

"An' you ast me ta' find out about the cabin too—it's a corporate rental owned by a company that is ultimately owned by the judge himself. I think it was one of the measures he used to hide assets from his wife."

Tran nodded. "Okay thanks. Ito, you were about to add something?"

"Sure was. After some more scrubbing of the radar logs, I can confirm my earlier thought about the radio transmissions. The first one originated on the beach in the vicinity of the bungalow where Lockwood's witnesses saw the guy. Nine seconds later, another transmission originated from out in the water..." he looked directly at Kenison, "...207 yards—not 200—away from the confirmed position

95

of the Marshal's patrol boat. Based on this data, I'm absolutely certain *something* was in the water off the beach near the bungalow."

"They have shark nets 100 yards off the beach in this part of the island," Torres said, "because there was an attack here a few years back."

"Thanks, Lieutenant. That's good to know," Tran said, "and good work, Ito."

"As far as air traffic," he continued, "there were no commercial flights near the time of the murders. The latest commercial traffic into or out of LPIA arrives at 11:00 p.m. and a guy at the tower said the flight arrived early that night due to high tailwinds. But radar did detect a few light aircraft in the area. I confirmed most of them, but one didn't have a transponder signal."

"That's it," Lockwood said. "That's the one we need to focus on."

"Judging from its trajectory, I'd say it most likely originated at the Nassau Paradise Island Airport, about nine miles away from LPIA."

"A small field I take it," Kenison said.

"Yeah," Ito said, "and it's been shuttered since 2012. It doesn't have government security anymore because everything of value has been removed, and they intentionally riddled the runway with bomblets so it couldn't be used for unsanctioned take-offs and landings. They have rent-a-cops out there now, primarily to keep the kids away."

"Okay, then. Viv, get hold of Lieutenant Torres and tell her we need transportation. I'm headed back to the bungalow. Wynken, Blynken, and Nod here are headed to that airfield," Tran said, motioning at Ito, Kenison, and Trigg.

"I'll call her right now," Lawrence replied, as she lifted her phone.

Starr checked her watch. "I need to get to the Atlantica Resort."

"Stressed are you, Doc?" Lockwood joked.

Starr pursed her lips. "I'm going to see Xochitl Brandon, Ms. Brandon's surviving child who was in the cabin when the murders took place. Both her parents and three of her grandparents are dead, but her paternal grandfather flew in yesterday to take custody. They're flying

96

back to his home in Indianapolis tomorrow, but last night I arranged time to meet with Xochitl today."

"I don't wanna' show my ignorance here, Doc, but what useful evidence can we possibly get from a kid who was asleep and didn't see anything?" Trigg asked.

"We don't know what this little girl may have seen or heard. Kids can be very perceptive to things around them. They're like sponges— they soak up whatever seeps their way. With the right handling, they can yield a great deal of helpful information."

"But I've always heard they suck as witnesses because they can be manipulated," Trigg rebutted.

"Anybody can be manipulated by crafty lawyers or sinister adults, Trigg, but our mission is to find facts that lead to evidence. Getting useful information from child witnesses is a different matter than putting them on the stand in open court," Tran said. "The prosecutors can worry about the kid's quality as a witness. If we do our job right, there'll be far more than a child's testimony to support our conclusions."

Lawrence interrupted. "Grace, the Lieutenant is in the base commander's office right now, but she sent one of her people. He's almost to the Embassy now."

"Thanks, Viv." Tran turned to the more junior members of her team. "You four can share that car; Lockwood and I will wait for Torres. We'll use the time to review the files on Secure Star. Viv, since you're the only one of us in DC right now, I'll need you to run down this business about who besides the clerk and Judge Oberlin might have known about the judge's pending decision on the *Goddess Frankenstein* case."

Field interviews weren't really the province of administrative assistants, but Tran had absolute confidence in Lawrence's ability to handle anything. They'd worked together a long time in two different agencies, and Tran knew Lawrence thrived on doing things that seemed difficult if not impossible.

"No problem, Grace. I'll get right on it."

"...And schedule some time for me to speak with Deputy Marshal Henri and Marshal Stupleton in that order, here at the Embassy please. Make sure they won't pass each other in the hall."

"Absolutely."

"And one more thing...Find out what you can about Lieutenant Torres."

The instruction immediately raised eyebrows, and Tran moved quickly to answer the unasked questions. "She's not a suspect. I just want to cover all the bases."

"Anything else?" Lawrence asked, feigned exasperation on her face.

Tran smiled. "I think that's enough for now, don't you?"

"I'll say!"

The group laughed at Lawrence's reaction, and their ad-hoc convocation slowly broke up as the agents parted ways for their next tasks. Tran stood and walked back to her temporary office across the aisle from Ito's and Lockwood walked to his on the other side of that.

Plopping into the chair behind her desk, Tran sighed as she considered the many daunting facets of the task ahead of her. "As the Brits say," she remarked aloud, "the truth will out."

Chapter 8: Backstory

Tran opened her laptop and began scanning the electronic files Viv had sent on the Secure-Star system. She searched first for the one pertaining to Ernesto Cabrillo. The Columbian drug lord was the only person they'd run across in the investigation so far that made an overt death threat to the judge, so starting with him didn't seem unreasonable. She read the case summary first, and then thumbed through the hundreds of forms and other documents contained inside. The fact that they were all in electronic form made the searching and manipulation of the case files much easier than had she had the actual bulky brown accordion files like they'd used *back in the day*, as her maternal grandmother used to say. She came to the document she sought—the trial transcript. She flipped it open electronically and turned first to the Case Summary.

Ernesto Sanchez Cabrillo headed the Sudamis drug cartel, the largest, most notorious criminal organization in Columbia. The Drug Enforcement Agency said the cartel had infiltrated most every level of Columbian society, and even had enough power to affect the South American nation's foreign policy. Its reach was vast and its tactics brutal.

On Cabrillo's order, the cartel had kidnapped three US DEA agents from their hotel rooms within hours of their arrival in Bogota to train the National Police of Colombia on US drug interdiction tactics and technology. After holding, torturing, and displaying them on TV for over a month, Cabrillo ordered two of the agents executed, and personally murdered twenty-four-year-old Marco Cruz, a first-deployment DEA agent, after hacking off his genitals and stuffing them in the young man's mouth. A former Cabrillo lieutenant, who'd entered witness protection in exchange for his testimony, said his boss had also sodomized Cruz before mutilating him, and then watched the life bleed out of Cruz, whom he wrapped in an American flag and then set aflame. When the horrific sight concluded, Cabrillo had the charred corpse dumped on the street outside the US Embassy in Barranquilla. The witness said the extreme brutality of the murder was motivated by Cabrillo's special hatred for Hispanics in America—traitors and children of traitors, he called them. Cruz's wife and toddler sons welcomed a third child one month after his death. The case made international headlines, and Cabrillo basked in the glory of his infamy, thumbing his nose at the United States and its "pansy President," as Cabrillo said in an interview. Within hours, US Special Forces launched a strike against Cabrillo's motorcade in Medellin, killing ten bodyguards, wounding three others, and nabbing Cabrillo whom they evacuated to a US aircraft carrier on patrol in the Caribbean. Three civilian casualties and immense damage to the shops, roads, and bridges where the strike took place were regrettable collateral costs for which the United States promised compensation.

A federal jury spent the past six months weighing the evidence of the multiple charges against Cabrillo and convicted him on all but a few minor charges that ultimately made no difference in his sentence. Through the trial, Cabrillo had repeatedly lapsed into fits of rage, defied the court's authority, uttered vile profanities, and otherwise showed contempt for all things American. With Oberlin's firm stewardship, the trial ended in multiple convictions, and it then fell to the judge to determine Cabrillo's punishment.

Oberlin had said in TV interviews after sentencing that the case weighed heavily on him for weeks beforehand, and that he'd deliberated long and hard on what to do. He admitted feeling negative attitudes toward Cabrillo before the trial but said his commitment to justice was far greater than his personal feelings. He also said that after the trial, images of Marco Cruz's charred, mutilated body, and the tears of his widow and babies influenced him significantly in deciding the sentence, assuring the reporter that victim impact was a fair consideration under the Federal Sentencing Guidelines. Since Congress had resurrected the federal death penalty, sentencing Cabrillo to death for these offenses was permissible and justified. Oberlin disfavored the death penalty, not because he fundamentally thought it wrong for the government to take human life, but more because overwhelming statistics showed a disproportionate application of the death penalty to minority defendants. In addition, new forensic techniques were increasingly exonerating convicted felons who'd spent years in prison for crimes they truly hadn't committed. This, however, wasn't among those situations. In this case, Cabrillo had not only admitted killing the "sell-out American pig," but he'd publicly gloated about it.

Tran shook her head in disgust as she read and recalled the facts of the case. After a time, she turned from the Case Summary to the actual transcript from sentencing day. Pushing back in her chair and raising her shoeless feet to the desktop, she began reading...

> Bailiff: All Rise.
>
> [Judge Oberlin enters courtroom. All parties and spectators stand, except Defendant Cabrillo and several members of the audience seated directly behind him].
>
> Judge: Please be seated, everyone. This court is again in session and the courtroom will come to order. I note counsel of record for both sides are present, as is the defendant. Counsel, are there any final statements before I announce sentence?
>
> Assistant US Attorney: No, Your Honor. The government is prepared to resume." [resumes seat].
>
> Defense Counsel: Your Honor, may it please the court, my client would like to make a statement on his own behalf.
>
> Judge: Counsel, it does not and will not please the court to hear any more of the sort of trash that previously spewed from your client's mouth. I will not tolerate it.
>
> Defense Counsel: No, Your Honor. We've worked with our client on a few prepared remarks he'd like to make before you pronounce sentence. We've fully advised him on proper courtroom decorum.
>
> Judge: And we've seen just how effective that appears to have been. [Sighing] All right, I will allow your client to make a final statement before sentence, but I admonish that you'd better assure he comports himself appropriately.
>
> Defense Counsel: Of course, Your Honor.

Judge: For your sake, counsel, I hope so, because I'll hold you responsible for what happens next.

[Court Reporter's note: Defendant Cabrillo stands to recite his statement]

Defendant: Your Honor— [lengthy pause; defendant drops papers to table]. I ask You, this Court, the United States Department of State, the U.S. government, and the President of the United States to suck my Columbian—

[Court Reporter's note: Defendant Cabrillo lowered his cuffed hands to his crotch and began to unfasten his zipper. US Marshals tackled Defendant Cabrillo before he could complete his statement or action.]

Judge: [shouting] Get him out of here!

Defendant: [shouting loudly] You're a dead man, you mother [expletive]. I'll kill you and everyone around you, just like I did that [expletive] [expletive] Cruz, [expletive] traitor to his own people. You're a [expletive] dead man you [expletive] [expletive] [expletive].

[Court Reporter's note]: US Marshals removed defendant Cabrillo from the courtroom by force. Defendant continued to shout obscenities in Spanish and English. Judge resumed speaking after Defendant departed.

Judge: Okay then. Since nobody has anything to say, I'll now pronounce sentence.

Defense Counsel: Your Honor, may we have a recess to calm and counsel our client? He has a Constitutional right to be present at his trial, and I believe he just got overcome by the moment.

Judge: [pointing gavel at defense counsel] Counselor, you're already on thin ice. A defendant's right to be present during trial is predicated upon his behavior during the proceedings. He has no right to disrupt these proceedings. His behavior throughout this trial has been grossly inappropriate, and I have no intention of giving him another platform to disrespect me and this court again. I am therefore continuing this hearing in his absence.

Defense Counsel: Your Honor, I object on the—

Judge: [shouting and interrupting defense counsel] Overruled!

Defense Counsel: But Your Honor—

Judge: Not another word, Counsel. Nothing you do or say will reverse my ruling, and if you don't like it, take it up on appeal. Now, we'll continue... [judge clears his throat]. I have considered the overwhelming weight of the evidence as to the particular inhumanity and callous disregard for law and human suffering involved in this case, and I have considered the defendant's reprehensible conduct during the course of this trial in terms of his likely rehabilitative potential. I have duly considered the effect of the defendant's offenses on the administration of justice in the United States, the pervasive reach of the defendant's violations, and most importantly the impact testimony of Agent Cruz's family, supervisor, and friends. I am particularly moved by the brave testimony of Agent Cruz's widow, Mrs. Mercedes Cruz. My heart and the hearts of people nationwide go out to Mrs. Cruz and all the families of the victims. It is not without great consideration that I impose a sentence, which for many reasons is one I view as the only sentence appropriate to this case. This court sentences the defendant, Ernesto Sanchez Cabrillo to death by electrocution to take place at a federal institution designated by the Commissioner of the Federal Bureau of Prisons. Subject to appeals, properly executed stays, or executive pardons, said execution shall take place not later than midnight sixty days from this date. That is all. This session is adjourned.

[End of transcript]

Tran closed the transcript and stood to stretch her muscles. Ernesto Cabrillo or members of his cartel looked good as suspects in the assassination of Oberlin's party, if for no other reason than because he'd threatened to do it only weeks before the murders occurred in the exact way he'd threatened to do it. Besides, taking out the innocent people around his intended target helped instill fear as a lesson to others who might cross the cartel, and it was consistent with its past tactics. If Cabrillo's reach extended into the Columbian government as the Drug Enforcement Agency suspected, Columbian military resources might have helped make it happen—that could explain some of the apparent sophistication with which the assassination seemed to have been carried out, Tran thought. If that proved to be the case, the whole affair could spin into something much greater because the President was more hawk than dove. He'd not let the Columbian government's assassination of a US official go unanswered, especially when the official was his friend. The Columbians surely would have anticipated the severe costs of such an act, but perhaps their anger about the US's illegal seizure of Cabrillo off the streets of Bogota had overwhelmed their good senses.

Walking tight circles around her small temporary office, Tran pondered the potential repercussions if the Columbian government played even a passing role in Oberlin's death. She glanced up, and through the glass walls on three sides of her space, and saw Lockwood hunched over his desk, presumably pouring over another Oberlin case. *Maybe he needs a break too*, she thought, moseying the short distance to him. She tapped on the frosted-glass door, opened it, and stepped inside. Lockwood rocked back, craning and rubbing his neck.

"Riveting stuff," he said.

Tran shrugged. "The Cabrillo transcripts were colorful."

"You think there's something there?" Lockwood asked.

"It's got all the makings, but it almost seems too easy a conclusion," Tran reasoned aloud.

He nodded and thumped the pages on his desktop. "Well *Goddess Frankenstein* here ain't a pleasure read."

"Is it as straightforward as Viv says?"

He pursed his lip and nodded. "Abortion, playing God with human genes, mortally disfiguring people—there's a lot here to piss off a whole range of people, and not just some kooky fringe-dwellers either." He paused and wrinkled his face.

"You're not buying it as a motive?"

"I don't think so, no," Lockwood answered.

"Why?"

He leaned forward and flipped the pages of the case file. "To be honest, there's just not much here. Oberlin held a hearing, but nothing out of the ordinary occurred. It's exactly what Viv said, a bunch of legal mumbo jumbo."

"Lawyers behaving badly?"

"Yeah. Oberlin asked a few questions and then said he'd take it under advisement. The whole hearing was forty-five minutes, with no real fireworks. There were a handful of protestors outside the courthouse, but nothing notable. The known threats were directed at the defendant, not the judge, and I've been reading up on the most outspoken stakeholders in the case. Even if I could rationalize an argument about why they'd take out the judge, it's inconsistent with their beliefs to kill the Deputy Marshals, the girlfriend, and especially the kid. And, I don't see that these people have the money and connections necessary to carry out something like the assassination of a federal judge at a secret location outside the country, protected by well-trained armed Marshals, all without leaving a trace of their presence."

"Not to mention that we'd still need a connection to the judge's unpublished decision," Tran said, nodding as she weighed Lockwood's gut read.

His preliminary conclusions had come pretty quick, but she couldn't argue with his reasoning. Besides, she'd learned to like gut instincts. Nine times out of ten, they were right.

"It just doesn't add up," Lockwood said.

Tran patted his shoulder. "Give it a little more thought, and challenge your conclusions as harshly as you can," she said. "If, after that, you still think that case is a dead end, we'll take it out of the running."

Lockwood nodded, and adjusted his body for round two of the case review. Tran went back to her office and sank into another case identified as a source of potential leads. This one involved two competing bio-tech companies, Bio-Drone Incorporated and Ajenatic Futures Incorporated, which sued one another for patent infringement and theft of trade secrets. Both companies had invested billions in genetic research that recently showed promise for curing several forms of cancer. More than a few scientific journals lent credibility to the research, and within days of their publication, both companies filed for patents. The drawback to making such a filing, however, is that one's work became a matter of public record, on which squatters and patent trolls were usually quick to pounce. In this case, the winner of the patent race stood on the precipice of a decades-long multi-billion-dollar stream of revenue, while the loser would suffer multi-billion dollar losses. The *Bio-Drone v. Ajenatic Futures* case could provide a powerful motive for bad behavior, but its appeal as a motive for Oberlin's murder escaped Tran. She flipped through the transcript, but nothing struck her as remarkable or even noteworthy. She flipped more pages:

Plaintiff's Counsel: Your Honor, I would submit that—

Judge: By all means, Counsel, please do so.

Plaintiff's Counsel: Excuse me, Your Honor?

Judge: I said, *by all means, please do so, Counsel.* You said you *would* submit, and I invited you to do so.

Plaintiff's Counsel: Uh, yes, Your Honor. As I was saying, I would like to submit that—

Judge: Again, I invite you to do so, Counsel. So get on with it.

Plaintiff's Counsel: Yes, Your Honor. I submit a tape-recorded conversation between my client's President and the defendant's Vice President for Research—

Defense Counsel: Objection, Your Honor! We have no way of knowing the legitimacy of this recording, and even if we did, state law requires two-party consent to the interception of a conversation, and that didn't happen here.

Plaintiff's Counsel: May it please the Court, these gentlemen had this conversation in the lobby of a federal office building, while awaiting separate appointments with an official. There's a sign in the lobby that puts visitors on notice that the area is under audio and video surveillance. Both men continued to have the conversation, so we argue that both participants in fact consented to having their conversation recorded.

Defense Counsel: That's ridiculous, Your Honor [yelling and standing to his feet]. The statute provides that—

Judge: I've heard enough, gentlemen. I'll allow this tape into evidence, Counselor, because it's being offered only to show your witness lied. You can use your charm and stunning good looks to try to persuade the jury it's unreliable and that they shouldn't give it any weight.

Defense Counsel: But Your Honor, that still doesn't—

Judge: I've made my ruling. Now sit down, Counsel [pointing gavel].

Tran rubbed her eyes and stopped reading the boring transcript. None of that section seemed particularly applicable to the issue at hand, so she flipped to another section of the file and began reading again. As she did, she heard the door to the outer office open. Seconds later, the door into the hallway outside her office opened. She looked up to find Lieutenant Torres walking toward her. Tran smiled and stood to greet the young officer. The expression on Torres's ash-gray face telegraphed that something wasn't right.

"What's wrong, Jessie?" Tran asked, opening her office door for the Lieutenant.

Tran didn't know Torres well, but the young lady seemed frazzled. She guided Torres to one of the guest chairs opposite her desk, and then seated herself in the other. She gently rested one hand on Torres's shoulder in an effort to reassure her and get her to talk.

Hearing Tran's question to Jessie, Lockwood left his office and walked briskly to Tran's.

"Uh, I, uh," Torres stuttered.

"It's all right, Jessie," Tran assured. "Take your time."

"I'm not sure, but I think I'm in trouble, Grace," she said. "I just got my ass chewed by the base commander. I don't know what I did to cause it, and he wouldn't let me explain."

"What happened?"

Torres shook her head. "I'm not really sure, to tell you the truth. I was on my way to the Deputy Commander's office to ask him to order the Hydrophonics Lab to give me the tracking information I requested. The Commander's yeoman stopped me in the hall to tell me the Commander wanted to see me immediately."

"Yeah."

"When I got to his office, I went in to speak with him like I always do, but he jumped out of his chair and chewed me out for not reporting-in properly."

The formal method a military member uses to report to a superior ranking officer was to walk to within a few feet of the officer, stand at attention, and render a crisp salute, while saying, "*Rank and Name* reporting as ordered, sir." However, such formality was rarely required unless the person summoned was in trouble. Routinely, even the sharpest military members otherwise responded to routine summonses merely by answering the call as fast as possible and asking, `You wanted to see me, sir?'

"I was shocked but, okay…So I reported-in formally, and he ignored me and pretended to read some damn thing on his desk, while I stood at attention, holding my salute. He didn't even look at me for about five minutes."

"Yeah, go on."

"So after a while, he finally looked up and proceeded to dress me down for seeking information that didn't concern me. He said they'd received Intel that some Al-Qaida cells were trying to steal a US military vessel in the region and—"

Tran saw extreme agitation on the Lieutenant's face as she reflected on the event. "…And what, Jessie?"

"He suggested in no uncertain terms that I might be helping them do so. I…I've never had my integrity challenged like that," Torres said, shaking her head and letting her mouth fall agape.

"Did he read you your rights?" Tran asked.

"No."

Tran nodded as though she'd just proven a point. The Uniform Code of Military Justice requires a military member who suspects another military member of committing a crime to read the suspect his or her Article 31 rights—informing them of the right to remain silent, that anything they say may be used against them, etc.—before further discussing anything possibly incriminating. Otherwise, evidence resulting from the discussion can't be used to court-martial them. Every commissioned officer is schooled on that obligation because Article 31 rights are much broader than civilian Miranda rights, which are triggered when a suspect is questioned while in custody.

"I can't believe he'd think I'd do something like that."

"He doesn't," Tran said. "If he truly thought you were helping terrorists, he'd have read you your rights, and you'd be in the brig under heavy interrogation right now. He'd be required to immediately issue notifications to a bunch of folks from his Navy superiors to NSA to CIA, and probably the Pentagon and White House too, each of whom would then get their hands in the matter. He'd only do that if he thought there was something to it. He was playing power games with you to rattle your cage. The question is why?" Tran looked at Lockwood.

"I tried to explain that I was seeking information to support your team, as *he* ordered me to do, but he talked over me and wouldn't hear anything I said."

"What exactly did you ask for, Jessie?" Lockwood asked.

"I got the air traffic reports no problem but ran into a wall when I requested sub-tracking data and hydrophone analyses for the last forty-eight hours. I assume that's the *information* Captain Ashmead referred to because those are the only unusual things I inquired about."

"You asked the Hydrophonics Lab for that information?"

"The air traffic information came from our radar tower, but yes, I requested the other stuff from the Hydrophonics Lab."

"Did they give it to you?"

"No, and it pissed me off," Torres said. "Agent Lockwood, if you know anything about the military, you know a Chief Petty Officer shouldn't tell a Lieutenant not only that she can't have information she requested, but that she'd better get the hell out of his lab or be detained."

"He spoke to you like that?" Tran asked.

"Yes, and got in my face too, like he was physically threatening me."

"What did you do?"

"I guess I could have reported him to the Deputy Commander, but I stormed out of there," she said. "I thought he might hit me."

Tran stood and looked Torres deep in the eye. "As long as you wear that uniform, as long as you hold any position of authority, don't ever cede your power."

"What do you mean?"

"I mean, you gave your power away by retreating. You are a United States military officer, and that Chief Petty Officer should comply with your instructions out of respect for or fear of you, Jessie, not because you ran and told on him to someone else who can help you."

"But I couldn't force him—"

"How do you know? How would he know?" Tran challenged. "Fake it if you must, but never let anyone see you doubt yourself or your abilities. Don't be stupid, of course. If you didn't want to risk a physical altercation with him, then you execute a power retreat, and return with reinforcements. You're a commissioned officer, and that carries power. You can have the Shore Patrol detain that man merely on your order alone. You can order other military members in the area to relieve him.

There are other things you can do, but you don't let people like that win."

"He apparently had orders from the C-O."

"You don't know what, if any, orders from the commander were, but even if he had them, it's a court-martial offense under the Uniform Code of Military Justice for him to disrespect and threaten a commissioned officer."

Torres stood from her seat, looking like someone who'd failed a basic test of officership. Tran patted her shoulder to soothe the sting she'd just delivered, but she hoped the young woman would learn something.

Tran turned to Lockwood, a telling expression on her face. "What do you make of this?"

"I think that terrorist stuff is a BOP-D," he answered. "He just doesn't want us to have that information for some reason, and that just makes me want it more."

"A BOP-D?" Torres repeated, her tone asking her question.

"Yeah, B-O-P-D…a big ole' pile of doo-doo," Lockwood explained.

Tran said, "I'm not a big believer in coincidence. I'm not sure what yet, but I think we may have stumbled onto something."

"You think this has any connection to our mission?" Lockwood asked.

"I don't know," Tran said. "But as Buddha once said, three things cannot be long hidden—the sun, the moon, and the truth."

She turned to Torres. "Let's go."

Chapter 9: Laying Plans

"What do you intend to do?" Torres asked.

Tran sat silently in the passenger seat as Torres drove the bumpy Nassau streets en route from the Embassy back to the base. She initially planned to march into the C-O's office, crush him with her authority, and demand an explanation for his interference with Torres's effort to obtain relevant evidence. Then, she'd subtly threaten the man's career, which would ultimately lead to her storming out with answers in hand. It sounded good when she first told Torres to drive her to the base, but she thought otherwise as she considered it *sans* anger.

Tran wanted information to help her investigation of course, but she also wanted to support Torres and bolster her legitimacy as a highly competent officer. But she realized her plan just might send the opposite message—that Torres was too weak to handle it on her own and needed someone else to fight her battles. Besides, that wouldn't get the President the answers he wanted.

Tran calmed herself and turned to the Lieutenant. "I don't like people getting in my way, Jessie. Your C-O may have a lot of power in his little world, but he'll need a hellauva lot more than he can ever hope to get if he thinks he can derail my mission."

"Navy Captain versus the Commander in Chief—I guess so," Torres agreed. "But Ashmead can still make things difficult for you around here."

"I know," Tran said. "That's why I've decided not to attack him directly. Instead, I'll deceive the heavens to cross the ocean."

Torres smiled. "Sun Tzu at his finest—the old open feint."

"I'm impressed—you know The Art of War," Tran said. "Yes, point west and go east."

Torres paused, seemingly waiting for Tran to elaborate, but Tran merely smiled and turned back to the windshield. She fell deep into thought as she fleshed out the rest of her plan, occasionally consulting her smart phone and then lapsing back into deliberation. Before long, the van crossed onto the base and pulled up to the front of the Headquarters Building.

"Wait here," Tran instructed. "It'll make things more difficult if I back your commander into a corner in front of you."

She hopped from the van and climbed the stairs with haste. After signing into the building under the watchful eyes of the building's Marine security, she made her way to the Commander's Suite on the first floor of the modern palatial building.

"May I help you?" an elderly woman greeted as Tran entered the Commander's anteroom.

"Good morning, Ma'am. I'm Special Agent Grace Tran, National Security Agency. I'd like to see Captain Ashmead please."

The woman squinted as she scanned a ratty calendar on the desk in front of her. "I'm sorry, but you don't have an appointment, Ms. Tran. The Captain's a busy man, so I'm afraid he won't be able to see you now. I can set an appointment for—" She flipped several pages of the calendar. "—Friday at 1:30?"

"Thank you, Ma'am, but I'd like to see the Captain now please."

"As I said, Ms. Tran—"

"Yes, Ma'am, I heard you, but I need to see Captain Ashmead immediately. This is a matter of national security."

Tran didn't wait for the receptionist's answer. Instead, she walked past the woman's desk and headed directly for the C-O's office.

"You can't go—"

The somewhat portly woman rocked a few times to create momentum enough to get out of her chair, but her stiff, perhaps arthritic knees fought against her. Tran entered the Commander's private office long before the woman could catch her.

The Navy Captain and a visitor were startled as Tran burst through the thick, solid wood double-panel doors and marched directly to Ashmead's desk. "Good morning, Captain," Tran began. "I'm—"

"I know full damn well who you are, Ms. Tran, but the question is who the hell you think you are, barging into my office like this?"

Tran turned to address the young man in civilian clothes sitting in the Captain's guest chair. She recognized him the instant he turned his face to her—the driver of the Shore Patrol car that chased her away from the sub-pen. "You'll need to excuse us."

"Don't you move a fucking muscle, Sailor," Ashmead barked at the man in the chair before turning to Tran. "You don't give orders around here, lady. I'm the Commander here."

"Captain, you'll be coming before your second Admiral's promotion board in ten months. If you want a chance of becoming a flag officer, we should talk...now."

"You threatening me, Ms. Tran?"

Tran feigned shock. "Threaten? Certainly not. I'm here to help you, Captain, but what I have to tell you—" She looked directly at the young man still sitting in the chair beside her. "I'm not at liberty to discuss it with just anyone."

Ashmead paused a moment, and then glanced at his visitor and bobbed his head at the door. The young man hopped from the chair and hurried to the door without another word. The Commander's receptionist followed behind him and closed the door as he exited. Tran seated herself in the chair occupied by the previous visitor.

Ashmead waited a few seconds more, then cleared his throat. "Now what the hell's going on, Agent Tran?" he demanded.

"Captain, the NSA has reason to suspect terrorist activity in this region," she said, recalling the Shore Patrolmen's admonition when chasing her away from the submarines. She knew the Shore Patrolmen had lied, but she could turn it to her advantage at the moment. Even if Ashmead had concocted the guard's lie in the first place and directed his troops to convey it to Tran, terror threats were the new norm post-9/11. Ashmead couldn't know what NSA knew or didn't know. He'd thus have

114

to reserve for the possibility that Tran spoke truthfully about the threat, especially because she spoke it with clear confidence.

Ashmead relaxed into his seat. "Really?"

"What I'm about to tell you is classified Top Secret, Captain, so you may not disclose it to anyone without a Top-Secret Clearance and a mission-essential need to know. I've come down here because we've had an intelligence asset killed in a cabin on the island a couple days ago."

"Yes, I heard about Judge Oberlin."

Tran responded as though Ashmead's comment was inconsequential, but it was actually quite significant. News of Oberlin's assassination had been kept under tight wraps. "The Judge's death was unfortunate, but one of the security guys killed along with him was our intelligence asset. His assignment as a Deputy US Marshal was a cover that gave him reason to be here at this time, and the Judge's death is my cover to investigate what happened to our asset."

Ashmead sat forward in his chair. "What was he working on?"

"We have credible information that an Iranian submarine smuggled a dirty bomb into the region after first stopping in Havana. They plan to mine the lanes into and out of AUTEC so it will appear that an accident at this base caused a nuclear detonation, thus discrediting the United States before the next round of talks on the Iranian nuclear program."

"I haven't heard any of this," Ashmead said. "I'm the senior US military official in this region. I should have been informed."

"That's above my paygrade, Captain. You probably didn't hear about it because this is a joint NSA-CIA operation, which we thought was under control. However, losing our officer has made the White House, the Director of National Security, and a bunch of other folks nervous about what happens next."

Ashmead thought for a second. "What's your confidence level in this information?"

"Very high. I've confirmed a few things I can't yet disclose, but the Pentagon will send a task force down here to respond since AUTEC isn't a Combat Operations base."

"We have resources to protect ourselves, Agent Tran. Don't worry about that."

"I'm not trying to insult you, Captain, but without combat aircraft or attack subs, AUTEC's military capacity is limited. You're more like a college research center."

"As I said, Agent Tran, don't worry about our capability to conduct armed operations."

"Okay, well, as I was saying, until the task force gets here, you're the only US asset in the area with any chance of stopping this thing from happening."

"You expect me to mobilize a combat operation just on your word?"

"You can validate me with the Director of National Security or the Chief of Naval Operations—hell, you can even call the President if you want—but whatever else you do, you need to move the assets under your command to DEFCON 4."

"I've received no orders to increase our Defense Condition status, Agent Tran, and I don't take orders from low-level NSA agents."

Tran stood and leaned over Ashmead's desk, speaking in a low, direct tone. "The agency estimates the loss of life and property at acceptable levels, so the physical fallout from this threat is purely local, Captain. The political fallout, however, will be felt around the world, starting on Capitol Hill. If this goes down on your watch, your career and the hope that AUTEC emerges unscathed from the budget wars will go down with it. I appreciate all the help you've given my team since we've been here, so I wanted to give you a heads-up. You and I—we're even now. What you choose to do with this information is entirely up to you."

Uncertain whether she'd accomplished what she came to do, Tran turned and headed for the door without awaiting a response from the base commander. Her stomach muscles tightened as she reached for the doorknob.

"Bullshit!"

Tran stopped and turned back to Ashmead. "Excuse me?"

The Captain stood and circled his desk as he approached Tran. "Did you really think I wouldn't see through your ruse, Agent?"

"If you have something to say, Captain, then spit it out."

"You didn't come here to do me no damn favors," he said, gloating as though he'd discovered something. "You came here because you need my help. NSA can't afford to let this thing to happen any more than I, but you want me to feel like it's my ass on the line, so I'd intervene. Isn't that the real truth, Agent?" He smiled.

"This isn't the US homeland, Captain," Tran resisted. "The agency can survive non-US casualties on foreign soil. The cold reality of the matter is that the power structure will conclude that this is just a tiny island nation full of a bunch of dark people with no oil or other vital strategic military or economic value to US interests. The rich Americans who come to play here will simply find somewhere else to vacation until things settle back to normal here."

Ashmead stared at Tran for what to some would be an uncomfortable period, but her years questioning witnesses gave Tran an appreciation for silence as a strategy. She stared back a while, then resumed her trek from the Commander's Suite. She opened the door and stepped into the anteroom, where the elderly receptionist glared daggers at her. Tran smiled and nodded politely at the elderly woman as she walked briskly for the outer door.

Ashmead followed her into the anteroom. "Bullshit," he repeated. "I was born at night, but I wasn't born *last* night, Agent Tran. I'm not as dumb as I may look, and I was the neighborhood champion at *Chicken* at the age of ten," he said. "The stakes have gotten bigger and the toys more impressive since then but commanding a warship on the front lines of freedom is pretty much the same damn thing. The tough-girl act suits you, Agent Tran, but if you want my help, you'll have to come right out and ask. Otherwise, I'm content to sit here and let this shit play out."

For a second time, Tran stopped and turned back to the Captain. She had him right where she wanted him. His smug grin prompted the urge in Tran to punch him in the face. But she remembered the many times her grandfather had talked to her about maintaining her cool in the face of conflict and facing problems with cunning instead of brawn. Pop-Pop, as his grandkids called him, was a pilot in the 332nd Fighter Group during World War II. As one of few black officers and pilots of the time, and an active participant in the Civil Rights movement in post-war Florida, Pop-Pop knew something about facing down difficulty. He made sure to impart it to all his grandkids.

Tran smiled as her whole body oozed defeat. "Okay...All right. We do need your help. We don't want this thing to happen, and if you can help us prevent it, you'll have the Director of National Security on your side when you go up for promotion—Admiral Ashmead."

"I'll do as you ask, Agent Tran. But rest assured, I *am* going to confirm what you've said here today. If you're misleading me, I won't be the one worrying about their ass."

"If you'll deploy your sub-tracking equipment and get me the tracking data Lieutenant Torres requested, we have a deal," Tran said.

"Then it's a deal, Ms. Tran. I expect your boss to live up to his end of this bargain. If not, I'll come for the both of you."

Inside, Tran bristled at Ashmead's threat. She found the man pompous, presuming, and condescending—the kind of person she liked to take down a peg or two, or several. But, giving in to her ego wouldn't serve her mission here, so she dug down deep to suppress her instinctive reaction. "I like you, Captain," she said, "so I'll offer you a pearl of wisdom. I hope you use it well."

"And what might that be?"

"Low-level NSA agents don't have the Senior Executive Service rank of a Vice Admiral." She smiled and then stepped through the doorway.

Chapter 10: Weeds in the Garden

Tran descended the stairs of AUTEC Headquarters and made a beeline for the van out front. Two people—one in uniform and the other in civilian attire—stood several few feet from the van, locked in intense conversation replete with energetic arm movements. The guy in civvies had his back to Tran and blocked her line of sight to the one in uniform, but she recognized from his garb that he was the same guy she'd dismissed from Ashmead's office, the driver of the Shore Patrol car. As she passed the pair en route to the van, Tran could see it was Torres speaking to the guy in such animated fashion. She remained absorbed by the conversation that it didn't seem she'd noticed Tran come from the building. Tran reached the van, climbed into the front passenger seat, and fastened her seatbelt, closing the door loudly enough that Torres would hear it.

As she waited for Torres to finish her conversation, Tran's phone vibrated the custom pattern that indicated an incoming text from Vivian Lawrence over the NSA's Secure-Star server. She fished the device from her pocket, entered her decryption code, and beheld the message.

Torres ended her conversation and then rushed to the driver's seat, her movements signaling frustration or perhaps anger. Tran observed as Torres climbed into the vehicle, and then offered an expression that inquired about the sidewalk discourse.

Catching her eye, the Lieutenant grimaced and shook her head in resignation. "Good help is hard to find."

"More than you know," Tran agreed.

Torres fastened her seatbelt, started the engine, and pulled away from the curb. "Where to, Grace?"

"The cabin please."

"As you wish." Torres maneuvered the van through the narrow parking lot, turned onto Nimitz Road, and pointed the van to the front gate. Clearing the initial traffic congestion at the entrance to AUTEC, she turned to Tran. "So, how did your meeting with Captain Ashmead go?"

"I think we'll get everything we need," Tran answered.

Torres nodded, but her repeated glances and expectant demeanor showed her pressing desire for more detail. Tran smiled, but offered nothing else. Instead, she turned and stared out the windshield for a few minutes before her phone vibrated several more times. Tran promptly studied each of the messages that popped into her inbox, and sent responses to a few of them, leaving Torres in silent suspense as they made their way back to the sight of the murders.

A short time later, they reached the crushed-shell road leading from the main road to the cabin. As the van turned, the ride grew even bumpier, thus rousting Tran from her electronic tether to Washington.

"Who was the young man to whom you were speaking back there?" she asked.

"Petty Officer Endicott, the newest sailor in the Protocol Office. His suit was pretty sharp and all, but I didn't authorize him to be out-of-uniform today. And he seems to have a perpetual attitude with me."

That didn't sit well with Tran. "Stop the car," she barked.

"What?" Torres asked, surprise in her tone.

"I said stop the car!"

Torres pulled the van to the side of the road at once. As the wheels ground to a halt on the rocky surface, Tran threw off her seatbelt and kicked the door open. "Get out," she ordered.

Befuddled, Torres did as instructed, hastening around the front end to Tran's side. "What's the matter, Grace?"

"I thought I made it clear that I wouldn't let anyone screw with my investigation, Jessie. If you cross me, the fact that I like you won't keep me from putting you in prison for so long, you'll fart dust by the time you see the sun again."

For a second time in the same day, Torres had been dressed down by someone of superior rank. "What? I don't know what—"

"I work for the NSA, Jessie. Did you think I wouldn't find out?"

"I don't know what you're talking about," the Lieutenant protested.

"Don't you?"

"No, Grace. I don't. Maybe you can just tell me what I did to piss you off?"

"I'm talking about that young man back there—Endicott. He drove the car that tailed me the other morning as I went for a jog. He and his partner threatened me away from the sub-pen. The same car followed us to the cabin yesterday and then again to dinner last night."

Torres's expression showed surprise. "You sure you're not mistaken, Grace? Why would he do that? That makes no sense. And he doesn't have a partner"

"Then I suppose it makes even less sense that he was just in Captain Ashmead's office, deep in conversation when I barged in a few minutes ago."

"What? What business would he have with the C-O?"

"Perhaps you should ask him."

"I asked him why he was at Headquarters and in civilian attire when he was supposed to be home on sick leave today, caring for his wife. He said he wanted to review his selection file for his next promotion board—said he wanted to assure everything that should be in the file was in fact contained there. Funny thing is, he's not up for promotion for two more years."

"You're suggesting you didn't know he was in the C-O's office?"

Torres looked Tran dead in the eye, her demeanor taking a new tone. "I'm not *suggesting* anything, Agent Tran; I'm *telling* you. I had no idea he went to see the Commander, and I have no idea why. As my subordinate, he shouldn't have done so without me knowing. We work in the friggin' Protocol Office, so he's damn well aware of that...I told you, that guy has an attitude problem."

"You strike me as neither stupid nor incompetent, Lieutenant, so I don't believe for one second that you're in the dark about this. I think you knew full well he was there, and you know exactly why. In fact, I think you're part of whatever is going on here."

Torres's expression showed a mix of disbelief, annoyance, and anger, but she managed to control of her tongue and temper. "Look, *Agent* Tran, I'm a lot of things that are far from perfect, but a liar isn't one of them. Whatever it is you think I've done, you're wrong, and I'm offended that you'd question my integrity without even giving me the courtesy of telling me what you think I did. So how about you stop with this…whatever you're doing and just tell me what the hell you're accusing me of?"

Tran raised her brow and turned to the officer. "Your actions suggest you don't value your future very much, and your involvement in whatever Ashmead is doing tells me you value your liberty even less."

"Yes, Agent Tran, I know you work for the President himself, and I'm sure you can scuttle my career with a single phone call. But regardless of what you think, I haven't done anything that would get me put in jail for any length of time. Hear me loud and clear, Agent Tran: I have to put up with a lot of shit at home and I have to put up with shit every day at work, but if you keep talking to me the way you are, you won't have to worry about getting me tossed out of the Navy, because I'll take off this uniform before I ever let anyone—including you and the President himself—impugn my integrity."

Tran stared at Torres for a moment as she sized up the young bundle of conflicting messages. Then, she pushed her way passed Torres and grabbed the door handle. "I need to get to the crime scene."

"Now wait just a second, Agent Tran—"

Tran climbed in the van, closed the door, and then pulled the safety belt across her lap, waiting for Torres to get behind the wheel. Her mouth agape, Torres held her gaze on Tran through the window a few seconds more, and then hurried to the other side. She slammed the door with more force than normal and started the engine. The gear remaining in *Park*, she hesitated and then angled her body toward Tran.

"So that's it? You're just going to tell me to take you to the cabin now? No further discussion of the fact that you just accused me of something and didn't even tell me what? It's just *never mind* about the fact that you threatened my career and my freedom? That's a load of horseshit, *Ma'am*."

"I don't want to talk about this any further right now, Lieutenant."

"Well I do. You can't just say something like that and then drop it, Agent Tran. As someone recently pointed out to me, I'm an officer of the United States Navy and you just questioned my integrity. I assume you damn well have evidence to support those charges, and I want to know what it is."

Tran looked at Torres who held the eye contact for as long as Tran gave it. "People in hell want ice water, Lieutenant. Now, do your job and take me to the crime scene…now please."

Torres glowered a moment more, but then firmly put the van in *Drive*, mashing the gas pedal nearly through the floor. The rear wheels spun on loose shells covering the road surface, and then sent the vehicle bounding down the road, fishtailing a few times at the start. The chill inside the van might have been uncomfortable to many, but Tran thrived on its intensity.

It didn't take long before they reached the cabin's driveway and seconds later, the large fountain at the front door. Tran climbed out of the van and then turned back to a fuming Torres.

"Get back over to the Hydrophonics Office and get the tracking information I asked for. Be back her in thirty minutes."

"Yes, Ma'am," Torres answered, not even looking at Tran.

No sooner had Tran closed the door, the van pulled away at a pace more rapid than normal. Tran watched it disappear over the crest of a hill, and then turned for the cabin's open front door. There were a lot fewer people fussing about than the day before, but Agent Darden stood in the center of the main room, coordinating the Evidence Recovery Team's activities. He saw her the moment she stepped inside and met her half-way across the floor.

"Morning, Grace—Well, I guess maybe its afternoon now, isn't it," he said, checking his watch. "So I guess I should say, *good afternoon, Grace.*"

"Hey Bob, how's it going here today?"

"Good. I think we're getting some stuff you can use."

"Don't tease a girl like that."

Bob chuckled. "Of course. Well, first thing is the footprints from behind the cabin. They're a size 7 or 7½ print—"

"That's a pretty small foot," Tran observed. "You sure you got a good impression?"

"The impressions from the back yard were mediocre at best," Darden admitted. "They're pretty shallow—only the aft left quarter of a left tread. Your man Lockwood said witnesses saw the suspect run to the water from somewhere near the rear fence line, so we took impressions on the beach side of the wall too. Those were much better, probably because your suspect jumped off the wall and landed solidly on the ground which at that location is composed of mud and clay from the yard as well as sand from the beach. We were able to confirm the prints inside and outside the yard came from the same set of shoes."

"Is that helpful?"

"Might not be to most folks, but as the Deputy Assistant Director told you, I'm the best at this."

"And modest too, I see," Tran joked.

"Yeah, well the shoe prints in the sand have an uncommon pattern on the bottoms that allowed us to hazard a good first guess about their origin. The partial bloody handprint from the top of the wall made us ninety-eight percent certain."

"A handprint?"

"Well it's not exactly a handprint, like with finger ridges. This was more like a smudge from a glove, but the rough texture of the wall took a little bite out of whatever left it. The material comes from a small textile company in Guangdong Province, China. It's primarily a domestic product or else sold in Southeast Asia because it doesn't meet the fireproofing standards for clothing in the US."

"That's useful. What about the blood?"

"Belongs to the victims. We also recovered five high-velocity rounds from the bodies—all with their brains torn to mush."

Darden withdrew a small plastic evidence bag from his pocket and handed it to Tran. All five fatal rounds were contained there.

"Our database says these are hollow-point, nine-millimeter rounds from a Norinco QSZ-97."

"These were made for sniper hits," Tran surmised as she studied the slugs. "Norinco—that's Chinese, right?"

"Yeah. It's designed to do maximum damage to human tissue and organs, so killing the target only requires a hit in the approximate area of a vital organ," Darden explained. "This is a new weapon that's still being beta-tested by the Chinese Army. The Naval Intelligence Service, CIA, and even your agency tell us it hasn't been distributed outside a few favored Army units. But, there's something even more special about this thing."

"Now you really have my attention, Bob."

"We think the weapon that fired those rounds was used in four other murders."

"Which?"

"The Vietnamese Minister of the Interior a year ago; a political dissident in Cambodia a few months later; a former Russian FSB officer in London; and, an Israeli tourist in Malaysia six months ago."

"A tourist? That seems out of keeping with the others," Tran noted.

"Unless the *tourist* was Mossad."

Tran nodded. "Yes, an Israeli intelligence agent might be a person someone might have an interest in killing. The question is who?"

"Afraid I got no answers for you there, Grace."

Tran considered the new information. "All the hits were in the Asia-Pacific rim, except the Mossad agent and now Judge Oberlin."

"That's a ways outside my jurisdiction," Darden said, bending to reach into a briefcase at his feet. "Here's a summary of everything the evidence has told us so far. Your assistant, Miss Lawrence, asked that I send an electronic copy to her, but I wanted to clear that with you first."

Tran nodded her assent as she texted instructions to Viv on what to do with the materials. Darden handed a thick, spiral bound report to her, motioned as though tipping the brim of an imaginary hat, and turned on his heels, fading into the buzz of activity in the room. Tran seated herself at the kitchen table and opened the report.

She'd scanned the entire document once and had done a more detailed read-through on the first third of the report when she sensed someone walking up on her. She looked up to find Rick Henri standing before her. "Marshal Henri," she said, surprise in her tone.

He nodded in greeting and offered a full grin of bright white, perfectly aligned teeth. "At your service, Agent Tran."

"What are you doing here?"

"Looking for you."

She flipped the evidence report closed. "Why?"

"I heard you were looking for me." He noted her quizzical expression. "Your assistant, Ms. Lawrence, called me to schedule an interview with you."

Tran nodded. "Ah yes. Well, when we do interviews, we typically do them at our offices, and not in the middle of a crime scene."

Tran stood, tucked the report under her arm, and gave him her full attention. For the first time since hearing anything about Deputy US Marshal Rick Henri, Tran really looked at him, beyond mere acknowledgement of his presence. His five-foot, eleven-inch frame understated a powerful athletic build only partially concealed by Hollywood-cool threads. A thick mat of wavy dark hair cut to military standards covered his head. His olive skin looked as smooth as a baby's bottom, except along his prominent jawline and dimpled cheeks which were covered by a light layer of dark fuzz that matched his hair. His features suggested he carried an interesting mix of ethnicities, but Tran couldn't hazard a guess at what they were. As she studied his features, her gaze came to Henri's eyes. The deep, transparent orbs emitted hints of crystal blue, flannel gray, and peridot green which sparkled subtly with

126

his movement, like glittering flashes from a pure diamond in bright light. Speaking to her, Henri seemed to look into her core, sparking discomfort in Tran, not so much because it was creepy, but more because she felt exposed.

"So who wants to be typical?" he asked. "Certainly not me, and from what I hear, you're not that type either."

"Right," Tran dismissed.

Henri smelled good—really good. It wasn't the powerful overwhelming aroma of a men's fragrance she noted, but something different. It was masculine on one hand, but gentle on the other. It reminded her of something she couldn't identify, but whatever it was, it was appealing. As much as she wouldn't acknowledge it, Tran found Marshal Henri immensely attractive, at least physically, but she'd foiled many good-looking threats to national security in her career. Still, it took a moment before Tran realized she'd been staring into his eyes for longer than appropriate. She snapped back to reality, hoping he'd not detected anything out of the ordinary about her reaction to him.

"So, I'm all yours, Grace. May I call you Grace?" he asked.

"Why don't we just plan to meet at the time Vivian scheduled for us, back at the Embassy where my team is working?"

"I was just there, and they told me you weren't available. So I came here."

"Not being there doesn't mean I'm here, Marshal Henri."

"And yet, here you are."

He chuckled, but Tran offered no visible reaction.

"I do work for the US Marshal Service—it's kind of our business to find people, you know."

"I know," Tran said as she lifted her phone and opened its calendar. "It appears we're scheduled to meet in forty minutes."

"Half of which will be consumed by the drive back to the Embassy. I figure we can get a jump-start on your interview on the ride back. I have a car, so I'm happy to be your chauffer."

Tran looked at him blankly. He carried a high-performance weapon just like she did, probably had similar firearms training, and they'd be alone wherever he might decide to take her other than the Embassy. If Henri had any involvement in what happened to Oberlin, this would be an ideal opportunity for him to do something to keep Tran from finding the truth of it. But Starr's read on him seemed inconsistent with the nefarious thoughts coursing through Tran's mind at the moment, and she herself didn't perceive maliciousness from him. Still, as Lockwood remarked, deception was a key strategy for people up to no good.

"That would be improper," Tran resisted.

"How so? We'd be sharing just a ride, not an intimate moment."

"It could create the appearance of familiarity, even though none exists."

"Relax, Grace. It's not all that serious a deal. We're just driving from a crime scene to a federal building together over the course of twenty minutes."

Tran hesitated.

"You sure this isn't about something else?" Henri asked.

"Like?"

"I could say something obviously wrong like, maybe you find me irresistibly attractive or something, but it's probably more like, you didn't yet have time to review my file which you wanted to do before talking to me."

Tran smiled. "And maybe you thought that showing up early for your interview would let you take control of the time and place of our meeting, thus throwing me off my game."

Henri laughed. "I studied *The Art of War* too, but no, that wasn't it."

"What does Sun Tzu have to do with this?" Tran asked.

"The General said the successful commander controls the time and place of battle—surely you know his work." He paused to await her reply. He'd correctly guessed Tran's paradigm, but she let him struggle with the possibility that he'd figured wrongly. "It seemed as though you—well, I just thought you wanted to talk to me. Frankly, I expected to be interrogated sooner than this."

128

Tran stared at him for an inordinate length, but this time intentionally. She wanted to observe his reaction to silence and direct stares where conversation was otherwise expected. Finally, she lifted her phone and pressed one key. A muffled voice answered on the other end.

"Would you be so kind as to let the Lieutenant know I won't need her to pick me up from the cabin. I'll catch a ride with Deputy Marshal Henri," she said when Lockwood answered. "We're leaving now and should bet there in twenty minutes or so." With that, she put her phone away and said, "Okay, James, to the Embassy."

Henri smiled. "Right this way, Ma'am." He bowed and opened his arm toward the cabin's front door.

Tran turned and waved at Agent Darden as soon as she caught his eye, then maneuvered around Henri on her way to the driveway. Outside, he nodded at one of the several plain fed-mobiles parked in the circular driveway around the fountain, and she headed directly to it. Henri rushed to open and hold the front passenger door for Tran. She thanked him, and then opened the car's rear door. She plopped into the back seat and reached for the door handle. Henri's face contorted with surprise.

"You did say you wanted to be my chauffer, didn't you?" she asked. She didn't wait to hear his answer, but instead pulled the door closed, and scooted her way across the big bench seat.

Chapter 11: Familiarity Breeds Contempt

The car pulled out of the driveway and turned onto the crushed shell road that would take them back to town. Settled in her seat directly behind Henri, Tran watched him closely as his eyes scanned the road outside and then rolled across the rearview mirror every few seconds. Each time, his eyes met hers, his lingering expression revealing that he hadn't expected Tran to hop in the rear seat to truly be chauffeured to the Embassy. That was why she'd done it, at least in part. Her position behind him would also enable her to unload several rounds into the back of Henri's head before he could move a muscle, if that became necessary.

Henri smiled, shook his head in disbelief, and gently positioned his hands at the ten o'clock and two o'clock positions on the steering wheel. As they traveled to the Embassy, she scrutinized his every move, giving particular attention to his eyes. He'd have to fix her position in the back seat before he could aim a weapon at her with any degree of accuracy, and his eyes would be the first tell. Tran also noted the route he drove because the Embassy was a direct path from the Cabin. Deviations would arouse her suspicion.

"So, what can I answer for you?" Henri asked.

"You can answer my questions when I ask them, Marshal Henri."

"Well of course, Grace. I meant what questions do you have for me?"

"I know what you meant," Tran said.

She fell silent and Henri begrudgingly followed her lead. They rode the rest of the way in an awkward silence of which both were keenly aware.

Henri took the most direct route to the Embassy, arriving seventeen minutes after leaving the cabin. As Tran lowered her window and withdrew her Consular ID, the Marine guard recognized her. "Good afternoon, Special Agent Tran. Everything okay?" The other two guards emerged from their positions, one with an automatic rifle from the gatehouse and a third with a canine came from the opposite side of the gate.

"Yes, Corporal. Thank you. Deputy Marshal Rick Henri is with the United States Marshal Service, and he's with me," she said, nodding at her driver.

"Yes Ma'am," the guard answered as he turned to Henri. "Be that as it may, Sir, I still need to see your identification please."

"Of course, Corporal." Henri withdrew his badge and credentials and passed them to the young man outside.

"Please stand-by, Sir," the man said, stepping back into the gatehouse.

The dog and her handler circled the car as a crusty armed jarhead in front of the car stared hard at everyone in it. A short time later, the guard stepped from the gatehouse and returned Henri's credentials. "You may proceed, Sir," he said, waving them through the gate. The security barrier in the road sank into the ground, and the car pulled into a designated visitor spot along the front of the Embassy. Moments later, they sat inside the conference room in the team's office suite.

Tran reviewed the file on her computer while Henri sat in awkward silence. Lockwood entered the room, and pulled out the chair next to Tran, directly opposite Henri.

"So, which of you is good cop and which is bad?" Henri asked.

Tran snapped up from the computer screen. "We don't play games, Marshal Henri. Besides, this isn't that sort of setting anyway. You're a colleague. We're asking routine questions here to officially clear you of involvement in this matter."

"Yeah, that's the boss's position," Lockwood said, "but I haven't made up my mind quite yet."

"So, you're the bad cop, I see," Henri said, nodding at Lockwood.

"Let's just cut to the chase," Tran said. "I've read your report about the night of the murders, but I have to ask, why did Marshal

Stupleton order you to break pursuit? You were only a hundred feet or so behind a fleeing suspect, so it seems counter-intuitive that she'd order you off."

Henri hesitated before offering an answer. "Look, from what I hear, Agent Tran, you and your team are pretty sharp, so I'm gonna' be candid with you."

"So you wouldn't be candid if you didn't think we were sharp?" Tran challenged. She didn't really expect an answer to that question, but Starr had said Henri liked to control his conversations with people. Tran intended to control this interrogation, and thus wanted to keep Henri off-balance.

"Of course not. It's just a manner of speaking. What I mean," Henri continued, "is that I'm not gonna' give you some politically correct bullshit answer. I'm gonna' give you the cold, hard truth. Some folks really don't like that about me, but I'd prefer to shoot straight and deal with the fallout later."

"And what does straight-shooting look like in this situation?" Tran asked.

"Stupleton's carelessness makes her dangerous and I'm gonna' do whatever I can to prevent another tragedy."

"Consequences be damned, huh?" Lockwood jabbed.

"She's a bull-headed, controlling bit—" He realized the words about to spill from his mouth at the same time his brain reminded him to whom he was speaking. "—a bit. She wants to show everyone she's smarter than they are, large and in-charge. Every good idea has to be hers or it's not a good idea. The fact that I might have collared the suspect was more than she could handle. She wanted to be the one who saved the day."

"Save the day?" Tran repeated. "Your protectee and his party were murdered. I'd hardly call that a *save*."

"We didn't know for sure that Oberlin and his party were dead at that point, but no doubt it crossed her mind. If so, she would've been thinking about how badly her ass would be hanging out as head of the protection detail. If she couldn't prevent the murder, the second-best thing was capturing or killing the suspect personally. That would show she's superior to the idiots working for her."

"So you think she waived you off so she could be the hero?" Lockwood summarized.

"Yeah, I do."

"Doesn't sound like you think much of your boss," Tran said.

Henri sat forward in his chair and leaned on Tran's desk. "Look, I'm sure you know Stupleton and I have history with each other, so let's not go through all this crap. I didn't like Stupleton one damn bit but liking one's coworkers isn't a requirement of the job."

"You're right," Tran agreed, "but respecting them enough to perform your job is."

"You're right too, Agent Tran," Henri said. "I make no bones about the fact that I had a lot of trouble with that when it comes to Stupleton. Her need to over-compensate for enormous insecurity she only thinks she hides from everybody makes her judgment bad, and when peoples' lives are on the line, I've got no use for that shit."

"Evidently," Tran said. "Two letters of counseling and a formal reprimand, on top of the suspension without pay in your file, all at the hands of Supervisory Marshal Stupleton."

Henri leaned into the back of his chair. "What can I say? The woman's a moron. I don't understand how she keeps this job, and especially how she's *my* boss—she must have compromising pictures of some big-wig."

"So this is a personal thing with you two?" Lockwood asked.

Henri shrugged. "Maybe it's becoming that way now, but it didn't start out like that. Over the years, I've come to see that Stupleton is an idiot, and idiots do idiotic things. I can forgive that up to the point of it costing peoples' lives. It's just wrong that we let people entrust their safety to us if we can't do our jobs right."

"Is that what happened with this fugitive apprehension debacle?"

Henri paused and looked to the wall, agitation clearly showing on his face. He sighed. "Yeah that's exactly what happened. I obeyed

133

that woman's ridiculous orders, and a little girl got killed because of it. I should've just taken the shot and put that mother f—" He stopped himself mid-phrase again. "I should have just shot the guy like my gut told me to and ignored Stupleton's order. That girl would still be alive."

"Your ass would be in a sling though, wouldn't it?" Lockwood said.

Henri chuckled, more from the irony of the facts than because he found anything funny. "Maybe you didn't realize it, but I'm fairly accustomed to that situation, at least where Stupleton's concerned."

Tran glanced down at the file. "Let's go back and discuss everything you know from the moment you guys were assigned to Oberlin's protection detail."

"Where do I start?" Henri invited.

"How about the beginning," Tran answered.

Henri sighed heavily and then began to recount a story, much of which he'd repeated many times in the prior few days. He explained when they first learned they'd been detailed to protect the judge, when they knew their destination for the trip, and the planning details. He delved into the security information they'd been given in advance, his knowledge of Judge Oberlin's activities, and just about every other aspect of the Detail's mission.

Tran and Lockwood listened intently for nearly three hours, occasionally interrupting with questions and comparing minute details of his recollection to previous times he'd given his account. He discussed the other members of the protection detail and explored the lives and connections of the deceased members of his team. Tran estimated his consistency at ninety percent, even with minutia. Liars generally avoided the minute details because it was hard to keep them straight, especially in an involved accounting of an issue. On the other hand, high accuracy could mean his story was well-rehearsed. But since Henri related the same facts and concepts without using the exact same words and phrases, since he answered quickly without having to think about basic facts, and since he looked them in the eye with each answer, Tran believed his facts were more likely than not true.

"So lemme' go back to your relationship with Stupleton," Lockwood said. "It's pretty clear you think she's an incompetent bitch," he summarized. "Why not leave? With your record—at least before Stupleton shit all over it—you could have gotten a transfer within the Marshal Service or to another federal agency—hell, even outside federal service."

Henri looked to the ground for a moment. "I've asked myself that several times, Agent Lockwood," he said. "Truth is, I don't know really. Except for the Stupleton part, I love my job and I love my agency. I feel like I'm using the skills and abilities the Big Man Upstairs gave me to support an honorable purpose. I shouldn't have to leave my job because some dim-witted, fat-cat bureaucrat who forgot or never knew what it's like on the front line put this idiot over me and a lot of good men and women."

"So this is a cause for you?" Tran asked.

Henri shrugged. "Maybe a little. You've probably pulled all our service records, so I'm guessing you know this was the first mission for Marshal Liang. He's a good guy to his core, who really wants to do something good for the country and for other people. He's dreamt of being a U.S. Marshal since he was seven, running around pretend-shooting bad guys on the streets of Chicago's Chinatown. He carries the weight of the world on his shoulders. I don't want him to think Stupleton is an example of what the real world or the Marshal Service is all about. Marshal Oseefah is a little older than Liang, but there's a similar story there."

"By similar, you mean the sexual harassment thing?" Tran asked.

Henri snapped his head around toward Tran. "I suspected Stupleton had some sort of personal interest in him, but I didn't know he filed a sexual harassment complaint," he answered.

Tran hadn't said he filed a sexual harassment complaint against Stupleton—Dr. Starr had only surmised Stupleton's carnal interest in Oseefah from her conversation with him. Still, Tran didn't correct Henri's misperception because it could help elicit information. "What do you know about that?"

"I know Stupleton is a sad, lonely middle-aged woman with a overinflated ego on the outside and a tiny sense of self-worth on the inside, and she has power over a young, unattached guy she finds attractive. I've seen that adversely affect her decision-making and attention to detail."

"Such as the decision to deploy your team the way it was deployed a few nights ago?" Lockwood asked.

"Exactly." Henri explained that he and Stupleton had had tense discussions when they deployed at the cabin that night. He said he believed the distribution of assets was less than optimal and urged a different plan. But, Stupleton ended the discussion by saying she was the agent-in-charge who was paid to make that decision.

"There are a few things we've learned about that night that baffle me as well, Marshal Henri," Tran interjected.

"Join the club," Henri agreed.

"What if I told you that Marshal Stupleton received huge cash payments a day before and a day after the judge's assassination?" she asked.

Henri sat straight up in his chair, and then stood, bringing his hand to his forehead and sweeping it down his face. It seemed as if he tried earnestly to repress a curse or two. "You sure?" he asked, wrinkling his brow.

"We're running down details now, but we're sure it happened," Lockwood answered.

Henri deliberated the information but didn't seem to know what to make of it. "I...I suppose there's no other explanation for it—like the sale of a house or an inheritance from a recently dead auntie or something?"

"We've not made that determination just yet, Marshal Henri."

"I don't believe it," Henri said.

"I'm never surprised anymore by the capacity of people to surprise us," Lockwood added.

"No, I mean, I really don't believe it," Henri clarified. "Stupleton's a real piece of work, and Lord knows I have my issues with her, but I just don't think she'd ever do what you're suggesting."

"Wait, you're saying you wouldn't believe the cold, hard facts that show she received as-yet untraceable funds in an off-shore account right around the time of Oberlin's assassination?" Lockwood asked, incredulously.

Henri resisted the idea. "I'm saying those cold, hard facts don't fit with what I know of Terri Stupleton. She's a lot of things, but a murderous conspirator sell-out isn't among them. She's a die-hard jarhead patriot to her last fiber—America first, my country right or wrong, American exceptionalism—all that stuff. Those are more than catch-phrases to Stupleton. She thinks this nation is perfect in every way, and I just don't see her doing anything like assassinating a government official for money."

"The facts speak pretty loud," Lockwood said.

"There's nothing more deceptive than an obvious fact," Henri said.

Tran quickly noted the Sherlock Holmes quote—it was among her favorites from the legendary sleuth. And in this case, it perfectly expressed her own gut reservations. Someone with the moxie to pull off an assassination like this wouldn't be so stupid as to leave a blatant marker that pointed right back at them. Of course, the First Rule of Assassination was *Kill the Assassin.* Dead men tell no tales, so a guilty party would be well-advised to eliminate the chance that a co-conspirator might later blackmail him or trade him for advantage if it ever became necessary. An appropriately blatant trail of evidence to Stupleton could be someone's effort to put that rule into play. Of course, that would mean Stupleton was somehow involved.

Another thought suggested someone set Marshal Stupleton up as a fall-guy—or girl, in this case. In the criminal arena, good trial attorneys often won cases by offering the jury an alternative suspect. It didn't have to be true; it just had to be credible enough to make them believe. In one of the most notorious cases of the 20th century, *if it doesn't fit, you must acquit* became the mantra of a skilled jurist who did just that. Maybe this was one of those situations.

Through the glass walls, Tran saw Dr. Starr re-enter the suite, returning from her visit with the surviving child of Judge Oberlin's girlfriend of the moment. She closed her electronic portfolio and stood from the table. "Thanks for your time, Marshal Henri."

"So you're done with me?" Henri asked. He looked Tran deep in the eyes, smirking slightly enough to make her wonder whether he was joking with her.

"For the moment," she answered. "But you know how these things work—based on the course of the investigation, we may have some more questions for you later." Tran smiled ever so slightly, nodded, and headed for the door.

"So have you concluded I'm not out to hurt you?" Henri asked.

Tran stopped at the door, holding it partially opened. "Excuse me?"

"The car this morning," Henri said. "It was more than humor that made you jump in the back of my car. The truth is, you have your doubts about me, right? I put my hands at the ten and two o'clock positions on the steering wheel, so you could easily see I'm no danger to you. None of us on the protection detail are a danger to you, and we're not involved in the judge's murder, except that we failed our duty to protect him."

"You have an active imagination, Marshal," Tran said.

Henri nodded. "Yeah, I do. That's what makes me really good at my work. I can envision the possibilities of every situation," he said. "In this case, you called your team before we left to apprise them you'd be leaving the cabin with me, a potential suspect in five murders. Then, you gave them an ETA beyond which time they'd know to come looking for you if they didn't hear from you. You released the safety snap on your holster as you entered the car, and you sat directly behind me where it would have been difficult for me to get a bead on you if I'd planned to shoot you on the ride back. You, on the other hand, could easily cap me in the back of my thick skull. Did I get it right, Agent Tran?"

Tran stood at the door and stared at Henri for a moment, noting he was smarter and more observant than she initially thought. "Why Pigmeat?" she asked.

Henri wrinkled his brow. "What?"

"I saw in the file that the code name you folks gave Oberlin was Pigmeat. Who picked it and what's the significance?"

Henri chuckled, this time because he found humor in her question. He stared back for a few seconds before answering. "I picked the name, and as far as its significance—well, I could tell you, but then I'd have to kill you."

Chapter 12: Too Much is Not Enough

Dr. Starr tossed her briefcase on the desk and uncharacteristically plopped into one of the guest chairs in her office. Tran tapped lightly on the door, more to avoid startling Starr than to obtain permission to enter.

"How did it go?" Tran asked, stepping into the room.

Starr sat upright and motioned Tran to the other guest chair. "Xochitl Brandon is a typical eight-year-old all-American girl in most ways, but she's suffered far more than her fair share of emotional trauma. Her dad died from cancer when she was five, and each year since, she lost a grandparent—all from age-appropriate natural causes. She may have been too young for significant memories of her father, but I'm sure her little mind felt something missing. She certainly sensed her mother's sadness and depression in the years afterward, and she would've been old enough to remember her grandparents. And now this…"

Starr waved her hands in the air, indicating the hullaballoo of the mother's and brother's murders, the federal agents buzzing around her, the investigation, and everything else she experienced in the last few days.

"Even with all this, Xochitl appears to be quite a little trooper. If she's subconsciously burying the trauma of these events, it'll manifest somehow somewhere down the line, but for now, this little girl is managing to hold it together. Her surviving grandfather says she's something of a prodigy on the violin."

"Did she offer anything useful?" Tran asked.

"She didn't actually see anything that happened that night, but something she said struck me as quite interesting."

Tran was intrigued. "What?"

"She said she heard someone say, *in the pipe five-by-five down here, so I'm good to go.*"

Tran interjected, "Are you paraphrasing or—"

"No, those were her words. She spontaneously volunteered that exact phrase—*in the pipe five-by-five down here, so I'm good to go*—without prompting from anyone," Starr reported. "It's a peculiar phrase that's beyond the comprehension of most eight-year-old girls, and I'm sure it's beyond Xochitl's."

"Why are you sure?"

"I probed several different ways about the meaning of the phrase and how she uses it in other contexts. Her responses suggest she's merely regurgitating something she heard and didn't reflect an independent mastery of the phrase or its component parts."

"You're saying she doesn't know enough about the words to use them on her own?"

"Exactly."

"How confident are you in that assessment?"

"Ninety-nine percent, Grace. This young lady is a violin prodigy, and there's a good deal of credible research that says children with musical training have greater neural development than their peers. This may translate into substantially better memory and factual recall."

Tran knew the phrase—actually, the two phrases—herself. She heard them in the military. Her aviator friends used *in the pipe five-by-five* to indicate their aircraft were in operable condition or they were on course to achieve their missions. Her Army friends used *good to go* to indicate readiness. Other people used it too, but when she heard it, it always made her think the user was or had been military. She didn't know whether her reasoning was right, but she explained as much to Starr.

The psychologist chuckled. "It's an interesting coincidence that this case seems to be developing a slight military stink to it," she said.

The unmarked government cars that followed her, the unusual difficulty getting AUTEC tracking data, and the unrequested but fortuitous assignment of AUTEC's Protocol Office to support Field

Team Six had already ignited a hint of distrust in Tran's gut, but Starr's remark buttressed her hunch. On some level, Tran began to feel AUTEC was connected to Oberlin's murder, but she struggled to justify her feeling. The convergence of random occurrences didn't lead to the logical conclusion that AUTEC was involved in Oberlin's assassination.

"Why do I have the feeling you're trying to lead me somewhere, Deanna?" Tran asked.

Starr sat up straight. "Oh no, Grace. I'm not trying to lead you anywhere. I'm just asking whether you think there's a connection between the two."

Tran chuckled. "It is a capital mistake to theorize before you have all the evidence."

Starr shook her head and smiled when Tran offered the oft-repeated phrase in reply.

"I'm curious," Tran said. "Based on your knowledge of him thus far, how would you size up Captain Ashmead?"

Starr considered the question. "Without assessing him clinically, I can only answer based on what I know about those who show similar behavior patterns. Generally, people who fit his profile loathe appearing impotent or irrelevant, especially if it is forced on them by circumstances beyond their control or other people. They fear being insignificant, forgotten, or pushed aside. At the other extreme, they relish the limelight, especially when they can appear in control, decisive, and victorious. You'll find the characteristic playing out in situations that have languished under the leadership of others."

"You're saying he has a hero complex?"

"That may be a bit oversimplified, but yes, Grace. That's generally correct," Starr said.

"Given his military record," Tran said, thinking aloud, "I'm sure he's had command of nuclear weapons at some point in his career. That means the Navy would have had him do a Personnel Reliability Profile."

"Good idea. That should give me some clinical data on which to base an assessment," Starr said. "I'll pull his military records."

Lockwood and Henri stepped into the hall outside Starr's half-glass wall as the former escorted the latter out of the suite. Starr waved nonchalantly as they passed.

"How was his interview?" she asked, nodding at Henri.

"It went well." Tran also watched as the pair walked out of view.

"So what do you think?"

"It's my turn to play shrink now?" Tran joked. "Deputy Marshal Rick Henri is an intelligent, competent, self-assured professional. He's hyper-observant, cool-under-pressure, and strategic in his thinking."

"So you believe him," Starr summarized.

Tran nodded as though reassuring herself of a conclusion she'd just reached. "Yes, I do. Integrity is of paramount importance to people like him. I don't see him plotting to take out his own protectee unless ordered to do so for a reason he found extremely compelling. If that were the case, he wouldn't have taken out the innocent people around his target. If he was involved in the plot, he'd own it—maybe from a place he thought we couldn't reach him, but he'd own it and he'd be brazen about it."

"Does that mean you also give him a pass on having knowledge of the plot, before or after?" Starr pressed.

"I think your prior read on him is dead-on, Deanna," Tran said. "Given his personality, Henri would see having advanced knowledge of the plot and doing nothing to stop it the same as actively assassinating those people. I don't believe that's in him in the normal course."

"I agree," Lockwood bellowed as he entered Starr's office. Since the ladies occupied the guest chairs, he rounded Starr's desk and sat in the plush leather chair behind it. "That guy wouldn't even throw under the bus the very woman who tried to scuttle his career."

"You're talking about Stupleton?" Starr asked.

"Yeah. We gave him the opportunity to point the finger at Stupleton, a woman who has caused him a fair amount of trouble. Even though he could have deflected all suspicion away from him and put her in the crosshairs, he wouldn't do it—despite the fact that we indicated we were leaning that way," Lockwood said.

"We delved deep into several areas he didn't particularly want to talk about, and he gave us straight answers," Tran added. "He acknowledged weaknesses in his position and didn't try to explain away every little discrepancy. Those are indicators of truth. Guilty people tend to give precisely the same well-rehearsed responses when you dig into their backstories, or else they avoid talking details altogether. Henri eagerly challenged us when we impugned his integrity, and while his answers were consistent, he didn't use the exact same verbiage to discuss it."

"Yeah, and the evidence team reported that only one of the Marshals showed anomalies in their polygraph results," Lockwood added.

"Let me guess," Starr said, "Stupleton."

"Guess there's a reason you got the doctorate, Doc," Lockwood joked.

"They call it a lie detector test, but the machine doesn't test the truth or falsity of a person's statement," Starr said. "It only measures autonomic responses that may indicate whether a person is being deceptive. It can easily be misinterpreted or fooled."

"That's why they're not generally admissible in court," Tran said. "But they're good tools for an investigation, especially with those who can be manipulated."

"You think that'll be the case with Stupleton?" Lockwood asked.

Tran shook her head. "Stupleton has her issues, but I don't think she's an idiot," Tran answered.

"I can tell you for sure, she's not stupid," Starr said. "Over-zealous, impetuous, controlling, short-sighted—those are all words that describe her, but stupid isn't."

"Well, whatever the case, Lockwood, I want you to look into her military connections to anyone or anything here at AUTEC."

"You recall that she retired from the Marine Corps, right?" Lockwood said.

"Yeah, but that's not it," Tran said.

"You have a theory?" he asked.

"No, a nagging dissatisfaction," Tran answered. "The deeper we dig in this case, the more random, senseless anomalies and coincidences we find."

"Which you don't believe in," Lockwood said.

"Calling something a coincidence is a copout for not doing the work to find the facts," Tran said, pausing to work through a thought. "We've found a few as-yet unexplained things about Stupleton and a few as-yet unexplained things involving AUTEC. As far as I see, none of them have clear relationships to each other, and even fewer seem to have anything to do with Judge Oberlin or his people. The common denominator is that they all seem connected to AUTEC."

"So you do think they're related?" Starr asked. "Or, at least you're wondering."

"I have no facts to suggest that, Dr. Starr," Tran answered.

"But you don't have all the facts," Starr said. "Perhaps you can get some of those answers from Marshal Stupleton."

Tran smiled and nodded. "We have about an hour before she's due here," Tran said, checking her watch. "Let me brief you on what Darden's team found at the scene."

"I was going to ask," Lockwood said.

"The evidence team recovered traces of a Chinese textile. We think it is material from the assassin's clothes or maybe his parachute," Tran said.

"Did we find something that conclusively shows he used a parachute?"

"No, it's pure speculation at this point, but it fits the facts," Tran said, doing her best to mask her frustration.

Based on the known facts, Tran developed a working theory about how the assassin accomplished his mission. She knew the *what* and part of the *how* but had yet to discover the *who* and the *why*. She'd hoped to be further along in the process by this point. Uncovering the rest of the *how* would get her there.

"The pathologist pulled these from the bodies." Tran withdrew the bag containing the rounds and handed it to Lockwood.

He studied the singed chunks of metal. "These are hollow-point, high-velocity, nine-millimeter rounds," he said.

Tran nodded. "From a Norinco QSZ-97."

"Chinese?" Lockwood asked.

"Yes," Tran said. "The particular weapon that fired those rounds appears to have been used in the assassinations of a Vietnamese government official, a political dissident in Cambodia, a retired Russian FSB officer, and an Israeli tourist."

"Assassins don't kill tourists," Lockwood said. "That tourist was probably Mossad."

"An Israeli intelligence officer?" Starr asked. "Is this going where I think it's going?"

"I don't know," Tran said. "But this is the second hint of foreign involvement, and neither of them spells good things for how this resolves."

"You think the President would retaliate for this?" Starr asked.

"I think the President won't tolerate the assassination of a US official by a foreign government, especially if that official was his good friend. I think the President will want solid, indisputable answers before deciding a course of action, but once he decides, he'll be swift and clear in his response. That means we need to be damn sure of what we report."

"But what Chinese interest is served by assassinating a U.S. judge?" Lockwood wondered aloud. Just as Kenison liked to follow the money, Lockwood typically looked to see who benefitted from whatever the issue might be.

"I don't know, but it suggests we need to look really hard at what Oberlin was involved in. We need to scour his cases again, and maybe widen our search," Tran said.

"Agreed. We should probably get the agency doing an analysis on the textiles and these fragments," Lockwood said.

"Already done," Tran said. "I asked Viv to circulate the fabric analysis results to the Strategic Research Directorate."

"Good move," Lockwood agreed. "SRD is pretty sharp and they're like a dog with a bone. If there's anything to find, they'll find it."

The inner door into the suite swung wide, and Kenison, Trigg, and Ito walked briskly inside. They hurried to Starr's office and formed a semi-circle around Starr and Tran, eager to report their findings over the last several hours.

"So, the airfield has been closed for some time like Rique said," Kenison began. "But it's been used for unsanctioned activities, including three nights ago."

"By whom?" Tran asked.

"It's mostly rocket clubs and radio-controlled airplane hobbyists that trespass the field, but some local hoodlums that hang out there and the rent-a-cop on-duty that night said a small aircraft took off around 2315 hours, headed southwest."

"An 11:15 pm take-off from an unmonitored field?" Lockwood said. "I don't suppose they got an N-number?"

"Nope, nobody saw the tail number, I'm afraid. In fact, nobody saw the plane. They only heard it. The rent-a-cop said a car had approached and stopped at the gate a while earlier, but it turned around and went back toward town before he could get in his golf cart and get over there," Kenison said. "I re-conned the area and found a hole cut in the fence."

"I don't suppose he saw the car's plate?" Tran asked.

"No. It drove off without turning on its lights," Kenison answered. "But he thinks he chased the same white car away from there a few days earlier."

Tran's subtle expression and head movement showed her keen interest in the information. "How does he know? It was dark after all."

Kenison turned to Trigg, prompting the latter to speak. "He's a car buff who can identify any car by its shape, head- and tail-lights, the sound of its engine. I'm a car guy too, Boss, so I tested him. He's not as good as me, but he knows his stuff."

Trigg went on to explain that the security guard had spotted someone standing beside a white Dodge Avenger parked at the locked gate at the main entrance to the airport. "He says it's fairly common for random people to drive up to the old airport, stop at the gate, and do a

147

three point turn before heading back for town. But this driver, he said, parked his car, got out, and stared through the fence for an extended time. The guard said they don't usually get too excited about chasing people off for just coming to the gate, but they'll chase them off if they linger too long. This guy stayed long enough to annoy, so the guard hopped in his cart to go shoo him away."

"Did he get a good look at the guy?" Lockwood asked.

"He said the guy stared directly at him until the cart got about 100 feet from him, spat a wad of gum on the ground like he meant to say *screw you*, and then drove off just as the guard reached the gate."

"So he didn't get a good look?"

"Not really," Kenison said. "But he gave us the best description he could."

"What is it?" Tran asked.

"We might be able to do better than explaining it, Boss," Kenison replied. "I'll let Van Gogh here explain."

He turned and nodded at Ito, whose gleeful smile usually preceded a snarky remark or stupid joke, and occasionally something groundbreaking. Ito maneuvered his well-worn laptop from his side to a balanced position on his forearm. He flipped it open and deftly toggled its keys one-handed, giving rise to an image that flickered onto the screen. "I put the guard's description into a program I designed to make artists' renderings of suspects. Here's what we have."

Everyone's eyes dropped to the computer screen for several moments, and then came back up to peer at Ito, who in turn looked at Tran. The black-and-white image showed a charcoal sketch of a young, medium-height male in generally good physical shape. He had broad shoulders, a thick build, and a few strands of wavy hair sticking out from beneath a baseball cap with an undefined emblem on its front. The center of his face lacked any identifying detail that would have given a clear picture of the person-of-interest, but the guard had been too far away to make useful observations. Ito toggled a button that changed the view to a similar image, this time with a pair of sunglasses covering the man's face.

148

"The guard couldn't remember whether the guy had specs on or not," Ito said. "…so, you get both."

Tran stared at both images, and while she felt a sense that she could know the person, she also knew it wasn't enough to narrow the field of suspicion to anything useful. If it was anything near accurate, however, it could rule out anyone carrying the common traits of African Americans, Hispanics, and Asians, unless the person was racially mixed which might not produce the usual ethnic markers. It also ruled out women, and really tall or really short people. "How confident was the security guard in his description and how confident are you in your rendering program?" Tran asked of Ito.

"I have ninety-nine percent confidence in my program's algorithm," Ito said. "I'm still coding it, but future enhancements will improve its detail, not its accuracy, which is based on the input. I can't attest to the security guard's observations. He's a 30-year-old dude riding around in a golf cart for a living, so maybe he's not the brightest bulb in the box," Ito said, "but whatever he reported, I put in the program."

Tran glanced up from the screen once more, this time staring directly at Ito. "A little dismissive there, isn't it, Agent Ito?" Tran teased. "There's a certain guy named Tiger who rides around in a golf cart on TV every Sunday, and he's the best there ever was at his art…handsomely rewarded for it too."

"You know what I meant."

"Yes," Tran replied, "but that guy's observations could be key to breaking this case. Let's not assume anything about our witnesses or evidence."

"You're right, Boss. I didn't mean it that way."

Tran smiled, winked, and turned to Starr. "Does this tell you anything, Doctor?"

Starr had already been studying the image but leaned forward to study it more closely. "Eyewitness testimony is usually vulnerable to attack by crafty defense lawyers on three bases," Starr said. "Visibility may have been in question at the time, poor human capacity for facial identification especially under stress, and lastly, the process used to obtain a visual identification."

"It was a clear day and it was a natural setting instead of a line-up or a mug-shot review," Kenison said. "So, the first and third factors aren't really issues here."

"I think you're right," Starr said, nodding. "Juries often rely on eyewitness identifications to convict, but there is a substantial body of evidence to suggest eyewitness ID is highly fallible. And, eyewitness confidence in testifying has proven a statistically poor measure of accuracy."

"So you're saying this is useless?" Trigg asked.

"Not at all," Starr said. "I'm just saying we need to take it with a grain of salt." She studied it closer. "I'm not a car girl but look at the sketch of the car next to the driver," she said. "This is remarkable detail from which I can clearly identify the make and model of the vehicle, and even see dirt on the front hood of the car. If this is any measure, this may reflect an accurate illustration of what the guard says he saw and what was input to the program."

"I'm more interested in something else you said," Tran added. "If the guy loitering at the gate spat out a wad of gum, we might be able to extract DNA if we can find where he spit it."

"I'm a step ahead of you, Boss," Kenison said. "I asked Agent Darden to get his evidence team out there to search the spot. The guard says he knows exactly where it is."

"Excellent work, Agent Kenison," she said.

"What's that?" Trigg asked, pointing to the bagged rounds in Lockwood's hands.

"Bullet fragments from the bodies," the senior agent answered.

Trigg opened his hand. "May I?"

Lockwood passed the slugs to him as everyone watched the former bomb technician begin to study them. In quick time, Trigg said, "these are high-velocity, hollow-point rounds from a QSZ-97. If I remember right, that's a close-range precision weapon designed to maximize internal damage. Last I heard, the Chinese Army was beta-testing these things in a few of their elite units."

He returned the bag back to Lockwood, the latter's wide-eyed expression betraying his momentary awe of the rookie's munitions knowledge.

"I'll be damned," Lockwood said. "You have experience with Norincos, Trigg?"

"They didn't call me *Trigger* for nothing," the rookie answered, smiling. "I got real familiar with all kinds of explosives and weapons in Afghanistan. If you think the Chinese didn't have a role in all that shi.... uh, stuff that went on over there, you got another think coming. They armed whoever was fighting us."

"Well I suppose you're good for something after all, Rookie," Lockwood said.

"Agent Darden sent that report direct ta' me," Lawrence chimed from the screen on Ito's chest. Everyone turned to the device as Ito spread his arms wide and moved his laptop aside, so they could see her clearly. "I'm already washing the data through the NSA database. I'm still waitin' to see if there's anything on the bullets, but somethin' just popped in on the fabric, Grace."

"What's that, Viv?" Tran asked.

Lawrence leaned in close as she paused to read something on her computer screen. After a few seconds, she leaned back and looked into the camera. "Okay, CIA says the fabric comes from a wing suit, like Kenison suspected."

"What's their confidence in that information?" Lockwood asked.

"High enough to identify the wing suit as the Kui-3 model," Lawrence replied.

"Anything else, Viv?" Tran asked.

"Uh, just to close the loop on your friend from Protocol," Lawrence said. "It don't seem like she's up to no good. I looked in all the usual places and ain't found nothin' dirty on her. I still got a few more things to check out, but so far, she looks good."

"Thanks, Viv. Keep me posted." Tran turned back to the rest of the team.

"Boss, I have some intel about Suspect Number One," Kenison joked.

"If you're referring to Marshal Stupleton, she's not quite a suspect yet—no more than anyone else on her Detail," Tran corrected.

"You might change your opinion after you hear my report," Kenison warned.

Intrigued, Tran nodded prompting Kenison to elaborate. He reported that he and his contact at the Treasury Department's Office of Terrorist Financing and Financial Crimes spent a long time tracing the money backward from the Cayman Island bank account bearing Stupleton's name. The money came into the account from another Cayman Island account at a bank across town, and before then, it came from a numbered account in Switzerland. They continued to trace the funds through banks in Lebanon, Luxembourg, and Singapore where the trail seemed to originate. Unfortunately, Singapore's bank privacy laws thwarted their ability to dig further. They'd enlisted the aid of a national security liaison at the State Department, but he warned not to expect much if anything from the Singapore government, and certainly nothing fast.

"That's not all, Boss," Kenison continued. "Homeland Security dug up one-way air reservations for Stupleton from Lyndon Pindling International Airport to Brunei, Cambodia, China, Vietnam, and Indonesia, respectively."

Tran wrinkled her face. "In her name?"

"Not exactly but close. The tickets were in the names of her deceased grandparents," Kenison said, "—the actual names of her grandmothers, and distortions of her grandfathers' names."

"And we know this how?" Tran pressed.

Kenison withdrew a notepad from his hip pocket and scanned its pages. "The background investigation done for her first military security clearance shows her grandmothers' maiden names were Teresa Heryon and Anne-Marie DiSpenza. Her grandfathers were George

Wertz and James Vick. Homeland Security found flight reservations in the exact names of the grandmothers, in addition to some for Georgia Wertz and Jane Vick. All leave from Lyndon Pindling International and have connections that ultimately go to the destinations I mentioned."

"I guess it's only coincidence that none of those countries have extradition treaties with the US," Lockwood said.

"How about hotels or rental cars?" Tran asked. "Any bank accounts in any of these places?"

"We found no rental car transactions, but we did find a reservation in the name of Teresa Heryon at the Heryon Hotel in Yogyakarta, Indonesia."

"Wait," Starr interrupted. "The name of the hotel is Heryon, like the grandmother's maiden name?"

Kenison nodded. "Ironically, yes." He went on to explain how the FBI tracked Stupleton's credit cards but found no activity outside the US. Even the international air tickets and Indonesian hotel reservation weren't showing up on her credit cards. Searches for transactions in the names of her likely aliases also came up empty. Kenison acknowledged that anonymity might have helped an unknown accomplice provide Stupleton with resources he overlooked, but thus far, he'd found no unusual financial behavior from Stupleton.

"Did you get anything on her polygraph test?" Lockwood asked. "That might help us focus our investigation."

Kenison smiled. "Yeah. The examiner said Stupleton showed deception only on one question: *do you have, or have you had any relationship with any party that may have compromised your duties with respect to the protection detail assigned to Judge Oberlin?*"

Starr winced. "That's not the best-structured question for a polygraph exam, in my opinion. It's too broad and too given to interpretation, especially if he didn't hone in on something more precise later in the exam."

"He asked several versions of the question, and each time, her answers indicated deception," Kenison said.

Pursing his lips, Kenison stopped speaking and feigned interest in a random piece of wall décor as he stifled a grin. His expression suggested he had something else to say, but kept it to himself. Tran guessed at the perhaps embarrassing nature of the matter, and then prompted him to disclose it. "I'd clean your clock in poker, Kenison," she said. "You might as well just say it. After all the years we've worked together, you should know you can't hide anything from me."

The younger agent's grin blossomed into a full-blown chortle. "Our boys in the Bureau searched her apartment. They didn't find a smoking gun or anything, but they did find her diary in which she confessed her deepest, darkest secrets." He sniggered.

"Go on," Tran pressed.

"Apparently, she does have an *interest*, shall we say, in Deputy Marshal Oseefah," Kenison replied.

"Do tell, girlfriend," Lockwood joked.

Tran sighed and rolled her eyes as she shook her head. "Decorum, gentlemen. Decorum," she reminded. "Did you review the actual diary entries or just hear about them?" Tran asked.

Kenison struggled to maintain his composure but acknowledged that he'd seen Stupleton's actual diary entries about the youngest member of her detail. Skipping the sordid tidbits, he summarized Stupleton's expressions of lust for her young Nubian subordinate. Though she wouldn't with most others, Tran implicitly trusted the quality and completeness of Kenison's work, and accepted his representations, but he nonetheless passed her the transcripts of Stupleton's diary. Tran spread them over the table, shaking her head at Stupleton's foolishness. For someone long of Washington, Stupleton evidently hadn't learned the Richard Nixon principle: if you want something to remain secret, don't write it down. But Tran knew the Marshal couldn't have anticipated anything remotely like the circumstances now befalling her.

"What about her phone records, emails, and other communications?" Tran asked.

"There's a little color there too," Kenison said, taking on a more serious demeanor. "Her cell phone records show she's received multiple calls from various burner phones at odd hours of the night and day." He handed a summary of the communication records to Tran.

"Every one of them is only a few seconds long," Tran noted, scanning the documents.

Kenison nodded. "The tech team says they're not long enough for actual conversations, but they're plenty long enough for high-speed computer exchanges."

"So, we think she has a high-speed communication device out there somewhere?" Starr asked.

"I don't know, but the agency's MYSTIC program intercepted her calls in a mass collection of data," Tran said. "So we've got her calls and her metadata."

"Tell me there's something useful in those calls," Trigg pleaded.

Kenison shook his head. "No can do, bro—at least not yet. The agency collected the call data, but there was no probably cause to listen to Stupleton's actual phone calls—"

"—and no warrant," Starr added.

"—before these events," Kenison finished. "But they did store her calls along with a billion others in case of events just like this. I'm told the Office of General Counsel is seeking a federal warrant at this very moment, so we can listen to her conversations."

Tran's phone vibrated in her pocket. "I need to take this," she said, fishing it out and reading the incoming number. She stood and walked out of Starr's office. "Special Agent Tran."

The caller spoke the cryptic words expected of people in his office, and Tran answered with the reply expected of people they called, confirming the recipient was the intended recipient of the sensitive information he'd convey. Tran listened in earnest to the caller's report, and after a time, ended the call. She turned to look back to her team, fully absorbed in serious conversation. Though she'd not seen or heard him exit the room, Lockwood was no longer among them.

Tran sighed. She appreciated the hard work they'd been putting in, but she felt frustration creeping in. Each new piece of evidence led in a different direction, some of which felt wrong, illogical. She wondered whether she'd made incorrect presumptions early on that started the team in a direction completely off from whatever was really afoot. The call made her feel it even more.

Chapter 13: The Queen Regent

The time had come. Supervisory United States Marshal Terri Stupleton arrived for her long-anticipated meeting with Special Agent Grace Tran in a setting where one of them clearly had charge and the other...didn't.

"Right this way, Marshal," Lockwood said as he opened the conference room door.

He motioned to the table, behind which Tran and Starr sat, an open folder on the table. Stupleton pushed passed Lockwood as he held the door and paused just inside the room as her eyes met Starr's. As in a cut-rate cinematic production, they stared daggers at one another for a noticeable moment. Starr offered only a blank, unrevealing expression, but if looks could kill, Starr would have fallen dead on the floor as soon as Stupleton looked in her direction.

Tran stood as the Marshal entered, quietly debating whether to shake Stupleton's hand or pass on that formality. It might be a pointless gesture given the relationship they'd thus far developed, but at the same time, she saw no point in fueling a fire. She went with her gut.

"Thanks for coming, Marshal," she greeted, extending her hand.

Stupleton looked askance at Tran's outstretched arm and then quickly seated herself. She tossed her oversized purse onto the table, and heaved a thick file, the label of which read *Oberlin, J.*, onto the surface next to it. "I'm sure you've been looking forward to this for a while now, Tran, so let's just get this over with."

Tran resumed her seat beside Starr and Lockwood took position next to Tran, the trio facing their guest symbolic of an old-west stand-off. "I actually have been looking forward to speaking with you, Marshal," Tran replied.

"Well don't expect me to be your whipping girl, because—"

"—Not at all, Marshal. That's not the point of this meeting," Tran said. "Your perspective on the events leading up to the murders will be invaluable in piecing together a complex puzzle."

"If that's what you want, then I guess this'll be a short meeting," Stupleton retorted. "Everything I know is in my written report."

Inside, Tran bristled at Stupleton's combative demeanor, resisting the urge to reach across the table and knock out several of Stupleton's teeth. She wasn't particularly proud of it, but Tran knew she possessed the capacity for hot-headedness just like her Pop-Pop, but like him, she'd trained herself to keep it under wraps most of the time. Aside from the fact that she and Stupleton had both been strong military women who now had civilian careers in male-dominated fields, they had little else in common. Tran had found nothing to even remotely like about the woman, but her military side reminded her that liking someone wasn't a prerequisite to working effectively with them. Tran took a cleansing breath and then responded.

"I appreciate that you filed a report, Marshal, but I'm sure someone with as much as experience as you knows a written report can't possibly cover everything that might be relevant."

"You accusing me of omitting something else from my report?" Stupleton challenged. "You're a real piece of work, aren't you?"

Tran stared as she tried to decide the best way of diffusing Stupleton's hostility. "Okay," she began, nodding as she thought it through. "Okay, Marshal, why don't we just put this on the table? You and I have had our differences, and that's okay. As professionals, we don't have to agree on everything or even like each other to do our jobs. In addition to hearing your insights as head of the Protection Detail, it's a common approach in this sort of investigation to rule out the people closest to the case—you know that."

"Now you're telling me what I know? Jesus."

"It's not that—" Tran began.

"Well, I'm not talking to that one," Stupleton said as she leaned back in her chair and jabbed a thumb in Starr's direction without even looking at her. "You wanna' talk to me, you need to get her outta' here."

"That's not happening, Marshal. Dr. Starr is part of my team, and you don't get to select my team or what they work on."

"She's had an axe to grind with me for a long time," Stupleton rebutted.

Starr's only reaction to the Marshal's allegation was a stolid glare. After nearly a minute, she said, "In the interests of full disclosure, I told Agent Tran about our past interactions, Marshal, but I am not concerned about possible bleed-over from our past to this case. The facts here will speak for themselves."

"That's a bunch of headshrinker bullshit, Starr, and you know it," Stupleton screamed as she exploded from her seat. Her face reddened and her fists clenched.

In Tran's experience, people like Stupleton drew strength and encouragement from their ability to intimidate and manipulate people, to shake their confidence, confuse and derail them, but Starr's reaction offered nothing of the sort. Though effective, Starr's lack of reaction and persistence in driving toward a conclusion could agitate someone on the edge, especially if they felt cornered. Like other visitors to the Embassy, Stupleton had to surrender her weapon upon entry, but weapon or no, Tran didn't have it in her to coddle temper tantrums, especially from an adult. No, it required a proportionate response.

Tran exploded from her seat, everything about her posture conveying readiness for combat. "Sit down and get hold of yourself, Marshal. I know your history with Dr. Starr, and I have full confidence in her objectivity."

"Well I don't. She can't be objective about anything involving me," Stupleton said.

"That's unfortunate for you because your confidence in the members of my team is irrelevant."

"I'm not gonna' let this bitch scapegoat me again."

"The facts we've uncovered suggest you're anything but a scapegoat, Marshal. They make you look very good as a conspirator in the murders of Judge Oberlin and his party. If you don't want to help clear yourself, so be it. I'll proceed with the investigation, note that you refused to submit to questioning, and I'll fry you like a battered chicken. Your reputation in the law enforcement and protection community will be shit. Now sit your ass in that chair and let's do this."

Tran motioned to the empty chair and waited until the Marshal sat in it. When Stupleton complied, Tran resumed her seat, reorganized her papers, and calmly asked, "Did you study Judge Oberlin's docket for possible threats before he departed?"

"Of course," Stupleton answered. "I conferred with his clerk and researched several cases the clerk identified as possible threats."

"So you knew about the Cabrillo case, the Goddess Frankenstein case—"

"Yes, and the AMAGS case, the Ajenatic case, the Shelton case, his ex-wife's threats, hostile commentary from a laundry list of famous ex-girlfriends, and a bunch of other crap too," Stupleton said. "Are you trying to say we didn't work up a proper threat profile?"

"I'm not trying to say anything, Marshal. I'm just asking questions," Tran said. She shifted her line of inquiry. "Has someone close to you passed away recently?"

Stupleton wrinkled her face. "What?"

"According to your records, both your parents passed away over a decade ago, but I wondered whether an aunt or uncle, or someone else close to you may have passed recently?"

"No," Stupleton scoffed. "Maybe I have extended relatives still kicking around somewhere out there, but everyone close to me is long dead. I have no husband and no kids. Satisfied? Now why the hell don't you just tell me what the fuck you're getting at, Tran?"

"Did you have an investment pay off? Maybe you cashed-in some stocks or bonds?"

Stupleton scoffed again, sounding like an antsy horse. "No, no, and no."

"I should have known that would be your answer because you would have had to file an executive branch financial disclosure form, which you have not," Tran said.

"Now that your crack investigative skills have uncovered the obvious, how about you just get to it?"

"Marshal, have you had any kind of financial windfalls lately?" Tran pressed.

"For the last time, no."

"Okay," Tran said, writing a few notes. "On the night of the murders, you had two of your six-man detail on the boat, one circulating the grounds, one inside the cabin, and two on relief. Why did you distribute your assets that way?"

Stupleton sighed heavily, apparently exasperated at having to answer that question again. "Look, I put my assets where I thought they'd be best suited for the mission at hand."

"But under your arrangement, only two Marshals could respond immediately to any emergency with your Protectee. Why? That seems inefficient."

"You've been talking to that sorry ass Henri, I see."

"He disagreed with your decision?"

"Don't treat me like a fool, Tran. I know you interviewed him already, and I'm sure he filled your head with a bunch of his crap. He probably thought he could melt your panties off with his piercing green eyes and what he sadly thinks of as wit."

Tran neither acknowledged nor denied her discussions with Henri, but merely stared at the Marshal, letting silence do its crafty work in situations like these. Stupleton went on talking about her rocky history with Henri, all their conflicts, confrontations, and disagreements, and the reasons she'd had him suspended without pay. She revealed her plans to get Henri fired after this mission because he questioned her orders in the middle of an emergency.

"Let's talk about that, Marshal," Lockwood interrupted. "Your team member's reports indicate you ordered Henri to break pursuit even though he had the suspect in sight and expressed certainty he could catch the guy. Why? I wouldn't have given such an order."

"Well we aren't talking about you, are we, Lockwood?" she snapped, her neck muscles tensing as she slightly bared her teeth.

Stupleton rolled her eyes, and then explained that at the time, she didn't know the status of the judge and his party. For that reason, she wanted her most senior Deputy Marshal at the scene with the Protectee. She could intercept the suspect, but Henri was closer to the scene and would have known better what to do than the other members of her detail if there had been further issues—a second shooter, a medical emergency, a fire in the cabin, or something else. Since she herself couldn't get to the cabin before Henri, she wanted him to be with the judge more than any of the other Deputy Marshals.

"So you value Marshal Henri?" Lockwood surmised.

Stupleton pursed her lips, subtly rolled her eyes, and droned out a monotone reply. "As the scene commander, I made use of the resources available to me, Agent Lockwood."

She offered a succinct, non-committal answer, which Lockwood didn't seem to appreciate. He creased his brow in a way that signaled annoyance to anyone who knew or could read him. "I'm sure you did, Stupleton, but what I'm trying to establish is whether or not you think Henri is an asset to your team."

"He's a waste of his daddy's squirts," she said. "I'm not sure who he's blowing to keep his job, but I don't trust him any further than I can throw him. He brings nothing to the table, and that's why I'm canning his ass when we get home."

Silence hung in the air for a few minutes as Tran considered Stupleton's words. After some time, she blurted, "Now that's just not true, is it, Marshal? You don't think Henri brings nothing to your team."

"S'cuse me?" Stupleton demanded, wrinkling her face. "You think you know what's in my head better than I do? I know you think you're some kinda' hot-shot super-agent who's better than everyone at everything, but that's a little ridiculous, even for you."

Tran sat forward in her chair. "If you ordered Henri back to the cabin because you wanted his skills and experience on-scene in case of an emergency with the Protectee, then you obviously found him of greater tactical value than others in your detail, including one who's a combat-hardened former Navy SEAL. If you sent Henri back to the cabin for some other reason—like maybe you didn't want him to catch the suspect—then you must have felt he had the wherewithal to do it."

"You're twisting my words," Stupleton objected.

"I'm doing no such thing. I'm trying to understand what you're telling us. But from what you've said, I can only conclude you're not being truthful or else you have no idea why you made the decisions you made that night. Neither is good," Tran said.

"Like I told this one," Stupleton said, thumbing at Lockwood, "you use the resources you're given, not necessarily the ones you want."

"And did you know Judge Oberlin would soon be announced as a Supreme Court nominee?" Tran asked.

Stupleton's eyes grew wide. "I—I didn't know. Why wouldn't they brief me on something as important as that?"

"Operational security," Tran answered. "You didn't have a need to know, and that kind of political information could be misused."

"You don't think it's an important consideration in determining how to safeguard my Protectee?" she demanded, raising her voice.

"No, I don't," Tran replied. "Your assignment was to protect that man and his party from threats during this trip. Who may have wanted to harm him might have changed given his status as a Supreme Court nominee, but the threat of death, kidnapping or other grievous harm would have been the same."

"No, it's not, actually," Stupleton argued. "We might have—"

"You knew he'd received death threats for the Cabrillo case. What harm could be worse than that, and how many entities could have greater resources and sophistication to carry it out than the Sudamis Cartel? Your preparation should have embraced the worst likely scenario, so nothing should have been any different whether you were protecting a whistleblower, a mob informant, or a Supreme Court nominee."

"That's just not—"

Tran cut her off. "Your bosses and the White House evidently didn't want you to know, and that's that."

The room was silent for several seconds before Starr launched a few questions. "When were you notified of the assignment to protect Judge Oberlin on this trip?" she began.

"About a month ago."

"You've worked with Henri a number of years now, certainly long enough to have reached your conclusions about his abilities. If you had such doubts about him, why didn't you remove him from your team before taking such an important assignment?" Starr pressed.

Stupleton pursed her lips and contorted her face into an expression of utter contempt. "People like you love to sit on the sidelines and take pot-shots at those of us who make critical decisions in the heat of the moment, Starr. You don't get that we have to be creative and sometimes make it up as we go. We rarely get to choose who we work with."

"I know that perfectly well, Marshal, but sometimes, you do," Starr rebutted. "You know that from personal experience, don't you?"

"You fucking bitch," Stupleton said, standing abruptly from her chair.

"Marshal," Tran warned.

"It's all right, Grace," Starr said, gently grasping her boss's arm to still her. "Your insults don't offend me, Terri, but if they make you feel better, then by all means, call me whatever you like."

"You think you're fucking clever, taking a swipe at me because my old boss transferred me off his team to a desk job in Podunk, Arkansas. That was all based on your damn lies. You undermined me by telling them I was some kind of crazy nut."

"Sit down, Marshal," Tran warned to no avail.

Undaunted, Starr continued. "You've apparently rationalized that the consequences that befell you after our last case together were my fault, but the truth is, choose the behavior, choose the consequences. I didn't make you act the way you did," Starr said. "I only shared the facts and offered my professional opinion about their implications. What your superiors chose to do with that information is not my issue."

"Really? You're really gonna' sit here and hide behind a bunch of psycho-babble bullshit?"

"It's interesting that in both the prior case and this one, you've endeavored to make someone else's actions the focus of discussion rather than your own," Starr said. "It prompts me to ponder your motives."

"And your effort to hide behind psycho-babble makes me wonder about yours."

"I see a pattern with you, Marshal," Tran said. "Issues between you and your commanding officer ended your military career, and then there were a couple of skirmishes with teammates during your early years in the Marshal Service. An apparently vicious confrontation some years ago caused you and Dr. Starr to part on bad terms, and now there's this bad blood between you and Rick Henri."

"*Rick Henri?*" Stupleton repeated. "Rick Henri, not Marshal Henri? Are you fucking him now?"

This seemed a clear attempt by Stupleton to redirect the focus of the issue away from her to Tran and Henri. "There you go again," Tran said, shaking her head in resignation.

She stood from the table as she removed a document from her folder and shoved it across the table at Stupleton. "These games are a waste of my time, Marshal Stupleton. If you want to take this opportunity to give your insight, then sit down and do so. If not, then get out. I have other things to do than cajole you as you play out your histrionics."

She paused to give Stupleton a few seconds to think as the latter's eyes darted up and down the two-page document. Seeing no hint of capitulation, Tran gathered her papers and walked toward the door. "Escort her out," she said over her shoulder.

"Wait," Stupleton said.

One hand on the doorknob, Tran stopped and turned back to Stupleton, but said nothing. She waited.

"You're a master game-player, Tran," Stupleton said. "You whet my whistle by tossing something like this at me and then pretend you're outta' here, knowing I'd ask what this is." She brandished the page Tran had given her.

Still, Tran said nothing. The women stared at one another for a second or two before either broke.

"I'll answer your questions," Stupleton snarled, "but you need to tell me what the hell this is first."

The report from the Treasury's Office of Terrorist Financing and Financial Crimes showed two large transfers of money into a Cayman Islands bank account bearing Stupleton's name. Tran found it useful for her meeting with Stupleton but felt far from satisfied that it proved anything conclusive. It showed a lot of money in an account with Stupleton's name, and it showed that the money came from another Cayman Island account after multiple transfers across the globe. It was neat, pat, and clean—too much so for Tran's tastes. The trail seemed complex enough to look like someone tried to hide the money trail, but not complex enough to look like the work of a true professional money launderer. Tran had seen far more elaborate transactions orchestrated much more effectively in an effort to hide money for substantially less risky nefarious actions than assassinating a US official with ties to the President. This just seemed too easily uncovered and too amateurish to be the real deal. But Stupleton knew none of that, so Tran decided to use it for whatever it might yield.

"Given your line of work, I think you're familiar with Trace Reports from OTFFC," Tran answered, meandering back to the table. "Who will you blame for that?"

"What is this? What are you implying, Tran?"

"Nothing," Tran said. "I'm merely showing you evidence from OTFFC of a bank account in your name which received a half-million-dollar deposit contemporaneous with the assassination of Judge Oberlin and his party."

"Are you trying trick me into something?" she barked, "or are you setting me up?"

"This report came from the Treasury Department and it shows your hand in the cookie jar. You—or your criminal defense attorney—can feel free to verify it independently if you like."

Stupleton's mouth fell agape as she studied the papers. "I don't have an off-shore account, and I damn sure don't have a half-million bucks."

"Evidently you do," Lockwood said, nodding at the paper on the table.

"This isn't my money," Stupleton protested, pushing the paper back at Lockwood. "I…I…" she stammered, shaking her head. "…I see how this looks, but damnit, I'm tellin' you, this isn't mine. I don't know this bank and——"

"You had knowledge of Oberlin's schedule and location," Tran said. "You controlled his security detail, which, despite the protest of an experienced member of your own team, you deployed in a manner that made it easier for your accomplice to kill your Protectee. Afterward, you also ordered that same skilled Marshal who was in hot pursuit and about to apprehend your accomplice to break pursuit. Then, you received a half-million-dollar payment for a job well-done. That's the picture I'm seeing, Stupleton. You had motive, means, and opportunity to kill the Judge."

"Someone's setting me up," Stupleton shouted, panic in her voice. Tran wondered whether the fear stemmed from the fact that someone was actually setting her up or because she'd been caught.

"Who would have a motive to set you up by giving you five-hundred thousand dollars?" Starr asked.

"I don't know…Henri maybe."

"Where would he get that kind of money?" Starr asked. "You really think he's involved?"

"Wouldn't surprise me."

"Why is that?"

"He hates me. He'd throw me under the bus in a second," she said.

"Would it surprise you to know Henri defended you?" Tran asked. "He had every opportunity to implicate you, even with this evidence staring him in the face, but he didn't. He admitted that the two of you have a history of issues and that he didn't particularly like you, but he was also emphatic in insisting that you'd never be part of

167

something like this."

Stupleton fell silent as she gawked at the page.

"Is it your accomplice at the base you've been calling?" Tran pressed.

The Marshal looked up from her semi-dazed state. "What?"

"Is your accomplice at AUTEC?" Tran repeated. She noted hesitation on Stupleton's face. "We have your cell phone records, Marshal. We know you made several calls to a telephone number at a base exchange. Either way, I'll hunt down whoever you've been calling or you can make it easier on yourself and tell me who it is."

Stupleton thought for a moment, apparently contemplating the calls she'd made to AUTEC. Finally, she answered. "I, I did call an old Navy friend at the base a few times recently," she said.

"Who?"

Stupleton explained that she'd called a Master Chief Petty officer with whom she'd previously served on active duty and had briefly dated many years earlier. He now served as the Non-Commissioned Officer in Charge of AUTEC's Shore Patrol. She first called him after learning Oberlin would vacation here, so she could get the *lay of the land* about the area, its criminal elements, and any potential threats. She'd called him a second time for emergency assistance in securing the crime scene right after the murders, and the third time to thank him for dropping everything else he had to do in order to help her, no questions asked.

Observing Tran's expression, Stupleton spontaneously explained why the Master Chief couldn't possibly have had anything to do with the assassination. Foremost among her reasons was that she'd never told him why she needed the information she sought, so he wouldn't have known Judge Oberlin would be there. After the murders, she'd only told him she needed his men to secure a restricted area until additional support from the US Marshal Service arrived from the States a few hours later. Citing compartmentalized classified information, she'd given him no explanation of her need, and as a combat veteran and security expert, he understood the need to compartmentalize sensitive information. He'd not even hinted about knowing any details of her requests.

Tran tried not to show it, but she realized Stupleton's information represented the first independent confirmation of a connection between AUTEC and the cabin before the assassination. That was significant.

"So this Master Chief was your co-conspirator?" Tran pressed.

"Co-conspirator? I told you I had nothing to do with this thing. Before a few days ago, I hadn't talked to Jerry in probably eight or nine years."

Nobody on Field Team Six had found any contacts between the two, except for those to which Stupleton already admitted. While it was possible that they used burner phones, go-betweens, or some kind of secret code to communicate, it appeared on the surface that Stupleton spoke truthfully about their connection.

"Alright, Marshal," Tran said, shifting her posture and her inquiry, "do you know anyone by the name of Teresa Heryon or Anne-Marie DiSpenza?"

"Why are you asking that?" Stupleton challenged.

"How about George Wertz or James Vick?"

"Judging by the fact that you're asking me those questions in the way you asked them, it's clear you know those were my grandparents," Stupleton said. "What do they have to do with this?"

"Are you planning any trips any time soon, Marshal?" Tran asked.

"No, I'm not, but I'd like you to tell me why the hell you asked about my grandparents and then moved on to a new subject-matter, just like that."

"This isn't a new subject, Marshal," Tran said. "They're quite related."

"For God's sake, give me at least a shred of professional respect, Tran. Stop playing games and tell me what you're getting at," Stupleton pleaded.

Tran closed the file and pushed it aside. She leaned closer to Stupleton's face. "All right, Marshal Stupleton," she began. "Why do your dead grandparents have pending flight reservations to countries that don't have extradition treaties with the United States?"

The Marshal wrinkled her brow. "What?"

"They all have reservations booked out of Lyndon Pindling International Airport for tomorrow night."

Stupleton's mouth drooped open. "This can't be a coincidence," she said after a few seconds.

"That's something on which we agree," Tran said. "How about you explain that to me?"

Stupleton glanced up, staring into the ceiling as she thought, her mouth agape. "I…I'm not sure what this means, Tran, except that someone is clearly up to something, or else there's a hell of a coincidence afoot here…and I don't believe in coincidence," Stupleton said.

"Something else on which we agree," Tran noted.

The Marshal shook her head. "This is outrageous. I didn't kill the Judge, Agent Tran, but these facts—if you're not bullshitting me to coerce me into a false confession—make me look complicit in all of this. The chances are slim to none that it's coincidence that a half-million bucks shows up in an account with my name on it, when there are plane tickets in the names of my grandparents leaving from Lyndon Pindling right after the assassination of someone I'm assigned to protect."

Stupleton fidgeted in her seat and snapped open her briefcase. She withdrew a pen and pad and began writing notes. She appeared to be starting her own investigation.

Surely, she must know better, Tran thought.

"If I had any sense, I'd ask for a lawyer, but I didn't do this," she insisted at elevated tone. "I'll be damned if I let anyone frame me for something I didn't do. I'm a Marine, goddamn it, and nobody calls me a traitor and lives to say it again." She seemed to emerge from her angry tirade as she realized how her words could be misconstrued. "…I didn't mean you," she assured. "I mean whoever's trying to make me out as a murderous traitor. I'm gonna' rip off their head and shit down their neck."

Tran leaned back and applauded. "Bravo, bravo, Marshal Stupleton. Your righteous indignation might be moving, if it were genuine," she said.

The Marshal's head snapped up so she stared directly into Tran's eyes, her own burning with intensity. "You challenging my integrity?"

"I've seen much better actors than you concoct a well-acted performance to throw us off their trail—you know, toss out some sequins and put on a show with such razzle-dazzle that we're blinded to the truth."

"Then you'd better have the proof to back it up, Tran, because nobody impugns my honor and integrity without sacrificing a chunk of flesh. If you can't lock me away or kill me, I'll come after you with both barrels."

Unphased, Tran nodded and pressed on. "Maybe this is how you bluster your way through things, but the polygraph detected your lies."

"Polygraph, schmalygraph," Stupleton yelled, growing excitable once more. "That damn hunk a' junk doesn't tell you anything."

"It told us you lied, Marshal."

"Well it's wrong. I didn't lie about a single thing."

"So you lied about *several* things?" Tran asked.

"You think this is funny, Tran? My career and reputation are on the line here."

"I don't think it's funny at all, Marshal, which is why I'm looking to you for answers. Why would the machine read deception in you?" she pressed.

"I don't know."

"Yes, you do," Tran yelled. "You know but you won't say."

"Don't contradict me," Stupleton growled, her face growing flush. "I said I don't know."

Tran fished the polygraph report from her file and slammed it to the table in front of the Marshal. "The machine indicates deception on your negative response to the question, *do you have or have you had any relationship with any party that may have compromised your duties with respect to the protection detail assigned to Judge Oberlin? Why?*"

"For the umpteenth fucking time," Stupleton screamed, pounding her palm on the table, "I don't know why that goddamn machine says what it says, but I had nothing to do with the assassination of all those innocent people. Even if I could somehow take out the judge, why would I hurt that woman, a little kid, and my own team members for Christ's sake? I did not do this, do you hear me?"

Tran paused, inserting a break in the steady rise of tension in the room. Then, she spoke more calmly. "Marshal, you're being evasive with me about something. I won't fully clear you until I know what it is and I'm satisfied it has nothing to do with Judge Oberlin's death. You might as well come clean about it right now, because I will find out what it is."

Stupleton sighed with the intensity of an angry bull snort, pushed away from the table, and stood. She turned her face away from her interrogators and paced around the room. Tran watched for signs of cracks in the Marshal's façade but saw none. Instead, Stupleton's body language told of the disgust, anger, and frustration she evidently felt, tinged with uncertainty, fear, and shame. Much of it followed the profile of someone falsely accused, but the shame was something else. That's what Tran hoped to get at. She felt reasonably certain that the Marshal's deployment plan that left her alone with Deputy Marshal Oseefah might have been the source of Stupleton's evasiveness. But, confronting Stupleton with her diary entries would only humiliate the woman to no good end, so she decided not to do so, at least for now.

"All right, Marshal," Tran said as Stupleton paced. "Let's just go over this again. Let's start at the beginning."

For the ensuing three hours, Tran, Lockwood, and Starr bombarded Stupleton with questions. They reviewed in painstaking detail the facts and circumstances Stupleton previously related, often asking the same questions in different ways—it was often difficult for liars to remember their lies They used a seemingly erratic style of questioning, abruptly shifting their inquiries without apparent pattern. The methodology had been designed to off-balance a suspect or witness to test the veracity of their replies and the conviction of their beliefs.

They finished the interview at nearly 7:30 p.m. when it became clear the session had worn down the team nearly as much as it had Stupleton. The members of Field Team Six not present in the conference room sat in an office at the end of the hall, quietly observing the session on Ito's computer, carefully fact-checking as many of Stupleton's assertions as possible. They'd compare notes later.

Tran stood abruptly and began collecting her papers. "Thank you for coming in, Marshal Stupleton. I think we have enough for now, but I may want to speak with you again. Agent Lockwood will escort you back to the entry control point."

Having never used it, Stupleton collected the file she'd brought with her and stuffed it into her oversized bag. She pushed her chair back and stood in the same motion. "Are you done suspecting my team now?" she asked.

Tran smiled. "We'll be in touch."

Chapter 14: Good Times

The day had been another long one, and it wasn't over yet. The team members deferred their work for a little downtime followed by another late dinner, after which Tran planned a late-nighter to review information headquarters had sent earlier in the day. The AUTEC coincidences had been nagging at her for some time, especially since Stupleton's information offered a solid connection to the events at the cabin. AUTEC's possible involvement in the judge's death or a cover-up made no sense whatsoever, yet that seemed to be the implication. Tran discussed it with Starr as they ascended the outside stairs of the Visiting Officer's Quarters, bound for their adjacent rooms, directly above their colleagues. Tran craned her neck to look down the street. A plain blue sedan sat parked on the side of the road, facing the side of the VOQ onto which Tran's room opened. She could make out at least two silhouetted heads in the front seat of the car—but at least they'd had creativity enough to change vehicles, Tran thought.

"Okay, I guess that's something to consider," Tran said, ending their conversation for the moment. She reached into her briefcase and withdrew the room keycard. "I'm gonna' shower and check email before dinner."

"Did we decide where we're going?" Starr asked.

"I don't know. Didn't seem like we could get more than two people to agree on any of the suggested places," Tran said as she opened her door. "I'd just as soon that it be somewhere close."

"Marco's doesn't sound good to you?"

Tran laughed. "The food was pretty darn good, that's for sure, but it's too heavy for this late. And, it's too far. I'm fine with a fast-food burger."

Starr wrinkled her face in apparent disgust as Tran shook her head and pushed her door open. "We'll figure it out," she said. Closing the door, Starr agreed.

Throwing her bag and keycard on the table, Tran stepped out of one shoe and flipped the light switch. She kicked off the other shoe as she peeled off her suit jacket and turned for the bathroom. A dark shape moving toward her caused a sudden knot in her stomach, but before she could react, a large black hand reached for her mouth.

"Please don't scream, Agent Tran," the man said.

Tran brought her right arm across her body atop the man's arm and knocked his hand away from her mouth. At lightning speed, she drove her elbow into the man's nose with as much force as she could summon. He absorbed the full hard blow and stumbled back several steps. That created all the space Tran needed to withdraw her Glock from the holster on her hip, in one motion flipping off its safety and taking a bead on the center of her assailant's forehead.

Rebounding from the blow and swinging his left arm to the barrel of Tran's weapon, the man reacted quicker than anyone Tran had ever encountered. His swift strike knocked the weapon from her grip. She drove the heel of her right hand into his nose, again knocking him back. The man recovered and raised one arm to deflect Tran's follow-on attack while punching forward with the other. Tran moved to the right and grabbed the man's wrist. Spinning to the rear, she pulled forward with all her might, launching his body toward the door. He flew like a bag of potatoes over Tran's shoulder and landed on a table that imploded under his weight. Tran had enough time to grab her weapon, brace herself, and level the Glock squarely between his eyes.

"If you even twitch, I'll blow your head off," she barked.

The door to her room burst open, and Tran quickly retrained her weapon on the body coming through the door. In an instant, her mind recognized Starr on the other end of another outstretched Glock, and then reacquired a target-lock on the man on the floor. Starr too figured things out in a few milliseconds and trained her weapon on the downed intruder.

"I can't believe I got my ass kicked by a girl," the man groaned. "I'm gonna' slowly sit up so we can talk. Please don't kill me."

As the man did as he represented, Tran and Star had an opportunity to really look at the attacker. They recognized Marco, the restaurateur in an instant, except he'd lost his heavy island accent. He held his hands in the air, away from his body and moved at a turtle's pace.

"Please don't shoot me, ladies," he said. "That would make for a very inauspicious end to my day."

"You have two seconds to tell me why you're here," Tran said, "and why you carry a Beretta." She nodded at the holstered matte black handgun in his half-opened jacket.

Marco smiled. "Uh, what if I told you I'm not really a restaurant guy?" he asked, leaning back against the wall. Neither Tran nor Starr answered. "My name is Marcus Quizby. I'm CIA."

The revelation surprised Tran and mentally knocked her back a step or two. On the outside, she showed no reaction. "As far as I know, you're a Bahamian restaurateur," she said her tone conveying disbelief.

"Marco's is a real restaurant, but as far as me being the owner, that's my cover. It wasn't hard when we paid the real Marco a princely sum to take an all-expense paid vacation for six months. The young girl there, I hired off the street to do most of the cooking I claimed was mine," Marco said.

Tran nodded at Starr, who lowered her weapon, activated its safety, and tucked it in its holster. She'd have more than enough time to put a few rounds through Marco's brain before he could even think about trying to take Starr's weapon, and she was marksman enough to do it. Starr inched closer and then removed the Beretta from Marco's holster. She tossed it in Tran's direction, and then patted Marco down.

"He's got no I.D.," she announced to Tran.

"Sorry," Marco said. "It's down there." He nodded toward his crotch.

Starr followed his head motion. "You really are trying to get shot, aren't you?" she asked.

176

"I'm not being vulgar, Dr. Starr. I have ID in a flap inside my undergarments. You wouldn't expect me to carry a card in my wallet that says *CIA Operative* in big black letters, would you?"

"Are you suggesting you carry such a card in your boxers?" Starr sarcastically rebutted. "What's your validation code?"

Quizby rattled off an alpha-numeric code, which Starr memorized. She opened her phone and placed a call to the Agency's Operations Desk.

"This is Special Agent Deanna Starr, ACN: 0924-1965-D on a mobile encrypted line," she said to the nasal voice that answered.

After a brief silence, the voice offered the proper reply, indicating that Starr's identity had been confirmed by voiceprint identification.

"I need a National Security Asset Validation," she said.

Starr listened to the instructions on the other end, and when prompted for an Asset Control Number, repeated the alpha-numeric code Quizby had given. A few seconds later, the voice confirmed that the number corresponded to Central Intelligence Agency Field Operative Marcus Quizby. The lady recited a physical description of Quizby as Starr listened and studied the photo that appeared on her phone. The procedure existed to prevent US agents from mistakenly terminating one another in situations precisely like this. Starr nodded to Tran, who accepted the gesture as confirmation that Quizby checked out okay.

"All right, Operative Quizby," Tran said. "Why the hell are you in my room?"

"May I?" Quizby asked, motioning to stand.

Tran nodded, but kept her weapon aimed squarely at his head. Intelligence agents had been known to go rogue. Starr unholstered her weapon and retrained it on him as he stood from the floor until he unfolded to his normal five-foot seven-inch height, his hands still at ear level.

"I came to give you something you might find helpful, Agent Tran." He nodded at the bed, in the middle of which lay a thick brown folder.

"What is it?"

"Mana from Heaven for you."

Tran glanced at Starr, tacitly asking her to keep Quizby in her sights as she holstered her own weapon. She reached for the folder.

"A Vivian Lawrence from your agency queried the National Intelligence Database for information. The query sent an alert to my handler, who did a little investigation of her own and realized there could be a connection between our cases," Quizby explained.

As Tran opened the folder, her gaze fell upon a black-and-white photo of a medium height, burly white man with a thick moustache and an odd, insubstantial shock of hair atop his head, both of which looked manufactured. The page on the inside front flap identified the presumptive name of the target as Alex *Last Name Unk*, a/k/a *Single Best Solution*.

"Who and what is this?" Tran asked, flipping through the pages behind the photograph.

"That may be your assassin," Quizby said. "We pulled that photo from security cameras at Lyndon Pindling International Airport about four weeks ago."

"What makes you think this is my assassin?" Tran asked.

"It's a long story. May I put my hands down?" Quizby asked.

"Maybe," Tran said. "Why the hell didn't you just approach me professionally with this information instead of breaking into my room? You scared the shit out of me and nearly got yourself *capped*, as they say."

"Mine is a continuing operation against opponents who've shown themselves sophisticated and crafty," Quizby explained. "They've infiltrated some highly secure places to carry out their work, which suggests they've infiltrated the security operations of some key NATO players, including us. I have no way to know who may be surveilling either of us, so extreme caution is a way of life for me. Outside the restaurant—which I heard you dis, by the way—I can't have any ties to your team." He shrugged and smirked. "I got into your room in a way that wouldn't give anyone any reason to suspect a connection between us."

Tran still felt the agitation and adrenaline from the fright he'd given her, but at least she'd made him keep his hands in the air for an extended time. She figured that had to be almost as painful as the three-quarters squat she held for twenty minutes when she smarted-off to her gym teacher back in high school. Tran shrugged. "You can put your hands down, Quizby, but you've got some explaining to do," she warned.

"I guess you're entitled," he said. "Where to begin… So, as the whole world now knows, NSA routinely monitors global communication for activity of interest to those of us in the national security business. Random monitoring picked up communication traffic from China to a location just outside of Lompoc, California."

"—Home to Air Force Space Command's 30th Wing at Vandenberg. I'm sure that grabbed someone's attention," Tran said.

"You're as quick as they say," Quizby said, nodding confirmation. "The Joint Functional Component Command for Space is housed at Vandenberg, and it's also the headquarters of several top-secret projects. Needless to say, calls from one of our most aggressive espionage adversaries to that area do tend to get our attention."

"You tracked the numbers?" Tran asked.

"The calls came from a burner phone and went to another burner phone, which further aroused our curiosity. Out of an abundance of caution, we began routinely tracking calls into the region, and through a series of complicated maneuvers which I won't go into right now, we determined that the person receiving the calls from China is Captain Lee Whitehead, United States Navy. He also happens to be the Executive Officer for the Commander of JFCCS."

Tran nodded. A "purple-suited outfit," the Joint Functional Component Command for Space was comprised of members of all branches of the U.S. military along with Department of Defense civilian employees. In that kind of unit, it wouldn't be unusual for a Navy officer to report to an Air Force General. Connections between US military members of such rank or position and any foreign government would certainly garner the attention of US security officials. They weren't

179

completely disallowed. There could be a number of valid reasons for contacts between senior U.S. military officers and foreign governments and people, but federal and military law required the U.S. military member to formally report them and obtain approval to maintain them. Quizby explained that Captain Whitehead had made no such disclosure.

"Why would Captain Whitehead be getting calls on a burner phone from a burner phone in China?" Starr asked.

"We wondered that too, Dr. Starr," Quizby said. "That's why we put surveillance on Captain Whitehead."

"This is interesting, Quizby, but I'm waiting for the part that explains you breaking into my room," Tran said.

"We didn't intercept anymore calls to Whitehead from the original burner phone, but six weeks ago, he began receiving frequent late night and weekend calls from a series of different burner phones. The numbers changed after two or three calls. Each time he answered, he'd go outside to take the call or otherwise excuse himself if he had company."

Tran nodded. She recognized several indicators of potentially unauthorized clandestine activity in the facts Quizby relayed. They were more than sufficient to set off alarms for counter-intelligence agencies.

The CIA agent continued. "The calls were made using encryption software, but we were able to decrypt some of their conversations. Over a series of brief calls, they discussed monetary transactions and used the phrase '*single best solution*' and the word '*target*.'"

"I agree that merits watching, but it doesn't explain you breaking into my room."

"The intelligence business is about piecing small bits of information together, Agent Tran, so you'll have to bear with me to get the full flavor of the situation," Quizby said, chiding her impatience. "A call from one of those burner phones originated in Mong Cai, Vietnam, a small town on the Chinese border. We tracked that same phone across the Pacific Ocean until it placed another call to Captain Whitehead, this time from the airport here in Nassau."

"Did he not turn off his phone aboard the aircraft?" Tran asked.

Quizby looked at Tran from the corner of his eye and smiled. "It's pure fiction that we can't track cell phones when they're off," he said. "I guess there are some things even NSA doesn't know."

Now, the picture grew clearer for Tran, but not totally. Quizby revealed that in a separate operation, CIA, British Intelligence, and the Israeli Mossad had been trying for some time to capture an international assassin known only as Alex, also referred to by many who dealt in that line as the *Single Best Solution*. The intelligence services always found themselves a step or two behind Alex, but a brand spanking new analyst at CIA headquarters, while reviewing routine transcripts of the calls, noted that Captain Whitehead used the phrase, 'you are the *single best solution* to our problem' in a couple of his conversations. Based on that, he made a WAG that the person calling Captain Whitehead might be the elusive assassin known as Alex. He immediately alerted his superiors.

Tran was a big believer in the Wild-Ass Guess. She normally referred to it as a hunch, an instinct, or a gut feeling, but *WAG* was completely fitting. She always encouraged her team to follow them when they experienced them. Quizby explained that the rookie analyst's WAG was enough to get Quizby dispatched to the Bahamas two months ago. Vivian Lawrence's query against the National Intelligence Database a day ago seeking information to help Tran's investigation suggested the possibility of a connection between Quizby's mission and Tran's investigation, so his bosses cleared him to read Tran in on the Agency's knowledge of Alex.

"Okay, I get it," Tran said, subtly nodding to Starr, who holstered her weapon. "But what makes you think *this* is Alex?" Tran asked, nodding at the photo in the folder.

"Based on the time the burner phone went active, we guessed the approximate time the caller arrived in the Bahamas and then narrowed down the arriving flights to the one the caller was most likely on. Security footage in the airport shows the guy in the photo getting off the aircraft and immediately making a call at the precise time Captain Whitehead received a call from that number. In checking the passenger manifest, we found he booked his ticket using an alias known to be linked to Alex. A flight attendant confirmed that man was the guy in the seat reserved for the Alias."

Tran nodded as she considered Quizby's information, but she didn't quite buy it yet. He noticed. She had different information than the CIA agent. "All you really know is that this guy sat in a seat reserved to someone who used one of Alex's purported aliases."

Quizby thought about it. "Yeah, maybe," he admitted, "but the flight attendant confirmed his photo."

Tran smiled at Starr and then turned back to Quizby. "Someone I value once informed me that eyewitness testimony is often the least reliable form of testimony. Besides, think about the number of passengers a flight attendant sees on a route into a popular vacation destination. Unless something unusual happened to make the guy stand out, the flight attendant probably doesn't remember the occupant of that seat."

"Nobody reported anything out of the ordinary on the flight," Quizby said, thinking back to the field interview.

"My evidence team recovered size seven or seven-and-a-half footprints from the ground around the cabin. From this photo, I'd guess this guy would need a size eleven or twelve shoe to support his frame," Tran said.

"Seven is a pretty small foot."

"Not for a woman," Tran said.

"That's not consistent with what we know about Alex," Quizby said. "But...maybe it explains why we've not gotten much on him."

"How about you tell me what you know about Alex?" Tran said.

Quizby explained that intelligence services from several countries had compiled a sparse dossier on the alleged assassin. Their information came from witnesses who claimed to have seen Alex, and a few pieces of hard evidence supposedly from Alex himself. He was a skilled assassin trained in multiple deadly arts. His nationality hadn't been confirmed, but he frequented countries in the Pacific Rim. No one seemed to know his home country, but best guesses included China, Vietnam, or Cambodia. The International Police Agency—Interpol—

credited Alex with twenty high-visibility assassinations in the last decade. His loyalties seemed to run first to himself and then to the highest bidder. His services were expensive—a minimum of $3.5 million paid into a Swiss Bank Account. CIA had attempted to track Alex's money through several countries across the globe, and multiple shell corporations, trusts, and fictitious names, all to no avail.

After ninety minutes of briefing, Quizby came to the end of what the CIA knew or thought it knew about Alex. Tran found none of it especially helpful to advancing her investigation, but it did give her some things to consider. "I don't see a connection between Whitehead, Ashmead, Alex, and Oberlin."

"Well," Starr interjected, "based on my comparison of their military records while we've been talking here, I can confirm that Whitehead and Ashmead have a greater connection than the fact that they're both senior Navy officers. They're former classmates at Annapolis, and it appears they participated in some of the same clubs."

Tran agreed the bits of information were starting to suggest a picture far different from the one she suspected when they first got this assignment. But, if Alex was in fact the assassin they were hunting, what did Whitehead and Ashmead have to do with Oberlin's death and why?

Tran turned to Quizby. "Even if Alex is my triggerman, I'm looking for a lot more than him. Hired assassins are instruments of someone else's will. *That's* who I'm ultimately after. Give me a day or so to review your file, Quizby, and I'll circle back to you."

"Well mon," Quizby said. "Ya' cert'ly knows ware ta' fine me, dontcha' now?"

"I think I'm starting to feel a yen for *da' bess' eats on da' whole island*," Tran said, smiling.

Quizby turned and started toward the bathroom but stopped after a few steps. "One more thing, Agent Tran," he said. "Torres is clean. She recently passed an SSBI to get her clearance for her assignment to AUTEC, and we did a supplemental check of her recent financials, online activity, and communications. I also searched her quarters. There were a few salacious emails between her and her boyfriend, but otherwise, she's spic-and-span."

Having passed several Single Scope Background Investigations in her career, Tran knew the SSBI probed deep into a person's life, including activities people thought were private. If neither the SSBI nor Quizby's supplemental check into Torres had found anything untoward, Tran could feel reasonably comfortable about the Lieutenant, presuming she could rely on Quizby's word. She was nonetheless surprised by Quizby's remark—she'd never told him of her reservations about Torres. She raised her brow as she looked at him. "Why would you suspect anything else?"

"I didn't, until Miss Lawrence started poking around in government databases for information about the Lieutenant," he replied. "When I saw that, since Lawrence works for you, I thought maybe you had some concerns, so I initiated my own check. I'm just sharing what I learned."

Quizby nodded at Tran, and then resumed his trek toward the bathroom, leaving Tran and Starr wondering what he was about to do. He knelt to the floor near a large twelve by twelve return-air vent on the wall beside the bathroom door. With his bare fingers, he twisted the screws around its edges, removed it from the wall, and then shimmied into the vent shaft, which seemed far too small to accommodate the body of an adult male. Nonetheless, Quizby disappeared up into the wall, pulling the grate back into place behind him. As his feet lifted out of view, a series of fading bumps and thumps inside the wall signaled his departure.

Chapter 15: Trust but Verify

Tran completed her morning routine, dressed, and gathered papers she'd spread over the half of the bed her tossing and turning didn't destroy in the night. She peeked out the window just as Lieutenant Torres pulled up in the van. She checked her watch: 0540.

Tran opened her briefcase and fished a hard-plastic case from its depths. It contained four pin-head pips on black felt, displayed like fine jewels from a Beverly Hills boutique. Lifting her smartphone, Tran scrolled its aps to find the one installed by the NSA's tech team, and then entered a series of numbers and thumbed a button. An electronic meter on the app came alive, indicating that she'd successfully activated the first of the pips. Tran took the tiny black dot from the case and removed its protective backing, letting it stick to her finger. Satisfied, she gathered her things and hurried downstairs to the parking lot. The team wouldn't leave for another twenty minutes, but Tran saw an opportunity to talk privately to Torres. She guessed the officer's conspicuous absence the last few days stemmed from their less-than-pleasant interaction in their last conversation.

Tran kicked and crushed the loose gravel on the pavement as she walked to the van, sending a guttural grumble through the otherwise quiet air. Without looking in Tran's direction, Torres turned and climbed into the driver's seat, firmly closing the door behind her.

Yep—still pissed, Tran thought.

That Torres didn't flinch when Tran tapped the driver's window supported Tran's speculation that Torres retreated into the van to avoid her. Tran tapped a second time and then motioned for Torres to step outside. After a moment of obvious internal debate, Torres did so, but

185

left the door ajar and the radio blaring, perhaps signaling her desire that the conversation be brief.

"Good morning, Jessie," Tran began, her voice soft and gentle.

"Ma'am," Torres said, looking over Tran's shoulder.

As she observed Torres head-on, Tran noted another possible reason for the young officer's avoidance behavior. Beneath several layers of strategically applied concealer, foundation, and blush, dark patches surged across the skin around Torres' right eye and extended down her cheek to the underside of her chin. Her lip sported three small blisters where the epidermis had obviously been broken but had started to heal already. Torres had done a yeoman's job of blending her makeup to hide it, but her skills couldn't compete with Tran's experience as an expert observer and student of human behavior. The blemishes were elongated ovals with imperfect edges, each about the size of an adult fist. Since the bruises covered Torres' right side, Tran theorized that a left-handed person had caused them. The extent of bruising indicated three, maybe four separate impacts as the span was too wide for a single punch. That kind of injury might be explainable if Torres' duties required occasional physical confrontation with people—the Shore Patrol or Navy Seals, perhaps—but the roughest service a Protocol officer experienced was dealing with namby-pamby politicians or flag officers who thought their shit didn't stink. The bruises might also be explained if Torres were into Judo, kickboxing, or some other voluntary hobby, or even rough sex, but poorly concealed bruises made Tran feel an ill sensation mixed with anger.

"What happened to you, Jessie?" Tran asked.

"Ma'am, nothing happened to me. I'm here on time—even a little early," she answered.

"I'm not talking about your punctuality, Jessie. I'm talking about your face. What happened?"

Torres did her best not to, but she flinched ever so slightly at the mention of her face. Tran interpreted the reaction as shame, perhaps horror at realizing someone had seen what she tried so hard to cover.

186

"Nothing happened to my face, Ma'am," Torres retorted, still denying eye contact.

The response confirmed for Tran that something for which there is no justification had happened, something Torres didn't want to discuss. Had there been an explanation for it, most people would offer it freely, without concocting a reason on-the-spot. Over the years, Tran had grown adept at discerning when people were making up stories to explain away damning evidence or avoid uncomfortable facts, especially when they had to do so on the spur of the moment. Those instincts didn't fail her simply because this was a personal matter rather than a case.

"That doesn't look like 'nothing,' Jessie. It looks like someone punched you pretty hard."

Her back against the van, Torres stood erect and thrust something into Tran's stomach. "As ordered, Ma'am."

Tran looked down her frontside to a manila envelope Torres held against her stomach. She grabbed it and casually flipped through its contents in the dim mix of parking lot lighting and daybreak. Torres had delivered the AUTEC air and marine tracking data Tran had requested.

"Thank you, Lieutenant." Tran paused to consider how to start the conversation she really wanted to have. Superior rank, power, and experience didn't entitle Tran to this conversation with Torres, or anyone else who shared what appeared to be her situation. "It doesn't take NSA training to see something isn't right here. I've seen this—"

"—With the respect you're due, Agent Tran, if you have orders for me, I'll carry them out to the best of my ability because I've been detailed as your liaison officer. But, if my own clumsiness caused me to slip on the stairs at home, it's not the NSA's business and it's certainly none of yours."

"That's what you're going with—a clumsy fall down the stairs?" Tran asked. "I've heard that almost as many times as 'the doorknob hit me in the eye' or 'it's my fault; I made him do it because I annoyed him.'"

187

Torres snapped her head directly at Tran. "I'm a Navy officer who graduated at the top of her class. Do you really think I'd let any man hit me?"

"Jessie, this kind of thing happens to women at all levels—successful career women, housewives, and yes, military officers," Tran said.

"Yeah, well, even if it did happen in my personal life, it's just that—personal."

Tran inhaled and exhaled deeply, feeling a bit out of her depth. As a skilled interrogator, she'd dealt with uncomfortable, embarrassing situations many times, but helping a victim of domestic violence come to grips with their situation and take steps to fix it required a whole other set of skills, which Tran didn't feel she possessed. Torres needed someone trained in this area to help her. Still, Tran didn't feel she could let it go.

"So, if it's personal," she said, "you're assuring me that neither Captain Ashmead nor any goon reporting to him had anything to do with the bruises?"

"Of course not," Torres answered, umbrage in her tone. "I'm a Navy officer, and I'd never accept that kind of treatment—Navy personnel wouldn't behave that way anyway."

"I believe members of the military are a cut above the norm for the most part, Jessie, but Tailhook showed us that even the best of the best can run astray," Tran said.

"The Tailhook sex abuse scandal was a long time ago, Ma'am, and we've come a long way since then. Now, if we can return our focus to the mission at hand, that would be appreciated. I can do girl-talk with my friends."

Which you are not, Torres didn't say but Tran heard it loud and clear.

"I won't press the issue right now, Jessie, but this is another instance when you must exercise your power—and I'm not talking about physical power. I'm talking about the power of your will, the power of your brain. You can win this, and you're not alone—high-ranking military officers and other very accomplished people—of both, or all, genders, I might add—have been sexually and physically abused. Some of them have gone on to do great things, but sooner or later, they all have come to grips with their situations. You need to do that too."

"There is no situation, Agent Tran. How many times must I say it?"

"Ok, ok, Jessie, but—"

"How about I call you Agent Tran and you call me Lieutenant Torres?" she snapped.

"All right, Lieutenant, but I'm here if you need me."

Torres turned away and offered no response.

Tran waited a few moments in case Torres changed her mind and decided to open up about whatever was happening to her. After a time, it seemed clear that wasn't going to happen, and Tran reluctantly pressed on with the business of her day. She knew she wouldn't—couldn't—let it go completely.

"Ok, well, I'm glad you're here a little early, Jessie, because I think you're pissed about the way I treated you recently. I want to explain—"

"You don't owe me an explanation. You're a senior SES officer conducting an investigation for the President of the United States. I was wrong to think we'd started to develop a friendship or to expect even a modicum of common decency and respect from you."

"Ouch," Tran said. "Maybe I deserved that, but there's a reason, Jessie."

"Lieutenant," Torres corrected.

Tran wouldn't usually explain herself to witnesses or suspects, but she felt differently with Torres. She wanted to share her reasoning in the hope it might contribute something useful to the Lieutenant's personal and professional growth. Torres's behavior and body language, however, conveyed a distinct disinterest overtop a layer of hurt and distrust. Even so, as much as she disclaimed a desire for Tran's explanation, she didn't try to stop it nor did she retreat from it once Tran began.

"I don't believe in coincidence, Jessie, so the convergence of questionable facts suggests someone at AUTEC may be somehow connected to the deaths of Judge Oberlin and his party."

"What facts?" Torres asked.

Tran hesitated. If she was wrong about Torres, candidly answering her question could be tantamount to sharing information with the assassin or his co-conspirators. But Tran began to sense Torres was one of the good guys, and aside from mentoring the young officer, bringing her into full confidence could mean developing a valuable asset inside AUTEC. It was one of those gut instincts, those hunches Tran encouraged her team—including herself—to heed.

"I'm going to read you in on my case, Jessie, but you must keep this information absolutely confidential. You may discuss it with anyone on my team, but no one else—no one." She awaited Torres's agreement, but it didn't come. Tran continued anyway. "A few days ago, I received a call from the White House Chief of Staff and the Director of National Security. They told me the President wanted to see me…"

Tran gave Torres the deep detail of the case. She told Torres about the air traffic data from Lyndon Pindling Airport, the witnesses on the beach, and the mysterious radio transmissions followed by the assassin's apparent escape into the water. She explained how the facts led them to AUTEC where the unusual behavior of its officials raised additional questions.

"On top of all that," Tran continued, "government vehicles have been following me and my team since shortly after we arrived. Your subordinate, Petty Officer Endicott, drove one of those vehicles. Despite the fact that my security clearance is higher than anyone's on this base, he and a Shore Patrolman ordered me away from the sub-pen."

"I never authorized him to perform duty with the shore patrol, and he never reported any of this to me," Torres said. "You sure it was Endicott?"

Tran nodded. "Cell phone tracking confirmed it."

Torres contorted her face as though doing so would help further develop her thoughts. "Our VIP dossier on your team listed your individual clearance levels, so he knew you had clearance to be anywhere on the base."

"After ordering me away from the sub-pen," Tran said, "he and his partner trailed me back here to the VOQ and then parked down the street where they could see me as I entered and left my room. Don't look at this very moment, but the car is still there now," Tran assured. "In any event, a day later, I found Endicott meeting with Captain Ashmead, which you said you knew nothing about."

"That was the day I saw him in civvies outside Building One?"

Tran nodded. "And this information—" she brandished the envelope Torres had just delivered "—at first glance looks inconsistent with other information we've received. Against that backdrop, I never requested support from the Protocol Office and yet, there you were with an official reason to be in the middle of everything my team would do and everywhere we'd go."

"As I said," Torres insisted, "Captain Ashmead ordered me to support your team during your time on the island."

"I know what you said, but to be blunt, I don't know you, Jessie. You seem like a fine, patriotic officer doing her duty to the best of her abilities, but in my line of work, you learn quickly that the masks people wear are often tools of deception. You could be an Oscar-worthy actress."

"So I'm a suspect in the assassination of Judge Oberlin?" Torres asked.

"At first, I found it hard to believe you didn't know your subordinate was having closed-door meetings with your C-O, but we'd not be having this conversation if I considered you a suspect," Tran replied.

"Then you've concluded I'm not part of whatever you think is happening. May I ask what convinced you?"

"People caught in elaborate lies don't usually continue talking about it. They change the subject to something they didn't lie about. When I implied you were part of whatever's happening and then dropped it abruptly, you did the opposite. You wanted to defend your honor and integrity by delving into the facts which you challenged at every turn. You talked in specifics rather than generalities, and your representations were consistent. Those aren't hallmarks of a conspirator."

Torres paused to think. "So that obnoxious bitch routine was just a test?"

Tran looked at her askance, a little impressed by her capacity to be both subtle and brazen at once. The miffed officer had found a way to throw cutting barbs without crossing the line of insubordination. "I suppose you could say that—about some of it. I meant what I said about not giving up your power or letting people see you doubt yourself, Jessie."

Torres nodded. "So, that's it? Based on your gut feelings, you concluded I'm not guilty of conspiracy to kill five people? What if I'm just an Oscar-worthy actress like you said?"

Tran shook her head. "My gut instincts help focus my investigations, but I always support them with facts. Yours checked out."

"You invaded my privacy," Torres summarized. "That's what you're really saying."

Tran chuckled and half-jokingly replied, "As long as you wear that uniform, you have no reasonable expectation of privacy from the government."

"I don't believe this," Torres said, shaking her head. "You're asking me to believe that a senior Navy officer—an Academy graduate, a decorated combat veteran, someone I deeply respect—would conspire to assassinate a federal judge. You want me to accept that the US government can secretly crawl up my ass for a look-see any damn time it wants."

"We don't yet have enough facts to conclude that anyone at AUTEC is complicit in the assassination of Judge Oberlin, but yes, Jessie, I'm asking you to accept that possibility."

Torres's pallid gaze telegraphed her sense of shock, betrayal, and doubt—feelings an idealistic Lieutenant Tran felt years earlier when a three-star general grabbed her breasts, made lurid suggestions about what he'd do to her, and threatened her career if she reported him. Grinning in flagrant dismissal of her indignation, he reminded her that *rank has its privileges* and said she should just *get with the program*. Lieutenant Tran had worked hard through four years at the Air Force Academy to earn her place as a Distinguished Military Graduate and to be the best in her field. She whole-heartedly subscribed to the high moral and ethical code the Academy had drilled into every cell in her body.

Before the three-star encounter, she thought all other military officers subscribed to it too, especially senior officers, lest they wouldn't have made it to such revered ranks. Finding reality very different from the ideal shattered the faith Tran placed in those above her and made her question everything she'd come to believe to that point. She wallowed in disappointment for longer than she cared, but then heard a talk show host comment about unfairness in the world. "You have to let go and let God," the woman said. Tran eventually managed to do that, but the event left a lasting mark. She liked Torres and hoped to ease her into the realities of the professional world in such a way to spare her the unpleasant awakening she herself experienced.

The sounds of doors opening and closing some distance away caught Tran's attention. She looked up to see Starr and Ito emerging from their rooms onto the exterior hallways, en route to a timely team rendezvous in the parking lot. The approach of other people signaled an end to the time for private conversation. Tran hurried to finish her comments.

"Listen, Jessic. You're smart, driven, and capable. I think you have a very promising future, wherever it may take you. Don't let anyone or anything knock you down, at least not for long. It's unfortunate that this kind of crap happens where you don't expect it, but the world isn't always a nice place. Some people are fine, upstanding citizens who contribute positively to society, but some lie, cheat, steal, and consistently fail expectations. You can't let it shake you. Find a lesson in all of this, and then get on with it. I learned this under difficult circumstances. The faster you do, the better off you'll be."

She squared her body to Torres's and looked her over as though inspecting her uniform. Torres wore the same pair of conservative stud earrings she'd been wearing each time Tran had seen her since they first met. That would do, Tran thought.

"Your left earring is a little loose," she announced. She reached for Torres's earlobe, but stopped a millimeter shy. "Permission to touch?"

With Torres's nod, Tran's left hand gently grasped the tiny jewel from the front, while her right firmly pressed its backing onto the thin metallic post that pierced the fleshy lobe. It took only a split-second, and when Tran's hand withdrew, Torres felt only what she expected. She knew nothing of the small pip stuck to the back of her earring.

Tran smiled and patted Torres on the shoulder.

"Good morning, ladies," Starr greeted as she neared. "Did we all have a good night's sleep?"

Tran and Torres both smiled in acknowledgement, the latter turning her head slightly away.

"I don't know about y'all, but I slept like crap," Ito announced, coming up behind Starr. "I couldn't seem to settle my brain—"

"A lack of REM sleep certainly explains your dull wit," Kenison joked. The group heard him before they actually saw him. Kenison came from the hotel lobby, carrying a cardboard tray with six lidded cups in one hand, and a single cup from which he drank in the other. He raised the tray toward his colleagues. "Rigging caffeine IV's is a bit impractical, so I got you guys some cups of get-your-ass-in-gear."

"Dude, I knew you were good for *something*," Ito said, taking the nearest cup.

"That's not yours, Doofus," Kenison chastised. "I know you prefer yours like a milkshake, so *that* one's yours," he said, nodding at a cup in the opposite corner of the tray. "I put in your little flavored creamer and some pink stuff. Guess I should've written *Princess* on the side, so you'd know which was yours."

"Man, if you're looking at me as your princess, we both got big problems," Ito said.

194

Kenison shoved his own cup into the spot vacated by the one Ito took and selected another from the caddy. "And this is for you, Jessie. I noticed you like two spritzes of cinnamon hazelnut and one half-and-half in yours." He handed her a particular cup, smiling deep in her eyes.

"Thanks, Agent Lockwood," she replied.

Kenison's eyes grew wide as though he'd seen something frightening. He began to correct her. "No, I'm Keni—"

She smirked and turned away, perhaps pleased that she'd forced a reaction from him.

"You rang?" Lockwood's voice bellowed from the dark. The big man moved quietly through the darkened lot until he'd nearly reached the group. "You got one of those for me too?" He reached for the coffee caddy without awaiting Kenison's reply.

Trigg stumbled out of his room a few seconds behind Lockwood and lumbered toward the van. He said nothing to announce himself.

"Damn, Trigg, you look like something out of that zombie show, *The Running Dead*," Kenison said.

"Me and morning don't get along too well," Trigg grumbled. He yawned and rubbed his eyes.

"How very unmilitary of you," Kenison said, chortling. "You don't act like a guy who did two tours in the sand and woke to reveille every morning."

"I act like a guy who left active duty 'cause he never liked that crap in the first place."

"Looks like we're all present and accounted for, so let's bust a move as we used to say in college." Tran nodded at the van, prompting everyone to climb inside. "We've got a lot of ground to cover today."

Tran caught Lockwood's eye in the low morning light as everyone piled into the van. He cocked his head and scrunched his cheek, a sign of poignant thoughts shooting through his brain. Tran knew Lockwood suspected she knew something important he didn't. She looked away, rounded the van, and climbed into the front passenger seat.

195

Torres turned toward her backseat passengers. "Sounds like you folks have a busy morning on tap," she said. "I'm happy to drop you at the Embassy and run back out to pick up some breakfast for you."

"Whoa, Lieutenant," Lockwood said, staring at her face. "You go to Fight Club after work last night?"

Torres quickly turned back to the windshield, reducing the amount of her face visible to those in the back seat. She peered at Lockwood in the rearview mirror. "No, I, uh, I tripped over my own feet going down my back stairs last night. I fell pretty hard," she explained. "My face hit the wall, but I'm okay—just embarrassed by my klutziness."

"Looks like you went a few rounds with Ali and the bee stung you bad," he said, laughing boisterously.

"You really know how to charm a lady first thing in the morning," Torres rebutted.

Kenison punched Lockwood's arm—the one with which he held his coffee. "Yeah, man, shut the hell up."

"Ow, ow, ow," Lockwood exclaimed, the hot liquid spilling onto and through his pants.

"Serves you right, old man," Kenison chided.

Tran shook her head and rolled her eyes. "Thanks, Lieutenant. That would be very helpful," she said, redirecting the conversation.

"That's why you're the protocol officer," Kenison said from the second row. "You take such good care of us." He smiled as he peered at Torres in the mirror.

Torres shook her head and playfully rolled her eyes as she fired up the van's engine. A second later, she pulled out onto the road, taking a different route to the main gate, one that took them right passed the government vehicle Tran had mentioned earlier. Tran watched Torres look as nonchalantly as she could at the two heads in the car, both of which turned away from the approaching van.

Twenty minutes later, the team members sat in their offices, catching up on emails, reviewing where they'd left off the night before, or making calls to others crazy or driven enough to be at work at that hour. After some time, Tran stood from her desk and walked into the hall, calling into the air, "everyone to the conference room please."

Tran waited at the head of the table as her team filed in one-by-one, morning gloominess still hanging on their faces, Tran and Kenison excepted. Kenison closed the door behind him, then turned and paused as he looked upon his colleagues.

"Damn, y'all look like zombies," he announced. "Cheer up folks. God has given us a brand new day on this side of the dirt. Be happy and rejoice in it." He laughed boisterously as he walked to an empty chair.

"Pipe down, man," Ito said. "You're way too loud for people who haven't had their second cups of coffee." He plopped into his chair, placed his laptop and Ito-pad on the table, followed at once by his head.

"I'm good, kid," Lockwood claimed. "You young'uns mistake old age for bad mood. It just takes me a little longer to get going, that's all."

"Speaking of old age, you know how you can make a sweet old lady say the F-word?" Kenison asked, energy in his voice. "Get another sweet old lady to yell *Bingo!*"

Groans, grimaces, and eye-rolls rippled over the room. Not wanting to encourage Kenison, Tran stifled her outward reaction as she laughed only on the inside. Her *Ba Ngoai*—Vietnamese for maternal grandmother—and her cronies were cut-throat bingo players, and Tran had seen them demonstrate the vicious truth of Kenison's joke. And, as her *Ba Ngoai* used to say, *there's always some truth in a joke.*

"You just watch it, junior," Lawrence said from the Ito-pad. "I'm one a' them old ladies, and it don't take no *bingo* to make me say the F-word—and I ain't in no bad mood neither. I been up two hours. Did my calisthenics, got in three miles, and finished my morning smoothie."

"You mean that spinach-flax seed crap you grossed us out with the other day?" Ito asked.

"You don't know what you're missin'," Lawrence rebutted.

"Okay folks, let's get started," Tran said. "I know you're already working particular angles of the case, but there have been some important developments overnight. I'll give you the thumbnail version."

Tran regaled her team with the *meeting* she and Starr had with Quizby, conveyed his information, and passed around the file he'd given her. Afterward, she shared her interpretation of the information and its impact on the case. "Any questions?" she asked.

Lockwood cleared his throat and lifted the photo of Alex from the file. "I'm curious why they think this is Alex. The person who committed the murders got into and out of the cabin, executed five people, including two well-trained Marshals, and hardly left a trace."

"I gotta' agree, Boss," Kenison said.

"Plus," Lockwood continued, "he supposedly committed multiple assassinations in different countries around the world, but never let himself get caught on camera anywhere, including London—the most surveilled city in the world. If this guy is the international assassin he's supposed to be, it's awfully odd that he'd suddenly let himself get photographed like this—no discernible disguise, full-on face and body coverage."

Starr gently took the photograph from Lockwood. "And the footprint from the scene," she added, shaking her head, "It doesn't match a burly guy of this man's height and apparent weight."

"Agreed," Tran said. "CIA's info about the overseas phone calls is interesting, but I don't think the guy in that photograph is our assassin. For the reason you cited, Dr. Starr, I think we may be looking for a woman. And the language little Miss Brandon reported makes me think the assassin has a military background."

"What language?" Lawrence asked.

"I'd guess *Five by five and in the pipe* and *good to go*," Trigg said. "That's military jargon if I ever heard it."

Tran nodded.

"You think she's U.S. military?" Trigg asked.

"If the calls CIA tracked are in fact the assassin, then there's a clear connection to the U.S. military, but I don't have a firm read on whether she's a US military member," Tran said.

"This file suggests she may live in Southeast Asia. An American would probably stick out like a sore thumb there," Lockwood said.

"Maybe," Tran said. "But maybe not if she's mixed like me."

"I don't get how the phone calls connect to Oberlin," Ito said.

"I wondered about that too," Tran said. "CIA tracked the calls to a Lee Whitehead, a U.S. Navy Captain who serves as Executive Officer to the Commander, Joint Functional Component Command for Space."

"Now that's something," Lockwood said.

Tran agreed. "It's either connected to this case or it may be our next case."

"I'm still missing something, Grace," Starr said. "No doubt it's a red flag we should care about, but why do you think it connects to the assassination of Judge Oberlin?"

Tran cleared her throat. "Quizby said the assassin used one of several pre-paid phone numbers to make an encrypted call to Whitehead from Lyndon Pindling Airport here in Nassau a week before the murders. Whitehead and Ashmead attended Annapolis at the same time—Whitehead graduated a year ahead, but their time overlapped. They were in some of the same student activities."

"Cha-ching!" Kenison exclaimed. "Houston, we have a connection."

"It's tenuous right now, but we need to run it to ground," Tran said. "This new information means we need to shift our activities a bit. I'm going to invite Captain Ashmead for a chat. Dr. Starr, I need you to get to the airport. The flight crew of the plane that may have brought Alex to the island is due to land at Pindling in about an hour. Interview them and let's see what they really remember about Alex."

"Will do, Grace," Starr said. "By the way, I did have a chance to review Captain Ashmead's Personnel Reliability Profile."

"Anything useful?" Tran asked.

"Confirmation, I suppose," Starr answered. "Several psychologists have reviewed Captain Ashmead's PRP over his career, and while there are minor differences from person to person, a consistent view of his personality arises in the assessments. They suggest Captain Ashmead is a *guardian* type with borderline narcissistic

199

personality tendencies. He needs to feel important, in control, intelligent, and adored."

"Thank you, Doctor," Tran said, nodding. "I know just how to use this information when I talk with him." She looked to her notes and then turned to the Rookie. "Trigg, I want you to have a visit with Marshal Stupleton. We need to ferret out Master Chief Byron's connection to the case, and she may be able to help with that."

"Happy to, Boss," Trigg answered, apparently pleased that Tran trusted him enough to go solo on this one.

Tran nodded as she took a flash drive from her pocket and tossed it to the other end of the table. "Heads-up, Ito," she warned as it arced toward his face.

Ito said he wasn't a morning person, but his morning lethargy didn't dull his lightning-fast reflexes. "What's this?" he asked, snatching the device out of flight.

"That's the tracking data from AUTEC. Lieutenant Torres gave it to me an hour ago. Go over it with a fine-tooth comb in comparison to this." She tossed another flash drive. "The second one contains the satellite feed for this area over the last ten days—a gift from our friends at NRO."

"Oh man," Trigg exclaimed, seemingly shocked. "I can't believe you got anything from the National Reconnaissance Office. My old platoon leader told me it was like pulling teeth to get stuff from those guys, even when we were hunting Bin Laden in the Hindu Kush."

"Guess it depends who's askin'," Lawrence said. "Grace is a bad-ass. They know not to mess with her."

Tran smiled. "It helps to ask nicely."

"—yeah, and work for the President," Lockwood chuckled.

"NRO keeps a bird in geosynchronous orbit above the southern US approaches for drug interdiction and anti-terror efforts," Tran said. "When I explained what I needed, they were happy to help."

Ito fired up his laptop and plugged in both flash drives, eager as a kid in a toy store.

Tran turned to Kenison. "I brought something for our numbers geek too." She tossed a third flash drive and a thick document down the table. "These are recent communications intercepts. Analyze them with special attention to the numbers highlighted on the hard copy."

"What am I looking for?" he asked.

"Anything into Lompoc, California from overseas, especially Southeast Asia or the Bahamas. You're authorized to listen live-time to any calls that strike your fancy involving those phone numbers. An analyst at headquarters has been detailed to support your monitoring efforts."

Kenison flipped through the document as his eyes scanned the list of marked numbers, some of which were US-based. The NSA's widespread interception of phone calls had been a topic of hot debate in the media and on Capitol Hill in recent months and tapping the calls of American citizens seemed to aggravate matters even more. It had even proven to be career-ending for some US officials. "You said I could listen live-time?"

"Yes," Tran confirmed. "The General Counsel's office is getting a FISA warrant as we speak, but we can't wait for the bureaucracy to catch up."

The Foreign Intelligence Surveillance Act created the FISA court, a judicial check-and-balance on the activities of U.S. intelligence agencies. Except to the extent it affected her work, Tran left the politics of the issue to the Director of National Security and the agency General Counsel.

"*Seeking* a warrant?" Starr repeated.

Tran heard the concern, loud and clear. "Yes, we're seeking it, Dr. Starr. Time is critical and the national security risks have just increased tremendously."

"But, there's—"

Tran raised her hand to waive off Starr's forthcoming comment. "One of the numbers belongs to a pay-as-you-go phone bought with a g-card."

"You're shittin' me?" Lockwood said. "Someone used a government credit card to buy a burner phone that's now in the midst of our case?"

Tran nodded. "And by my read of the law, the fact that the buyer used a g-card to buy the phone makes it US government property," she said.

"And the government doesn't need a warrant to listen-in on its own phones," Lockwood added.

"Every federal employee is told on day one that their conversations on government lines and equipment are subject to monitoring," Tran reminded.

"So the court petition is icing on the cake?" Starr asked.

"It is," Tran said, "on the chance we need legal back-up."

"Do we know whose number this is?" Kenison asked.

"That particular one belongs to Captain Ashmead," Tran said.

Lockwood sat up straight. "He's officially a suspect now?"

"He's someone in whom we have an interest," Tran explained. She turned to the team's senior agent. "Lockwood, I'm convinced something's awry with Petty Officer Endicott. People of his rank don't usually meet with the C-O behind their supervisor's back without something else going on. I want to know what, so I want you to go get him and sweat him. Don't hurt anything more than his ego, and don't break too many rules, but I need him where Ashmead can't communicate with him. Call me when you have him."

"Standard protocol dictates that we present our warrant to the base Judge Advocate and let the Navy detain him for us," Starr reminded.

"We're not doing that," Tran said. "I don't know who if anyone under Ashmead's command is involved in this, so I can't risk operational security for the sake of protocol."

"You do know some admiral in DC is gonna' get his panties in a wad if civilians snatch active Navy personnel off an active Navy base, right?" Lockwood asked.

"I do," Tran answered. "That's why the Director of National Security has a bunch of shiny stars on his shoulders. He can deal with the admiral's panties." She turned to the Ito-pad. "Viv, can you stop by The Old Man's office and brief him first this morning? Just tell him I'll need cover from the top for this, and he'll take it from there."

"Sure, Boss," Lawrence said, "and I'll see what I can dig up on Endicott—might just find a reason to hold him incommunicado. As for The Old Man, he loves me—no way he'll tell me 'no' to anything."

"It must be your endless charm, Viv," Lockwood joked.

"Don't start with me, Lockwood. I told you before, I ain't in the mood for your kinda' malarkey first thing in the mornin'," Lawrence warned, playfully shaking her finger at the screen.

"Unless there's anything else for the good of the cause," Tran prompted. She waited for any comments or questions, but hearing none, she pressed on. "Okay then, let's move out. I'll take Torres with me, but until further notice, the rest of you avoid using AUTEC resources, including the Protocol staff. Use the Embassy's motor pool instead. And Viv, you should probably find us off-base accommodations in case things get ugly."

Chapter 16: Power Play

The car pulled up in front of Building One, and Tran unbelted herself as she opened her door. "Park the car and then come on into the Commander's Suite, Lieutenant."

With that, Tran bounded up the wide stone stairs and went inside, flashing her credentials to the guards. As she approached the Commanding Officer's office, his administrative assistant jumped quickly from her seat and rounded her desk. She obviously remembered Tran's last visit.

"Oh, no you don't, Missy," the woman firmly asserted, placing her flattened hand against Tran's stomach. "You're not going to bust in there again without an appointment."

Tran glanced down at the wrinkled, age-spotted hand feebly trying to push her back. Her training and instinct told her to disable an assailant in situations like this by grabbing the wrist and twisting it back with force enough to off-balance them. After that, Tran would have multiple options to dispatch the assailant with various degrees of permanence. But she'd not do that to the insistent elderly lady who could have been her grandmother.

"My apologies, Ma'am," Tran said. "I need to see the Captain immediately."

The woman leaned in close and said in slightly louder than a whisper, "If you try what you did last time, Ms. Tran, I'll kick your rude behind from here to next month. You get my drift?"

The determined old woman acted the way a good administrative assistant would—zealously protecting their boss's time and keeping him on schedule. Tran valued that trait in her own admins, but it bothered her in this context. The woman appeared younger than that age at which the elderly were bestowed the privilege of saying whatever they pleased with impunity, but she was close enough. Looking to the nameplate on the woman's desk, Tran devised a different approach.

"I'm very sorry for my prior behavior, Mrs. Barrett," she began. "I got wrapped up in what I was doing and didn't stop to think about how I came across. I'll not do so again, but this is important."

The woman sucked her teeth with apparent satisfaction at confronting Tran. "It was important the last time you were here and behaved so rudely too, Ms. Tran, but as I said then, the Captain is a busy man. He can't just drop everything any time someone wants to see him about something. I can make an appointment for you first thing tomorrow."

"Thank you, Ma'am, but I think the Captain will want to hear what I have to say—"

"...And if you behave a might better than you did before, young lady, I may be able to fit you in this afternoon, but it's out of the question that you're going in there now."

"It's about his promotion to admiral," Tran stressed, "but time is of the essence. I need to see him now."

She paused as she clearly debated what to do.

"It's okay, Sally," a familiar voice grumbled in the background. Ashmead emerged from his office, wearing the brown khaki casual uniform of the day. "We can let this one through. I have a few minutes."

Tran smiled politely and thanked the woman before walking past her to Ashmead's side. As they turned and retreated to the inner office, Mrs. Barrett closed the doors behind them. A pungent odor smacked at Tran's nose as she walked through a haze hanging at eye and nose level.

"Have a seat," Ashmead directed, motioning to the chairs in front of his desk. He rounded them, pausing long enough to retrieve a burning stogie laid across the top of a coffee mug. He took a deep drag on the brown cigar and blew out a thick white smoke as he plopped into his high-back leather chair.

Tran seated herself. "You know it's a violation of about ten different regulations for you to smoke in here, right?" she said.

Ashmead leaned back and took an even longer drag on the cigar, holding the smoke in his lungs a minute and then exhaling in Tran's direction. "As commander of this base, I'm the law here, Agent Tran."

"I suppose it would change nothing if I showed you Defense Department and Navy regulations you're bound to comply with and uphold as commander of this base?" Tran asked.

Ashmead didn't answer, but instead snuffed out his cigar against his left palm heel, never taking his eyes off Tran. She watched and wondered about his bizarre behavior. Perhaps it was supposed to show his toughness, or maybe it was supposed to intimidate her. It did neither. It only showed what an idiot Ashmead could be, but Tran offered no outward reaction.

"Somehow, I don't think you came here to lecture me about smoking regulations," Ashmead said. "Did I hear you say something about my promotion?"

"Yes, you did."

He smiled widely. "Your boss made good on the promise?"

"Not exactly."

Tran's legal training made her disinclined to ask questions the answers to which she didn't already know, but unlike eliciting live testimony in court, the consequences of making that tactical mistake were minimal in this situation. She didn't yet know with any certainty whether Ashmead was involved in Oberlin's death—before or after—but the facts seemed to scream louder and louder each day that *something* was afoot. If her hunch didn't pan out, she might look a little stupid to Ashmead, but she figured the Captain already thought himself far sharper than Tran in every way. Besides, she felt confident she could rescue the situation without harming her mission. Thus, she decided at that very moment to risk it and follow her hunch.

"We made that promise in exchange for your good faith assistance in avoiding a potential nuclear incident."

"And that's exactly what I gave," Ashmead said. "I increased my surveillance of all air approaches to the sector, deployed all my anti-sub systems in the region, and delivered the tracking data you requested."

Tran raised her eyebrow. "And the chain of custody with that data?"

"The chain of custody is solid, Agent Tran. I retrieved it myself, reviewed it, and gave it directly to Lieutenant Torres who gave it to you."

"Are you sure?" she asked. "You didn't pawn that off to an underling?"

Ashmead leaned forward and pointed two fingers at Tran as his brow formed deep crevices that signaled displeasure. "I know you're not Navy, Ms. Tran, but it's unacceptable in the military to second-guess the commander—or make him repeat himself. You get me?"

Tran stared at the Captain without speaking or offering expressions from which he might read anything. After a pause, she shook her head and asked, "I guess you thought we wouldn't figure out that the sub-tracking data was altered?"

"What are you talking about?"

"You've served on ships under combat conditions, so you understand the use of redundant sources to confirm the integrity of actionable information, Captain. We do too, and the story our back-up sources tell about the accuracy of your tracking data isn't good."

She shook her head to dramatize her point, then paused to gauge Ashmead's reaction. He did a good job of muting a deer-in-the-headlights expression, but Tran noted his pupils dilated and his movements turned sticky and awkward, just for a moment. He also pursed and licked his lips quickly. He reached for the snuffed-out cigar stub he'd tossed haphazardly into the dry coffee mug, and then fished a lighter from his desk. He took an inordinate amount of time lighting it, after which he gave it several puffs until the flame did its job.

Stalling, Tran thought.

He blew out a thin, steady stream of smoke. "I just don't know what you're talking about, Ms. Tran."

She smiled. "That's all you have to say?"

"I don't know what to say. I don't know what the hell you're getting at." Ashmead stood and walked to a window overlooking the main thoroughfare onto the base. He peered outside and blew his smoke into the glass.

"We know about your classmate at Vandenberg, Captain," she prompted.

"And just what is it you think you know?" Ashmead challenged, not looking at Tran. He paused to let her to answer, but she didn't. "Go on, tell me." He waited a second time before continuing his taunt. "You don't know shit, do you, Ms. Tran? You're trying to bullshit me into admitting something, but it won't work."

Ah, so there's something to admit, Tran surmised. "We know about the overseas connection."

"Do you like trout, Ms. Tran?"

"Trout?"

"Maybe sea bass, tuna…let me know because I can tell you a few better places for your fishing expedition than here in my office," Ashmead said, moving his cigar-holding fingers in circular motion above his shoulder.

Tran stood and joined Ashmead at the window. Looking out at the scene with him, her left hand subtly probed the periphery of the window frame on the side of her opposite the Captain. With a wiggle of her finger, she pressed a small metallic pip into the lower outside edge of the frame where it would remain hidden by drapes. "NSA isn't much interested in a junior enlisted guy who blindly followed the orders of his C-O. We are, however, interested in senior officers with access to lots of classified information and equipment who commit acts like these." She turned to face Ashmead head-on. "Petty Officer Endicott will get a deal in exchange for telling us everything."

Ashmead whipped his head toward Tran. "Endicott is an active duty sailor under *my* command. If you want him, you're gonna' have to go through me. I could order him not to say a word to you—if I had any reason to do that, which of course, I don't."

"Maybe you could do that, if you had access to him, which of course, you don't," Tran taunted. "We're bringing him in as we speak."

Ashmead abruptly turned his whole body squarely to Tran. "As long as that man is a sailor in my command, I own him. He's US Navy property and no DC bureaucrat is gonna' tell me otherwise. You best not mess with my sailor without my permission." He turned, took several paces toward his desk, and reached for the phone.

"Don't do that, Captain," Tran warned, her body rotating to match Ashmead's movement. She raised her hands to her hips, in the process pulling back the flap of her jacket. Her motion *accidentally-on-purpose* exposed her holstered Glock, on which Ashmead's eyes instantly fixed. His face turned red as the arteries in his neck bulged.

"You threatening me?" His tone sounded a mix of disbelief and anger.

Tran shook her head. "I'm just saying, if you try to interfere in my investigation, I'll have to detain you. It'll make ugly headlines and I don't especially want that."

"I've had enough of your shit, lady. I warned you once already. This is *my* fucking base," Ashmead said, jerking his head to emphasize *my*.

"Then perhaps we should reconvene at my office, Captain."

"Fat chance. As Commander of this installation, I'm barring you and your team from all AUTEC facilities, effective immediately. Security will escort you to your rooms at the Q, where you'll have ten minutes to pack your shit and get the hell off my base."

"Really, Captain?" Tran asked. "You really want to go there?"

"Nobody comes in here and threatens me—and I don't give a rat's ass that you carry some fabricated, self-important civil service rank. This is a military matter, and the only ranks that mean anything here are military ranks."

Tran knew that as base commander, Ashmead had the power to ban people from premises he commanded, but thwarting the law was a prohibited use of military command authority. Tran was certain she'd ultimately prevail but going through formal channels would take more time than she wanted and cause more difficulty than she needed. Ashmead liked to play Chicken—after all, he'd earlier gloated about winning the title as neighborhood champ as a child. Tran slowly rounded his desk and resumed her place in one of his guest chairs. She crossed her legs, shook her head, and sighed. "Admiral is slipping away from you each time you open your mouth, Captain. They don't make flag officers of felons."

"Don't gimme' that bullshit. You were never gonna' do anything to advance my promotion in the first place. You just came in here and fed me a line of bullshit to get what you wanted."

And it worked, Tran thought but didn't say. "As I see it, Captain, this little stand-off will end in one of two ways. One, you'll do something stupid, force me to hurt you, and we'll cart you out of here cuffed to a stretcher in front of all your people. Or, you can walk out of here under your own power and come to the Embassy, where we'll have a little chat. If there's no problem, you'll be back in the Captain's chair in a few hours." She nodded at his rich Corinthian leather chair. "So what's it going to be?"

Ashmead followed her eye motion to his chair, and then seated himself in it. "It must be your damn time of the month, lady, because your hormones are evidently screwing up your thinking," he growled through gritted teeth. "I'm a damn Navy SEAL. I could gut you like a fish before you even think about grabbing that little pop gun on your hip. But practically speaking, I command hundreds of armed Shore Patrol troops, every one of whom is legally bound to obey my orders. If I send them to detain you, you might be able to stop one or two if you're real lucky, but you can't defeat them all."

Tran nodded. "Do you really think your troops would assault a federal agent just because you tell them to?"

"My sailors and Marines don't know you from Adam's housecat, Tran. As far as they know, you could be a foreign spy with a fake badge. They do, however, know I'm their commanding officer. They're trained to follow orders without question. That's called military discipline, and it's what wins wars."

"Surely you realize I'd never give you the chance to order anything like that," Tran said. "And by the way, you'd have as much success gutting me as you would gutting a Megalodon." She figured everyone who made a living by the sea knew of the sixty-foot hundred-ton prehistoric shark.

"Well I'll be damned," Ashmead said, laughing boisterously as he pulled the cigar stub from his mouth. He leaned back in his chair and put his feet on his desk. "Maybe I should just call you Agent *Tranny* 'cause I never met a chick whose balls were bigger than mine."

In unphased defiance, Tran laughed along with him for a few seconds before taking on abrupt seriousness. "You're right, Captain. You really will be damned if you continue the path you're taking. Since you like practicality, consider that I'm here on orders of the Commander-in-Chief on something of personal importance to him. I can pick up my phone and have him relieve you of command and bust you down to Seaman Basic in the next five minutes and those troops you think will do your criminal bidding won't be yours to command anymore."

Relieving Ashmead of command would damage his career beyond repair and his ego even more, and Tran knew she really could set that in motion with a phone call, but stripping a commissioned officer of rank was more than a notion. It required the due process of a court-martial or discharge board which, again, would take more time and hassle than Tran cared for at the moment. Even so, Ashmead didn't strike her as one to think that far ahead. She sized him up as intelligent, but his smarts were easily overwhelmed by his pompous zeal. That made him well-suited for staring down an enemy who used force, but not so much with an opponent who used power.

"This little dust-up," she said, sweeping her right pointer and index fingers to and fro between them, "will make national headlines, and the NSA will take the opportunity to clean up its image. It'll tell the press you've been implicated in a terror plot and provide convincing evidence in support. The media will be all over a juicy story about a murderous, traitorous senior US Navy officer who graduated the Naval Academy. Every media outlet in the country will crawl up your ass with a microscope and look under every rock, vying to find something even more salacious than the last network about you, your wife, your children—anyone and everyone close to you. You'll be publicly shamed. It'll be even worse if we come to blows over this. You'll get quite familiar with a Federal guesthouse—maybe even Guantanamo given your terrorist connections."

"You don't know who you're fuckin' with, *Tranny*," Ashmead growled.

"What I know is, I represent a government that prints its own money and buys ink by the barrel," Tran said. "I won't lose this."

"I represent that government too, and *I'm* a highly-decorated military officer."

Tran stood and straightened her suit, her weapon still visible on her hip. "As am I. The difference is, our Commander-in-Chief is on *my* side."

A single, loud knock at the door stopped Tran cold. She considered that Ashmead might have pressed some sort of concealed panic button, so she could only imagine what might be on the other side of the door. She prepared to draw her weapon and fire if necessary.

"Come," Ashmead yelled after a pregnant pause.

Mrs. Barrett opened the door and then stepped aside to let Torres enter.

"Good day, sir," Torres greeted her C-O. Then she turned to Tran. "Ma'am." She hesitated a moment as her gaze oscillated between Ashmead and Tran, apparently sensing the tension in the air. "Uh, I've interrupted something. Shall I wait outside?"

"No worries, Lieutenant. We're done here," Tran said. "The Captain and I have decided to continue our conversation at the Embassy, right Captain?"

Ashmead stared wide-eyed for a few seconds, clearly deliberating what to do. Tran hoped he'd decide correctly, but she was ready if he didn't. Her phone vibrated, the caller ID showing Lockwood's name and number. Staring at Ashmead, she lifted the phone to her ear.

"Tran." She listened as Lockwood reported that Petty Officer Endicott had been detained coming from his girlfriend's flat at the beach.

"Great. Thanks for that information," she said, deactivating her phone. She turned her full attention back to Ashmead.

"I trust that was important enough to keep me waiting," he said.

"Captain Whitehead, Executive Officer to the Commander, Joint Functional Component Command for Space," Tran said, waving her phone to suggest her comments arose from her just-ended conversation. "My colleagues are inviting him for a chat just as I've invited you. Between Whitehead and Endicott, your opportunity is closing. Now's the time, Captain."

Ashmead remained silent as Tran studied his face.

"An hour?" Tran suggested.

With that, she turned and walked for the door. "Let's get back to the Embassy, Lieutenant."

Torres came to attention and saluted her commanding officer, then turned and fell in step behind Tran.

"Belay those instructions, Lieutenant," Ashmead bellowed.

"Sir?" she asked, turning back to look at him. Tran stopped short and turned too.

"Effectively immediately, I'm reassigning you from NSA support duties. I have other needs for my Protocol Officer."

"But sir, I—"

"Dismissed, Lieutenant."

Chapter 17: Nassau Hold-'Em

Lockwood laughed into the phone. "So, they just told you to find your way back on your own?"

"Pretty much," Tran answered.

"You need a ride?"

"I walked. The VOQ isn't far from Building One. But I do need you to get everyone back here—we're checking out. I had Viv make arrangements for us at the Atlantica."

"I suppose the lesson I take from all of this is piss off high-ranking people so I get to stay in first-class resorts on the government's dime."

Tran chuckled. "You would, wouldn't you?"

"Seriously, Grace, I know you have your ways and all, but I don't get why you left him unattended. We've tipped our hand. If he's involved, he now has motive and opportunity to warn his accomplice and conceal evidence."

Tran walked to the door of her room and pulled open the curtain over the window beside the door. As she suspected, the shore patrolmen who'd followed in a car as she walked back to the Visiting Officer Quarters had taken positions on the walkway on both sides of her door. The larger of the two was unfamiliar to Tran, but the black-haired, blue-eyed pretty boy was Petty Officer Jones. Together with Torres's subordinate, Endicott, he'd chased her away from the submarine pen a couple days earlier. She flashed them a friendly smile and then let the curtain fall back into place as she retreated deeper into her room. She pulled a small scanner from her briefcase, activated it, and waved it around the room until it rendered its report: negative for active electronic listening devices in the vicinity. From an abundance of caution, she switched its function to activate its signal-jamming feature.

"I'm counting on it," she answered, a grin clear in her tone.

"So what are you saying?" Lockwood asked.

"I left a pip in his office. It picked up a call he made the minute I was out of earshot. I think we got him," Tran said.

"Don't tell me he confessed to the whole thing?" Lockwood joked.

"Not quite, but he gave us some good stuff. He's clearly concerned about our investigation."

"What?" Lockwood probed.

A knock at the door demanded her attention. "Let's go, ma'am," a voice on the other side instructed.

"I'll tell you more when I see you." Tran answered. "Right now, my babysitters are about to unceremoniously evict my mixed ass from my room."

"Roger that, Boss. Hang on—we'll get there as fast as we can."

Tran ended the call and tucked her phone into her pocket. Ashmead's eviction of her team from the base and his hasty reassignment of Torres were flexes of his command power. She could override him with a phone call, but they confirmed her suspicion of the Captain's predisposition to misuse his authority. In her experience, many officers who reached the lofty heights of the O-6 pay grade grew intoxicated by the sense of their own power, but Ashmead's case seemed excessive. If he'd abuse his authority to interfere with a Presidential envoy and senior level counter-intelligence agent in the course of her duty, it wasn't beneath him to bug her room, install pinhole cameras, search their belongings while they were out, or undertake other nefarious actions, like complicity in the assassination of a federal judge.

Her fast capitulation to Ashmead's eviction order was a tactical feint in response to a poorly conceived mistake by her adversary—one she'd later turn against him. Captain Ashmead was a reasonably intelligent, accomplished military officer by many measures, but being the Commanding Officer of an isolated installation had apparently given him a sensation of absolute power that made him arrogant. Time and time again, it was a siren song that sealed the fates of sailors and powerful men alike. That sort learned the hard way that all but the Ultimate had to submit to a higher power. Tran didn't yet know the precise nature of Ashmead's transgression, but his conduct made Tran certain it had some connection to her case. Whatever its nature, he'd reached into something far beyond his depth. It seemed he was about to lock horns with Tran.

The shore patrolmen knocked at the door again, this time with greater force and clear distemper. "Open this damn door right now," the angry voice commanded. "I won't ask again, Ma'am."

Tran put the device into her briefcase and returned to the door. "Petty Officer Jones," she said as she opened it. "How nice to see you again."

Jones stood on Tran's right side, a half step in front of his larger partner on her left. The bigger man pushed the tip of his boot across the threshold, evidently to stop Tran from closing the door on them if she were of a mind to do so. Their faces somber and stern, Jones said, "Yes, ma'am. Are you ready to go?"

Tran stepped slightly to the side to give them a clear view of her packed garment bag and bulging briefcase sitting neatly on the floor just inside the room. "As you see, I myself am ready, but I must await my team so they can get their things. They're en route now, and in a few minutes, we'll be out of your hair." Her smile provoked no reaction from the men's stone faces.

The larger patrolman looked hard at Jones, who looked back at him briefly. "It's been more than ten minutes, Ma'am," he said. "Our orders were to give you ten minutes and then escort you off base."

Tran sucked her breath and repressed the response she really wanted to give. Instead, she said, "I understand, Mr. Jones, but as I said, my team is en route. They're coming as fast as they can. Once they get here and get packed, we'll be out of your hair."

Jones hesitated and looked over his shoulder to his colleague. The man nodded. Jones turned back to Tran. "I'm sorry Ma'am, but you need to leave now."

As he grabbed Tran's left arm, she planted her feet and pulled backward, oscillating her glance between his hand on her arm and his face.

"Take your hand off me, Sailor," she barked. "It's a federal offense to interfere with a federal agent on official business."

Jones pulled harder. "Sorry, Ma'am. Orders are orders."

Again, Tran resisted. "You don't' have to obey illegal orders, Mr. Jones."

"Look, bitch," the larger patrolman interceded. "Do as you're told before I have to hurt you."

Without warning, Tran launched her right palm into Jones' nose, stunning him and knocking him back against the rail separating him from a twelve-foot fall to the parking lot. Blood erupted from the delicate vessels in his nose, painting the walkway a deep crimson as Tran pulled her arm loose. She used her body's recoil to power her left palm into the bigger man's nose just as he moved forward to grab what his partner had released. As he staggered, Tran snap-kicked his leg dislocating his kneecap and dropping him to the ground in a heap like a sack of potatoes. She struck him twice more at the temples, knocking him unconscious.

"Gentlemen don't behave like that," she said, catching her breath.

She turned back to Jones as he groaned, the dazed sailor collapsed against the guard rail. She gently cupped his head into her palm and then forced his forehead into the wall beside her door. The violent motion left an irregular circle of blood on the wall and a second unconscious sailor on the ground. Tran scanned the area for witnesses to the ninety second brouhaha but saw no one. She pulled the dazed bodies into her room and closed the door.

Three minutes later, a car pulled up in the parking lot below her room. Tran hurried to look out the window, unsure whether she'd see more of Ashmead's men bounding up the stairs or the members of her team. The hood of the van displayed the emblem of the United States Embassy. Relieved, Tran opened the door and stepped out onto the walkway. She yelled down at them as they disembarked the van.

217

"You've got about five minutes to get your things out of your rooms," she said. "I have something to finish in here and I'll be right down."

Tran went back inside her room and scribbled a note. Almost as soon as she began, the door burst open as if it had been propelled by explosives. Lockwood and Kenison rolled inside and took up defensive positions with their weapons drawn. Starr, Ito, and Trigg flanked them high and low, to the left and right of the doorjamb. Startled, Tran quickly drew her weapon and dropped into position, contorting her body to acquire a target. She relaxed when she realized who had burst into her room.

"You okay, Grace?" Lockwood asked, seeing no immediate threat in the boss's room.

"What the hell?" Kension asked, his gaze falling to the floor.

Tran stood and followed Kenison's eyes to the thing he found so curious. The unconscious shore patrolmen lay face down on the floor just outside the bathroom. Using ripped bed sheets, Tran had blindfolded, gagged, and hogtied them in two tight bundles, one as still as a midwinter night, and the other beginning to stir.

"We saw all the blood out here," Lockwood said motioning toward the door.

Tran nodded. "Long story. I'll tell you later."

The team members dispersed to their rooms to gather their things. Tran removed two twenty-dollar bills from her purse, folded them with the note she'd written, and tucked them into the bindings of the still unconscious Shore Patrolmen. She stood, examined her work for a second, and then double-checked the tautness of the makeshift restraints. Satisfied, she collected her bags and departed the room.

Ten minutes later, with Lockwood at the helm, the Embassy van pulled out of the VOQ parking lot onto AUTEC's main thoroughfare, Field Team Six fully packed and on board. They'd go first to the Atlantica Resort to resettle their belongings and then return to the Embassy, where the grizzled Marine from the gatehouse kept company with Petty Officer Endicott, courtesy of the Embassy. As the vehicle passed through AUTEC's main gate, Tran lifted her phone and punched in a number. It rang twice before someone answered.

"Good morning, Master Chief," she greeted. "This is Special Agent Grace Tran. I left something for you in my room." She ended the call and returned her phone to her briefcase.

"So Boss," Kenison said. "What's up with the doofi in your room?"

"The what?" Trigg asked, wrinkling his face.

"Doofi," Kenison repeated. "You know—one doofus, two doofi."

Tran chuckled. "Two of AUTEC's finest thought they'd invite me to leave before I was ready," she said. "I told them otherwise."

"Why aren't we arresting them?"

Tran shook her head. "They're just a couple of young, testosterone-filled boys looking to make their marks in the world. They thought they were doing their patriotic duty by following their C-O's orders. They have no idea he used them for his own illegitimate ends. I won't scuttle their futures because of that."

"I saw you'd written something down," Starr said. "Care to share?"

Tran laughed. "When it became clear during my conversation with Ashmead in his office that we were headed for a conflict, he reminded me that he commanded hundreds of armed men. He said I might be able to stop one or two of them if I was really lucky, but I couldn't defeat them all. So, my note said, *Tell Ashmead it looks like Lady Luck is on my side*. I also left them forty bucks to pay for the sheets I destroyed."

"I'm impressed you know how to hogtie something, Boss," Trigg said. "You grow up on a farm?"

"I grew up in suburbia, Trigg, but I read a lot." Tran smiled.

"You're taunting them," Starr said.

"Ashmead took the bait. I'm now setting the hook," Tran answered.

"A man like him really won't like that you bested his pawns," Starr said. "He'll like it even less that you're throwing it in his face. He'll really come after you now, Grace."

"I'm counting on it," she said, "and I suspect his anger will make him careless, especially now that we're out of his reach."

"He took the bait all right," Kenison said.

"You have something?" Tran asked.

"Yeah. Earlier this morning, we intercepted a call from his office to Lompoc, California. He called from a number that didn't appear on the list you gave me, Boss, but the number he called was. Through voiceprint ID, my Tech Services guy confirmed with ninety-nine percent certainty that the speakers were Captains Robert Ashmead and Lee Whitehead."

"That's good stuff, kid, but what did they say?" Lockwood asked, swerving to avoid a rough spot in the pavement.

"They're typing up the official transcripts but, uh—sorry, Boss, but—"

"I'm a big girl, Stefan. I can handle it," Tran assured.

Kennison nodded. "—Ashmead said, *'It's me. The bitch knows we faked the sub-tracking data.'* Whitehead told him to calm down, to which Ashmead yelled, *'she's summoned me for questioning in an hour.'* Then he said, *'All this pussy-footing around is bullshit. It's time to go on the offensive instead of just hoping that tenacious bitch will go away.'*"

Tran smiled. She liked that Ashmead considered her a tenacious bitch. It meant she was doing something right and her instincts were spot-on. Besides, Ashmead just confirmed his connection to the Oberlin case.

"And what did Whitehead say in response?" Starr asked.

"He told Ashmead they needed to think carefully about their next move, and that he hoped they'd come up with the single best solution to the problem. Ashmead replied that 'hope is not a plan'."

"Any indication what that plan might be?" Starr asked.

"They didn't go into it. Whitehead had to get off the phone to tend to something else. It seemed pretty clear from their discussions that they don't want *the old man* finding out about whatever they've done."

"Who's *the old man?*" Trigg asked.

"*The old man* usually refers to the highest authority in a unit," Tran said. "That's what we call General Sharp."

"Clearly, they're trying to cover something up, but what?" Lockwood wondered. "We've found nothing otherwise linking them to the Judge, so what do they gain by assassinating him?"

"How would two senior Navy officers benefit from the death of a federal judge and/or the members of his party?" Tran asked, thinking aloud.

"And if they didn't actually do it themselves, why would they help whoever did do it cover it up?" Starr added.

"More importantly, who would have gotten them into it?" Lockwood asked.

Tran shook her head as the van bounced and bobbed its way along the streets. "The answers are out there somewhere," she said. "We've missed something."

"Is it possible the girlfriend was the target was the target and Oberlin was collateral damage?" Trigg asked.

Tran considered the thought. "You're absolutely right to question our presumptions, Trigg. Doing that every once-in-a-while gives us a reality check. But in this case, my gut tells me Ms. Brandon is the collateral damage and we're on the right track here with Oberlin. But, let's keep that in mind as we consider the evidence here."

"Well, I can confirm for sure the AUTEC sub-tracking data has been manipulated," Ito added.

Lockwood hit a pothole, bouncing everyone in the van to and fro.

"You need me to take over the helm there, Sir?" Trigg asked.

"Don't make me stop this car, Junior," Lockwood playfully warned, pointing his finger in the rearview mirror.

"What did you find?" Tran asked of Ito.

"I'll show you when we get somewhere I can unpack my stuff, but the long and short of it is, NRO's thermal imaging data confirms that something emitting a heat signature held station off-shore at that location the night of the murders and put out of the bay shortly after midnight. Its egression route took it directly back to AUTEC. Amazingly, however, AUTEC tracking data doesn't show any of that."

"I assume you accounted for timing?" Kenison asked.

Ito pursed his lips and wrinkled his face, scoffing at the notion that he didn't. "Of course. When I analyzed the data beneath the AUTEC images, I found evidence that some of the original data were erased and replaced with data about the same location but from twenty-four hours earlier."

"So, it's like someone cut a square from a photograph and pasted into the bare spot a same-size, same-shape piece of another photo of the same spot the day before," Tran summarized.

"Exactly."

Lockwood hit another hole in the road, shrugging his shoulders as his passengers cast annoyed stares.

"CIA and Navy Intelligence examined the satellite images of the object detected off-shore the night of the murders," Ito said. "They confirmed that the object's physical specs match known U.S. technology and expressed no concerned about its presence. They strongly suggested that my inquiry end there, saying any additional information would have to come from the Old Man."

"Such a high authority level," Kenison said. "That means that thing has major national security implications."

"Agreed," Tran said. "What they're talking about is the Orta-class submarine prototype."

"I'm pretty well-read on all kinds of weapons systems, but I never heard of an Orta-class sub," Trigg said.

"With good reason," Tran replied. "The program is a classified, special access program known only to a few at the highest levels of the U.S. command structure. The joke is that the Orta can crush the heart of the enemy before he even knows he's in danger. There are two prototypes, both of which are at AUTEC for testing. Only one boat is operational—they call it the *A-Orta*."

Reluctant snickers rippled over the group.

"What exactly is it?" Trigg asked.

"As Ito illuded, details about it are kept close to the vests of those in the Orta program office," Tran replied, "but as I understand, it's not the typical kind of vessel that usually comes to mind when one thinks of a U.S. submarine, like a fast-attack boat or ballistic nuclear sub with hundreds of crewmen aboard."

"Jessie did say the term *submarine* includes single-person submersibles and remotely operated drones," Kenison said.

"Judging from the satellite photos, I'd guess the Orta is bigger than either of those things," Trigg said, giddy excitement.

"It supposedly has tactical and strategic capabilities beyond anything ever deployed by any military power in history," Tran said. "It carries a traditional payload in addition to advanced first-strike nuclear technology."

"Advanced first-strike technology—what the hell is that?" Lockwood asked.

Trigg shrugged and wrinkled his brow. "The twitter verse has been abuzz for years with rumors of new U.S. military technology, like plasma bursts, electromagnetic pulse bombs, sonic weapons—some other stuff."

Kenison laughed. "That sounds like a sci-fi movie."

"Yeah, but that's the scuttlebutt nonetheless."

Refocusing their discussion, Tran interrupted. "The exact details of the Orta program aren't germane to our case, but the program itself could be. Our Old Man says it's the kind of technological leap that gives us military capabilities light-years beyond anyone else, like the first atomic bomb, the cruise missile, or the stealth fighter when they came online."

"That could explain why a foreign agent might be involved in this," Kenison said.

Tran nodded. "It might if we knew what *this* was."

"Yeah, something's wonky about this," Kenison said.

"The phone tracking evidence connects someone from northern Vietnam or southern China to Captain Whitehead," Tran thought aloud. "So it wouldn't be an illogical jump to theorize that one of the programs run by the Joint Functional Component Command for Space where Whitehead is the executive officer could be connected to that person who also showed up in the Bahamas where Judge Oberlin was killed."

"How do you guess Ashmead figures into it?" Kenison asked.

Tran pondered the question. "I think it's either directly related to Ashmead and AUTEC, or one of these officers enlisted the other's involvement for unofficial reasons."

"You mean something personal, like a favor?" Trigg asked.

Tran nodded. "Or perhaps a threat or extortion."

"Regardless," Starr added, "it's still unclear why either would want to kill Judge Oberlin."

"I agree," Tran said. "I'm certain the answers are right beneath our noses somewhere."

"Or maybe the kid is right and we're barking up the wrong tree entirely," Lockwood said. "Our theory right now is based on the premise that the person who killed Oberlin is the assassin for whom the CIA is looking. Maybe we've only looked for evidence to support our theory and ignored facts that might lead elsewhere."

"That's called a confirmation bias," Starr said.

The rookie wrinkled his brow. "What's a confirmation bias, Doc?"

"It's an error in inductive reasoning, a mistake some researchers make by selectively seeking and interpreting information to prove their preconceived beliefs rather than critically assessing what the data actually says."

As he continued addressing Tran, Lockwood glared at Starr in apparent dismissal of her psych-jargon. "Yeah, as the kid and I suggested, our murderer could be someone who acted for reasons completely independent of the Orta program."

224

In the deepest regions of her mind, Tran had to admit Trigg and Lockwood's suggestion had at least some possible merit. Still, she couldn't dismiss what she felt inside, and that had always served her well. "You're right about the possibility, of course, but my gut tells me otherwise, Ian."

"And we know how you love gut hunches," Lockwood said. "Whatever happened to, *it is a capital mistake to theorize—*"

"—*before* one has data," Tran said in slow, staccato fashion to emphasize the words. "If you know the literature well, you know Sherlock Holmes often made wild-ass guesses. He simply deferred making them until after he had facts on which to base them. In our case, we don't have all the answers yet, but far too many facts line up logically to dismiss them as coincidence."

"You know he was fictional, right?" Lockwood laughed.

"Or is he?" Tran rebutted. "Sir Arthur Conan Doyle based the character of Sherlock Holmes on a doctor with whom he'd worked who was known for correctly reaching major conclusions based on minute observations."

Lockwood playfully shook his head. "You're a real piece of work."

Tran smiled. "I am indeed. Whatever the case, Ashmead will soon meet us at the Embassy, and I suspect we'll start getting some answers to fill in the blanks. I'll provoke him into revealing the linkage—he won't be able to help himself. I plan to run a standard play on him, so I'll need everyone in position to monitor his movements after he leaves."

Starr exhaled deliberately. "I can't overstate the danger inherent in that approach."

"I realize that, Doctor, but we must uncover what's going on here sooner rather than later," Tran said. "This carries some risk, but it'll flush out the rats."

"Well, we're all set up on all his electronic communications," Kenison said. "And Lockwood and I can get in position to tail him pretty fast."

"I'll fit his car appropriately while he's in with you," Ito said.

"Viv," Tran called into the air. "I'll need you to visit with our friends in Tech and be sure they're ready to track his car," she instructed.

"No worries, Boss Lady. I'll head down there right now. I'll have 'em eatin' outta' the palm 'a my hand in no time flat," Lawrence answered.

Turning onto the grounds of the Atlantica Resort, Lockwood guided the van through a wide, gentle curve. As they rolled toward the main lobby, the enormous pastel palace shot up from the ground like Jack's beanstalk. Everyone fell silent as they gazed upon the opulence around them, from the tip of the property all the way to its front entry. The van stopped at the main entrance and everyone piled onto the sidewalk.

"Good work, Viv," Lockwood said surveying the hotel lobby.

"This ole lady can still do something right, eh?" Lawrence said.

"More than you know, ole girl, more than you know," the senior agent replied.

"Yeah, that's what I thought," Lawrence said.

The team checked into the suite Viv had reserved for them on the seventh floor, and then went up to stash their gear. The spacious, well-appointed suite boasted a living room equipped with plush leather massage sofas and an 80-inch television, what appeared to be original oil paintings, a kitchenette and wet bar, a sauna, hot tub, and three bedrooms, each with bathrooms that featured 10-head steam showers. They'd have to sleep two to a room but the amazing amenities—which were nicer than their homes—worth the sacrifice. For now, though, they had no time for the indulgences. After stowing their equipment and oohing and awing over their accommodations, they hurried to get back to the lobby and loaded themselves back in the van, bound for the Embassy.

Moments later, they endured the usual security checks at its front gate. As the young guard prepared to wave them through, Tran addressed the senior, grizzled Marine supervising the process a few feet behind.

"Gunny, I'm expecting Navy Captain Robert Ashmead soon," Tran said. "Would you be so kind as to personally escort him to us?"

"Aye-aye," Ma'am," he replied as he saluted.

"And Gunny," Tran continued, "please alert me immediately if he arrives here with anyone other than a driver."

The guard nodded, saluted, and again waved them through the gate. As the entry barrier sank into the ground, Lockwood drove to the front door of the Embassy and pulled into the same reserved space from which he'd taken the motor pool vehicle.

As the team disembarked, Ito stood on the ground and craned his neck to survey the four-story, far less than five-star, lime-green building. "We should have worked from the Atlantica," he said.

"Aww quitcherbitchin', Princess," Kenison chided. "If this was meant to be fun, it wouldn't be called work, now would it?"

"Dude, that's the second time you've called me princess. Maybe we need to give careful though to the sleeping arrangements at the hotel," Ito rebutted.

"Don't flatter yourself, Cupcake. You're not my type," Kenison joked.

They passed through the interior security check point and walked briskly down the hall, Tran and Lockwood bringing up the rear.

"Ian," Tran began, "I'd like you and Dr. Starr to handle Endicott's interrogation. I'll interview Captain Ashmead in our conference room. I want him to see Endicott, but I don't want him to have a chance to speak with or hear him, and I don't want Endicott to know Ashmead is here."

When the possibility of a conspiracy surfaced in an investigation, the team often used such tactics to scare suspects into giving up information that could damn their co-conspirators. Properly applied, the fear of harsh penalties or the promise of lenience were often very effective in turning malleable suspect into founts of useful knowledge. While Ashmead may not be that type, Endicott certainly was. When Dr. Starr joined the team, they'd grown much more skilled at manipulating suspects, especially those who thought themselves smarter than they really were.

"You got it, Boss," Lockwood answered, nodding eagerly.

Tran checked her watch. "Ashmead should be here in fifteen minutes. Until then, I'm going to review the case file. I feel like we've missed something, but I'm not sure what."

"No worries, Grace. I'll bring Endicott to the suite in thirty minutes or so."

"Touch base with Viv beforehand to see if she found anything useful on Endicott. Also, Darden called while I was in Ashmead's office. His team confirmed the saliva from the wad of gum at the old airport matches the DNA profile in Endicott's medical records."

"Well I'll be damned," Lockwood mused. "This is getting interesting."

"It's about to get a whole lot more so," Tran said. "Contact headquarters and have them pick up Whitehead. I don't care what they talk about, but I don't want Ashmead to be able to reach him in any way for 24 hours after he leaves us."

"I'm on it."

"And be sure Endicott hears you order the detention of a Navy Captain."

Lockwood smiled. "Happy to, Boss."

As they reached the door to their temporary offices, Tran saw the crusty Gunnery Sergeant approaching from the opposite end of the hall, Petty Officer Endicott walking in front of him.

"Grace," Lockwood said, as he watched his quarry approach. "I've been waiting patiently for you to fill me in on the CIA guy in your room."

"Have you?"

"I figured you'd get around to it when the time is right, but I kind of hoped it would have been right by now."

"You know about OPSEC," Tran said, smiling as she teased.

"Don't give me that operational security crap," Lockwood dismissed. "My clearance is nearly as high as yours, so unless you're

228

saying this is above my clearance—" He paused to let the words hang in the air.

Tran trusted Lockwood, but she enjoyed giving him a hard time in jest. She smiled. "You'll never guess in a million years," she said.

"Ashmead? Am I warm or cold?"

Tran shook her head. "You're double digits below zero."

"Stupleton?"

"You're so cold, you're a block of ice."

"As someone I know well might say, it's a capital mistake to theorize before you have data," Lockwood paraphrased. "Gimme' a hint. Is it someone I'd know?"

"Hey mon, may-be we de-scuss dis ova' some nice Switcha and da' bess eats ya' eva' dun et ba-for," Tran said in her best Bahamian accent.

Lockwood wrinkled his face in disbelief. "You're shittin' me. Marco—the restaurateur?"

"Muddasick!" Tran exclaimed. She smiled and winked at Lockwood, then turned the door handle and stepped inside their office suite, leaving him in the hall.

Chapter 18: The Watergate Maxim

The agents split off to their own tasks, and Tran retreated to her office to pour through the files again. The answers were hiding there, waiting to be discovered.

Jack Oberlin was a fifty-five-year-old divorced father of two, with a long list of famous, even infamous wealthy girlfriends, relationships, and ties. The file photo showed him as a muscular man with dark hair, a square jawline, and deep turquoise eyes that made him very physically appealing to a wide audience of sexes, orientations, and personal pronouns, and reports suggested his charisma, wit, and knack for being in the right place at the right time made him what some referred to as a media darling, others a media whore. He didn't present the typical profile of the respected, highly accomplished jurist destined for the Supreme Court. But he'd been on the bench nearly eighteen years, and he'd deftly handled some of the stickiest cases before the bar. He didn't hail from a moneyed family, but he was evidently wicked smart. His academic prowess took him to Princeton undergraduate and Harvard law where he shared housing for a few years with a guy who'd one day sit behind the desk in the Oval Office. He did two tours of active duty in the U.S. Air Force Judge Advocate General's Corps, followed by an honorable tenure as in-house counsel for several multinational conglomerates, followed by an appointment to the bench of Montgomery County, Maryland, just outside of Washington. He retired from the Reserves as a lieutenant colonel in the Air Force Judiciary. Tran knew all that information from her initial review of Oberlin's background, and it didn't seem particularly relevant to what had developed in the case so far.

She pushed Oberlin's dossier aside and looked at those of his girlfriend and Deputy Marshals Declan O'Keefe and Samuel Fakmann. Likewise, she found nothing new in their files, so she moved to the notes she'd taken throughout the investigation to date, starting with Marshal

230

Stupleton's first interview. She made a mental note to supplement her written notes with whatever Trigg found in his follow-up with her today.

The desk phone screeched an ear-piercing tri-tone that ripped her attention from the pages and nearly prompted her to defensive posture. As she lifted the handset, the gate guard informed that he'd just cleared Captain Ashmead and a Lieutenant Jacobsen through the front gate. He said someone would escort them to her office once they got through Security at the Embassy entrance. Tran acknowledged the information and thanked the guard before hanging up and organizing the mess of papers she'd spread over the desktop.

In the process, something caught her eye. She'd written that Marshal Stupleton confirmed she'd checked all of Oberlin's cases for possible motives or threats, *including the Cabrillo, Goddess Frankenstein, and AMAGS cases.* Tran recognized all the captions as cases on Oberlin's docket, but she recalled that members of her team had briefed only *Cabrillo and Goddess Frankenstein.* The last one—AMAGS—had not been briefed by anyone, at least not to her. Stupleton had identified the case as a possible source of a threat to Oberlin, but it was not clear why, Tran wondered. She lifted her cell phone as she stood and walked out of the office to intercept the Embassy escort, Ashmead, and Lieutenant Jacobsen, whoever that may be.

"Viv," she said when Lawrence answered the other end. "Listen, I just have a second, so I have to be quick. Can you pull the AMAGS case from Oberlin's docket?"

"Yeah, I saw that one on the list," Lawrence said.

"I saw it too, but none of us briefed that case in detail to the team," Tran said. "Stupleton seemed to think it had some promise as a potential source of threat."

"Okay, I'll pull it, Boss."

"Thanks, Viv. One other thing…Ashmead arrived here with someone named Jacobsen…a lieutenant. Need you to find out who that is pretty quickly and get back to me."

"I'll get back to you right now, Boss Lady," Viv answered. "Lieutenant Jacobsen, Eric G. is the Navy Judge Advocate General officer stationed at AUTEC. I ran across that name when we were talking about nabbing that shore patrolman off the base."

"Great. You're amazing, Viv."

"Tell me sump'in I don't already know," the woman joked. "You know I'm here to make your life easier, girl."

"And that you do, Viv. That you do," Tran said. "Okay, one more thing—at least for now…"

"Sure thing, Grace? Waddoyou need?"

"Call me in forty-five minutes or so."

"No problem—'bout anything in pa'tickalar?"

"I just need a strategic interruption."

"Ah, got it."

Tran heard the understanding nod in Lawrence's tone. "Okay. Gotta' go."

She ended the call just as the Gunnery Sergeant made eye contact with her.

"Your visitors, Ma'am," he said, walking them to her side. Tran smiled and nodded her thanks.

"And Ma'am," he said as he began to turn, "I have a package I've been holding for you in the other room. I'll give it to your senior man." He smiled and then stepped smartly down the hall, leaving Tran and her guests alone.

"Thank you for coming in, Captain," she said, looking him squarely in the eye. Then, she turned to the junior officer. "Lieutenant." She nodded and extended her hand.

"Ma'am, I'm Lieutenant Eric Jacobsen, Judge Advocate General Corps." He shook Tran's hand.

Tran knew pushing Ashmead into fear of prosecution might prompt him to lawyer up, but she didn't think she'd pushed him that hard yet. "Special Agent Grace Tran, NSA." She opened the door to the suite and stepped aside. "Gentlemen," she prompted, nodding at the far side of the reception area. "We'll head through the door there and go into the conference room immediately on the other side." They proceeded in orderly fashion.

Ashmead sat in the middle chair on one side of the table as soon as he reached it. The Navy lawyer waited for Tran to seat herself before taking a chair and pulling a pen and notepad from his briefcase. Tran opened the discussion.

"I've asked you to come here to talk as part of an official investigation, Captain." She activated a voice recorder and conspicuously placed it on the table in front of the men. "For the record, this conversation will be recorded."

"Before we begin, I'd like a little clarification, Agent Tran," Jacobsen said. "What exactly is the nature of your investigation?"

"I think I'd like a little clarification, myself," Tran said. "In what capacity are you here today, Lieutenant?"

"Didn't you first tell Captain Ashmead you were here to investigate the death of an NSA intelligence asset?" the lawyer asked, taking on the demeanor of a character in a Perry Mason courtroom drama. "Then, you told him your purpose in coming here was to help prevent the detonation of a dirty bomb smuggled in by an Iranian submarine. Which is it, Miss Tran, or maybe it's something else completely?"

"It doesn't particularly matter," Tran replied. "I have come to believe there are a few issues with which I believe Captain Ashmead can be helpful."

"Well I believe I have an issue your lies and deceptions. The Captain and I have discussed your interactions with AUTEC personnel, and clearly, your investigation is targeted at something other than what you've indicated. So, why don't you stop playing games and cut to the chase. What's your end-game?"

Ashmead sat barrel-chested across the table, smiling— gloating—at Tran. She turned back to the lawyer. "And why don't you stop playing games and answer my question, Lieutenant? Do you represent Captain Ashmead individually, or are you here in your capacity as the base Judge Advocate officer?"

"He's the base commander." Jacobsen said, his tone dismissive.

"Indeed, he is, but that doesn't answer my question, Lieutenant," Tran rebutted. "You're assigned to the base legal office. Do you represent Captain Ashmead?"

"I just need to be clear about what's going on here, Agent Tran," he said. "You implied in your earlier conversation with Captain Ashmead that he violated US and Navy laws and regulations," Jacobsen charged. "Under the Uniform Code of Military Justice—"

"—You know, Lieutenant," Tran interrupted, "I once had the pleasure of working with Air Force Major Dixie Moran—the best trial lawyer I've ever seen in action. She told me that good showmanship could never substitute for good preparation."

"I'm not here for a stroll down memory lane, Agent Tran."

"Nor am I," she countered. "Had you adequately prepared for this meeting, you might have known that I have a law degree and ten years of active duty in Air Force Special Investigations under my belt," Tran said. "I know military structure and military attorney ethics. Now, I ask the question again, Lieutenant: do you represent Captain Ashmead?"

"The Captain asked me to attend this meeting to—"

"Focus, Lieutenant," Tran sharply interrupted. "The question I asked was whether you represent him. It's a simple yes or no question. If you represent him, we can have a more detailed conversation once your clearance is verified. So, for the last time, do you represent Captain Ashmead in connection with his visit here today?"

Jacobsen hesitated in silence, clearly considering his reply. That told Tran all she needed to know. An attorney who truly represented someone in the legal sense of the word wouldn't hesitate to say so, but Jacobsen apparently couldn't bring himself to answer the question directly. An awkward silence filled the air as Tran held her piercing gaze on the young lawyer as she waited for him to answer her question.

Frustrated, Ashmead saved him from stumbling over the question. "Oh, shut the hell up, Jacobsen," he barked. "I can't believe you let this woman push you around. What the hell kind of lawyer are you anyway?"

234

"An ethical one, it appears," Tran said. "Correct me if I'm wrong on anything, Lieutenant, but he's assigned to the base legal office, not the Area Defense Services office. Therefore, his duty is to advocate and defend the best interests of the United States government, not to defend criminally charged Navy personnel. As an attorney, a Judge Advocate General officer, and an officer of the court, he knows that lying in an official investigation could get him court-martialed, disbarred, or both. It doesn't appear he's prepared to take that risk by going on record as your defense lawyer in this case, and you're wrong to put him or anyone in your command in an ethical quandary like that."

"Bullshit," Ashmead yelled.

"You seem to like that word," Tran said.

"If you suspect the Captain of wrongdoing, you must give him his Article 31 rights," Jacobsen said.

"I said shut up, Lieutenant," Ashmead yelled. "In fact, get the hell away from me. I don't need you—I'm the damn Commander." He paused as the lawyer looked at him in disbelief. "Go on, get." Ashmead waved his hands as though to shoo a fly.

Jacobsen stood from the table, fumbled to grab his briefcase, pen, and notepad, and then hurried from the room with his figurative tail tucked between his legs. When he'd gone, Tran looked back to Ashmead. "He was trying to protect your legal interests and you belittled him, Captain. Article 31 of the Uniform Code of Military Justice—"

"I have the right to remain silent, I have the right to an attorney, anything I say can and will be used against me in a court of law—all that crap. That's what you mean?" he interrupted.

"Most people know them as Miranda rights, but yes, that's what I mean," Tran said.

"Lady, I've been a command officer over fifteen years. Do you know how many times I've spouted that meaningless legal bullshit to some dumb drunk asshole who beat the hell out of some other dumb drunk asshole?" Ashmead screeched.

"I'd hardly call respect for the Rule of Law meaningless bullshit, Captain," Tran said.

"Whatever," Ashmead huffed. "I know that bullshit by heart."

"So, you're waiving your Article 31 rights?" Tran asked. She knew Article 31 didn't quite apply in this situation because she wasn't a military member questioning Captain Ashmead about possibility criminal activity, nor were they even on a military installation. Miranda warnings, which people were entitled from civilian law enforcement, weren't even in order because Captain Ashmead wasn't under arrest or otherwise detained, so this wasn't a custodial interrogation. Still, she wanted enough evidence in the record to defeat any arguments a crafty defense lawyer might use to muddy the water in any subsequent trial activity.

"What do you want, Agent Tran?" Ashmead growled. "Lives depend on me running my command, and every minute I'm here in this shithole is a minute I'm not doing that," he said, motioning around the conference room. "I don't plan to be here long, so if you have something you want to ask, then get to it."

"Okay, Captain. Let's do that, starting with your relationship with Captain Whitehead."

"Who?" Ashmead asked.

"You can save some of your valuable time if you stop with denials that neither you nor I believe," Tran said. "We know you've been in recent and frequent contact with your old Academy friend, now the X-O for the Joint Functional Component Command for Space."

"Yearbooks and org charts are public records, Agent Tranny. Do you have a point?"

"I do," she replied.

Lockwood stepped into the suite's inner hall, engaged in conversation with Petty Officer Endicott on his left. Tran looked overtly in that direction as Lockwood positioned his body so Endicott had to face away from Ashmead to look at Lockwood.

"Excuse me a moment," Tran said as she folded her papers and stood.

"Where are you going?" the officer demanded, gawking in disbelief. "You're wasting my time."

"Please excuse me for just a second. This is important," she said.

"My time is important too, Agent."

Tran said nothing, but instead walked out of the conference room to meet Lockwood and Endicott in the hall. She felt Ashmead's eyes follow her as she departed, but not with the lustful quality of stares she often felt as she walked away from a man. Annoyance and aggravation weren't the same as admiration.

In the hall, Tran stood beside Lockwood as he re-introduced her to Endicott, the latter of whom shook visibly. Tran greeted him and briefly explained the reason he'd been invited to the Embassy. Despite an obvious effort to prevent it, his voice cracked as he took in the detail of the NSA's desire to speak with him. He also expressed concern about reporting late to his duty station.

"Your C-O knows you're involved in a national security investigation, Mr. Endicott," Tran said. "I'll be sure he knows you're not shirking your duties." She flashed a reassuring smile.

"Tha...Thank you, Ma'am," he stammered. "Am, uh, am I in trouble?"

"I won't sugarcoat it, Mr. Endicott. This is a serious matter that can land you in prison for thirty years. But to be frank, the guy who tasked me with this investigation—the President of the United States—isn't interested in you as far as the case goes. So, be truthful, forthcoming, and candid with us and I'll get you back to work in a couple hours. Mislead us and I'll bring the full weight of both the White House and the Pentagon down on you. Understand?"

"Yes ma'am. I, I do."

"If you understand me, then nod your head like you're excited about something," Tran said. Endicott nodded in exaggerated fashion, and Tran responded with exaggerated delight. She smiled, nodded, and shook his hand. "Okay then. Go with Agent Lockwood, and I'll join you shortly."

"Yes, Ma'am," Endicott answered.

Tran nodded and turned for the conference room.

"One more thing, Boss," Lockwood said, leaning close to Tran as he pushed Endicott in the opposite direction. "Torres is back with breakfast," he whispered. "Looks like she fell down the steps again too."

"Eh, you can eat mine for me—I'm not all that hungry anyway," Tran said, "but save my coffee."

Lockwood nodded and then escorted Endicott out of the hall to an unused office down the main corridor. Tran returned to the conference room and resumed her seat across from Ashmead. "Well, Captain, I guess I need to revise my approach to our discussion here."

Ashmead smiled. "Endicott told you to go to hell, did he?"

"Quite the opposite, but he and Captain Whitehead do change things."

"More fishing," Ashmead dismissed. "You'd blast me right out the gate with cold, hard evidence if you had any. The fact that you're not doing so speaks louder than anything you might say." He checked his watch. "You have thirty-seven minutes left before I walk out of this building. I suggest you use your time wisely."

Tran laughed. "I've found that there are almost always multiple ways to achieve a mission, and I don't give a rat's ass which way gets me there, as long as I get there. Right now, Petty Officer Endicott is ready to piss his pants at the thought of spending most of his life in prison, where his lily-white butt will look like fresh meat to hardened thugs who've been caged for so long they have only vague memories of what a woman looks like. He doesn't find that an appealing future for himself, so he's spilling his guts about your orders to interfere with my investigation. We already know about his trips to the old airport, the unsanctioned take-off, and your single best solution," Tran said. "We know the A-Orta took station off-shore from the Judge's cabin to pick up the assassin."

Ashmead sat stone-faced for a second before leaning closer to Tran. "We both know an active duty military member won't spend one second in a hardened prison, Tranny. If he's convicted, he'll go to a much more humane military prison, and since he was only following orders, he'll be out in no time."

Ah, Tran thought. *He's admitting that Endicott acted on orders.* "Maybe you're right that he'd be sent to Fort Leavenworth, but Endicott doesn't know that. Besides, there's always the possibility the court could conclude that he's a terrorist, in which case he goes somewhere more severe—Guantanamo perhaps."

To Tran's surprise, Ashmead merely shrugged.

"You'd really let him sacrifice himself to protect you?" Tran asked.

"Sacrifices are pleasing to God—Hebrews 13:16," Ashmead said, cracking a wide smile.

Oh no he didn't just quote the Bible to justify this, Tran thought. Her paternal grandmother—Grand, as all the grandkids called her—and Pop-Pop regularly took little Gracie to Sunday school, Bible study, and when she hit her teens, the 7:30 service at the New Beginnings Fellowship Church. Tran didn't continue her regular attendance into adulthood, but she still went on special occasions and anytime she felt a need for a reminder of God's presence in the world. She maintained a glancing familiarity with scripture, which she whipped out whenever it felt appropriate.

"Righteousness and justice are more acceptable to the Lord than sacrifice—Proverbs 21:3," she parried.

Ashmead scoffed. "Get off your high-horse, Tranny. Every military man knows he could be called to make the ultimate sacrifice at any time. Endicott would be doing just that in a way, except he'll survive it."

"I'm awed by your principled leadership," Tran chided.

"You have no idea what leadership requires."

"You evidently think it requires trampling the rule of law and disregarding the welfare of your subordinates."

"People like you can't see beyond some dusty, two century-old papers rotting on a shelf in the basement of some stuffy old building."

"If you're referring to the Constitution, then you're right," Tran snapped. "I don't see beyond the foundation on which our nation is built."

"Protecting America in the twenty-first century requires bold, decisive action, and sometimes, that means bending the rules."

"Is that how you and Whitehead rationalized this nefarious plan?"

"Who?" Ashmead asked.

"Play coy if you want, Captain, but at this moment, he's telling my colleagues how you conceived of finding the *single best solution* to your problem," she said, again using a phrase the two officers had used in private conversation. She watched his face for tells. He made a valiant effort to hide them, but he also pursed and licked his lips as his movements grew momentarily erratic—the same nervous responses he showed when confronted with the falsified tracking data. Tran knew she'd hit a nail on the head.

"I have no idea what you're talking about, Tranny," Ashmead objected.

"Yes you do, Captain. The question is whether you, Whitehead, or Endicott give us a statement first," Tran said. "Let's start with your orders for Endicott to monitor my investigation, the identity of the assassin, and a location where I can find her."

"I still have no idea what you're talking about, and you've now wasted another nine minutes of the limited time I'm giving you."

Tran's phone rang softly and vibrated on the table, garnering both hers and Ashmead's attention. "Excuse me," Tran said.

"Again?" Ashmead fumed. "I'm leaving in eighteen minutes whether you're done or not."

"Grace Tran," she answered.

"—If you choose to waste them, then go right a-damn-head," Ashmead continued in the background.

"Hey Boss Lady, it's me," Lawrence said from Fort Mead, Maryland.

"Uh-huh, Uh-huh," Tran replied, nodding. "Fully?"

"I'm calling 'cause you ast me to."

"I understand," Tran said.

"Is he listening to you talk?" Lawrence asked.

"Yes."

Lawrence giggled. "An' you just actin' like I'm sayin' sump'n important, aren't you?"

"Yes, exactly."

"Iss kina' funny. I ain't sure what to say right now, so I'm jus' talkin'."

"Yes, that's just fine," Tran answered. "That's exactly what I needed."

"Is he squirmin' in his seat?" Lawrence asked.

Tran looked overtly at Ashmead who eyed her as she talked. "Yes, that's right," she said. "That will be sufficient, yes."

"You 'bout to hang up on me, Boss?"

"Indeed. This has been very helpful. Thank you."

"Okay, but Imma' call you back in a bit. I mighta' found sumpin' on that case you ast me ta' look at," Lawrence said.

"Yes, please send an escort officer," Tran answered.

Tran ended the call and gathered her papers into a manila folder, which she pushed off to the side. "Looks like we don't need any more of your eighteen minutes, Captain Ashmead. We're done here."

He cocked his head and wrinkled his cheek. "Just like that?"

"Just like that." Tran stood and headed for the door to the conference room, stopping midway as she pushed it ajar. She turned back to a stupefied Captain. "As I said, there are always multiple ways to accomplish a mission, and I don't really give a rat's ass which way I get there, as long as I get there. You're dismissed, Captain."

The Naval officer sat motionless and silent, leaving Tran to wonder at the thoughts shooting through his mind at the moment.

"So what now?" he asked.

"Now, you go," Tran replied, jerking her head toward the door.

"But what of your investigation, Tranny? What of my detained sailor?"

"That involves decisions above my pay grade, Captain," she answered. "I'll report my findings to them and while they will certainly ask my advice on various aspects of the way forward, they'll decide what

241

to do about you, your sailor, and anything else related to this case. I suspect the Director of National Security will confer with the Chief of Naval Operations first, but you'll hear from us," Tran assured.

"What the hell does that mean?"

"It means the music has stopped and you're the only one without a chair. You may want to visit the Area Defense Services office now. They'll be able to actually represent you or refer you to a civilian lawyer."

Tran pushed the door the rest of the way open and stepped into the hall. She stood behind the thick glass door and propped it open with her foot, an obvious invitation for Ashmead to leave. She left her trigger hand free in case panic or desperation moved him to irrationality as he passed. If she'd done things the way she intended, Ashmead would be fearful that his co-conspirators were trying to save themselves by throwing him under the proverbial bus. He'd try to confirm by contacting them, but he'd not be able to reach them. He'd feel the walls closing in and his options dwindling, so he'd activate the backup plan she felt certain he had, but he'd do so under the watchful unseen eyes of Field Team Six. Her strategy gambled that the Watergate Maxim would bare this case wide: it's not the crime that does one in; it's the cover-up. She hoped Ashmead's panic would betray him, out his co-conspirators, and wrap up the case in a neat little bow.

The Captain slowly stood, straightened his uniform, and then walked briskly through the threshold in proper military fashion. Tran followed him to the suite door where the escort officer awaited. He paused and turned back to her.

"Thank you, Agent Tran," he said, smiling. "Me walking out of here confirms this whole affair is a charade, doesn't it? If you really thought I killed that judge and his people, you'd throw me in the brig immediately."

"The flaw in using the game of Chicken as a model for decision-making, Captain, is that the other side must fear the consequences of failing to yield." She returned his smile. "I don't."

She closed the door and returned to her office, confirmed that Ashmead had a role in some aspect of Oberlin's death. Now all she had to do was wait for him to prove it. She lifted her phone and sent a group text to the team: *the game is afoot.*

Chapter 19: Devil in the Detail

"...and so, she didn't actually recall who sat in the seat originally," Starr said, breathing heavily. "None of them did."

Tran didn't respond right away, but mulled Starr's report. She stared at her feet as they took turns landing in the sand in a predictable rhythmic pattern. Each step seemed to drive the new facts deeper into place among the thousands of other pieces of the puzzle in Oberlin's death.

"It's what I expected," Tran said. "But they do recall that the guy in the picture was actually on the plane?"

"Yes, and they remembered that he changed seats with a woman in business class."

"Why would a business class passenger want to change to a cattle class seat?" Torres asked, keeping pace with Tran and Starr.

"They said the woman complained about someone's perfume near her and this guy in back looked uncomfortable where he was."

"Which was where?" Torres asked.

"Last row, aisle seat, near the bathroom, aft doors, and galley," Starr said. "That may explain why airport cameras didn't capture an unaccounted-for female passenger getting off that flight. I checked: the ground crew entered the plane to restock the aft galley and empty the trash. They used a High-Lift to get sodas, ice, and supplies from the ground into the galley."

"Ah," Torres said, catching the doctor's point. "It would have offered an easy way for Alex to get off the plane unnoticed and without going through the boarding gate."

"What are you ladies gibbering-jabbering about up there?" Trigg asked from behind the trio.

244

"If you two would stop lollygagging back there and run a little faster, you could play too," Torres said, teasing the guys.

"That sounds like a challenge," Kenison rebutted, picking up speed.

Torres burst into full stride, leaving the group in her wake. Kenison struck out after her as Trigg caught up to Tran and Starr, panting relentlessly from the heat and quick pace. Tran chuckled at his obvious discomfort.

"You know you didn't really have to come for a jog just because I suggested group therapy on the beach, right?" she asked. "It just helps me clear my head sometimes."

"And what kind of psychologist would I be if I didn't support a group session?" Starr added.

"No worries, Boss. I used to do beach runs all the time when I lived in Daytona," Trigg said.

Tran didn't think her newest team member quite lied, but a polite exaggeration wasn't beyond him. With the Atlantica in sight, she increased her speed to full throttle for the last part of the run. Starr, then Trigg followed, barely matching her pace.

"I thought you had reservations about the Lieutenant, Boss. If so, why are we discussing case details in front of her?" Trigg asked between pants.

Tran heard the question but focused on hitting her maximum speed before reaching the end of her course. She increased her pace once again and stretched her legs as far as she comfortably could, leaving her running mates behind. She zipped past beachgoers laying in the sun while sandal-clad pedestrians moved quickly out of her way. She blew beyond her stopping point, and then suddenly relaxed, letting her momentum carry her as her legs slowed to idle speed and then a walk. She struggled to return her breathing to normal as she kept moving to let her heart simmer down gradually.

Starr and Trigg ran past her, and then slowed to a walk as they turned and traveled back to intercept her. Tran motioned for them to turn again and walk with her a little further down the beach. They could see Kenison and Torres approaching from even further down the shoreline, their exuberant competition having extended their run.

"I've made myself comfortable with Torres, primarily because I've been monitoring her, Trigg. You know what a pip is?"

"The self-adhesive micro-transmitter?"

Tran nodded. "I put one on her a few days ago. She hasn't revealed anything about our case to anyone and hasn't done anything to warrant suspicion. An SSBI and a supplemental CIA survey both say she's clean, and she's been working to find ways to help us get information."

"Torres knows nothing about the pip," Starr hurried to say as Kenison and Torres neared. "Make sure it doesn't slip out in conversation."

Trigg nodded.

"So, who won?" Tran asked as they arrived.

She saw the sweat running from Torres' brow had washed away some of the makeup she'd applied around her eye-socket, offering a subtle glimpse at the bruise she'd meticulously covered. In the time since Lockwood mentioned this newest bruise, Tran again in as gentle and tactful manner as possible broached with Torres her suspicion about their origin. The Lieutenant's demeanor changed in an instant, her spoken and unspoken communication conveying disinterest in speaking about it. Tran wanted to press the issue, but from her other dealings with domestic violence victims, she knew she couldn't save Torres, no matter how badly she wanted to. She could only empower Torres to make her own decisions and provide a supportive, non-judgmental atmosphere. When Torres was ready, she'd accept help and make her move. Tran only hoped it wouldn't be too late. The Lieutenant's reply jarred Tran from her thoughts.

"Is there any doubt?" Torres asked.

"I let you win. I wanted to enjoy the view," Kenison said.

Torres landed a playful swat on his bicep. "You'd better be talking about the beach."

"Is there any doubt?" he rebutted.

The sweaty group changed directions and headed back to the hotel's beachside entrance.

"How was your talk with Marshal Stupleton?" Tran asked of Trigg.

"Pretty good. She said the same stuff she told you—that she hasn't had contact with Master Chief Byron in a long time before getting this assignment and then again when she needed help securing the scene. She also said his unit helped her immensely with the administrivia of the initial investigation."

"Hmm," Starr muttered. "I wonder what that means—administravia."

"Clerical things like faxing, relaying messages, typing up and sending her reports back home to headquarters."

Tran stopped and grabbed Trigg's arm. Starr stopped along with them as Kenison and Torres—absorbed in conversation—continued ahead. "Wait, you're saying Master Chief Byron filed Stupleton's reports for her?" Tran asked.

"I don't know about the Chief himself, but someone on his team transcribed the notes she dictated during her examination of the scene immediately after the murders. Also, she used the Chief's personal wi-fi hotspot for internet access. I checked it out—the office's internet is encrypted but his personal one is unsecured."

"Bingo," Tran said. "That's how AUTEC got inside information before we arrived."

"It might also explain why things were left out of Stupleton's report when she thought she'd put them in," Starr said.

"You're defending her?" Trigg asked. "I thought you didn't like her."

Starr glanced at him sideways. "I don't like her at all, Trigg, but regardless, I must deal in facts as they are. This particular set of facts gives a plausible explanation for why things were omitted from her report."

247

"Yes," Tran added, "but we still have to wonder whether the omissions were intentional or negligent, and why Ashmead gives a hoot about Oberlin at all."

The group resumed its trek into the hotel, stopping again just outside the door. Kenison and Torres stood on one side of a black, thigh-high fence separating the walkway from the Ocean Breeze Café. They spoke to Ito who sat comfortably at an outdoor table inside the cafe, drinking an iced beverage with a small umbrella sticking from within. Bare-footed and clad in cargo shorts, mirrored sunglasses, and a beach shirt that exposed his hairless chest and navel, Ito stretched his feet to a nearby chair, his laptop straddling his thighs.

Tran sidled up to the trio, Starr and Trigg in tow. "On vacation are you, Agent Ito?" she asked.

"Multi-tasking, Boss," he replied. "Just got off the phone with Lockwood. He's still tailing Ashmead, right now down Atlantic Coast Highway. Apparently, the Captain decided to take the long way back to his office from the Embassy this morning. He went directly to an off-base bank, a Bahamian lawyer's office, and a small civilian airstrip. He also bought a new pre-paid phone at a drug store a few miles from the Embassy."

"Nothing suspicious in any of that," Kenison joked.

Torres said, "Captain Ashmead has a private pilot's license. He rents time in a Cessna 172 which he flies for fun on the weekends."

"Hmm," Tran muttered as she considered these facts. "Bank, lawyer, airport, untraceable phone—escape plan. Let's check into his destinations and any properties he may own or frequent, as well as the range of the aircraft he rents or has access to."

"I've heard him talk about great times he's had in a town called Sancti Spiritus in Cuba," Torres said. "Apparently, he discovered it while stationed at Guantanamo Bay a few years back."

"Cuba, huh?" Tran said. "The U.S. has no diplomatic relations or extradition agreement with Cuba."

"Not sure, Boss," Kenison offered, "but I think that's in range of a small aircraft."

"You're probably right. Do we have anything on his new phone number?" Tran asked.

"Lockwood called me after the purchase this morning, so I hustled on over to the store and got the phone's serial number from the sales clerk. That led me to its phone number, which I sent to the General Counsel's office. They're seeking a warrant for a live tap right now."

"How long will that take?" Trigg asked. "Seems like we might be missing out on what he's saying right now."

"It's not ideal, Trigg," Tran said, "but we have options."

"Yeah," Kenison added. "NSA has been capturing all cell conversations on the island for the last few days. Once we have the warrant, we can easily search the intercepted calls for those matching the new number, and then listen to the recordings."

"What if it's encrypted," Trigg asked. "He knows we're on to him, so why wouldn't he take precautions?"

"It's unlikely they set up an encryption system on a burner phone they just bought a few hours ago," Kenison said. "But, even if they did, our tech team is exceptional. It may take a little longer, but they'll break the encryption eventually."

"They should," Ito gloated. "I taught most of those guys everything they know."

"Yeah, well I was talking about *my* techie," Kenison corrected. "*He's* really good, and he's never been corrupted by your evil tutelage, by the way."

Ito scoffed at the playful sleight. "You apparently spooked old Ashmead, Boss. He's been calling one of Whitehead's pre-paid numbers every ten minutes or so, but to no avail. He hasn't left any messages."

"You mean *you* haven't found any messages," Kenison said with a smile. "My techie said Ashmead texted Whitehead a few times, saying things like 'call me now' or 'I'll handle this on my own' or 'I'm not waiting much longer.' It hasn't been anything especially incriminating."

"I'm surprised they haven't realized we'd be monitoring their communications," Trigg said.

"They probably think they're safe because they use different burner phones and avoid calling one another by name," Tran said. "A little bit of knowledge is a dangerous thing." She checked her watch. "Shall we do dinner tonight or do we need a break from each other for a few hours?" No one said anything, yay or nay. "Okay, then. Anyone who wants to, let's reconvene for dinner in an hour. Marco's sound good?"

Except one, the group's silence assented to the suggestion. Kenison explained that he was due to relieve Lockwood on watch-duty, and thus had to bow-out of the evening's eating fest. In a nod to the nature of their case, he'd grab a sub sandwich to take with him in the car as he monitored Ashmead over the next few hours.

Tran groaned at the young man's attempted humor. "Okay then," she said. "I'll head up to get showered and we can meet back in the lobby in an hour." With the team's nods, she turned to head for the elevators. As she did, she saw a familiar form in the background.

Naked to the waist, Marshal Henri sat at the outdoor bar of the Ocean Breeze Café with his wetsuit peeled off of his arms, shoulders, and chest. A small collection of empty bottles on the counter near him and a surfboard against the bar beside him, Henri seemed captivated by both the attractive barmaid and a soccer game on a wall-mounted TV.

"An old friend is here," Tran said, nodding in Henri's direction.

The team followed her motion across the patio. "Yo, Henri," Kenison yelled, inflecting a college football game tone.

Beer in hand, Henri turned in their direction, recognition immediately washing over his face. "Grace Tran," he called, rising from his stool.

His gait didn't suggest inebriation, but his mood seemed lighter and happier than all the times they'd seen him over the recent few days. He ambled casually toward them, smiling and extending his hand to shake the men's and his arms to embrace the women.

"Taking some R&R, Marshal?" Tran asked, overtly eyeing his sand-covered feet and less-than-business attire.

"*Administrative Leave Pending Investigation* is a wonderful thing," Henri said. "You get paid to sit on your ass, surf, drink beer, and do whatever the hell else you want as long as you're ready to come back when duty calls."

"Speaking of which," Kenison interjected. "I'd better get cleaned up and get moving—you know how Lockwood whines when people are late."

"Yeah, please wash every nook and cranny real good," Ito said. "I'm in the car after you, and I don't want to be choked to death by lingering aroma."

"Don't worry, little man," Kenison said. "As I get out of the car, I'll leave some aromatherapy for you."

"Disgusting," Ito chastised.

Kenison walked into the lobby, laughing as he departed. Tran shook her head and turned back to Henri. "Your whole team is on Administrative Leave?"

"Yes, until you officially clear us of involvement in Judge Oberlin's death and the Professional Responsibility Review Board decides we did nothing wrong—most of us, at least." Henri shrugged. "I don't know how Stupleton will come out of this. Oseefah and Liang have both gone back to the States while this thing plays out, and I'm just hanging around the island for a while," Henri explained. "I figured I'd rather do a little surfing, a little sight-seeing, and catch up on my reading at a fabulous resort instead hanging around my apartment in D.C."

"Is Marshal Stupleton here too?" Tran asked.

"I don't know and as long as I don't have to see or deal with her, I don't give a shit where she is." Henri shifted his focus. "So, how's your case coming?"

Tran paused. "We were just about to dress for dinner at Marco's Restaurant. Would you like to come with us—to dinner?"

"Why Agent Tran, are you asking me out?" Henri joked.

She rolled her eyes. "I'm asking whether you'd like to join fellow federal agents for dinner."

"I hear it's the hottest restaurant in town," he said. "I'd be delighted to have dinner with you, Grace."

Again, she rolled her eyes and shook her head. "One hour, in the lobby," she said. "And put on some real clothes."

In groups of one and two, the team retired to their rooms for the hour of prep before departure. Tran undressed and stepped into multiple streams of piping hot water from jet-heads above, beside, around, and below her. The powerful waves of water soothed her as they washed over her body, taking with it the sweat, sand, and dirt from outside and the stress of the last few days. The hot steam gave her a rejuvenating facial far better than any she'd get at one of the froufrou spas several of her friends frequented on occasion. After thirty minutes oscillating between hot steam and hot water, Tran found herself actively repressing small twangs of guilt in her gut, spawned by memories of her frugal father banging on the bathroom door when a fourteen-year-old Tran took long hot showers. Each time, he reminded her of the cost of the hot water she was pouring down the drain. Today, she silently rejoiced that she'd never have to see the bill to fund the indulgence.

Her mind eventually crept back to the investigation, to its missing pieces. Even amateur private-eye and police dramas embraced the old axiom that finding a murderer meant identifying her motive, means, and opportunity. The team had established the means and opportunity for the murders of Judge Oberlin and his party, but the motive remained elusive. That nagged at Tran, even in the bliss of her hot steam shower.

She exited the shower and grabbed a large, fluffy towel which she gently wrapped around her body like a sarong. She took a second one to dry her hair. The little voice in her mind peppered her with questions about what the missing motive might be. Her gut told her the answers were somewhere in the facts they already knew. They'd just overlooked something.

"Well, you know at least one damn place to start," Tran said aloud, answering her tacit questions.

She walked out of the bathroom to the desk in the bedroom. Starr stood before the large vanity mirror next to her bed on the other side of the room. She'd already donned a fresh outfit and was putting the final touches on her retouched hair and makeup.

"I'm heading down to the gift shop before we go—my nephews have their fifth birthday coming up and I want to get them something."

"Make sure you get something that makes lots of noise since you can leave their house after your visit," Tran joked. "Your brother will love you for it."

"You have an evil streak deep down inside, don't you, Grace?" Starr said, chuckling. "But that sounds like a great idea."

An aunt herself, Tran laughed boisterously at the thought. "I'll be down in a bit. I want to check something first."

She opened her computer and entered the security code as Starr left the room and closed the door. When the device unlocked, Tran scanned her inbox for the most recent message from Vivian Lawrence and found it quickly. Lawrence had summarized the nature of the case:

'Boss, attached is the official court file from the AMAGS case you asked me to pull. It involved a lawsuit under the Freedom of Information Act where a defense contractor sought the release of documents related to a contract with the Environmental Protection Agency. EPA refused to release the documents, citing national security, after which the plaintiff sued for a court order requiring the release of the documents. Judge Oberlin ultimately decided the case in favor of the government.'

Most of that seemed like routine stuff—certainly not a motive to kill five people. Companies lost Freedom of Information Act lawsuits all the time, and as far as Tran knew, no FOIA case had ever been motive to murder the judge who decided it. That was probably a major reason this case wasn't considered a likely source of a security risk to the judge. Tran opened the email attachment and began reading the case file.

Many of its paragraphs and words were blacked-out to keep someone from reading them, but the record still offered useful information. *AMAGS*, the American Missile and Guidance Systems Corporation, was a large defense contractor that attempted to use the Freedom of Information Act to get classified government documents relating to a multi-billion-dollar contract awarded to one of its competitors. The U.S. Environmental Protection Agency argued that AMAGS only sought the documents to delay the acquisition of a satellite system to study polar ice melts due to climate change. Agency officials decided not to let a sore loser improve its bargaining position by exploiting sensitive government information and abusing the U.S. legal system. As a result, it invoked *Exemption 1* of the Freedom of Information Act—the National Security exemption—to withhold the documents. The ensuing lawsuit landed on Judge Oberlin's docket. To help him decide the case, Oberlin ordered an *in camera* review of the disputed documents, meaning only he would see them. EPA lawyers objected to giving even him the documents because of national security concerns, but Oberlin overruled the objection. He noted that, in addition to being an experienced trial lawyer, he retired as a lieutenant colonel and held a top secret security clearance. "I know how to keep secrets," he chastised. Within days of his secret document review, he ruled in favor of the government. End of case. No smoking gun in any of that.

Tran continued to paw her way through the voluminous file, mostly finding nothing of apparent significance to her case. But, roughly eighty percent into it, her eyes fell on something of interest, something that harkened back to her active military service—a small annotation in the corner of a contract data sheet identifying the funding agency: *Department of the Air Force/JFCCS/81265-92465-061195-111898*. She had no idea about the numbers beside the words, but the text touched on facts related to her investigation, albeit tangentially.

Tran checked her watch. She should have been down in the lobby, but she'd obviously been distracted. That she still wore a bath towel was evidence of that. She grabbed her cell phone and pressed a speed-dial button.

"We were just about to send out the search party," Starr said, answering the call.

"Sorry, Doc," Tran said. "I may have stumbled onto something in the AMAGS case file. I want to stay here and see where it goes—I'm not especially hungry anyway."

"You sure? We can wait a little while if you want—a little starvation won't hurt us."

"I'm sure. This may be nothing or it may be the break we need. I have to follow this while my mojo is hot," Tran explained. "You guys go on, enjoy a good meal. I'll brief you on what, if anything, I find."

"This reminds me of that night we saw your favorite jazz singer in concert," Starr said.

To anyone not a member of Field Team Six, the comment would have been an odd, out-of-the-blue remark, but every member of the team had pre-set code words or phrases other members of the team could use when circumstances indicated a need to confirm whether their teammate was in need of help or whether they were okay at the moment. Starr's oddly placed comment provoked Tran to speak the right words if she was all right or say anything else if she was under duress. If the latter, the rest of the team would soon arrive at Tran's room, weapons drawn and ready for action.

"Yes, Nancy Wilson was amazing that night, wasn't she?" Tran replied, uttering the right words. Nancy had been Pop-Pop's favorite jazz artist too, and over years of the two of them enjoying his collection of jazz LPs, reel-to-reels, and compact discs down in his mancave, he'd passed to his only granddaughter his love of jazz and a particular appreciation of the stylings of the late, great, incomparable Nancy Wilson.

"All right, Grace. Sounds like everything is good and you're sure you don't want dinner," Starr said.

"I am."

"Can we bring anything back for you?" Starr conceded.

Tran shrugged, oblivious to the fact that Starr couldn't see her gesture. "Surprise me."

"Okay. We won't be long."

"Later," Tran answered, turning attention back to the file.

Now with a narrowed focus, she flipped the electronic pages, somewhat yearning for the good ole' days of hard copy paper files which part of her found easier when trying to compare pages. Her subconscious scolded her for her curmudgeonish thinking and reminded her that technological advances had their advantages. The point was reinforced for her as her eye caught the page-count in the lower corner of the screen: 2,363.

Tran selected the computer's *Search* feature and typed in *JFCCS*. For an electronic search, the process took an inordinate amount of time, making her innate impatience surface for a moment. Chuckling in her mind, Tran noted the irony that she felt annoyance at having to wait a few seconds for something that would once have taken a few days.

Eventually, the e-search revealed only the one use of *JFCCS* she already found. She searched again, this time using *Air Force*. The search returned two results, neither of which were helpful. She searched again using the names of Ashmead and Whitehead, AUTEC, Orta, and several other terms, all of which gave the same unhelpful results. Then, she typed in the long, odd number from the contract data sheet: *81265-92465-061195-111898*. It seemed meaningless, but she figured it was there for a reason. After a few seconds, the search returned numerous instances where the first segment of the number appeared throughout the record.

Tran examined each instance sequentially. Each time the number appeared, it was accompanied by large blocks of redacted text, yielding an incomplete understanding of its meaning. Switching tactics, she opened her NSA secure portal and logged-in to the agency's intelligence database, where she searched several different ways for anything relating to AMAGS, litigation involving the company, and EPA polar ice studies. She also looked for AUTEC and JFCCS information. The agency's secure database told her significantly more, including the fact that the Department of Defense had supplied both funding and personnel to the EPA's efforts on a research project known as *Brimstone*. Indeed, the EPA lawyers who argued the case were actually Department of Defense lawyers seconded to the EPA for the purpose of Brimstone research. Tran found the additional information enlightening, but it didn't reveal much about the case itself, what specific documents were in dispute in the case, or why major parts of the trial record had been redacted. With her security clearance, she should have access almost any U.S. government document, classified or not. That might yield additional insight that would let her rule out the AMAGS case as a motive for Oberlin's murder or find a relationship between the two.

A knock at her door screamed for her attention. She quickly scampered to the door to shoo away the housekeeping staff or someone errantly thinking they'd come to their buddy's room. When she looked through the peephole, an eyeball stared back at her, filling the entire viewing area. It could be a drunk guy being playful in a rascally kind of way, or it could be someone trying to prevent her from getting a look at him for a nefarious reason. Tran stepped to the side of the door and scanned the room, looking for her weapon. Unfortunately, it rested safely in its holster across the foot of her bed in the other room. She slowly backed away from the door.

"Grace? You in there?" a somewhat familiar voice called. "I can see your shadow under the door."

"Whoever you are, I need you to step back from the peephole."

"Uh, sorry. It's Rick, Rick Henri."

Tran returned to the peephole, this time seeing Henri's mug with a silly grin across his face. He'd changed from his wetsuit into a blue, patterned sport jacket with a red silk handkerchief sprouting from its pocket, and a light button-down shirt open at the collar to display the thin gold chain dangling from his neck. His hair had been neatly coiffed in a manner that screamed night club or male model more than suspended federal agent.

"What do you want, Rick, Rick Henri?" she asked.

"I've been waiting for you in the lobby, and then I heard you weren't coming. I came to check whether you were avoiding me or something. You decent?"

Tran smiled and then unlocked and opened the door, pulling her towel tight against her body. "I'm always decent."

Henri's eyes nearly popped out of his head as he struggled to avoid looking like he was checking her over, even if he was. He clearly hadn't expected to see this, and his stammer showed it. "I…I uh… I was uh…"

"Come on in," she said, motioning at the sofa as she turned for the suite's bedroom.

As he followed her inside, his silly grin matured to an eager smile. It lasted until Tran stopped at the threshold leading into the bedroom where she turned back to him, her expression not at all the one he expected.

Tran jabbed her finger into his chest, saying, "I meant come into the suite and have a seat while I get dressed—something I'm pretty sure I can do myself."

"I'm sorry. I didn't mean to—"

She rolled her eyes and then disappeared into the bedroom. "Don't worry about it," she called as she closed the door. "I should have been dressed thirty minutes ago but I got caught up in something."

"Uh, yeah Dr. Starr mentioned that. I thought maybe you were just trying to avoid me—playing hard to get or something."

Tran emerged from the bedroom clad in a T-shirt and jeans, brushing her damp hair as she walked past Henri on the sofa and plopped onto one opposite him. "Hard to get?" she repeated. "That would imply you're trying to get me, now wouldn't it, Rick?"

He laughed as he stared at her, his eyes having difficulty staying at her eye level. "How would you feel about getting got?"

She stared warmly at him for a moment. Then: "I thought you were going to dinner with the team."

"And I thought you were too," he said.

"I was planning to, but I stumbled on something that I need to run to ground. I'm not really hungry anyway, so I opted to stay here and work. You didn't need to forgo your dinner on my account."

He smiled as he stood and walked to the chair beside Tran and seated himself. "I only accepted the offer because I thought you'd be there. I don't really have much of an appetite either—at least not for food," he said, staring deep in her eyes.

She smiled and stared back. "I—" From the bedroom, her phone rang a familiar, particular pattern that signaled an incoming call from Agent Kenison. "Uh, I should get that," she said, excusing herself.

She stood and walked into the bedroom to retrieve her phone. The moment she activated the *Talk* feature, Kenison began speaking frantically.

"Boss, we've got a big problem," he yelled. "This is an emergency."

Chapter 20: Turning Tides

"Wait, slow down, Stefan. I can't understand you," Tran said into the phone.

"Sorry," he replied. "I just got off the phone with my Techie in DC. He said the warrant for Ashmead's new cell phone came in so he immediately pulled and listened to the intercepts from earlier today."

"Yeah."

"He's called Alex back to the island to kill you, Boss."

"What?" Tran asked.

"He's getting the assassin to come back here to take you out."

"How do you know?" Tran asked.

"That's what my Tech intercepted, and voiceprint identification confirms that it's Captain Ashmead talking."

"Did you hear the intercepts yourself or is that the Tech's interpretation?"

"I haven't listened to them myself yet—I wanted to call you right away. I'm sending the audio file to your Secure Star box now."

"Thanks. Send it to the whole team. I'll listen to it, and we'll figure out our next steps later. In the meantime, calm down and think clearly."

"I will Grace but be aware that these intercepts are several hours old, while we were waiting to get the warrant. We don't know where Alex is coming from. If our theory is right, Alex arrived on the island a little over a week ago to do the job on Oberlin. He could still be here on the island or in close proximity."

"I know, but we still need to approach this rationally. Acting on emotional impulse leads to mistakes," Tran cautioned. "Stay on Ashmead as planned until further notice."

"Roger that, Boss," he replied.

Tran ended the call and turned to find Henri half-way to her. "What's wrong?" he asked.

Tran waved the phone in the air. "Kenison says they intercepted calls between Ashmead and the suspected assassin. Evidently, the Captain has enlisted Alex's help to take me out of the picture."

"Shit," Henri yelled, his eyes growing wide. "So, what do we do?"

"We?" Tran asked. "This isn't your job, besides the fact that you're on administrative leave."

"I don't give a shit," Henri said in an elevated tone. "I'm not just gonna' sit around twiddling my thumbs while some ass-wipe tries to hunt you down, administrative leave or not."

Henri's outrage seemed genuine. She appreciated it. "Let's not jump to conclusions," she said. "Kenison's sending me—" The phone chimed, signaling a new email "—or I guess I should say, he sent me the audio file."

Henri walked to Tran's side. "Let me hear."

Tran clicked to open the newest email in the box, and then again to open its attached audio file. She switched on her speaker phone for Henri's benefit. They heard Ashmead's voice first:

'It's me. Where are you?' Ashmead said.

'Where I am is not concern for you. What you want?' a brusque tone demanded.

Deep and sinister, it sounded like a creature from the depths of hell as depicted in any number of horror flicks.

"That's a voice scrambler," Henri announced. "I've heard them plenty in pursuing involuntary witnesses and kidnappers."

Tran nodded and then resumed playing the recording:

'I know you already left the area, but we have a big problem developing. I need you back here to take care of it," Ashmead said.

'I told you not call me 'til tree month after job done,' the voice chastised.

'I know, and I wouldn't contact you, but this is a dire emergency. We have a big problem unfolding here.'

'You keep say, *we* have problem, *we* have problem. What you mean, *we* have problem?' the voice asked. 'I got no problem.'

'Yes, you do because I've got an NSA agent hot on my trail. I want you to get back here and put her permanently out of the game.'

'As I see, *you* have problem. *You* problem not mine,' the voice resisted.

'Look, this tenacious little bitch has already uncovered key parts of the plan, and I'm sure that sooner or later, she'll figure out some other things that lead her right back to me.'

'Again, I not see how that concern me,' the voice answered.

'Listen, *Moo Shoo*,' Ashmead barked, shifting his tone and manner. 'I'm not asking you; I'm telling you: get your boney little rice-eating ass back here quick-time and eliminate this little problem before it gets big. I didn't start this thing and I didn't kill those people—you did that, remember? If I go down for that judge's death, I won't go alone.'

'You know nothing of me. You can do nothing, so you threats are nothing,' Alex snapped.

'I know more than you think—how you get your money, where you live, how you travel. My men saw your face when they plucked your sorry ass out of the bay, and there are all sorts of cameras aboard that ship. Would you rather gamble that I won't tell them everything I know, or you wanna' get back here and do what you're so good at?' Ashmead asked.

'My service not free, you know. More body, more money, and I not cheap.'

'I don't know how much they paid you or any other agreements they made with you, but there won't be any more money on this one. Your payment is staying out of prison or off death row. After all, a bunch of governments around the world—including some not so nice ones—would love to get hands on you, if you get my drift.'

There was a long period of silence in the recording, almost prompting Tran to stop it midstream. But just as she was about to deactivate it, she heard Ashmead talk again.

'You there? I don't have time for this shit, so if you're going to do something, you'd best tell me now. Otherwise, I'll make my own arrangements.'

'Okay, okay. I not far—I coming back. I take care of problem, and when I done, you and me discuss your manners.'

'You threatening me?' Ashmead screamed. 'Bitch, you don't know who you're fucking with. I will gut you like a fish.'

The person on the other end offered no response.

'Hello? Hello, are you still there?' Ashmead asked.

Silence.

The recording ended and Tran looked to Henri.

"Can we jump to conclusions now?" he asked.

The situation was serious, but Henri's question made Tran laugh.

"Well, we definitely have enough to grab Ashmead now," she said. "I still can't figure out the why of this thing though."

"What are you confused about?"

"Maybe you can help with something. Stupleton said she reviewed all the major cases on the judge's docket."

"She did, yes."

"This AMAGS case was one we didn't debrief because it just didn't seem relevant. You know anything about it?" Tran asked.

Henri smiled widely. "In fact, I do. Stupleton mentioned the cases on Oberlin's docket but she didn't really tell us anything about them. I looked them up myself before coming down here, but information about that particular matter seemed pretty limited. Everywhere I turned, things were 'restricted' or 'denied,' or else any written documents were mostly blacked out."

"Yeah, it's kinda' hard to miss that, isn't it?" Tran agreed.

"Even as a kid, telling me I can't do something is like daring me to do it, like chumming the water," Henri admitted. "Since I went on

Admin Leave, I've had a lot of extra time, only so much of which I could devote to surfing and hanging out at the bar. So, let's just say I found something more constructive to do."

Tran chuckled, remembering Henri's background. "Well, show me yours, I'll show you mine," she joked.

Henri smiled at the double entendre. "Okay. That case involved a—"

"Skip the basics," Tran said. "Tell me what you learned."

"The first thing that struck me as odd was that the Defense Department funded and staffed an Environmental Protection Agency contract called Brimstone."

"I saw that," Tran agreed, recognizing the code name from her file research.

"Those two agencies have never been closely allied, especially because military operations have always created huge environmental issues, including chemical leaks, fuel spills, fallout from weapons testing, and noise and emissions pollution from base operations. I'm told their chiefs can't even stand to be in the same room with each other. That all made me wonder what could possibly make them work together on the same project, and guess what I found?"

"What's that?" Tran prompted.

"Nothing. I couldn't find a single public document to support the idea that the EPA and the Defense Department are working on any joint projects—no budget requests, no expense reports, no oversight committee testimony, no staffing reports—nothing. Using some of my contacts, I did find that there's been heavy com traffic between Vandenburg Air Force Base and EPA headquarters in Washington all throughout the FOIA lawsuit with substantial upticks around the hearing dates."

"Okay, but if they did have a joint project for which you simply couldn't find a public statement, that would explain the communications related to the lawsuit," Tran said.

"Except that the contract for Brimstone is funded solely by Department of Defense money controlled by the Joint Functional

263

Component Command for Space. If it truly were a joint project, there would be EPA funding sources listed on the contract documents or evidence of money transfers from DoD to the EPA to reimburse the EPA for its work on the program. There's none of that, so either they're lying about and concealing interagency money transfers, which they'd have no reason to do, or the EPA is donating its scarce funds to DoD, or the idea that this is a joint DoD/EPA project is just a ruse and the JFCCS is running the program while just pretending it's being run out of the EPA."

"—Which would create huge legal and compliance problems for both agencies," Tran noted.

"Agreed, Henri said. "Then the question is, why would they want to pretend a program is being run by EPA when DoD is really running it?"

"And why it needs to be kept hidden from public view," Tran added.

"And by the way," Henri added, "if there were any public documents or statements about this Brimstone or other collaborations between these two agencies, I'd have found it. I'm damn good at what I do."

"Okay," Tran said, sorting all she knew about the case. "Captain Whitehead is the X-O for JFCCS, and he's also a college crony of Ashmead. We know they've been in contact with each other recently, and that Ashmead has been desperate to reach Whitehead since I showed him a bit of our hand."

"And we know their communications increased significantly around the AMAGS lawsuit over which Judge Oberlin presided," Henri said.

"That case is mixed up in this somehow," Tran said, pausing to consider her next step. Finally, she blurted "The documents."

"What?"

"It's gotta' be in the documents Oberlin looked at," she explained. "The release of the documents is what the two sides were actually fighting about, so Oberlin decided to review them *in camera*. That means he as the presiding judge and looked at the documents in dispute to decide whether there truly was anything so sensitive about them that they shouldn't be released to the requesting side."

"Yes," Henri said. "I recall that. He ruled that the government did *not* have to release the documents. Are you thinking AMAGS was so pissed about the decision that they decided to kill him?"

"Maybe it was whoever succeeded in getting that contract," Tran said, thinking aloud. "I'm not sure, but I think the key to getting sure is in the actual documents."

Tran hopped off the sofa and dashed back into the bedroom to grab her laptop and then returned to the living room sofa. She called up the AMGAS case file and electronically flipped its pages, this time looking for something specific. She searched in silence for an extended period while Henri sat watching her, unsure what if anything he could do or say to help, or whether the best way he could help was to keep quiet while Tran pursued whatever had triggered her mind. After some time, she reached the end of the file and pushed the computer aside.

"They're not here," she announced.

"What?"

"The documents Oberlin reviewed aren't included in the case file—at least not the electronic version. I want them."

She lifted her phone and punched the speed-dial button for Vivian Lawrence.

"Hey, Boss Lady," Viv greeted from Fort Meade, a smile patent in her tone.

"Viv, I need you to get me the actual documents Judge Oberlin looked at during the AMAGS case."

"I done gave you all there was on that case, Boss Lady," Lawrence answered.

"I think we missed something because the actual documents in dispute aren't part of the electronic casefile you sent me."

"Maybe *they* overlooked something at the courthouse, but I didn't," Lawrence protested. "I double and triple checked—I gave you everything they gave me. I even drove over there to lay my own eyes on the court records."

With Lawrence still on the phone, Tran scanned the entire computerized AMAGS casefile again. "Viv, I need you to check with the court again, because I don't have the documents themselves. They're referenced in the transcript, but they aren't here."

"All right, Grace, I'll do it 'cause you ast me to, but I'm tellin' you, I already got everything there was to get on that case."

"You're probably right but check anyway, Viv. Call me back to confirm what you find," Tran said, "I'll be waiting."

She hung up the line. Tran flipped the electronic pages once more, and then engaged Marshal Henri in a detailed review of what they'd learned about the case thus far. He questioned her assumptions and picked at her logical leaps, helping her identify and answer weaknesses in her theory of the case.

***

After an hour, there were still missing pieces to the puzzle beginning to take shape, but Tran felt even more convinced that Ashmead, Whitehead, and the AMAGS case were connected to Oberlin's murder. The main irritant in her gut was that she hadn't satisfied herself on the questions of why or how. What would it profit Ashmead or Whitehead to kill Oberlin or to help his killer? After all, assuming the correctness of her working presumption that Ashmead and Whitehead were connected to the EPA, Oberlin had ruled for them, not against them. Maybe, she mused, her team had missed something more telling. Whatever the case, the answers lay in the documents Oberlin reviewed.

"—and I simply don't believe in coincidence," she said, summing up the situation for Henri.

"As much as I hate to admit it, Grace," he said, "I agree with you. But there's another thing I think we agree on."

"And that is?" Tran prompted.

"That I'm no longer a suspect in your case," Henri said. "Seems like maybe you've officially come to that conclusion since you've invited me into your investigation." He shrugged and creased his lip. "—at least that's what it seems like."

Tran smiled. "A long time ago. I'd never have let you get this close me if I hadn't."

A brief silence fell over them as Henri's grin grew wider. "So, you think we're close, Grace?"

Tran suppressed a smile, replacing it with a flat, un-telling expression. "The facts, Marshal Henri. Let's stick to facts."

At that moment, Tran's phone vibrated the ring pattern she'd assigned to Lawrence. She quickly snatched up the device, both because she was eager for the information she expected to get, and also because it offered an easy way out of the slightly uncomfortable direction of their conversation. "What did you find, Viv?"

"Boss, you ain't gonna' believe this 'cause I sure as hell don't…"

"Believe what, Viv?"

"Judge Oberlin's clerk—or I guess, his former clerk, now—said all the hard files related to the AMAGS case were stolen out the courthouse last night."

Tran shifted in her seat. "I don't believe—"

"—in coincidence," Lawrence said, completing her boss's mantra. "Me neither."

"Obviously we're on the right track, but to where?" Tran asked, thinking aloud. "Do you believe him, Viv, or might he be lying about this?"

"You know I got a good nose for sniffin' out bullshit, Grace, and I don't think this is one a' them situations. 'Sides, I checked out his story with the Marshals in the building, and also with an old boyfriend who now works for another judge there. This seems real legit at this point, and real professional too. The only thing missin' was the casefiles we want. And, mysteriously, the security cameras in the whole building stopped working right for seventeen minutes last night at 2:23 in the morning."

"Seventeen minutes, huh?" Tran shook her head as she thought. For someone to get into a federal courthouse, disarm its surveillance

267

systems, swipe the entirety of files related to a particular case—and nothing else—reactivate the cameras, and then exfiltrate the scene without leaving a trace of their presence required sophistication far beyond the typical criminal mind, and likely some skilled insider help. The question was, how *inside* was that help. Tran sighed. "Okay. I'm done pussyfooting around with this. Take it upstairs, Viv, and tell The Old Man I'll call him in an hour."

"You got it, Grace. On my way."

Tran tossed the phone on the sofa, frustration, perhaps annoyance wrinkling her brow. She sighed and subtly shook her head.

"The Old Man?" Henri asked.

She nodded. "Lieutenant General Keithe Sharp—the Director of National Security. He's a decorated Raptor pilot-intelligence officer with over 2,500 classified missions."

"I've seen him on the news a few times," Henri said.

"He's wicked smart, well-connected, and politically astute," Tran continued, "and his integrity is beyond reproach. I worked for him in two assignments on active duty. When he got plucked to be DNS, he personally asked me to come with him. He's a great guy—the kind of boss you want to have your back when you do work like this."

"My boss would just as soon plunge a knife in mine," Henri said.

"Sucks to be you," Tran jabbed.

She laughed in earnest, and Henri right along with her, but an awkward silence fell over them at the end of their chortle. Tran realized he was staring at her and she at him. It wasn't a cold glare or empty stare that would put someone on edge, but something more innocent, more adolescent.

"Uh," she began, breaking eye contact, "the way I see it, we can't do any more on this right now, so why don't we join the others for dinner?"

Henri checked his watch. "They left over an hour ago. Think they'll still be there?"

"They like to eat," Tran said. "Let me finish dressing and you can drive me—and this time, I'll sit in the front seat." Tran smiled as she walked into the bedroom, and still visible to Henri from the couch, grabbed her holstered Glock. She strapped it to her side. "All right, I'm ready."

Henri laughed, shaking his head. Moments later, the pair exited the suite and walked down the hall to the elevator.

"So, Air Force, eh?" Henri asked. "Did you come from a military family?"

"Born and bred," Tran said. "My Grandfather—Pop-Pop we called him—was a Red Tail back in the day, and Dad's a retired Colonel from the Air Force Judiciary. I've got two uncles who were also Air Force—one Special Ops and the other a flight surgeon."

"Damn," Henri said, only half-pretending to be impressed by Tran's pedigree. "You Trans don't play, eh?"

Tran laughed and shrugged. "Tran is my mother's maiden name, and my professional name, but no, we don't. What about you?"

Henri chuckled. "I figured you knew all about my background by now, being that I was a suspect in your investigation."

Tran shook her head. "We can just pretend I didn't do a deep background check on you," she said.

"Okay then. Let's do that," Henri agreed. "So how far back should I go?"

As they rode down the elevator and stepped into the lobby, he spoke about his background as though he'd met Tran as he might have met any other attractive woman in any other social circumstance. Tran found the conversation much easier than expected.

They reached Henri's rental car and strapped in. He started the engine just as Tran's phone vibrated. She answered the call and then quickly held her pointer finger in the air, signaling Henri to hold on what he was doing.

"Yes, General," Tran said, a different sort of properness about her. "I was going to call you in thirty minutes—"

"I know, Grace, but I wanted to reach out to you as fast as I could because I think you've grabbed a live wire," Sharp said.

"What do you mean, sir?"

"After Viv briefed me on your situation, I tried to do a little digging and I hit some of the same barriers you did. Well I don't like that, Grace, so I flexed a little muscle."

"Were you able to get anywhere, sir?"

"I don't make a habit of throwing my rank around or threatening people, but there are times when these stars on my shoulders, the title I carry, and my relationship to the occupant of 1600 Pennsylvania Avenue do offer some perks. I growled at one of the Joint Chiefs' executive officers, but yeah, I got somewhere. As I'm sure you've guessed, the break-in wasn't a crime of opportunity committed by some thug looking for a quick payday. I'm still expecting additional information, but the documents you're looking for were taken because they reveal the true nature of the EPA's joint project with DoD."

"We've theorized that the joint project between DoD and EPA wasn't quite what it appeared to be," Tran said.

"Your instincts are dead-on, as usual, Grace," the General said. "It's well-hidden under several layers of bureaucracy, but Project Brimstone isn't about polar ice melts. Long story short, Brimstone is an effort to militarize near-Earth orbit through the use of directed energy weapons technology—the ultimate Strategic Defense Initiative."

"Oh my God," Tran gasped in less than professional fashion. "That would give the U.S. a first-strike capability to destroy targets on the ground from an orbital weapons platform without warning."

"Yes, it would destabilize the global balance of power," Sharp said, "and it's illegal. It violates international law and about twelve different treaties to which the U.S. is signatory."

"Congress would need to authorize something like that, appropriate funds for it, and would probably want to exercise oversight of it," Tran said.

"Damn straight," Sharp huffed, "and the President would have to direct anything with such potentially substantial consequences. Brimstone would guarantee American military superiority over old nemeses as well as rising threats like China, Pakistan, and India. They'd have no notice and no ability to defend against it, and that could provoke them to launch a preemptive strike before we ever deployed it. I can assure you, neither I nor he knew anything about it."

"Thank you, sir," Tran said. "That narrows the focus of my investigation, but things may get especially rough from here on out."

"I'm going to have to see how far up this thing runs in the establishment, but you do what you have to do, Grace," the General said.

Tran bid her boss goodbye and disconnected the line. She sat in stunned thought for a moment.

"That sounded juicy," Henri said, hinting for details.

"We're going to have to take a raincheck on dinner," she answered. "And I think we've got clear direction on our next steps."

"How so?" Henri asked.

Tran gave him a brief explanation of The Old Man's revelations, at the end summarizing what she took from that information. At first, Henri seemed unimpressed.

"Yeah, but the Strategic Defense Initiative has been around since the Regan years. It's nothing new," he said. "I'm not getting where this technology is a motive for murder now."

"Maybe I'm not being clear," Tran conceded. "We've had SDI programs since the 1980's, but at that time, they were focused on creating a weapon that would shoot down incoming missiles in flight. Brimstone is different. It would allow the U.S. to destroy any perceived enemy at any time for any reason, merely by pushing a button, without ever risking an American life. And at the same time, Brimstone would deny an adversary any warning of an impending attack against which they had no ability to defend."

"No damn wonder a foreign agent would be interested in the technology," Henri said. "But I'm not connecting on how that translates into motive for AMAGS to kill the judge."

Tran paused. "I think this information means that to find Oberlin's killer, we've got to look at the case with a more inward perspective."

Henri considered her remark and thought perhaps he'd misunderstood her…until he didn't. "You mean to suggest someone in our own government orchestrated the murder of a federal judge?" he asked, almost dumbstruck. "But he ruled in favor of the government."

"It is upon the logic rather than the crime upon which you should dwell," Tran said, a nod to Holmesian methods of investigation. "At the outset of this case, we assumed the murderer might come from one of Judge Oberlin's cases—a disgruntled litigant angry about a decision he made against them, something that cost them a lot of money," Tran explained. "But what we learned today may suggest we were wrong in part of our presumptions."

Henri wrinkled his brow. "I'm not following, Grace."

"Think about it," she pressed. "DoD lawyers masquerading as EPA mounted a vigorous case to resist the release of government contract documents to anyone, including Oberlin. There were multiple motions and countermotions about the issue, costing both sides a small fortune in legal fees over what is usually a fairly routine thing in most civil trials. When Oberlin, in Solomon-esque fashion, decided to do a private review of the documents, the government filed a petition with the Foreign Intelligence Surveillance Act court to take the case away from him. When the FISA court declined jurisdiction over the case, the DoD/EPA team appealed to the Supreme Court, which denied cert."

Henri rolled his eyes. "I know you're not talking about a breath mint, are you?"

"Sorry," Tran said, "certiorari. It means the Supreme Court declined to hear the case, which means the lower court's ruling stood. After that, Oberlin reviewed top-secret Project Brimstone documents, which they went to a great deal of effort to hide from people outside their group—"

"—which we now know was because the documents may have disclosed illegal activity which could cost someone millions of dollars and send people to jail," Henri said, digesting the conversation.

"Exactly," Tran agreed as she continued to tease out her thoughts. "And while Oberlin ruled in their favor, he was nonetheless an outsider who knew of their illegal actions. On top of that, he was a media hound who frequently showed up on TV and liked the limelight."

"So, the government was pissed that the Supreme Court declined to hear their case, so they killed Oberlin?"

"No, but whoever was giving direction to the government's lawyers in the AMAGS case felt vulnerable because Oberlin had seen what was in those documents. They didn't trust him to be judicious with what he'd seen, and there's an old saying that dead men tell no tales."

"Okay, let's assume you're right about all of this so far. We connect Oberlin to the EPA, Project Brimstone, and probably Whitehead, but I see no relationship between all of that and AUTEC. We see a connection between Whitehead and Ashmead," Henri said, "but do you really think he'd risk his career and his freedom out of friendship with an old college buddy?"

"We know a little more than that because we know Ashmead and Whitehead were in frequent conversation around the AMAGS case, and the phone intercepts confirmed his involvement, at least after-the-fact. Why he'd be involved isn't totally clear—yet," she replied.

Again, Henri sat in silence, absorbing the enormity of Tran's theory. "Yeah, Grace," he said after a few minutes, "the theory makes sense, but the idea that the Pentagon had something to do with murdering a federal judge…?"

"Defense Department people are probably among the highest caliber people you'd find anywhere. But it's a big agency that doesn't always move in tandem with itself," she explained. "As with any large group, there are always a few bad apples. Research in behavioral ethics shows that even good people make can bad decisions, and that the choice to do so is situational. We now need to start zeroing in on Ashmead's particular motivation."

"Killing a federal judge is huge for anyone but especially these folks under the circumstances. I don't imagine Ashmead or Whitehead made the decision to do it on their own, much less that they carried it out by themselves. Are you prepared for what it might mean if you're right, Grace?"

Tran's turn to think in awed silence. Finally, she spoke. "We go where the facts lead," she said. "The Old Man may have to pick up the pieces, but we're going to do what we have to do. The President tasked me to get these answers for him, and that's damn well what I'll do."

"Okay, so what's next then?"

Tran shifted in her seat as she turned to face Henri directly. "Can you guys get me a secure place to hold a warm body for a few hours until the agency plane gets here from DC?"

Henri smiled with glee. "Absolutely I can," he said, smiling. "We were working out of a satellite U.S. Marshal Service office on the second floor of the Embassy since we got here. It's been shuttered because of budget cuts for a few years, but it has a small holding cell in which we can accommodate a guest for a few hours. And, all the members of the protection detail have been sidelined while you sort things out, so the space is unused and available."

"Amen for interagency cooperation," Tran said. "Get it ready. I think you'll soon have a new occupant for it." She lifted her phone and dialed Lockwood.

"Hey Boss," he answered. "Want me to bring you something back from Marcos?"

"No time for that," she replied. "Are you in a place where you can talk?"

"Yeah. There's nobody here but us and Mr. Marco, and he's in the back prepping our dessert orders. What's going on?"

"Huddle the team and put me on speaker."

"Standby…" He pressed a button on his phone. "Go ahead, Grace. We're all here."

"Thanks, Lockwood. I'll explain more later but for now, there have been some significant developments in the case, Tran said in a quieter tone than normal. "We need to move now. Lockwood, I want you and Kenison to go get Ashmead. Bring him gently if possible but bring him nonetheless."

"With pleasure," Lockwood said, glee oozing in his tone.

"Marshal Henri and I are headed to the Embassy right now, and I need the rest of you to meet us there as soon as you can."

"We're leaving this minute, Grace," Starr answered.

Tran ended the call and turned back to Henri. "I'm assuming you'd care to accompany me, but I can have them come get me if you'd rather not?"

Henri chuckled. "That'll make for an odd first date, but I'll go happily wherever you are."

Tran rolled her eyes and shook her head. Henri chuckled again and then put the car in gear. Fifteen minutes later, the pair arrived at the Embassy to meet up with the rest of the team. They cleared the security checkpoints at the main gate and the Embassy's main entry, then went straight to the second floor Marshal's Office.

Henri flicked on the lights and then walked to the back of the suite, Tran following in step. The layout of the space was similar to the visitor's office suite assigned to Field Team Six, but it was less well-appointed and considerably less maintained. Boxes of old files and unused equipment were piled atop desks alongside unplugged lamps, photos of past government officials in-office when the satellite location was last active, and random chairs were stacked in and about spaces that would have been used by employees. A few spots had been cleared and cleaned for the Protection Detail's advance team, but the Marshals actually protecting Oberlin's party didn't use the space after their protectees arrived on-island since their primary duty was to be where the judge was.

"This is the holding cell," Henri announced when they'd reached the back of the suite.

The small space existed for those occasions when prisoners passing through or captured on the island awaited transport to the continental United States. It would be a short-term solution, but it would be appropriate until the agency jet got there from Washington. Tran surveyed the room. It had windows across the top of one wall to let natural light into the room, but no one outside had easy view into the room, and no one inside the room could get to them without a ladder or other assistive device. There was one door into and out of the cell area, which opened onto an anteroom with a metal rectangular interrogation table and four chairs. Four bolts secured the table to the floor, and a thick iron loop protruded from its middle, the place at which chains could be tethered. Camera equipment kept vigilance on the table and as well the entry to the cell room. The anteroom had another door that opened to a large square room of side-by-side, dull gray, metal desks where the resident Marshals would work. A slightly raised, glass-enclosed cubicle for the Supervisory Marshal stood century over all the rest opposite the other desks in the room and just to the left of the main pathway through rabbit warren of desks. Beyond that was a bright, windowed waiting room for those having business with the U.S. Marshals and a small reception desk to greet them. The room's windows looked down into the parking lot on the far side of which was the gatehouse, home to the Embassy's Marine guard. Tran felt satisfied the place offered sufficient protection against the probability that Ashmead could escape them if he panicked when she clued him in to the reality of his situation with the cold hard brutality she intended.

"This will do," she said.

"I'm glad it can help you out," Henri said, smiling. "Uh, so shall we continue our prior discussion until they get here?"

Tran grinned but politely declined. "Major Dixie Moran, an old Air Force colleague of mine, once advised me that good showmanship could never substitute for good preparation."

"That's your way of saying you need to work right now?"

"I think I should review the file once more before I confront one of my prime suspects," Tran said.

"Makes sense," he conceded. "I guess, uh, I guess I'll just, uh, sit at my desk over there, and maybe review a few things too, 'til they get here."

Tran nodded and then retired to the anteroom. She put her laptop on the table and called up her case notes. She wanted to review the details before Ashmead arrived. But first, she wanted to update The Old Man on what she was doing and to formally request exfiltration of the suspect. And perhaps he might have an update for her. She dialed Sharp and he answered on the first ring.

"You calling to tell me you've got this case packaged in a nice little bow, Grace?" his gravelly voice asked.

"Not quite, sir," Tran replied. "I'm about to interrogate Captain Robert Ashmead. If you've been following my case notes in SecureStar, you know there's another Navy officer at Vandenberg who appears to be involved, and maybe a few other military personnel too. Also, the assassin—I want to bring him in, but I have to find him first."

"I know you like everything completely buttoned down before you close the books on anything, Grace, but the world has continued to spin while you've been down there on this boondoggle—some serious shit too. The President wants you on one of them, so I can't make any promises."

"All due respect, sir, the President also wants the triggerman. I'll get him, but I need a little more time."

The General laughed. "You're like a dog with a bone," he joked. "I'm up-to-date with your notes, so I'm aware of Captain Whitehead. Field Team Four is already on the west coast, so I'll send them after Whitehead. As for the triggerman, if your suspect is in fact this infamous assassin as you suspect, then there are already a bunch of other alphabet agencies looking for him. I can't afford to commit scarce resources to something that's already being handled by another agency."

"But the other agencies don't have me, Sir. I can get this guy. I'm sure of it."

"No promises, Grace," The Old Man said. "I can give you a little more time, but I mean a *little*. Wrap it up ASAP."

"Yes sir," Tran conceded.

"And Grace?"

"Sir?"

"Be careful. I'll send the plane as soon as we're done here."

Tran ended the call with the Director of National Security, partly saddened at his answer. She half-wished she hadn't called him.

"Sometimes it's better to ask for forgiveness than permission," Henri said, walking up behind Tran and patting her shoulder.

"That's your modus operandi?" Tran asked. "Do first and deal with the consequences later?"

Henri shrugged. "Sometimes it's the disruptors that force innovation and evolution."

Tran shook her head, knowing he'd answered truthfully. Her phone vibrated, telling her she had an incoming text. Lockwood had just parked the car downstairs, with Ashmead in tow. Tran replied with instructions to bring him to the Marshals' office on the second floor, just above the main entrance.

"They're here," she told Henri. "Let's take him to the Interview Room first," Tran said.

"Haven't you already interviewed him?" Henri asked. "This guy's a criminal who murdered my friends and a little kid, to say nothing of the Judge and his lady friend. Let's treat him like the rat bastard he is."

"How do you really feel about this, Henri?" Tran joked. "I get that you want him to feel the wrath of justice, and that'll happen. But I want more information out of him first, and to get it, I need to work around his ego that's as big as this island."

"So, you're going to pander to him?"

"Manipulating and pandering aren't the same thing," Tran said.

Tran heard noise from the hallway, indicating someone's arrival, most likely Lockwood, Kenison and Ashmead. She went to the waiting area, and opened the door, but found no one there. She went to the door into the hallway and surveyed up and down the mostly dark and empty corridor. From the far end, a familiar *ding* rang out to announce the arrival of the elevator car. As the mechanical sounds of opening doors shot down the hall, a spate of profane exclamations in a familiar voice assaulted her ears. Having been in active military service, she'd of course heard them all before, but the hallway of the United States Embassy wasn't the place one expected to hear them. Nonetheless, they confirmed that Captain Ashmead hadn't well-received this recent invitation to the Embassy.

Lockwood pushed a cuffed Robert Ashmead out of the elevator and down the hall toward her. Kenison brought up the rear. "Look what

278

the cat drug in," Lockwood greeted. "Found him at the marina messing with a small powerboat. He had this on him." Lockwood handed her a clear plastic bag. "I asked ERT to get over there to sweep it for evidence."

Tran examined the plastic bag. It contained two passports—one with Ashmead's correct name and the other with something fictitious—a navigational chart, two thick wads of cash, a small caliber weapon, a Swiss Army knife, four cell phones, and a few other items. She looked Ashmead up and down. He wore civvies rather than his uniform, but his cap clearly showed his Navy rank insignia.

"You fucking bitch," Ashmead said. "You have—"

Kenison delivered a swift, open-palmed swat to the back of the Captain's head. "A little decorum, sir. That's not how real men address a lady."

Tran subtly waved her hand at Kenison, warding him off as she examined the bag of items. "It's okay, Stefan. The Captain's a little emotional at the moment, so we'll forgive the conduct unbecoming an officer and a gentleman," she said, referencing an offense written into the Uniform Code of Military Justice. "Please come in, Captain Ashmead."

She stepped aside to allow the trio access to the suite, unfettered by her body in their way. Ashmead glared at her, obvious anger burning into her. "You have no idea who you're fucking with, Tranny," he growled.

"I'm glad to see you again," she replied. She nodded at the door leading from the waiting area to the back office. "Interview room, please."

Kenison pushed Ashmead across the waiting room, through the doorway, and into the hallway. Lockwood, then Tran followed. Marshal Henri hurried from his cubicle to join the group. When they reached the interview room, Lockwood forced Ashmead to sit in a chair by kicking the back of his knees while applying downward pressure to his shoulders. The Captain nearly collapsed into the chair as Tran took post in one across from him. Lockwood and Kenison retired to positions on the wall directly behind Ashmead. Henri moved into the corner behind Ashmead, to Tran's right. He could see Tran and hear everything that would transpire.

"Please remove his cuffs," Tran began, nodding at the zip ties pulled tight around Ashmead's wrists. She waited for Kenison to cut the hard-plastic bindings. "Thank you for coming, Captain."

"Like you gave me a choice, bitch."

Kenison moved toward the officer but stopped as soon as he caught sight of Tran's telling eyes.

"No, I guess I didn't, did I?" she conceded.

"This is the mother of all fucking mistakes on your part, Tranny."

"Save the threats and indignation, Captain. We have solid evidence on digital recording that you called in a hit on me, the tenacious bitch that I am," Tran said. "That alone is enough to cage you up for a very long time, but the evidence is very compelling that you misused your command to aid and abet the assassination of a federal official and conspired to commit multiple murders, including an innocent little baby."

"You like trout, Tranny?" Ashmead asked.

"There's no fishing here." She withdrew her phone and played the recording of Ashmead's conversation with Alex. "My boss, Lieutenant General Sharp, is at this moment informing the President and the Chief of Naval Operations of your arrest and the nature of the charges against you. That's the beginning of a long humiliating chapter that ends with you behind bars for the rest of your life."

"Is this supposed to scare me, bitch?"

"I don't give a shit whether it scares you or not," Tran said. "Frankly, I think you may be too stupid or too full of yourself to even know you should be scared. The fact is, tomorrow morning, you'll wake up in the custody of the U.S. Marshal in a jail cell back in the states. I'm perfectly willing to just throw you in that cell over there—" she said, pointing "—until the NSA transport arrives for you. However, I've decided to offer you one and only one chance to reduce the sentence you'll eventually get."

Agents Star, Ito, and Trigg bolted into the suite, and hurried to the conference room, where everyone else was gathered. Starr sat beside Tran while the other two took positions on either side behind Tran.

"Care to explain yourself, Captain Ashmead?" Starr asked.

"Screw you, bitch."

Starr raised her brow. "Perhaps my official profile of your intelligence and capability missed the mark."

"What the hell are you babbling about?" Ashmead barked.

"Your reaction is atypical for offenders of high intellect. Stubborn resistance and vulgarities at this point in the game correlate more directly with common thugs, drug dealers, murderers, and others arrested for vile street crimes. When caught dead-to-rights, the overwhelming preponderance of highly intelligent offenders who are also effective leaders usually explain their reasons. That doesn't seem to fit you."

"You people, you spineless, paper-pushing panties don't have the capacity to grasp the reasons for doing what I did," he said. "Why would I waste my breath saying anything to weak pussies who don't know their asses from a hole in the ground?"

"If you don't tell your story, your wife, kids, grandkids, subordinates, peers, and others who have known you throughout the years will see you as a traitorous baby killer. That's also how history will remember you. The achievements of your military career will be obscured by it."

"I am not a traitor or a baby killer," Ashmead screamed at the top of his lungs. "I did what I had to do to protect the country's future. That's my job as an officer of the United States military. It's people like you who are traitors, who will cause the deaths of millions of Americans because you don't have the fortitude to do what must be done."

Tran sat forward. "Let's talk about that, shall we...Mr. Ashmead?"

281

Chapter 21: Truth and Consequences

Tran rolled her eyes. "I'm tired of your babble, Mr. Ashmead," she said. "For the last hour, you've droned on and on about patriotism, but that doesn't provide relevant facts."

"Facts? I'll give you some facts, Tranny. Every little pissant country with a bomb has thumbed its nose at the United States whenever it damn well felt like it in the last ten years. They're not afraid of us anymore, and the spineless bureaucrats in Washington won't flex our military muscle."

"Just because we can do a thing doesn't mean we should do it. You're living in yester-year if you think we can deal with every situation that doesn't please us by threatening to send U.S. troops," Starr said.

"Diplomacy has its place, lady, but nothing is more convincing than a punch in the nose," Ashmead yelled.

"That's above your pay grade," Tran said sharply. "The Commander-in-Chief makes national policy decisions, not a pair of egomaniacal line officers who think their shit doesn't stink."

"I took an oath to defend the United States of America against all enemies, foreign and domestic, and—"

Tran interrupted. "You took an oath to support and defend the *Constitution of the United States* and to faithfully discharge your duties, Mr. Ashmead."

"It's *Captain* Ashmead, Tranny," he snarled.

"And it's *Special Agent* Tran, Ashmead."

"My duty is to make damn sure this great nation endures, regardless who stands against it. That takes the fortitude to do what's necessary, whatever the cost, even if the enemy is the U.S. government."

"Never mind trampling all over the rule of law required by the Constitution you're sworn to support and defend? Never mind obedience to the chain of command?" Tran charged.

Ashmead waved his hand in the air as though swatting an insect. "Don't give me that shit, Tranny. My duty as an officer of the U.S. military doesn't depend on some dumb-ass bureaucrat giving me permission to do it."

"Those sound like the rationalizations of a lunatic," Tran said. "Focus, Ashmead. We know about Brimstone and AMAGS, but it's not clear what you idiots thought you were doing by killing Oberlin, his girlfriend, a baby, and two U.S. Marshals who were serving their country."

"Idiots?" Ashmead repeated. "Idiots? Brimstone gives the U.S. the edge it will need in the rough years that surely lie ahead. When the shit hits the fan, you and every other fat-ass bureaucrat will be damn glad we did what we did."

"And the innocents you killed?" Tran prompted. "Will they be glad too?"

"That woman and child, and the Marshals were unfortunate collateral damage," Ashmead said. "I regret that they were in the wrong place at the wrong time, but you know what they say: the needs of the few are outweighed by the needs of the many."

"This isn't a sci-fi movie, Ashmead. It's real life, with real consequences."

"We wouldn't have consequences to deal with if that liberal judge had realized as much," he rebutted.

"He sided with the government," Tran rebutted.

"The word of U.S. military officers that the documents shouldn't be released was sufficient justification."

"The word of military officers who violated their duty, broke the law, and lied to their chain of command and the Congress of the United States—is that the word he should have accepted?"

Ashmead said nothing.

"So, he saw some sensitive documents," Tran continued. "He too was a senior military officer with a distinguished record of service to the Air Force Judiciary."

"He wasn't a real officer; he was a ninety-day wonder from Officer Candidate School who played soldier behind a cushy desk," Ashmead growled.

Tran felt exasperation welling her gut, but struggled to keep her composure. "My God! The man held a top-secret clearance at one point. He clearly knew how to keep military secrets."

"He held liberal, activist views that didn't serve the military's interests. They discouraged him from pawing through top-secret documents, but he nevertheless insisted. It seems he proved he couldn't be trusted. Besides, as I said, I had nothing to do with operational decisions about Oberlin. I was tasked to extract a classified asset from designated coordinates at a designated time. Since it was a compartmentalized covert national security operation, I didn't need to know any more than that."

"You run a research and development facility. Didn't you find it odd that someone would give you operational orders?" Starr asked.

"Nobody had to *order* me to protect my country, lady. I'm a Navy officer. It's what I do."

"If you didn't decide anything about Oberlin, who did?" Tran asked.

"I thought you had all the answers, Tranny."

"I have an answer, but I'm curious why yours and Whitehead's differ?" she said.

"What do you mean?"

"It seems your colleague from the brotherhood of real officers doesn't share your values. Whitehead says you made the call and you say you didn't?" Tran said.

"You're bullshitting."

"I'm told you conceived the idea."

"Bullshit. As you said, I lead an R&D command. How would I have even known about operational developments on the project without someone in program administration telling me?"

"You conceived the idea, and you hired the assassin for Oberlin just as you called him in to take me out," Tran pressed.

"If I was going to take Oberlin out, I'd have done it myself instead of hiring some chink-bitch to do it. And you'd have never known it was murder."

"Chink-bitch?" Tran said, raising her brow and trying not to show she'd just learned a new, very important fact.

Ashmead smiled. "Does that offend you?"

She laughed. "Racial slurs from old white men don't offend me," Tran said. "They reconfirm the predictable last resort of small minds, but the chink-bitch, as you say, intrigues me in an odd way. What do you know about her?"

"A little lesbo crush going on here? Can I watch?" Ashmead laughed. "I know your girlfriend comes from South China, and she's good…at the killing thing anyway. I have no idea how she is in the sack. She probably knows some of that ancient Chinese Ninjitsu shit or something, but she's supposedly the Single Best Solution to unique problems throughout the world. I understand she's helped us express U.S. dissatisfaction with—"

The sound of breaking glass interrupted Ashmead's remarks. His head micro-spasmed and immediately snapped back as his mouth formed up to deliver words or phrases that would never come. His opened eyes fixated on some unspecific point on the wall dead ahead, and two small streams of blood trickled steadily from his head, one from the right carotid artery and the other from his forehead.

Everyone in the room at once dropped to the floor and scanned the room to assess what had happened, the agents withdrawing their weapons in case they found the cause. Henri too reached for his weapon, but, as a temporarily suspended Deputy U.S. Marshal, he came up empty. Their eyes tracked to a few shards of broken glass on the floor along the outer wall, and then up to the window at its top. For several seconds, there was no movement and no sound of any kind but a low din filled the room as the agents began calling out their observations to their teammates. Finding no immediate threat to the team, Tran lifted her phone and summoned the main security checkpoint. "Shots fired, second floor Marshal's office. Lock it down," she yelled when someone answered. "Our prisoner is down."

"Aye-aye, Ma'am, but we didn't hear no gunshot or nuthin'" the young man answered.

"Lock it down, Corporal."

Sirens and flashing lights cracked the air, sending the entire building into a flurry. Office workers hunkered down and a Marine rapid response team deployed into the Embassy, ready to repel an armed incursion that didn't come.

After thirty-minutes, a systematic, room-by-room search of the Embassy yielded nothing, as did a review of building surveillance tapes. Kenison and Lockwood approached Tran as she and Starr finished a conversation with the Embassy security officer presiding over the process.

"This is interesting," Tran said as they approached. "Ashmead wasn't killed by a bullet. It's a hollow metal projectile through the brain."

"I'll need to see the post-mortem results to be sure, but it appears to have delivered some sort of toxin," Starr added.

"A blow dart?" Kenison asked. "From where?"

Tran nodded. "Security did a preliminary search but came up dry."

"You think this is Alex playing clean-up?" Lockwood asked.

"She did say she'd talk to Ashmead about his manners," Trigg said.

"And more importantly, he threatened her," Tran added.

"We found something interesting," Kenison said. "The glass on the floor blew into the room which means the shot came from outside. However, the glass in the waiting room blew out of the building onto the awning above the main entrance downstairs."

"So the second shot came from inside the Embassy?" Tran summarized.

"It appears."

"So how did she get in the building, and where did she take the shot?" Kenison asked.

"I called Agent Darden and asked for the Evidence Recovery

Team, Tran advised.

"That's all good, but I'm more concerned about getting you the hell out of here," Henri said to Tran. "You were the main reason the assassin came back to the island, and clearly this location is vulnerable."

"I agree with him, Boss," Lockwood said.

Tran tried not to roll her eyes. The guys meant well, but she wondered if they'd have the same reaction if she was male. Still, it was better than them not giving a crap.

"You know, we can use this," Tran thought aloud.

She explained that she could serve as bait to lure the assassin. The Atlantica's somewhat isolated location and the limited access to the seventh floor would make their hotel suite an ideal location, thus allowing them to choose the place of battle. They could position the members of the team at strategic locations around the hotel and use NSA satellites to monitor hotel grounds.

"We don't know how the assassin gets her information," Starr said. "How do we leak your location and the fact that you'll be vulnerable to her without being obvious?"

"I don't think we need to worry," Tran said. "Alex didn't amass a string of successful hits without having good intel. She'll find me."

"I don't like it. In our line of work, people may take shots at us, but we shouldn't invite it," Lockwood said.

Kenison agreed. "We can hunt this monster the traditional way."

"I can hijack video cameras all over the island and find this b— uh, woman, wherever she is," Ito said.

"I ain't too keen on it neither, truth be told," Lawrence chimed from the Ito-pad.

Tran mulled her team's objections. "We have what Alex wants," she said. "Plus, we'd control the place and conditions of battle."

"As Sun Tzu taught," Torres said.

"Precisely."

The group debated the best approach for several minutes more, but Tran eventually came to a decision. As warped as Ashmead's logic had been, he got it right when he said the needs of the few are outweighed by the needs of the many. The current facts presented a rare opportunity to capture an elusive and dangerous prey, the subject of numerous expenditures by agencies across the world. For that reason alone, Tran determined to proceed with the plan.

The team, Torres and Henri in tow, left the Embassy to the Marines and returned to the Atlantica, their two vehicles rushing through the streets like a VIP caravan across a city under siege. Once there, they made their way to the suite and swept it for explosives or other hazards Alex may have placed. Satisfied, the team convened in the living quarters. Tran pulled a white-noise device from her briefcase, activating it to prevent electronic eavesdropping.

"I've been thinking about a deployment plan," Henri said. "I recommend we put Starr and Lockwood in the lobby to cover the main hotel entrances, Trigg in the stairwell and Kenison on the roof to guard secondary pathways, and Ito in Security to monitor hotel surveillance systems. Grace, you'll be here in the suite, and I'll take post outside."

"No," Lockwood countered the second Henri finished. "I'll take post outside the room and you're in the lobby."

"All due respect, Agent Lockwood, your senior experience with crowd searches is better applied in the lobby. I promise, I'll take care of her."

Lockwood began to protest. "I won't have Grace exposed—"

"It's a good plan, with one modification," Tran interrupted. Lockwood's surprised expression demanded an explanation which Tran promptly offered. "My guess is that Alex is a careful planner. With the exception of Viv who hasn't been physically observable here on the island, she probably knows our team. I expect she'll be looking for each of you in relation to me. She may have seen Henri at the Embassy, but since he's not part of our team, there's a chance she won't expect his presence. Viv, I need you to get with the satellite team, and monitor this hotel and all approaches to it from above."

"And me?" Torres asked. All eyes turned to the Navy protocol officer.

"No offense, but you're not an agent," Kenison said. "You

shouldn't be involved in what may become a shooting match."

"I'm a U.S. Navy officer," Torres said. Everyone who wears the uniform must be prepared for combat at any time. I'm good at what I do."

"But—"

"You'd be good at the utility entrances," Henri said.

"Utility?"

He nodded. "Alex has evaded video capture all over the world. She'll anticipate video surveillance at the main doors and front desk," Henri explained. "It's not unrealistic that she'd enter through a less-monitored access point than the front door."

"In a place like this, everywhere is under video," Ito said.

"We take the situation as we find it," Henri said.

"But we don't even know who we're looking for," Trigg said.

"True," Tran admitted, "but based on the information we have, we can make some reasonable presumptions. Dr. Starr…"

"The techs say she used a scrambler on the phone, but voiceprint analysis suggest Alex is Asian or at least learned her early language skills in an Asian culture," Starr said. "She's most likely from the area around Guangzhou in Southern China, but some of her speech tags suggest Northern Vietnam as well. Based on these facts, we can assume she's a small-framed Asian female, probably around five feet, five inches tall and 120 to 130 pounds with dark hair and a fair complexion. She'll likely have a physical appearance that lets her get close to male targets, but her garb will be conservative, so she isn't an immediate spectacle."

"All right, folks," Tran said. "Let's go over the plan once more."

Field Team Six plus two huddled around a large coffee table and discussed their hastily drawn plan to lure and capture the assassin. They studied, challenged, hammered, and tweaked it until everyone felt reasonably comfort that it presented the best chance of capturing Alex while keeping everyone on the team alive. Afterward, they checked their gear, loaded weapons, and prepared to deploy to their assigned positions.

"Okay, I think we're as ready as we're going to be," Tran said as she stood. "Our biggest weakness is that we don't know exactly when

Alex will strike, so we must be vigilant 100% of the time. She, on the other hand, can lay in wait until it suits her—and it's possible she could try it at another time altogether, especially if she knows we expect her to make a run at me. But she has no reason to think we know she's been tasked to do that, so she'll think she has the element of surprise on her side. I want to bring her in alive if possible, but that's not a requirement. Your safety is. Don't take extreme risks. Any questions or discussion?"

Everyone shook their heads in a somber moment of realization, like troops on the battlefield preparing to engage the enemy.

"Okay then, let's get this bitch."

Chapter 22: Lying in Wait

It had been over two hours since the team dispersed throughout the Atlantica, awaiting a guest-of-honor who hadn't RSVP'd. A group with *Eternity Now Ministries* emblazoned on bright yellow t-shirts spilled from a bus into the lobby, where they mixed with Mai Tai-carrying attendees at the 60th Reunion of the Douglass High School Class of '54. Young families, honeymooning couples, and a bevy of bellhops also moved through the busy chamber. The scene conjured an image of rush hour in downtown Saigon, which Tran experienced first-hand during a long-ago visit to her Ba Ngoai's ancestral home in Vietnam.

The team carefully monitored the bustle for anyone or anything that might be Alex or a diversion to mask her entrance. Over secure radio, Torres reported nothing unusual at the service entrance, and Kenison confirmed everything remained quiet, and somewhat serene, on the rooftop. Trigg lamented a lack of activity of any kind in the stairwell, and Henri noted only a single visit to the seventh floor by verified housekeepers to prep the only other room on the floor for its next occupant, a visiting government muckety-muck from Canada. In the suite, Tran helped Ito monitor the hotel video feeds on her computer and listened to radio chatter through her earpiece.

After four more hours, Tran began to wonder whether she'd made terrible miscalculations in presuming the assassin would find her. She ignored a small voice in her head that chastised her for committing the confirmation bias error Lockwood previously mentioned. Her mind began work on a fallback plan to both capture the possible murderer of Judge Oberlin and rescue her investigation. Otherwise, an inglorious error in full view of the President and the Director of National Security would probably be irretrievably embarrassing, and worse than that, Tran hated being wrong as much as she hated losing. She resolved that would not happen in this case.

"All quiet in the lobby," Lockwood said.

"Status quo up here," Kenison added.

"Ditto," Trigg said.

"Nothing unusual on beachside," Starr said.

Then Torres: "Routine traffic in back."

"Nothing on eagle eye either," Ito said.

"Guys, we should keep the chatter down—it's less likely she'll make us," Henri said.

No one acknowledged his comment, which Tran knew that meant someone had hard feelings about Henri essentially telling them to shut up. Nonetheless, she had no time for ruffled feathers.

Tran stood and walked to the window overlooking the front parking lot. Not even the dark of night could obscure the island's innate beauty beyond the parked cars, vans, and buses. Silhouetted trees swaying in the breeze, and hundreds of tiny, sparkling lights in buildings on the dark mountains in the background created a different kind of beauty from that of day. Recalling joy and relaxation from family vacations to Hawaii, Tran longed for a time she could simply be in a place like this for an extended period, without worrying about electronic tethers to her office, couriers from the White House, or national security threats. The idea enticed her, but actually enjoying such serenity would take tremendous effort and willpower on her part—sad commentary on her mental state. Tran lacked a single clue as to when she'd become one of those people, those workaholics who couldn't relax and enjoy the life around them, but she recognized the symptoms.

Tran watched cars on the ground come and go, depositing vacationers or whisking them away to clubs, shops, or restaurants. Any one of them could be delivering Alex, or maybe none of them. *Why are you standing in this window?* she asked herself. *If she's out there right now, she could fire through this window and kill you like she did Ashmead.* Another part of her mind dismissed the possibility of a similar attack, at least not right now or right here. The Atlantica Resort stood alone on this part of the island, and the suite was on the seventh floor. It would take some sort of aircraft to get Alex high enough to threaten Tran, and Viv would see that coming a mile away.

"Hey folks, I've got a little problem here," Ito's voice called over the radio. "We've lost camera three."

"Camera three?" Henri asked. "Where's that?"

"It's the one at the front entrance," Ito said.

Tran stepped away from the window and walked back to her computer. She seated herself and began examining the different camera shots across the screen, noting one of the small squares showed only black. "Confirmed," she said into the mic. "Number three is out."

"I don't get it," Ito said. "Diagnostics say it's working fine."

"Look sharp, people," Henri said. "This could be it."

"What's going on, Ito?" Tran asked. "I need that camera back up now."

"I can't fix what ain't broke," Ito replied, intentionally invoking bad grammar. "Someone needs to get out there and physically check it."

"Where exactly is that camera?" Henri asked of Ito.

"It's on the lower northwest corner of the awning above the front door. It's supposed to see across the driveway into the front lobby. I could even see glimpses of Lockwood's fat head crossing the area."

"Guess that means I'm closest," Lockwood said from the lobby. "I'm moving out of position now to check it out."

"Starr, keep your eyes peeled," Tran said. "Forcing one of us out of position may be precisely what she's trying to do."

"I'm on it, Grace," Starr said. "I'm trying to cover my spot and Lockwood's."

After a few minutes, Lockwood came on the radio again. "I'm standing here outside the hotel under the awning. The camera is up kinda' high. I can't...reach it...very easily," he said, evidently making an effort. His voice faded slightly. "Hey, kid. Hey, come here a minute," he said.

A series of grunts and groans, and a flurry of *dude-what-are-you-doings* came over the radio.

"Shut up, kid, and lift," Lockwood said.

"Oh my god, man, like—you're breakin' my back," a voice said in the background.

"What's going on, Lockwood?" Tran asked.

Another grunt. "Uh...I uh..." Lockwood panted. "Sorry, Boss, I enlisted a little help to reach the camera. Looks like someone covered the lens with a black sock."

"A sock covered the lens?" Ito repeated.

"I don't see anyone with only one sock around here. There were some church people here a second ago, but they all shuffled into the lobby."

"How about the parking lot?" Henri asked.

"I don't see anyone suspicious—a couple bellhops but nothing unusual."

"What about that person standing near the awning?" Lawrence asked.

"What are you talking about, Viv?" Lockwood asked. "There's nobody here."

"Satellite says there is. They're standing stationary about fifteen feet from the door."

"Viv, I'm walking the whole front area right now. There's some bellhops in the doorway, but no one around here."

"I got 'em on thermal image, Lockwood. They're standing right at the door."

"How many times do I have to say it? There's nobody here, Viv."

"Okay, I'm going down there," Kenison said, nervousness in his voice.

"Negative, Kenison," Henri countered. "I can't afford to lose you off the roof right now. Trigg, get down to the lobby. Hurry."

"You still got a read on that person, Viv?" Kenison asked.

"Can you link me to the satellite feed?" Tran asked.

"Yeah, I still got 'em...wait a minute," Lawrence paused. "Uh, I got nothing now."

"What do you mean?" Tran asked.

"I mean I had a readin' right there one minute, and then nothing."

"Could it be a malfunction, Ito?" Tran asked.

"It's possible, Boss. It happens with solar flares, weather events, lightning—could be anything."

Tran ran multiple scenarios through her mind, trying to account for every possible explanation and alternative course of action. Suddenly, she had an idea. "Viv, contact Satellite Control and find out whether everything is operable on their end. Everyone, look sharp. I think Alex is making her move," Tran said. "Lockwood, get outside and get me a visual on the side of the hotel."

"What?"

"We're thinking in two dimensions instead of three," Tran said. "From 500 miles out in space, a satellite might not distinguish well between something at ground level and something fifty feet up."

"Damn," Starr yelled. "Most people don't look upward."

Tran heard grunting over the microphone, and on the video screen, she saw Lockwood dart from beneath the awning. "I'm outside now," he said, huffing. "I don't see anything up the side of the building."

A faint metallic clanging in the background made Tran wheel around quickly, but to her concurrent delight and disappointment, she saw nothing there. She wondered whether the excitement of the moment was playing tricks on her mind, making her hear sounds that didn't really exist—until she heard it again. She walked in the direction from which she thought the sound had come, carefully looking and listening for anything. A faint knocking rumbled through the air, not once, but twice more. She followed it each time, stepping nearer and nearer to the door of the suite. She froze in her steps when her eyes ran across the return air vent just inside the door at the bottom of the wall. In a flash, Tran withdrew her weapon and took posture to fire at whatever might come through it, but as she did, the room door beside it exploded open with tremendous force. In the split-second before she squeezed the trigger, her mind registered Henri entering the room, a crazed expression on his face and his weapon drawn.

"The vent," he yelled, his eyes scanning the room.

Movement pulled Tran's eyes to the vent as Henri fell to his knees, clutching his neck and crying out in pain. A thin stream of garnet liquid bubbled from beneath his fingers and sprayed the wall and tiled floor around him.

Tran threw her body toward the wall as she fired a single shot at the desk lamp, the bullet's impact sending shards of porcelain bursting across the floor and plunging the room into darkness. Only ambient light from outside illuminated the room and until her eyes adjusted, it was hard for Tran to see. But the assailant would likely be in the same boat, and it was difficult to get a bead on a target when one couldn't see it. Even if Alex wore night-vision equipment, the sudden change in conditions might give Tran the momentary edge she needed.

The vent cover clanged as it fell to the tiled floor, and a shadowy mass emerged from within. Tran pressed her body flush against the wall to present a more extreme angle to an attacker at once coming out of the duct and trying to line up a shot at her. Tran couldn't see it, but she heard and felt something whiz through the air and strike the wall beside her head. Tran answered with three short-burst rounds, apparently to no avail.

A meager kick grazed Tran's hand, suggesting the assailant had attempted to guess where Tran would be and took a shot in the dark. Its lackluster power was insufficient to harm Tran even a little, but its unexpected occurrence dislodged Tran's Glock from her grip. The handgun skittered across the floor and distracted Tran long enough for a fist to hit her face. The blow landed center-mass and knocked her several feet back. As she felt her balance ebb, Tran rounded her spine and relaxed into the fall, letting momentum carry her back, over, and up to a combat-ready stance. The shadow advanced, but Tran grabbed the fabric at the latter's neck, and yanked hard as she turned and dropped to her knees, sending the attacker violently over Tran's back. The shadow landed in a crumpled heap six feet away where the floor met the wall, but recovered quickly and hopped from the ground, immediately turning to resume her attack. Tran delivered two lightning-fast blows to the assailant's head, followed by a spinning back kick to her chest, all three blows connecting firmly. Tran's foot smashed the side of Alex's head, sending her head and body at high speed into the wall.

"You okay, Boss?" cracked the radio on Tran's hip.

The sound fixed Tran's location in the dark, and two muffled, staccato blasts exploded from the business end of an unseen firearm. They blew sizable holes in the wall where Tran had been, but as she evacuated that spot, Tran cast her radio several feet in the opposite direction, where two more shots destroyed it as it crashed into the floor.

Tran stooped low to the ground and swept her leg in a wide arc, striking and taking the shadow's legs, knocking her to the floor in a heap. Tran pounced on her, immediately grabbing the assailant's wrists and pinning them to the floor. Tran drove her forehead into the woman's face. She heard bones crunch and felt warm liquid spread into her hair, but she didn't know whether the sound and fluid came from her or her opponent. Whatever the case, Tran would have to defer her concerns about it to another time. Feeling for the assailant's weapon, Tran slammed the woman's left hand hard against the floor again and again and again, until it opened and let loose of the device in its grip. Tran felt a small sense of relief, but her negotiations were far from done. Tran knew a wrong move now could mean these would be her final moments on Earth—an event for which she felt nowhere near ready. But evidently, neither did her opponent.

The woman released a loud *kiai* that startled Tran as it was intended to do, and then brought her knee into Tran's back, sending waves of pain through Tran's spine. At the same time, she brought her arm across her body and plunged her elbow into Tran's face, knocking her to the floor and off of the assailant. The women hopped to their feet and readied for the next volley of assaults.

"You won't escape me," Tran said.

Alex yelled again and launched a rapid, relentless series of strikes and punches at Tran, alternating right and left and advancing with each salvo. Tran blocked and deflected each attack, stepping back to mitigate the force of each hit and watching carefully for an opening at which she could shift into offense. As Alex paused a split-second to breathe, Tran counter-attacked with a series of head, face, and body shots, each of which Alex blocked as handily as Tran had until Tran paused for air. The women delivered and sustained serious strikes to and from the other, battering, cutting, bloodying, and bruising one another throughout the brief but intense engagement, both seemingly aware that a stalemate favored Tran. Her team would soon arrive and that would make things more difficult for Alex.

A third *kiai* and the room's darkness masked the knife in Alex's left hand as she lunged. Tran stepped back to parry, oblivious to the precise moment the knife bit angrily into her shoulder, tearing into her flesh and severing muscles, tendons, and subcutaneous tissue. The immense pain sent Tran to a mental place she rarely went and taunted her deepest, most primal emotions. Her martial arts discipline had taught her to actively contain the well of rage lurking deep within her, but it also housed rich veins of adrenaline, resilience, and determination that had been decisive in previous confrontations. This was among the rare occasions she felt a small sampling of it would be appropriate.

As Alex came forward, Tran grabbed her collar yet again, rounded her back and fell to the floor, pulling Alex violently forward. The assailant arced in a circle over Tran's body, sailed through the air, and slammed into the plate window above the main entry. Like the desk lamp, the window exploded into a thousand shards that showered the floor inside the room and the parking lot and covered entry far below with sharp slivers. Alex's battered body crashed through the pane and plunged seventy-eight feet. Except for Marshal Henri's low groaning, the room was suddenly quiet. Though she couldn't attend him right away, Tran at least knew Henri was alive, which meant there was hope he would stay that way. First, she had to assure there was no further immediate danger to either of them.

Tran picked herself off the floor and staggered to the window, cautiously peering through the jagged opening to the ground below. Looking down the hotel's walls provoked the thought that perhaps Alex had scaled the outside wall. That would explain how she got to the suite unnoticed, despite the team's precautions. A crumpled body clad in black lay face up on the awning. The body didn't move and for several minutes, neither did Tran. Instead, she watched as a small crowd gathered on the ground, looking up at the awning or further up the hotel at her.

Behind her, Henri groaned, rousing Tran from her near-trance. She turned and hurried to the open suite door, where the downed Deputy Marshal lay in the midst of a spreading puddle of blood, grasping at his neck, trying to apply pressure to his own wound. Tran could see him starting to lose both his consciousness and his grip. He mumbled as Tran ripped fabric from his shirt, wadded it, and took over the job of keeping pressure on Henri's carotid artery. The task was far more difficult than it should have been, and for the first time, she felt the searing pain in her shoulder. Exploring its cause, she also noticed the jaded hilt of a small stainless-steel knife sticking out of her shoulder like the end of a dart buried deep in a corkboard, a deep red wetness matting in her shirt and jacket around the site. The dagger's pretty, decorative end betrayed the lethality of its business end.

"You're going to be okay, Rick," she assured.

Heavy footsteps thudded down the hall outside the suite and made their way toward the room. Tran's mind and body jumped back to combat mode, ready for a second wave attack, perhaps from unidentified co-conspirators of Alex and the deceased Captain Ashmead.

Lockwood rushed to and knelt beside her. "You okay, Boss?"

Kenison and Trigg deployed into the room in standard fashion to rout out and terminate any continuing dangers that might be lurking in the suite. Starr found the overhead light switch and turned it on before rushing to take over care of Deputy Marshal Henri. Lockwood grew alarmed as he examined Tran's condition, and it showed on his face.

"I'm okay, Ian," she said, firmly pulling the knife from her shoulder.

Lockwood grabbed her hand and held it in position. "You sure that's a good idea?" Lockwood asked, helping Tran out of her suit coat. He folded it into a compress which he applied to her wound.

"It hurts like a bitch but I think it got me only in the fleshy parts—nothing vital," Tran said. "How's he?" She nodded at Henri.

"His pulse is weak but steady," Starr answered. "He's lost a lot of blood, so we need to get him to a medical doctor fast."

"What's going on up there?" Ito asked over the radio.

"Tran and Henri are down," Starr reported. "We need a doctor now."

"There's a house physician on premises, and I'll alert Princess Margret Hospital—it has a level one trauma center," Ito replied.

Lockwood canvassed the room. "Where's Alex?"

Tran bobbed her head at the window, where Trigg and Kenison stood looking down below.

"I need someone down there to take control of the situation and the body," Tran said, her voice less present than usual.

"On it, Boss," Kenison answered, running out of the suite and nearly colliding with someone on his way into the room. He slammed the man into the wall, grabbing his one arm and pressing his own arm and elbow across his throat.

"What's the meaning of this?" a man demanded. "This is unaccept—"

"Who the fuck are you?" Kenison yelled.

Lockwood bolted into the hall, his weapon leveled at the man's head. "You got two seconds before I splatter your brains all over this hall."

The color drained from the catatonic man's face. "I'm the night manager here, my God. Please, please—"

"It's okay, Lockwood," Tran said. She peered around Lockwood at the ashen man. "I'm sorry for the mess and the disturbance, sir. Someone intruded on our party and things got a little rowdy."

"I...uh..."

Tran grimaced as she tried to stand. "Help me up, Lockwood." He did. She turned to the manager. "I'm Special Agent Grace Tran, U.S. National Security Agency," she said, trying to extend her hand. Pain made her rethink the action.

"Uh...uh..." he continued to stammer.

Tran paused for a moment as she looked around the room. "Don't worry about all of this. The U.S. government will take care of it," she said. "I suppose we'll need a late checkout. Agent Trigg will give you all the information you'll need." She nodded at Trigg who stepped forward and put his arm around the manager, gently guiding him out of the room as they spoke.

Cupping her right shoulder, Tran watched Trigg and the manager depart. When the civilian was in the elevator, she took a closer look at the room, stopping to stare at the open ventilation duct. She shook her head. Leaning against the wall, she ran her left hand over the wall, finding a rough spot at approximately ear level—the impact zone for whatever had whizzed past her head in the opening salvo of the night. Tran wanted whatever had embedded itself there. She used her nails to scratch away the tattered drywall so she could access the base of what she suspected to be a needle or dart.

"Get Darden's team over here. I want this place scrubbed," she said.

"I'll call him," Trigg said, re-entering the room. "I've got the manager handled, Boss. We're good to go."

Tran nodded, and then refocused her attention on the duct. She grimaced with the pain but dropped to her knees to peer into the long, narrow aluminum tunnel that extended deep into the wall. She could see clearly several feet into it, but the conduit turned and disappeared into the bowels of the Atlantica. *How in hell,* she wondered, shaking her head.

"Look here," Lockwood said. As Tran turned and looked up, Lockwood sauntered across the room, holding a gun in a used handkerchief fished from his pocket. "…a Norinco QSZ."

The weapon in Lockwood's hand was the same type that killed Judge Oberlin and his party. Under the circumstances, Tran guessed it was the actual weapon that killed them.

The hotel doctor arrived as he ran into the room, carrying a typical doctor's bag. "Where's the gunshot?" he asked, getting promptly to his business.

"Here," Starr advised. "But it's not a gunshot. It's—"

"It looks like some sort of hypodermic," the physician observed.

"Yes, and we have reason to believe it delivered a potentially lethal toxin into him," Starr said.

"What kind?" the doctor asked.

"It could be a blend of tetrodotoxin and Chinese cobra venom."

"Why do you think that?" the doctor demanded.

"It was used on another victim in a similar attack. I'll have our Evidence Team send over the toxicology report."

"That's good but this man needs help now." The doctor opened his bag and withdrew a number of instruments, tubes, and chemicals, and went to work on Henri. "This woman did this?" he asked, bobbing his head at Tran but not slowing his work.

"No," Lockwood snapped. "She's a victim too, and your next patient."

The doctor briefly glanced at Tran and then returned his attention to Henri. "What is your name, Miss?"

"Grace Tran," she answered. "National Security Agency."

"What seems to be the problem, Grace Tran, National Security Agency?"

"It seems, doctor, that I decided to block my attacker's knife with my shoulder."

"You seem quite alert," the doctor observed.

"Would I be more convincing if I screamed like a lunatic?" Tran asked, "because I'm perfectly willing to do that."

The doctor smiled. "Not necessary, Grace Tran National Security Agency. Let me save your friend here and then I'll be right there. Can you bear with me just a moment?"

"Do I have any other choice?"

He chuckled. "I suppose not."

"Yo, team," Kenison's voice cracked over the radio. "You guys aren't gonna' fuckin' believe this," he yelled, panting for breath.

"What the hell's the matter?" Lockwood barked.

"She's gone."

"Who?" Tran asked.

"The assassin—Alex."

"What do you mean she's gone?" Lockwood asked.

"She's not here—her body I mean," Kenison said.

"You got eyes on anyone, Ito?" Tran asked, unknowingly

snatching Lockwood's radio from his hand.

"I'm looking, but I don't see anything unusual, Boss."

Tran grimaced again, but this time not from pain. "I need all of you out there, right now. Scour the grounds and find her. She just got her ass beaten and thrown from a seventh-floor window. No way she's still alive. Someone must have taken her body. Find them." She noticed Lockwood's hesitation. "I'm in good hands, so go," she said, shooing him away. "Bring me that woman."

Chapter 23: Old Standards

"I see you're still faking sick to avoid work," Tran said as she walked into the room at Princess Margaret Hospital. "At least you look a little better than the last time I saw you."

"*What a Difference a Day Makes*," Henri replied, singing the old jazz standard by that name.

Tran laughed. "Keep your day job. Something tells me singing for a living won't work out well for you."

"Well maybe they'd pay me to shut up."

She nodded and smiled. "*They* aren't the only ones."

"But not you, I think. I think maybe you just couldn't stay away from me," Henri said.

"Professional courtesy," Tran corrected. "Can't stay long—my team is waiting in the van out front. We're on the way to the airport, but I thought I'd stop and see how you're feeling," she said, and give you this." With her uninjured arm, she tossed a box of Hawaiian Mauna Loa chocolates onto Henri's lap. He caught them and nodded his appreciation.

"Thanks for the medicine," Henri said, catching the candy. He nodded at the sling around Tran's arm and shoulder. "Looks like I'm doing better than you."

She looked down at her arm. "It's just a flesh wound. You should have seen the other guy."

Henri smiled. "I heard you threw her ass out the window."

"It doesn't pay to piss me off," she said, smiling.

"Did they find her body yet?"

Tran shook her head. "Judging from the damage to the awning above the main entrance, she hit pretty hard. I find it hard to believe she survived."

"I've seen some incredible things like that, especially with skilled martial artists—you're a black belt in Judo, right? I guess I'm singing to the choir."

"It wasn't a total loss. None of us ever saw her face, but we got a good DNA sample from the blood spatters in the suite and on the awning. From that, we've confirmed Alex is a female of Asian-Caucasian decent, likely between 25 and 35 years of age. During our fight, she attacked from a left dominant posture, so we think she's a southpaw. We'll analyze all the other information we've obtained and narrow down some key facts about this mysterious assassin. We also confirmed her weapon is the same one that killed Judge Oberlin and the others. And, the toxic dart used on you contained the same toxin that killed Ashmead."

"Why didn't it kill me too?" Henri asked.

"Medically speaking, it's because you're too much of a stubborn ass to die."

"Oh, that's the medical diagnosis, is it?" Henri asked, smiling.

"I believe someone may have taken liberties in paraphrasing my words," a voice boomed.

Tran and Henri turned to see the doctor entering the room, carrying a chart in hand. He opened and studied it for a second, and then closed it again. "Your vitals look pretty good, Marshal Henri, but I'd like to keep you one more night, just to be sure."

"No offense, Doc, but I'd rather put some distance between you and me—I don't like hospitals."

The doctor laughed. "Me neither, if I'm honest," he said. "I much prefer the beach or the green."

"Now you're talking," Henri agreed.

"All in good time," the doctor said. "I insist you give us just one more night though. The toxin injected into you is unlike anything we've ever seen. It's a cocktail of highly deadly poisons, including aconite,

305

tetrodotoxin—from the infamous deadly puffer fish—batrachotoxin, an extremely powerful cardio- and neurotoxin found in South America's poisonous dart frog—and I might add, it's ten times more lethal than tetrodotoxin—and concentrated venom of the Chinese cobra, one of the deadliest snakes in the world. The tox-lab says the compound has been manipulated at the molecular level to weaponize it by multiplying its toxicity by a factor of eighty. It could have lingering and potentially fatal effects. Your attacker clearly didn't mean for you to survive."

"And yet I did," Henri gloated.

"So you did," the doctor agreed. "You're one lucky bastard." He quickly turned to Tran. "Please pardon my French, my lady."

"Why am I such a lucky bastard?" Henri asked.

"At the right dosage, that compound would have killed even a strapping buff guy like you in a matter of minutes. You didn't receive the full injection. What you did get wasn't large enough to get the job done." The doctor shook his head. "I'm no crack investigator like this beautiful lady here, but I think that was a fluke."

"A fluke?" Tran asked.

"Yes. I read the toxicology report on the other victim, who was roughly the same size," he said. He turned to Henri. "You had only one injection site, but the other victim had two. The other dart—the one in the wall where the attack took place—contained the same toxin. Whoever shot you probably intended to use both darts on you, which would have delivered a fatal dose. Luckily, your shooter missed with the second dart. Otherwise, this fine young lady would have been visiting you in the basement of this institution rather than here."

"Be that as it may, I have better things to do," Henri began.

"Thank you, Doctor," Tran interrupted. "He'll be pleased to stay another night if that's your order."

The physician nodded, and then departed the room. Henri pushed himself up in the bed.

"*Pleased to stay another night?*" he said. "That's a little far-fetched. I'd planned to take you out somewhere quiet, have some wine and maybe a little soft music."

"Be that as it may, I have better things to do than waste time with your silly ass," Tran replied.

Henri smiled and folded both arms behind his head as he relaxed into the pillows. "So you've been thinking about my ass, have you?"

Now, Tran couldn't help but contemplate Henri's butt—the same as if someone instructed her to 'don't think of an apple.' One must think about the thing they're not supposed to think about in order to know what not to think about. Tran rolled her eyes and shook her head.

"The Director of National Security is expecting my report in-person tomorrow," Tran said. "And the President evidently has something he'd like to discuss with me."

"So, what is your report going to say anyway?"

Tran sighed as she spoke the thoughts she'd been thinking in deliberating her Report of Investigation. "Alex is still a loose end," Tran admitted. "I beat the hell out of her and threw her from a seventh-floor window, yet she may have walked—or limped—away from it, or someone stole her body, in which case she has a partner we need to get. Until I confirm she's dead, I'll suppose she's still out there somewhere."

"Are you concerned she'll come after you?"

Tran considered it. "She should be more worried about me coming after her."

"What about other suspects?" Henri pressed.

"Captain Lee Whitehead initially denied everything and blamed everyone else, but he caved when confronted with the evidence. Petty Officer Endicott's confession, Ashmead's recorded statements, and the phone tracking data made our case undeniable, and he eventually confessed—called himself a hero of the United States."

"So, let me guess, it was the professor, in the parlor, with the wrench," Henri said, mocking an old who-done-it game he played as a child.

Tran knew it well—like Ashmead had been the *Chicken* champ of his neighborhood as a child, she'd been the *Clue* champ of hers. "Whitehead conceived the whole thing. He called the daily shots on

Brimstone, he directed the defense of the legal case, and after they lost, he found the Single Best Solution to their problem."

"That bastard just can't take *no* for an answer," Henri joked.

Tran nodded. "He said he got Ashmead involved because Ashmead commanded the ideal location and the necessary equipment for the job. More importantly, Ashmead could be made to do as told without question. *Use all the right trigger words and people like Ashmead will cut off their own balls just because you tell 'em to*, Whitehead gloated."

Henri shook his head, agog at the intractable stupidity of some people and the innate mischievousness of others. "So, Ashmead gets off as an unwitting idiot."

"Besides the fact that he's dead, Ashmead's statements are sufficient to show he aided and abetted the assassination of a federal judge, conspired to cover-up five murders, and obstructed a federal investigation," Tran said. "It's too bad really—his service record was actually pretty good. But, as my Dad once told me, a man can be a great husband and father, a great neighbor, a great elder in his church his whole life, but he'll forever be a criminal after robbing just one bank."

"It's ironic that the guy's name is Ashmead," Henri said. "Did you know that *Ashmedai* in Hebrew was the king of the demons?"

Tran wrinkled her brow at the random factoid. "No, I can't say I knew that, really."

"Some investigator you are," Henri chided. "Ashmead not only caused his own downfall, but in making his subordinates follow his orders, he took them down along with him."

Tran shrugged. "My father used to say there are no victims in this world, only volunteers. For the bad choices he made, Master Chief Byron has been relieved of his duties and is facing a discharge board next month. Petty Officer Endicott was demoted two ranks and docked a month's pay, but he'll recover if he keeps his nose clean," Tran said. "Lieutenant Torres will be reassigned to the Navy Inspector General's office—a post she's wanted for some time now."

"You did that for her?" Henri asked.

"The lieutenant is a fine, capable officer," Tran said. "Her merit will serve her well."

"And having a mentor with the President's ear doesn't hurt."

Tran smiled. "Good people deserve support, even when you don't see eye-to-eye with them on everything."

"Are you talking about Stupleton?" Henri asked, rolling his eyes.

"I heard she's going into management training and then heading to a new assignment afterward."

"A desk job in Anchorage?" Henri asked. "That's more of a sentence than an assignment if you ask me."

Tran raised her brow. "Everyone I've ever met who's been to Alaska says it's beautiful and they love it. Stupleton will be just fine, if she so chooses."

"As long as I never have to work with her again, I'm good," Henri said.

"It sounds like there's an opening on your team," Tran said. "I hope they get someone good for that spot."

Henri smiled and then abruptly changed the subject, shifting back to Tran's investigation. "So, were you right about why Whitehead and Ashmead wanted to kill Oberlin and the others in the first place?"

Tran nodded. "As we initially thought, Oberlin was the intended target, and the others were merely in the wrong place at the wrong time. They wanted Oberlin dead because the Project Brimstone documents he reviewed in the *AMAGS* case showed that Brimstone armed a research satellite with a first-strike laser system that violates international treaties, and U.S. and international law. It also showed the Brimstone project officers misled the Armed Services and Appropriations Committees. After that jack-wad who leaked classified U.S. information and defected to Russia, the Brimstone folks didn't trust anyone outside their cabal— not even their superiors, other military members…and federal judges."

A dour expression washed over Henri's face. "How high does this go, Grace?"

"We think we cut off the head of the snake," Tran answered. "Ashmead and Whitehead were self-absorbed nobodies who endowed themselves with the right to decide how things should be rather than respecting the rule of law. They reasoned that what their superiors didn't know wouldn't hurt them. Bringing in the Single Best Solution gave them plausible deniability while fulfilling what they saw as their duty to defend the United States."

Henri shook his head. "Their hypocrisy made them betray the very thing they swore to protect."

"Ironic," Tran observed. She paused as she stared at Henri's crooked smile. "Well, like I said, my team is waiting downstairs. I should probably get going. Take care, Henri."

Despite the wires and tubes tethering him to a bevy of medical devices, Henri tried to get out of his hospital bed. Tran rushed to his side and pushed him back to the mattress. "This is no time to go rogue," she playfully scolded. "For once, follow orders and do as you're told."

"I'm not too good at that," he said. "But I might be willing to give it a try, if—"

"If what?" Tran prompted.

"What's it worth to you?" Henri asked.

She smiled. "You're kidding, right?"

"Dinner maybe?" He smiled back at her.

"Blackmail?" Tran asked.

"Nope, 100% Caucasian male through and through, but don't hold that against me," he said, grinning at his own attempted humor.

Tran chuckled as she shook her head. Feigning hesitation, she said, "I don't know. I guess I'd consider it if—"

"If what?"

"If you tell me why you chose *Pigmeat* as Oberlin's code name," she said, recalling one of their first conversations.

"As I told you," he began, "I could tell you, but then I'd have to—"

"Don't even go there, Henri," she interrupted. "You can't beat me even when you're in tip-top condition."

He laughed at her confidence and willingness to give back to him the same hard time he gave her. "You ever hear that 1968 hit song, *Here Comes the Judge*?" he asked.

"Hasn't everyone?" She wondered where his remark was going. "It was written by Pigmeat Markam," Henri said.

Tran chuckled as she shook her head. "I'll see you back home."

She turned and meandered down the hall to the elevator, noticing for the first time in a long time, a lightness to her spirit, a centeredness to her soul. She noted how odd the sensation felt as the doors opened, and she stepped inside. A moment later, she exited on the main floor, her mind continuing its aimless jaunt the whole ride down. Henri was a nice guy, with a sharp wit, a great sense of humor, and goals for his life. That he was easy on the eyes was icing on the cake. Tran enjoyed the time they'd spent together, but it had all been around the periphery of the case. Purely social or romantic situations were *a whole nuther thing*, as her grandmother used to say. It was possible that—

As Tran turned the corner to head for the entrance, something roused her from her thoughts, pulling her firmly back into her identity as a Special Agent. She felt a pair of eyes beaming directly at her, sending her into combat-alert mode. She relaxed as she noticed the owner of those eyes smiling a wide, genuine smile.

"Thought I might find you here," Torres said as Tran neared.

"I'm surprised but happy to see you, Jessie. I heard you got immediate orders to Washington—Inspector General's Office, if I recall."

She smiled, clearly unable to hide her glee. "Yes, and I'm sure I have you to thank for that."

"How do you mean?" Tran asked.

"You arranged it, didn't you?" Torres asked. "Lots of people want this job, which is really rated for a Commander, not a Lieutenant. I'm sure the Admiral didn't just suddenly on his own notice my application for the position out of the hundreds or thousands of officers who expressed interest in it."

311

"I was fortunate to attend a college that genuinely sought to build up its students and change their lives. I took issue with the grammar of their slogans—Never Underestimate You—but the message was compelling," Tran explained. "It fits you, Lieutenant. You're smart, ambitious, and capable. There's nothing you can't do if you resolve to do it."

"Thank you, Grace, for everything. You've been an incredible mentor—is it okay if I call you that—my mentor?" Torres asked.

Tran chuckled. "I've been called worse."

Torres chuckled. After a long pause, she continued. "…Uh, I heard what you said—you know, about ceding my power. I heard what you said and what you meant. But—"

Tran looked the young officer over closely yet again. Her uniform was dress-right-dress and in perfect order, and the bruising on her face had begun to fade. What remained seemed almost perfectly concealed by well-applied makeup. She looked good, but appearances weren't enough to make it in the world.

"Making big changes isn't easy, Jessie" Tran said. "It doesn't happen all at once, but if you keep pushing and keep having confidence in yourself, it will happen. Just don't wait until you have a hard fall. You may not recover from it."

--The End--

The highest proof of virtue is to possess boundless power without abusing it.

--Thomas Babington Macaulay, 1st Baron Macaulay

A Note from the Author

I hope you enjoyed reading *A Hard Fall From Grace*, the second Grace Tran story I've authored. In this story, the character of Navy Lieutenant Jessie Torres is loosely modeled on a dear friend about whom I'll tell you more below. In doing so, I'll use the character's name to speak about a real event, only because I wasn't able to connect with Jessie's family before publishing this story. Nonetheless, creating the character of Jessie Torres is one small way I chose to honor my friend, a victim of domestic violence. I believe we'll see Jessie in future books, and I expect she'll do her part to help prevent domestic violence, to help prevent anymore souls from joining my friend's fate. Let me tell you about it...

In the wee hours of October 22 and 23, 2013, in Volusia County, Florida, someone murdered a beautiful, talented, sweet young woman who is represented by Jessie Torres, along with her two beautiful young children. The murderer was Jessie's husband, a former gang member with a history of violence. He committed these heinous crimes out of jealousy, anger, rage, and a need to control Jessie. Faith teaches that Jessie and the kids have gone to be with the Lord, but the murderer robbed three beautiful souls of the lives God gave them and their family and friends of large pieces of their hearts. May God bless and keep the souls of the real Jessie, and her kids, and may He comfort, keep, and heal the family and friends they left behind.

A jury convicted Jessie's husband of first and second-degree murder, and the media reported that the jury voted 10-2 for the death penalty. However, state law required a unanimous vote to recommend the death penalty, so the murderer will instead serve the rest of his life in prison. I'm told he believes he'll likely be killed in prison because gang protocol punishes those who harm women and children.

The justice system convicted and imprisoned the murderer in this case, but Jessie and the children are still gone, taken prematurely and violently, and nothing can undo that. We can only commend this tragedy and our struggles to God, and remember Jessie, her children, and all the other victims of domestic violence in this country.

Jessie taught me a Spanish language phrase—*Broma In Serio*—which she translated as "joking but serious." It became the title of a chapter in this story, but there's nothing remotely joking about what happened to Jessie and her kids. It is, however, serious. I'm no subject-matter expert, but reports suggest nearly 25% of U.S. women experience violence at the hands of a current or former spouse or boyfriend during their lives, and that an average of three women are killed each day due to domestic violence. Especially in a nation purporting to be the home of the free and the brave, that's unacceptable.

President Theodore Roosevelt once said, "do what you can, with what you have, where you are." Jessie, the children, and all the other victims of domestic violence in this country cry out for all of us to do what we can to prevent domestic violence, to promote civility, and to encourage the resolution of problems in non-violent ways. Reverend Dr. Martin Luther King Jr. showed us it can work. At every stage, in every interaction, teach the boys and men in your life to treat the girls and women in theirs with respect and honor, always. No matter your place or space, be a leader where you are. Find an organization focused on preventing domestic violence, the abuse of women and children, and the proliferation of violence, and help advance their cause. Volunteer for them. Donate to them. Carry their messages throughout your circles. There are healthy ways to handle conflict, disappointment, and disagreement, but violence shouldn't be among them.

About The Author

Michael Murray is a Distinguished Military Graduate of the United States Air Force Reserve Officer Training Corps (AFROTC) who began his career as an officer-attorney in the U.S. Air Force Judge Advocate General Corps. On active duty, he served as a criminal prosecutor, contracts attorney, and general counsel to a military hospital. After completing his Air Force service, he served as a corporate attorney, a government administrator, and Chief Legal Officer for three multi-million dollar public and private entities. He has served on several corporate and non-profit boards of directors.

Michael earned his Bachelor of Science in Public Affairs from Indiana University-Bloomington's School of Public and Environmental Affairs, and a Juris Doctor from its Mauer School of Law. He is a 2d-degree black belt in Judo and has studied Tai Chi and Krav Maga. Michael's mother is a multi-talented artist and retired sales director, and his father a retired U.S. Army finance officer.

Michael is a speaker on leadership and management topics. He has been married to the same wonderful woman for over two decades and with her has two fantastic adult kids. He has three siblings, including a musical phenom, a clinical psychologist, and a U.S. Olympic athlete and fitness trainer.

Michael is also the author of _Intrigue at the Palace_ (available at Amazon.com) and has more novels in the works. Follow him on Twitter at @AuthorMMurray.

A Note from the Publisher

Dear Reader,

Thank you for purchasing, reading, and enjoying *A Hard Fall From Grace* by Michael Murray, the second Grace Tran story. We know you could have gone elsewhere to select your reading material, so we are honored that you gave us the opportunity to entertain, educate, inform, and impact you. If you enjoyed this story, please go to Amazon.com and write a favorable review of this book and Author Michael Murray and encourage your family and friends to buy their own copies. These are two of the best things you can do to help Mike gain notoriety, sell more books, and write more stories. And, stay tuned. Mike is already hard at work on his next novel, so keep your eyes and ears peeled.

If you'd like to get a special message or comment directly to Mike about this book or anything else, you can do so by going to our website and leaving us your name and contact information. We'll alert you about new books from Mike and other Cricket Cottage authors, characters, and books. We may even give you sneak peeks and special discounts that aren't generally available to the public.

Again, thanks for reading Cricket Cottage Publishing, LLC. We look forward to bringing you more stories that entertain, educate, inform and impact!

 **Cricket Cottage Publishing, LLC**